# THE
# FUND

## WES DeMOTT

LEISURE BOOKS        NEW YORK CITY

*To the beauty and spirit of those women who give
men a reason to give a damn about anything.*

LEISURE BOOKS ®

September 2004

Published by

Dorchester Publishing Co., Inc.
200 Madison Avenue
New York, NY 10016

ISBN 0-8439-5446-9

The name "Leisure Books" and the stylized "L" with design are
trademarks of Dorchester Publishing Co., Inc.

Printed in the United States of America.

Visit us on the web at www.dorchesterpub.com.

# THE MAN WHO KNEW TOO MUCH

Jamison pulled into traffic and stayed in the outside lane as he stopped at the light, the first car at the line. He sat there, looking everywhere while waiting for the light to change, wondering how long it would take them to find him.

A blue Ford pulled up beside him. Two men in suits—one fat, one ugly—sat in the front seat. The fat man must have felt Jamison's stare because he looked over and smiled, then turned to the Ford's driver. The driver leaned forward and both men grinned, looking at Jamison and bobbing their heads. Jamison watched the light, thinking maybe he'd seen them somewhere before, maybe in passing at work. When the light turned green he looked back again.

This time the passenger had a short-barreled assault rifle in his hand. The man's window was down and the gun was coming out in a hurry. . . .

# ACKNOWLEDGMENTS

As a former special agent of the Federal Bureau of Investigation, I want to thank the F.B.I. for the experiences that allowed me to write this book from an insider's perspective. The many fine men and women—and the occasional son of a bitch—in that elite organization are well represented in the pages of *The Fund*. Many will recognize themselves and smile or rage at the way they are portrayed. I call 'em as I see 'em.

I also want to thank the readers of *Walking K*, my first novel, for their incredible support. The enthusiasm we all shared over that book, and the fanaticism with which they sent their friends into bookstores to buy it, helped make *The Fund* a reality.

As always, thanks to my girls, Stacy and Kelsey, for thinking that I'm the best dad on earth, and my own parents for showing me the way.

Captain Richard Perkins (USN), a heroic aviator and respected skipper, has been a faithful friend since high school, and unknowingly served as an inspiration for pieces of many characters in my writing.

My love to the real Melissa Corley—an incredible woman.

# THE FUND

*"In the councils of government we must guard against the acquisition of unwarranted influence, whether sought or unsought, by the military-industrial complex. The potential for the disastrous rise of misplaced power exists and will persist."*

President Dwight D. Eisenhower
Farewell Address
January 17, 1961

# CHAPTER ONE

Peter Jamison hadn't heard a sound since seven P.M. His last three hours in the sprawling research center had been darker than normal and cemetery-quiet. Only emergency lights were burning, starry spots at each end of the hall casting eerie shadows along the corridor and through the glass beside his door. The FBI agents had gone, reeking of the power their credentials and a puny badge gave them. But they were sure to return tomorrow, and the next day, as long as it took to catch the person leaking information.

Jamison was rushing to finish his work and get down to Jonah's Bar. As the chief engineer on the Wombat's weapons modification, he always worked late and missed much of what happened in the world of happy hours, movies, and restaurants. He wanted tonight to be different because he needed the break, but the board of directors was making its final decision tomorrow and he had to make it an easy one. So he worked late, checking and rechecking every statistic, refiguring the costs, and confirming the allowances for manufacturing delays and conversion complications. He had it all on his desk, black-and-white documents and full-color charts—clear, concise answers to any questions that might be asked.

He raked his fingers through his thick blond hair, which much to the aggravation of management he wore in a shorter version of the surfer's cut he had in high school, back when good waves meant cutting school and weekends were spent surfing the hollow barrels of Cape Hatteras. He rubbed the back of his neck, then stacked his presentation. He felt confident, fully prepared, and ready for tomorrow's assault by the board.

At forty-seven years old, Jamison was the highest-paid division head at Dillon. He loved working there, even with the threats and fears that erupted after the leaks began eleven months ago. He'd made good time at Dillon after two years in the army and his late start on college. His hard work and confident leadership shot him ahead of the normal promotional curve. He was a blue-flamer, and he knew people said so when he wasn't around.

It hadn't hurt that Dillon's management liked him, in spite of the strain he put on some restrictive company policies. The aerospace industry was competitive, and fights over government contracts were fierce. Jamison had proven he was tough and would fight like hell for his projects. His quick movements, youthful face, and wild blue eyes always looked ready for a challenge, and Dillon had given him plenty over the years. He made good on every one of them.

He liked to believe those battles were the reason he stayed in such excellent shape, a corporate motivation to keep his lean, six-foot frame powerful. But it was a lie. Although Dillon provided a gym and encouraged its employees to use it, that wasn't the reason Jamison stayed strong and fast.

The unsettling truth was that he stayed fit, absolutely battle-ready, because the crazy man demanded it.

Jamison pushed back from his desk, locked the data in the credenza behind him, and tried to ignore little worries about tomorrow. "Okay," he said, "everything's ready. The target ident parameters, the accuracy data, and the cost projections. All my stuff's organized, so I guess I'm out of here. Time to knock back a few with—"

From out in the hall's gloom a sound slipped under his door and burrowed into his ears—the scrape of a shoe. Then a click followed, light as breath but mechanical as the antipersonnel mines that had laced the foot trails and paddies of Vietnam. He snapped off his desk lamp and turned the room to black.

The click came again. The doorknob was turning. Slowly, the shadowy glow of the emergency lights leaked into the room as the door cracked open. He watched with the quiet stealth of a predator, half thinking that he didn't have to worry because he was protected by Dillon's security force, but on some basic level doubting it. Then the alarm bell rang in his head and demanded that he trust himself for his own defense. He jumped to his feet and rushed for the door.

Like everyone who'd ever walked patrol in Indian country, he would always respect the value of speed. Regardless of how badly he wanted to flush the war's damage from his soul, a combatant still lived inside him, holding on to the skills that had kept him alive. Speed was his friend. Stillness too, at times, but speed was best when suddenly put on the defensive.

Jamison despised the way these old instincts controlled him, even as they propelled him across his office. He would often fantasize—it was his greatest fantasy—about how wonderful it would feel to be normal and expect nothing dangerous, to be able to turn slowly to the door and trust that its opening wouldn't bring a threat. More than anything he wanted to be normal, the gentle person he dreamed of becoming, his reason for choosing engineering at college. It was a gentleman's career, a cerebral job that would never require him to use his hands for anything more violent than erasing poorly placed dimension lines.

But Vietnam had spawned a craziness in Jamison's head, and right now, with a late-night visitor creaking open his door, the crazy man who ruled that part of his brain was shouting a basic rule of combat: Enemies are destroyed by overwhelming violence.

Two times, and two times only, the crazy man had totally possessed him. Jamison had felt violated then, dirty and used, as much a victim as the men he had killed. He never, ever wanted to relinquish control to the crazy man again and would do anything to keep it from happening. He closed in on the threat, praying that this was a false alarm. But the door kept moving. He grabbed the handle, threw open the door, and shot his hands at the intruder's neck, ready to break it if necessary.

Ted Bronovich stood frozen in the doorway, his right leg twitching in an attempt to get moving.

"Hey, slow down, it's me!"

Jamison jerked back his hands but kept his eyes on his boss's face, watching the kind of fear he'd never seen Bronovich show before. Not at work, and certainly not in the off-hours they shared together. His face mixed fright with resignation, the look of a person who sees some unavoidable disaster hurtling at him like a killer meteor, far off and small but closing fast. Some terrible event he has no power to stop.

"Damn, Ted, why sneak around in the dark? You trying to give me a heart attack?"

Bronovich didn't answer. He just shuffled side to side in the doorway, his sharp nose slicing through the air in front of him. He looked down the hall in both directions before he stepped inside Jamison's office. He wasn't wearing his jacket, the sleeves of his shirt rolled up to the elbows of his thin arms. His Christmas tie, a pattern of decorated trees and candy canes, drooped from his skinny neck.

Jamison reached to snap on the lights but Bronovich grabbed his hand. "I've just got a minute," he said, then glanced again down the hall. "Let's leave the lights off."

Jamison checked the hall before he closed the door and leaned against it. Bronovich's silhouette moved around in his office until somewhere over on the other side, completely lost in the darkness, his footsteps stopped.

"Okay, Ted, what's up?"

Bronovich took a heavy breath. "Peter, I shouldn't be telling you this, but I wanted to give you a little warning."

Jamison started toward him, but stopped. The darkness protected both of them and gave them the same advantage, so if he moved noiselessly to a new spot farther down the wall, Bronovich wouldn't know where he was.

"Thanks. Tell me what?" He moved right after speaking, hating that his mind still worked this way.

Bronovich's voice drifted to him from somewhere along the rear wall, near the corner.

"They've taken your project off the agenda for tomorrow's board meeting. I just found out. Knew you'd want to know."

Jamison took a noisy step forward, looked hard to find his friend in the darkness and get a look at what his face said.

"What do you mean, taken off the agenda? Another delay?"

Bronovich moved too, but then he spoke, making him easy to follow. "I wish. It's been canceled."

"Canceled? Why? I had approval from Casey."

"I know. Dead now, though. Sorry."

"The navy can't keep flying the Wombat without changes. Too many pilots have died already. You know that better than anyone. What's their reason?"

"Maybe your system didn't measure up, or it was a victim of economics. Maybe it's your old girlfriend's fault. I had nothing to do with killing it, so I really don't know."

"What about our jobs? Will my team be reassigned?"

Bronovich moved again. Jamison tracked him, but still couldn't see him.

"Don't worry, Peter. You're too valuable to lose. They're already talking about reassigning you to the attack platform of the F-35 Joint Strike Fighter. It's a great opportunity to work on an all-services, next-generation warplane."

"What about my team?"

Bronovich didn't answer.

"Ted, it's almost Christmas. Tell me they're not going to lay them off."

Bronovich walked through the darkness and stopped in front of Jamison. "I'm sorry, but yes. They'll be gone next Friday."

"Friday? Shit! Will they get severance pay?"

"They're contract workers, Peter. No severance, no guarantees. You know that."

Bronovich opened the door, letting the dim light of the hall drift in.

"Is Casey still upstairs? I want to hear it from him."

Bronovich stopped and lowered his voice as panic crept into it. "You can't go up there, Peter. They'd know I was the one who told you. With all the other leaks, they'd have my ass. Dillon is too dangerous these days."

"You're telling me."

"Yes. I am telling you. And if you make a stink, they'll just fire you."

Jamison shrugged, thinking that there were lots worse things than being fired. He stood still for a minute, feeling Bronovich's breath on his cheek. "Ted?"

"Yeah?"

"Why'd you risk this? Why did you come down here and tell me?"

Bronovich winced. "As a friend, I wanted you to know what was coming and give you a little time to prepare, a chance to do something. I doubt it's possible, but I wanted to give you the chance."

"I appreciate it."

"Well, actually, there is something else."

"Which is?"

"You know someone in the FBI, don't you? An agent with no connection to the investigation of Dillon's leaks?"

"Rich Blevins. Been friends since the army. Why?"

"You trust him?"

"With my life."

Bronovich rubbed his eyes. "Can you do me a favor, then? Will you tell him I'd like to talk to him? In confidence."

"About?"

"I've got a small problem, that's all. Nothing urgent, just whenever he gets a chance. Okay?"

"Sure. I'll tell him tomorrow. We box every Friday morning. Soon enough?"

"That'll be fine. Thanks. Our secret?"

"You bet." Jamison looked around his office, then came back to Bronovich. "I'm heading to Jonah's. Why don't you join me? We can talk a little, maybe help with each other's problems. What do you say? I could use your support around my design team."

Bronovich smiled, just slightly, and reached for the door. "No, I'm anxious to finish my work. The family's waiting."

"Understood."

Jamison stepped into the hall and watched Bronovich ease into the darkness, creeping along the shadowy walls until he was invisible, just the sounds of his footsteps coming back. When they faded out, Jamison grabbed his coat and briefcase and ran through the darkened halls. He cleared security and hit the cold air of another winter night in northern Virginia.

He drove along the southern shore of the Potomac, the Washington Monument's reflection bouncing off the black water. It was after eleven when he reached Jonah's Bar, and he was hoping the place would be empty and his team gone. But the parking lot was full and he had to park in the back. Trees shrouded this spillover lot and the spaces weren't marked. It was just a dark little slab of asphalt for employee parking.

He turned off his car but sat for a minute before opening the door. He understood his own limits, knew the pressure crowds put on him. He was already jacked up, so this might be a bad night to push the boundaries. Besides, what was he going to say anyway? You've been laid off, nice working with you, now goodbye? But he'd promised them he would come, so he bolted through the cold and entered the bar without slowing down.

Jonah's was a landmark, a comfortable old bar for people in the aerospace industry. It was the haunt of dedicated engineers who had never developed Potomac Fever. Judging from years of noisy conversations, the men and women who came here to drink didn't care about politics or international affairs or defense initiatives. They just liked to design, and then see their designs produced and working.

Tonight, Jonah's seemed overcrowded with sport coats and women's suits, the people wearing them crushed together too tight and laughing foolishly, desperately. Jamison stared into the churning mass, into the eyes that met his, and caught them searching, looking for some recognition. They had the same look of hope he'd seen as Saigon fell in '75, that sad plea of people begging to be noticed and saved, to be sum-

moned through the embassy gates and onto the rooftop
helicopters—quick salvation in the arms of caring
strangers. The desperation was better behaved and
nicely dressed, but Jamison saw it for what it was. Saw
it clearly.

He took a deep breath and pushed himself into the
crowd, worked his way to his team's table, and smiled
and shook his head when he got there. "Okay, wild
people, who's the designated driver here?"

Steve Harrison sat at the far end of the table with
three men on one side, and two women and a man on
the other. They'd saved the head of the table for Jamison but had used the spot to store empty glasses. Harrison waved for a waitress, then squinted at Jamison.

"You, Peter. You, sir, are the designated driver." His
slurred southern diction was loud and rose above the
noise of the crowd. "And I should tell you that we're
damn glad you finally showed up."

A waitress wriggled up to the table and Jamison ordered a gin and tonic. Then he turned back to Harrison.
"No way, Steve. You're not throwing up in my car
again."

All of them laughed at the old story, which made
Jamison sorry he'd said it. He'd come here wanting to
relay a hint of Bronovich's news, to give them some
kind of a warning that tomorrow would be a bad day.
Their laughter made it impossible. He glanced at their
faces and thought about their families, then looked into
their futures and saw how hard they would be. Defense
cutbacks and corporate downsizing had eliminated
thousands of jobs, and there was no way Dillon would
hold on to excess engineers in this tight market. If the
Wombat modification project died, it would be impos-

sible for them to find any kind of good work. There was nothing but suffering ahead for them, a holiday present from Dillon Aerospace.

He couldn't stay seated once that vision hit him. He stood up, dropped five dollars on the table, and tried not to rush his words but did anyway. "All right, folks, I've got to run. Just stopped by to tell you not to stay too late or drink too much. Those are the rules, my friends, and now you know them."

Seven pairs of eyes locked on to him. Harrison jumped up, wobbled, then sat back down. "My goodness, Peter, what's your hurry?"

"I just remembered something I need to do at the office. You people have fun, and don't be careless. I'll see you in the morning." He turned and left before they could argue.

He squeezed through the crowd and headed for the doors. He was lean, so he could slip in and out of spaces others couldn't and make quick progress for the exit. He was twisting his way past the bar in the middle of the room when a woman's arm stretched out to touch him. The arm was lean and muscular, and despite the cold weather outside, there were no sleeves covering it. No jewelry, either. Just a brilliant wristwatch encircling a thin wrist. The gold band fit loosely and slid toward the woman's slender hand as she stood on the rail and reached down for him.

Jamison had spent a hundred hours designing the watch, and eleven thousand hard-earned dollars having it handmade. It had cost more than all the watches and jewelry he'd ever bought for himself, but he'd spent the money gladly. He loved the woman who wore it so much that it had taken that kind of frivolous extravagance to express it. Anything less would have been profane. Despite all the women he'd dated over the years, he'd never felt that love for anyone before and was sure he would never feel it again. It was impossible. All the magical elements that blended perfectly to produce it would belong to this woman for the rest of his life. He had nothing left to give to anyone else and didn't even want to try again.

He was in slow motion now, moving through the crowded bar and looking at the slender arm scarcely a foot away from him. It took him a long, long time to get there. His heart was jumping, exhilarated, and hurting like hell at the same time. God, how he missed the warmth of that arm, wrapped around his nakedness, snuggling him close on cold nights, her hand caressing his body. This woman had been the one good and honest thing in his life, and had filled a spot in his soul that most people had no choice but to leave empty. Even now, as he suffered with the pain of losing her, he felt sorry for those who would never feel a passion like theirs.

The beautiful arm snaked through a wall of faces before her hand touched his shoulder and drained him of his strength. He slowed and allowed the hand to stay on him, let the long fingers run across his shoulder and along his neck, feeling like a faithful dog in his master's presence, trying his very best not to show it.

"Peter." Melissa Corley's voice was soft as gentle rain, almost too quiet to hear over the music, talking, and laughter. But it was the only sound he heard and it stopped him suddenly, glued him in place as her lithe body slid past the men who separated them.

Jamison was stuck and couldn't budge from his tight little space as she moved toward him, her dark blue dress a silky anomaly in the wool and cotton crowd. He saw pleasure crease the faces of two men as she squeezed past them. Jamison tried to ignore it and fought the demon of jealousy who wanted all of those close feelings for himself. He focused on Melissa as she moved through the men. She was beautiful. He was sure he would never see her differently, even though many of his friends didn't see her as he did.

Her skin was slightly dark, Mediterranean, as were the other features of her face. Her dark brown eyes seemed always to look past his face and into his mind. Her thin cheeks tapered to a slightly narrow chin. Thick brown hair framed her face with a soft curl, and behind that face was the best part: a mind he respected, an intelligent mind that had always been a stimulating challenge for him.

He didn't speak as she approached, unable to think of anything to say.

"Hello, Peter." The crowd pushed her body into his. "How are you?"

He tried not to look like a love-struck idiot but knew he wasn't pulling it off. "Fine, Melissa. I'm fine. Gosh, you look great."

At that instant he wanted to slap himself. Gosh? Had he really just said gosh to the woman he loved? Next time he would say something intelligent or just keep his mouth shut.

She kept looking at him. She smiled a little and tilted her head. "Thank you."

"Sure. You're welcome."

They stood in silence as the crowd jostled them, almost forcing her head against his chest. Jamison knew he couldn't take much more before he would throw his arms around her, so he forced himself to look away, over her head, searching around the bar for a distraction. He noticed things he'd never seen before—aircraft models on a shelf over the bar, a signed photo of the Blue Angels hanging on the wall, a tail hook from an F-14 mounted on a long plaque—but none of it held any chance of helping him. He was in her presence. Nothing else mattered. Except, of course, acting unaffected by her.

"Peter," she said, "I saw you come in a little while ago. I wanted to talk to you before you left. Do you have a minute?"

He leaned back, pushed his shoulders against the man behind him so he could look down into her eyes. "Oh? If you wanted to talk, why didn't you just come back to our table?"

She didn't blink, looking ready to compete with him as she'd always done. "I could have done that. I just thought it would have been rude."

"I didn't think things like that bothered you."

He would never understand how he said those things to her, didn't know where they came from, but always hated himself for letting the words out. He watched her eyebrows pinch together, just a little. No one else would have understood how badly he'd hurt her.

"You're right," she said, "I don't. Not really. But I didn't think you'd appreciate it if I interrupted your party."

Melissa's hands were on his arms, squeezing into his biceps. She was trying to keep some separation between them but failing against the pressures of the crowd. She closed her eyes and shook her head, swirled her brown hair around her face. The scent of Il Bacio stimulated his senses and suffocated him. She was wearing it when they first met and the scent always reminded him of what they'd shared and lost.

He grieved for Melissa and always would. He wanted her more than he could possibly want anyone but he couldn't have her. Not anymore. There wasn't any chance their relationship would survive. The battle between their employers had become a war that made them enemies, the conflict escalating every time newspapers hit the stands with one of her charges about Dillon's activities. Although he had been the one to draw the line that destroyed them, he was sure she would have done it if he hadn't. The death of their relationship had been inevitable, and they were both smart enough to know it.

Despite his pleas a year ago, she refused to pass over Dillon Aerospace in her hunt for justice. It was the kind of target she'd been after all her life. Nothing, she said, would stop her from destroying Dillon and other companies like it.

Even now, after a year to think about it, he still didn't understand how she could put her job before their relationship. Sure, he had balked about leaving Dillon, but that was only after she decided to go after them. He would have quit if he had to and found another job if she'd given him a little time. Now, of course, he wished he had. Wished it every night when he went to bed alone and every morning when he woke up the same way. Even more now as she stood in front of him with her hands touching his body. But at the time, neither of them had been ready to give up any ground, so the ground had cracked and shifted under them.

He tried to back away from her but the bar was too crowded. "I guess that was smart, not coming to our table. So, how are things at the Coalition?"

Melissa changed her tone, shifted into her lawyer's voice. "Fine, Peter. Are things okay at Dillon?" She looked down and studied his tie, smoothed it with her fingers.

"Yes, Melissa, everything's fine."

"Hmm." She lifted her eyes from his tie and licked her lips until her lipstick glistened, making him desperate to kiss her.

"Good, Peter, I'm glad. I heard a rumor about your Wombat project. I was worried about you. Worried about your job."

Jamison drew a deep breath, then exhaled. They had played this game before and Jamison was sure the rules weren't going to change now. She wasn't going to tell him anything, so there was no point in pressing her, even if she might know how he could save his project. He stayed silent in the noisy bar.

"Well, then, I guess my information was wrong. I'm glad for you. Really." She stretched up on her toes and kissed his cheek, so lightly it almost didn't happen. "Good-bye."

She looked him over once more before she turned and squeezed past the men between her and the bar. She walked through the opening they made, dragging his aching insides along with her. He watched until she was lost in the crowd, not even a sliver of her blue dress showing through the bottles, glasses, and elbows, then shook himself out of her spell and turned for the door, ramming his body through the human obstacles.

He needed room and ran outside. It was colder now, freezing, and he praised the icy wind that numbed his senses and cooled the skin Melissa had touched. He ran to his car, trying to shut her out of his mind. She was the most important story of his life, the most amazing woman he'd ever known, but regardless of how much he wanted to sort through the possible endings again, it was pointless. He had to shake his feelings, or at least hold them in check awhile longer. He had a job to do, an important job. His friends would turn desperate tomorrow, counting on him to save their jobs, their homes, their futures. He needed to focus.

He would go to the office and go over every detail again. Maybe find some way to change the board's decision.

He punched the code into his car's keyless entry system and the lock engaged. He froze, suddenly remembering trip wires and toe-poppers and all the men who had been lost to them because of a casual attitude in situations like this, angry that he still wasted so much of his life thinking about fighting and staying alive. It wasn't normal and he knew it, he just couldn't stop himself from doing it.

Could there possibly be a bomb? Was someone lurking around the dark lot? Was he standing on anything that might be pressure-sensitive? Or had he simply forgotten to lock the car earlier?

In less than a second the hairs on his neck prickled against his collar and sent a little shiver along his spine. He had locked the car; he remembered doing it. He took a big jump back, anticipating everything, or nothing, then ran around the car next to his. He crouched beside it and waited.

Three or four minutes passed. He didn't move but stayed low beside the next car, his eyes peering through the glass and watching for an attacker to rush from the shadows. But nothing happened. He began to shiver, and shivering always sucked when speed or deftness might be necessary. He stood slowly and scanned the area again. Then he crept to his car, looking for some sign of a break-in. He walked around it, noticing everything, wishing it had snowed so there'd be prints.

But there was nothing to indicate tampering or a break-in. His CDs were still on the seat, the player still in the dash, his briefcase on the floor. He'd learned a lot in the jungle, and the senses that had kept him alive over there were on full alert. He was combat-ready, *bladed,* as Lieutenant Blevins had called it.

He crouched beside the passenger door and turned away, covered his head with one arm as he pulled the door's handle, hoping he wouldn't have body parts blown off, or car parts blown into him, or any combination of the two.

The car didn't explode, so he elbowed over the floor and looked under the dash for unusual wires or a detonation cord. He climbed across the center console to check for a triggering mechanism attached to the driver's door.

Finally, he eased into the driver's seat, shut his eyes, and turned the key. The car sparked to life, and the suddenness of it twisted him involuntarily toward the door. He sat there embarrassed for a minute, then drove slowly out of the spooky lot, picking up speed as he hit the highway back to Dillon, wondering who had been in his car and why.

Ted Bronovich picked up the phone and called his wife, knowing she'd be upset that he was still at Dillon. He'd promised to come home in time to put their two girls to bed. It was one of hundreds of promises he'd broken since his brother died.

"Hi, honey. Sorry I'm not home yet. Are the girls asleep?"

"Yes."

He waited, hoping she'd say something else, something that showed she was still on his side, that she hadn't lost her share of his conviction. A security guard walked down the hall toward his office and Bronovich listened to the guard's keys jangling as he waited for his wife to speak. The keys' tinkling grew loud, then soft, and finally faded away. His wife was still silent.

"I'll be home in an hour."

"How much longer, Ted? I want to know how much longer this will go on."

"Hang on a minute." He walked to his office door and opened it, looked along the dimly lit hall, and listened carefully before closing the door and returning to his desk. "Not much longer," he whispered. "I'm almost done with this. Two more weeks, a month at the most. Then we'll start over, you and I and the girls. Something new and fresh, I promise."

"I'm counting on that, Ted. The girls and I are counting on you."

"I won't let you down. Don't worry. See you in an hour, maybe sooner."

He hung up and picked his younger brother's gold

wings off his desk. The navy wings were a reminder of the last time he'd seen him alive, suited up in his flight gear, grinning as if he owned the entire world, crouched on the boarding ladder of his Wombat aircraft as it sat on the transient line at Naval Air Station Oceana. That was how Bronovich wanted to remember his brother, a wild card, cocksure and ready from the day he was born.

He fondled the wings several times every day, just to cement his brother's grinning face onto his brain and use it to cover up the bloody image he'd conjured from the naval investigator's finding. The sanitized report said that his brother ejected safely when his Wombat's weapons system glitched the flight-control computer. His parachute opened but caught on a mountain ledge during descent. His brother swung in his harness all night, the high winds smashing his poor body against the rock face until every bone had been pulverized.

Jack Kane sat in his darkened office on the top floor of Dillon Aerospace, holding pictures of the two men in his hand, imagining his wife's and children's last minutes alive. It was part of his ritual, part of what made him so deadly—his willingness to live through this suffering again and again, and then focus all of his pain, all of his hatred, all of his vengeance, on whoever was next on the list.

His grief was an affliction he could hardly overcome anymore. As always, tears for his family came to his gray eyes and tried to work their way out. But they never succeeded. His eyes were pinched too tight to let them pass, narrow slits that saw only the evil he wanted to stop.

After staring at the pictures for twenty minutes—imagining what his family had said that night and remembering the gruesome photos that showed exactly what these men had done to them—he put them away and headed out the door, down the hall, ready. The photos had done their job, had started the acid pump and built up the pressure. They'd given him a thirst for blood.

But the executions were getting progressively harder for him, and this one would be no exception. He just couldn't tell exactly how much more difficult. The surge would still crackle through his big arms and destroy the man's life. There was no doubt about that. But resistance had been growing in his limbs during the last few months. A slowness had begun to govern his stride. His hands would wander a little before the kill. They were all signals of weakness, extra clutter for him to struggle with tonight besides Ted Bronovich.

For nineteen years this work had been a pleasure, a simple act of vengeance played over and over with a varying cast of characters. It was his way of purging himself of the poison of his family's death, or at least diluting it. It had never mattered if Kane knew the victims or not. Someone in the organization did and felt they had to die. Kane made the final decision, but he usually agreed with the recommendation. He understood that something had to be done about criminals, the evil men who hold good people at psychological gunpoint, causing them to lock their doors, watch their children, and patrol their neighborhoods and still know they can't stop the violence or protect their loved ones, then have to live with the pain and guilt when they fail.

Maybe it was just age that was making him soft, his

mountain of vengeance weakened and crumbling by the slow erosion of time. Fifty was only a couple of years away. He stopped at a glass panel dividing the long corridor and took in his reflection. He was still big and strong, still handsome. The hair had some gray, sure, and the big face showed the wear. But Kane was still hard and it showed, especially in the reflection of those dead gray eyes that were lost in the depths of the glass.

He learned nothing new about himself from the image, turned back down the corridor, and stayed in the shadows created by the emergency lighting. He was close to Bronovich's office now, and suddenly wondered whose name would be on the door next week. Strangely, he almost wished the name could stay. After all, Bronovich hadn't done anything to him, and he wasn't even sure his death would plug the leak. Compassion, or at least what he could remember of it, tried to turn him, tried to bubble to the surface for the first time since his family's murder. But he knew this was just weakness and nothing more. Bronovich, by guilt or bad luck, was caught in Dillon's spotlight, and Kane had taken on the task of killing him.

For the first time ever he tried to think of it as something other than murder, spent a little time twisting around the details. Could he cloak it in some kind of patriotic wrapper? Was there really much difference between this execution and the killing he'd done in uniform, back in the days before college, before Dillon Aerospace?

No, probably not. Killing was killing. A uniform didn't make any difference and bad people didn't have to live in a foreign country to be his enemies. Hell, there were plenty of enemies right here in Washington, and he was fighting a war against them. Fighting for all Americans. And winning.

He liked thinking that way. He almost smiled, thinking that he could get by just fine with that reasoning. A war, that's what it was. A war he hadn't started, but one he would be more than happy to finish.

At Bronovich's door he stopped and focused on his work, beat back the newborn pacifist crouching at the edge of his power. Jamison had been the last person to leave, about an hour ago. Everyone else had long since coded out and left the building. Everyone, of course, except Casey. He was still here. He would stick around until Kane was finished.

Kane moved his big frame with slow precision, looked through the office door sidelight, and saw Bronovich place those stupid gold wings on his desk and go for his coat. It was time to do it. If this got messy he didn't want to be screwing around with Bronovich in the hall. His pulse picked up and his nerves started to jump, his new weakness making it harder than ever before.

But what the hell, it had to be done. Or did it? Maybe the leaks were coming from a different division. Maybe they were all wrong about Bronovich. Was it possible? Could Bronovich be a victim of bad luck, a hardworking engineer who just happened to request the wrong files, files that contained information leaked to the press?

He thought about Bronovich's family, probably waiting right now for him to come home from work, the cute little girls who had sat in Kane's lap last month when he'd been there for dinner, asking Kane about his own dead family with shameless innocence.

He didn't know the answer and would not waste any more time wondering if Bronovich was the leak. He stuffed all his doubt into his bowels, his hands moving now with the skill of the beast that lived inside every man. But Kane's beast was well trained, mutated by two decades of lethal experiences into a creature of fatal efficiency. He gave the door a push, then pivoted into the opening.

"Bronovich."

The aerospace engineer turned to face Kane, dropping his coat at his feet. His gentle brown eyes snapped steady onto Kane, even as his whole body began to tremble. His small hands shook as he removed his glasses, banging them against his nose in a shaky rhythm. He looked foolish as he set them carefully on his desk before turning a photo of his family facedown. He squared his skinny body to Kane's, his delicate fingers clenched into tiny fists.

"Hello, Jack. I was afraid you might come see me."

Kane moved farther into the room, catching every twitch and movement Bronovich made, feeling ridiculously undermatched. Then he shut the door, closed his mind, and advanced silently on the terrified company man.

# CHAPTER TWO

Way out, at the very fringe of his consciousness, Jamison heard the clock's hands click into alignment with the alarm. He was still asleep but already moving, his hand flicking out from under the covers and toward the clock like an uncoiling spring. The alarm never rang, beaten by the unwanted reflexes that launched Jamison out of bed and threw him into action.

He was halfway across the room before his reflexes allowed him to slow down and force himself awake. He'd worked at Dillon until one-thirty in the morning and needed a couple more hours of sleep, but he wouldn't get them today. He kept moving around the dark room, fighting the temptation of his warm bed on this chilly morning.

He stopped at his dresser and leaned against it, rubbed his eyes into clearer focus, and started to make out objects in the blackness. As usual, the first thing he looked for was the picture of Melissa he'd taken several months before their split. There wasn't enough light to see the photo, but the frame was easily distinguishable. He stared at it, and through it, his mind retracing the roads of their lives that had separated them. He wanted to go back and eliminate the detours and wrong turns that led them apart, but it was an impossible task and he knew it. He started each day like this now, taking a new bearing based on where he'd been and the mistakes he'd made, determined to avoid making them again if life ever gave him another chance.

He hurried through a light breakfast, then stuffed some clean trunks into his gym bag. He stopped before closing the bag and thought about safety and how survival depended on being prepared, even if the threat was still unidentified. He took his Beretta out of the dresser drawer, checked to make sure it was fully loaded, then folded it between his sweats. He didn't know why he wanted his pistol and couldn't identify the warning thought that crossed his mind. Was it nervous jitters from working so late in a dead-quiet building? That his car had been broken into but nothing taken? More likely it was a cumulative effect. The swirl of events happening around him told his instincts to pack the weapon, and he trusted those instincts completely.

He got to the gym a little after six. It was a worn-out facility over a cheesy rent-to-own shop with iron bars over all the windows and a roll-up gate at the entrance. The dented steel door to the stairs was locked but yellow light filtered through the dingy glass of the second-floor windows, meaning Rich Blevins was already there. Jamison used one of the keys the old owner—a feisty little man with a bulbous nose and arms that still threw mean punches—had given them three years ago when they'd become regulars at the gym. The old man, a boxer who'd turned trainer, probably figured an FBI agent and an aerospace engineer were safe bets. They were polar opposites of the hothead youth and past-prime punchies who usually hung around the place.

Blevins was rapping on the speed bag when Jamison entered, making the small leather bag dance from the swivel under the round platform. At five feet ten, Blevins weighed a powerful hundred and ninety pounds and looked the way a boxer should. He was thick and stout and hard to knock down. His large hands were quick, and his brown eyes drew his narrow eyebrows together as they studied the continually moving bag. His face was big, squared off at the jaw, and his brown crew cut stood at attention like very short plumes on a medieval knight's helmet.

Jamison aimed his finger as he headed to the locker room. "Hey, you! I'm gonna kick the crap out of you this morning."

Blevins didn't look away from the speed bag and didn't break his rhythm. The bag took the pounding and snapped back instantly for more. "You're late. Take a while to build up some courage?"

"I'll be out in two minutes. Get ready to bleed."

He turned away and smiled at their threats, the taunts they'd been using against each other for twenty-five years. These words defined their friendship, and Jamison never expected them to change.

He slipped on black shorts over his plastic cup, then locked up his clothes and laced his shoes. He hurried back into the gym, pulling his gloves on with his teeth and stuffing the laces. He was freezing without a shirt, so he ran around the ring a half dozen times, shadow-boxing to get the blood flowing.

The ring's canvas, like the gym's floor, was stained with years of sweat, blood, and spit. Decades of foot-work had worn some pretty tricky slick spots on it. The ropes were filthy black in the corners, dark gray toward the middle. The light in the gym was bad, the air stank, and the heater had been broken for as long as they'd been coming. But it was their home gym, and Jamison had long ago stopped noticing the scars of brutality. He eyed Blevins as he climbed through the ropes and set the timer. "You ready?"

Blevins was stretching against the ropes with his back turned. "You bet."

Jamison hit the timer and both men moved to the center of the ring. They smacked their gloves together, and then raised their hands to protect their heads and bodies. As they went into motion, the seconds started to stretch by in long, disjointed ticks.

Blevins went on the attack right away and looked good doing it. He was moving more smoothly than he normally did, and his timing was excellent. Jamison kept having to adjust, change his jabs, and work hard to find an opening.

In the first few seconds of the third round Blevins landed a big punch on Jamison, his ears ringing like Sunday mass and warning him to expect another one soon. Jamison wanted to close his eyes and shake it off, but he forced them to stay open and ready for when Blevins came again. It took less than two seconds for Blevins to fire his left. Jamison blocked it and concentrated on the muscles of Blevins's right arm. They exploded, and as they did Jamison set his trap by feinting to the left and stepping back. Blevins kept reaching for contact with Jamison's face, following through until he was off-center and out of balance.

Jamison had him. He used his left to push Blevins's big hand out of his way, then buried his right fist into Blevins's face. As Blevins staggered back, Jamison hit him again, both blows coming all the way from his toes and opening a deep gash over Blevins's right eye. Thick, rich blood pumped out and oozed down his face. It was a good cut to work on.

He fired again while Blevins was still wobbling. He hit his mark, and then hit it again. Blevins was loose, dazed, his hands looking heavy. Jamison came again, and then again, working on the cut, opening it wider and wider until the blood ran hard, his punches splattering the red juice in a monochromatic shower. The blood ran down the sides of Blevins's nose and filled his eyes, blinding him. It was impossible for him to fight back but his fists were up so the fight was still on.

Jamison cornered him now, working the cut the same way Blevins had worked the speed bag earlier, smashing it with his left, then his right, then his left again. Now faster. Again and again and again while Blevins slumped against the ropes.

Jamison spat his mouthpiece onto the floor and screamed at the best friend he had in the world. "Go down, Rich! Damn you, go down!"

A referee would have called this fight, even though Blevins still held his hands up. But there weren't any referees. Only he and Blevins were in the ring. He crashed into the cut again and split the skin in a large arc that ran all the way from the top of Blevins's nose to the corner of his right eye.

"I said, go down!" he screamed. Jamison was an out-of-control maniac running loose in a civilized world, taking his crazy man out for an early morning walk, doing what he had to do to live with that damned beast. He hit Blevins again, harder than ever before, so hard it felt as if his forearm shattered. "Go down, damn you! Go down or I'm going to kill you."

Blevins was wide open. Jamison smashed into him again, spinning him around until his right knee buckled and he dropped to his left. Jamison stood over him, his right arm cocked and ready to finish it, his love for Blevins making him hate the words he screamed at him, the words Jamison needed to say as part of his therapy.

"Now get up," he said, surprised and disappointed that Blevins had actually dropped. "Come on, get on your feet."

Blevins's eyes looked closed, but it was impossible to be sure through all the blood. Blevins planted his left foot and tried to stand. Jamison drew back his arm to crush him as soon as Blevins straightened up.

Blevins held his head up, even though his hands were barely waist high. He tried to stand but fell down. Then he got on his knees and tried to push himself off the mat with his hands. Finally, he aimed his bloody face in Jamison's direction and shook his head—no.

It was over.

But the crazy man hated to see it end. After years of therapy, these matches were the only chance he had to get his pleasure. Win or lose, his pain or someone else's, these precious moments of bloodshed were his very best times. The crazy man dragged Jamison twice around the ring, smacking his hands against each other and crying out in some kind of bestial anguish. He circled back to Blevins, hoping to find him standing and ready for more punishment. But Blevins stayed down, blood-blinded.

Jamison slowly gained control, and after a few more minutes he got his devil bottled up, winning his second fight of the morning. He sat down in his corner, staring across the ring at Blevins, while he took deep breaths and worked the tension out of his shoulders. He was sure that lots of other people lived with demons, and he wondered what secrets they'd learned about dealing with their own.

A few minutes later he eased back to the person he wanted to be, the person he hoped and prayed would live alone inside his head someday before he died. He pulled off his gloves and dropped them to the canvas, walked over to Blevins, and knelt down. "Hey, you okay?"

Not once had Blevins hung his head. Even at the threat of that last blow, so frightening even his temporary blindness couldn't have hidden it, he kept his head up proud. Jamison admired that raw courage, that belligerent refusal to turn away from punishment, that insolent look of absolute fearlessness. It was the unshakable foundation of their friendship, the sacred ground on which they'd built their relationship long ago.

Blevins smeared a gloved hand across the gash over his eye, then pushed the leathery palm of his glove into his good eye, trying to clear the blood and get it open. "Yeah. I'll be all right."

"You sure?"

Blevins struggled to his feet like a child learning to

walk, staggering and unsure. "Uh-huh. Think so. Damn, you sure drew me off balance. I must have really telegraphed my punch."

Jamison helped his friend to his corner and sat him down, then reached into the dirty bucket for a sponge and squeezed yesterday's water out of it. He mopped off the blood so Blevins could see a little.

"No, it wasn't that. You caught me with that same combination last week, so I was expecting it. And I was having a good round. Come on, let's get you cleaned up. We'll put some butterflies on that cut and ice on the swelling."

They climbed through the ropes and headed to the locker room. Jamison felt bad for the damage he'd done, but last week he'd been the one to take the beating. He won today because of the lesson he learned then. That's the way life worked.

They showered and dressed. Jamison knotted his tie while Blevins checked and holstered his pistol, still a little unsure of his focus. "Today's your big day, isn't it?" Blevins asked, as he leaned into the mirror and checked for loose teeth. "Don't you do your dog and pony show for the board of directors this morning?"

Jamison grabbed his bag and checked Blevins's swollen eye once more to make sure the butterfly bandages were going to hold. "No, there's been a change, a bad one. I'll tell you about it later. I also need to ask you something for a friend of mine at work, a guy named Bronovich, but later, okay? Right now I have to get going. You ready?"

Blevins holstered his pistol, gave Jamison a suspicious look with his good eye, then picked up his bag. "Let's do it."

Jamison was on the road by seven-thirty, anxious to get to work. He would be there early, with time to organize his notes and be ready, if given the chance, to defend his work to the board of directors. Dillon had nothing else in the pipeline. If he didn't make something happen, there was nowhere else to assign his team, no option but layoffs if the project died. It was all the way to the mat on this one.

He parked close to the three-story research facility, double-checked the locked doors of his car, and ran to the entrance. People were already filling the halls. Guards and voices and ringing phones chased away the ghosts of empty corridors, making him feel silly for the fear he felt last night.

He put his presentation on his desk and wondered where the answers were hiding. Why had the board killed his project? What had gone wrong? He couldn't imagine the navy deciding the Wombat didn't need an upgrade of its weapons system. The plane had been in the air as long as the A-6 Intruder but with only half as many updates. Problems with the current weapons system made it a dangerous plane to fly. Pilots called it the Killer, but didn't laugh when they said it.

He started thinking aloud, his way to slow down and go over things carefully. "Okay, maybe that's it. Maybe the entire aircraft is slated for replacement and Dillon just found out about it from the Pentagon."

He rolled that idea around for a while, thinking maybe Dillon's decision to lay them off was just an overreaction, poorly thought out and maybe reversible. If the navy mothballed the Wombat, his team could redesign their system for another aircraft, maybe one of the next generation fighters. After all, Dillon wouldn't want to scrap all that great technology. They'd just re-design it for something else.

He hoped that was it. His team would just shift to an-other tactical jet and everything would be fine. But he kept working on other possibilities because he knew he was wrong. Bronovich had been clear.

At nine-thirty he called a staff meeting. His team-mates were smart people, and they had to know some-thing was wrong when he'd missed the board meeting. They deserved to know what he knew.

The people in the conference room looked worried and scared. All seven of his coworkers sat around the table but they weren't talking, and Harrison wasn't telling one of his jokes. Their eyes searched Jamison as he entered the room. They peered out from faces that blended hangovers, fear, and lost sleep into a weird mix of sad squints and tragic glances, the same kinds of looks he'd seen in emergency room lobbies.

"Good morning, everyone."

No one said anything.

"Look, I'm not going to bullshit you guys. I've got some bad news. Our project is dead, passed over by management."

Everyone reacted at once, shouting at Jamison, plead-ing for reasons, or turning desperately to the person in the next seat. Jamison didn't say anything. He let them live with it for a minute, and then held up his hands for quiet.

"Look, I'm just as confused as all of you. I want to know why this happened. If the minds on the board can be changed, we're the ones who'll have to do it. It's up to us to justify this project and we need to do it fast."

Harrison stood up. "What do you suggest we do, Peter?"

"First of all, don't bitch about it to anyone outside of Dillon. You all know what's been going on here since the leaks started. You know Casey won't tolerate any discussion with anyone unauthorized. Just go back to your office and try to dig up something. Start by looking at the project's costs."

"I don't get it," Harrison said. "Didn't we come in under budget?"

"We did, that's right, but maybe there's some aspect we're missing. Maybe something in the tail of the system, the long-term parts inventory, for instance. Or maintenance schedule, or retro-fit costs. Maybe we presented them poorly. I want everyone to get down in the weeds and take a close look in all those areas."

Harrison kept standing, waiting for more. "Is that it?"

Jamison pushed the hair off his forehead. "No, this is bad and I think all of you should get your resumes in the hands of your favorite headhunters. I'd be quick about it."

Several heads dropped a notch, as though they couldn't believe what he'd said. Jamison didn't want to say it again or lose more time. He turned and walked out of the room.

He worked all morning, tilting at any possible oversight but discovering nothing. He called Ross Casey's office two times and demanded a meeting, but his access to the vice president seemed to have died with his project.

At eleven o'clock he was wandering around his office trying to think of someone who could help. Casey had the answer, but he wasn't talking. Bronovich probably didn't know any more than he'd said last night, and Jamison couldn't imagine anyone else at Dillon who might know something *and* be willing to talk about it.

He leaned against his office windows, staring out at the bare trees in the courtyard between two wings of the building. His tired mind started to wander, and as always, it went straight to Melissa.

"Come on," he said out loud. "You don't have time for this."

She knew something, though, and Wombat was a reason to call her. He walked down to the lobby pay phones, hunkered into the phone box, and dialed.

"Citizen's Coalition Against Government Waste. How may I direct your call?"

The sound of the enemy made him flinch. "Melissa Corley, please."

"Just a minute, sir."

He was on hold with a few seconds to reconsider. This was a bad idea. He'd be better off—

"Hello, this is Melissa Corley."

Her voice laced its way through the line and snapped on his lights. He tried to hang up, to get rid of the phone that stuck to his hand, but he needed her and wanted her help. The whole team did.

"It's Peter. Can you talk?"

She didn't answer. Then, finally, "Why, yes, Peter, of course. I'm glad you called. Surprised, but glad. Hold on a second, okay?"

He heard her cover the phone with her hand and tell someone to please wait in her outer office.

"It's nice to hear your voice."

"Yours, too. You looked great last night."

She laughed. "That's nice of you to say. So what can I do for you? Or did you just call to say hello?"

He came straight out with it, didn't wait to see if extra time would make him more certain about what he was doing. "Do you think we could get together today, maybe at lunch? I need to talk to you."

The line was silent. He pushed the phone hard against his ear and listened to her breathing.

"Yes. I guess so. What time and where?"

"Twelve-thirty? You pick the restaurant. Someplace quiet."

She was checking her schedule. He could hear her open the leather book she always carried and turn some pages. "Twelve-thirty is fine. There's a Thai restaurant at 401 and the Little River Turnpike that doesn't get too crowded."

"That'll work. See you then."

He hung up in a rush and turned toward the lobby, logging in every face within possible earshot. Then he returned to his office, locked up his work, and headed to the secretarial pool to check out. He looked at Charlotte, a young secretary who'd only started at Dillon a year ago but had already earned his respect. She had short blond hair, cheeks that were a little too full, a short but sharp nose, and a keen look in her green eyes—a strange mix of round and angular features. She wore suits instead of dresses, as if declaring that she didn't intend to stay on this rung of the ladder for long.

"I'm taking off for a few hours, Charlotte, to take care of some personal business. Clock me out, okay?"

Charlotte looked up but didn't stop typing at her computer, somehow balancing their conversation with work. "Sure, Mr. Jamison, but you'd better see Mr. Casey before you leave. He tried to call you a few minutes ago, after the board meeting. You weren't in your office."

Jamison grinned and stared while his mind wondered what Casey was doing. Was he going to give Jamison a chance to plead his case, or did he already know he was having lunch with Melissa, the enemy?

He struggled with his nerves, trying like hell not to start any office gossip by acting strange. "Thanks, Charlotte."

He took the elevator up one floor, hurried down the long hall while tossing around what he knew of Ross Casey, trying to find something good to work with. Before the leaks Casey had been a pretty decent boss but a no-shit kind of guy. His simple motto had always been: *This is my pond. Do whatever you want away from work, but don't make ripples in my pond.* A career naval aviator, Casey earned medals in every military action from Vietnam to Beirut. When he retired from the navy and joined Dillon, he stopped flying and wearing uniforms, but those were the only changes. He still demanded obedience from everyone who worked for him. Once he made a decision, he didn't tolerate questions from anyone.

Back in the days before Dillon had become so factionalized and fearful, Jamison had actually enjoyed talking to Casey. He had used the types of weapons Jamison engineered and could accurately account for the human factor that made or broke a design.

The flooring turned from gray tile to burgundy carpet with a deep blue border. Overstuffed furniture, wood desks, and heavy wallpaper muted all noises in this executive hall.

"Hello," he said to the aging secretary. "I'm Peter Jamison, here to see Mr. Casey."

She didn't look up. "Well, Mr. Jamison, he has someone in his office right now. If you'll have a seat, I'll make sure he knows you're here."

Jamison thanked her, then backed away and pressed himself into the leather couch. He picked up a trade publication and flipped through pages he didn't notice.

After five minutes the old secretary spoke softly into her phone, then hung up and gave him a painful-looking grin that showed no teeth. "Mr. Casey will see you now."

Jamison headed toward the large mahogany doors, expecting the previous appointment to leave as he approached. When no one came out, he turned the handle and walked in.

Ross Casey was standing by some shelves behind his desk, speaking to a man who was leaning against the windows. Jamison didn't know him, but he did recognize something about the stranger's face—the severe loss of expression and the thousand-yard stare of empty gray eyes that had seen way too much death. Jamison knew the look far too well and could spot it two clicks away. He had worn it himself once, back when life was the prize and death was served to all who finished second.

Jamison had been lucky, extremely lucky. He'd managed to pry off most of his face after leaving Vietnam and returning to the World. He'd gone to therapy and attended work groups, talked to priests and mothers of dead soldiers. He'd healed most of the damage his killing had caused. Some men never managed to do it. Men like the one he faced in Casey's office.

"Come in, Jamison. Thanks for dropping by." He motioned for Jamison to sit, but it didn't look as though Casey was going to introduce him to the stranger.

Jamison looked at the two men and had no trouble reading the scene. This was going to be an ass-torching session, and he didn't want some stranger watching. He walked over to the stranger, stopped in front of the big man, and stuck out his hand. "I'm Peter Jamison."

The stranger didn't move, not a twitch anywhere. He just kept leaning against the window frame as he dug his eyes into Jamison's, his face declaring that he'd seen it all before. Finally, he reached out, gripped Jamison's hand, and started squeezing.

"I'm Jack Kane." Kane said his name as if it should have meant something, but probably nothing good. He strangled Jamison's hand.

Jamison squeezed back, applied enough pressure to turn coal into diamonds. Then Casey plopped into his seat. "Gentlemen," he said. "Gentlemen, let's get started here."

Kane looked over at Casey and loosened his grip. Jamison went for the fun of wrenching Kane's hand a second longer, just to see pain on Kane's face. It was only a small wrinkle, but at least a reaction. Jamison studied Kane's eyes, trying to show that he knew the address where Kane lived inside himself and that it didn't scare him. Then he walked over to the chair, turned it so he could watch both men, and sat down.

Casey swiveled in his seat so that Jamison saw him in

profile. He had an angular face with sunken cheeks. His skin was so lean it seemed to stretch across his jaw and skull, and his emerald eyes always looked as if they were locking on a target. Jamison had played a lot of basketball with Casey, back before the leaks had started, and knew Casey to be a fierce, unrelenting competitor. His face mirrored that personality.

"Jamison," Casey began. "I just wanted to make sure you're comfortable with my decision on the Wombat deal." He stopped and waited, made a quick glance at Kane.

Jamison leaned toward Casey, then glanced over to make sure Kane hadn't moved. "No, sir," he said, "I'm not. With all due respect, the Wombat needs a new weapons system more than any other tactical jet in the sky. I can't believe the Pentagon seriously thinks it can ignore the problems of the current system."

Casey shifted his profile and looked calmly at Kane. Then he clicked those green eyes back to Jamison. Any trace of friendliness that might have been there earlier was gone. "I'm sorry it came as a surprise, but I guess I couldn't expect you to understand the business side of our industry." He hesitated, then smiled. "Doesn't matter, we'll find something else for you to work on. Thanks for the hard work on Wombat."

Casey squared his chair to his desk and stood up. "That's all, Jamison. I just wanted to make sure you were clear on the situation." He produced a shallow smile that puffed out his flat cheeks. "Thanks for dropping by."

Jamison stood slowly. "Mr. Casey, I have to ask for something more specific. I can't go back to my team and tell them their contracts were written in pudding. I owe them more than that, sir, and so do you. They deserve to know where they stand."

Casey slapped his hands on the desk. "Listen to me, Jamison. We're in a tough business and I can't give your people any special privileges. Your little band of nitnoids are contract workers and don't deserve shit from me. So don't you dare come in here and make demands."

Jamison was up and moving as though he'd been sitting in a pile of red ants. He crossed the room, checking to make sure Jack Kane wasn't moving, too. "Is that what you think? My people worked their asses off for you, put in hundreds of hours off the clock to do a great job, and then you pull the plug, just like that." He snapped his fingers as he zeroed in on his boss's desk. "You owe us more than that. Come on, Casey. Have some guts and give me the truth. What's going to happen to them? Say the words."

Casey looked like a man about to fight, or not, but having to decide either way. He looked over at Kane, then came back and straightened up, leaning away from Jamison. "Get out of here, Jamison."

Jamison was ready to fight it out, right then and there, but he understood there wasn't any sense to it. This fight had already taken place and his team members had lost. He had to retreat, at least for now, with a desperate hope for a counterattack. He whirled around toward the door, thinking he'd better learn how to back down sooner.

Casey spoke again after Jamison took a few steps. "By the way, I understand you have some personal business this afternoon. Is that right?"

Jamison squared himself to Casey's question. "Yes, that's right. Is there some kind of problem with that?"

"No problem. Why would there be? I guess we'll see you later then."

Jamison looked at each man and walked out the door.

Casey watched the door close, then turned to Kane. "What do you think, Jack? Is Jamison a leak, too?"

Kane looked around the room, ramming those gray eyes into all the recesses. Casey flinched when they settled on him.

"I don't know, Ross. Yesterday I'd have said he wasn't. He was justified in requesting the information from closed files because he needed it. After all, we paid him to compare the old and new weapons systems. The information would've been damaging if disclosed, but . . ."

There it was, Kane's frustrating habit of stopping midsentence to preview what he was about to say. It pissed Casey off and reminded him that Kane always censored himself, even when talking to him. For years he'd tolerated the habit and not just because Kane scared him. He lived with the annoyance because Kane's immense power required that he put up with it.

"But what, Jack?"

"Well, the truth is that the information he's gathered over the last year is not what's been leaked so far. None of the files Jamison researched for the Wombat modification contained what the Coalition is using against us now."

"What happened yesterday to change your mind?"

Kane lifted his eyebrows. "I didn't say I'd changed

my mind. I said that until yesterday I'd have said Jamison wasn't the leak. I would appreciate it if you'd keep the distinction clear."

"Right, Jack. Sorry."

Kane continued, a little more slowly. "Lately we've had round-the-clock surveillance on several employees who had access to the leaked information. Last night our friend Jamison met someone from the Citizen's Coalition Against Government Waste."

"Really? Seems pretty suspicious."

"We checked Jamison's car but there wasn't much in it. Just a briefcase with a few innocent documents. We don't know what they discussed. He couldn't have said much, because they only talked for a couple of minutes. It was Melissa Corley, the woman he used to date, back before—"

Casey raised his hands. He didn't need Kane's help to remember when his career had started to come apart at the seams. He'd changed every company policy when the Coalition first began its attacks on Dillon. He became venomous, even deadly, when he discovered that one of his employees was leaking top-secret government information. Whoever was feeding facts to the Coalition was doing one hell of a job, turning over plenty of information the newspapers were anxious to print. The Coalition was close to making a public charge of criminal fraud, and that made the FBI begin an investigation into Dillon's leaks of military secrets. Casey was getting skewered by the press, the FBI, the Coalition, and his board of directors. They all seemed out to get him.

"So Jamison probably is the leak."

Kane took a book from Casey's shelf, opened the

cover, and read the flyleaf. "No, actually I don't think so."

Casey looked from Kane to the book, then back to Kane. He wished, as he had so many times before, that he was back in uniform, wearing a beautiful captain's eagle on his collar and four stripes on his sleeve, able to demand the answers and actions he wanted.

"Why not? What does Jamison have to do, hold up a sign? He's meeting with the Coalition, for God's sake. That's good enough for me. He must be a leak, too."

The book seemed to have all of Kane's interest now, his conversation with Casey a distant annoyance. "Like I said, the files he requested didn't contain the information leaked so far, and I don't think Jamison had any knowledge of it. Maybe he's collaborating with someone else here at Dillon. We just don't know, but we'll keep him covered until we find out."

"Damn it, Jack, why don't you just kill the bastard right now and be done with it?"

Kane reached up and rolled an earlobe in his fingers, staring away as though he hadn't heard.

"Okay," Casey said, "I guess that would leave some important questions unanswered, such as who he might be working with. Do it your way, but I'm getting my ass burned, so keep on top of it."

Kane had been leaning against the windows, but Casey's last words made him lurch forward, bringing his strong frame erect. He crossed the room silently, with long, noiseless strides. He was impossibly quiet for such a big man.

"I'll do what I have to do, Casey. You know I will." He looked lost, just for a second, before pasting those hateful gray eyes onto Casey. "But *I* decide who lives and who dies. Remember that."

Casey struggled against the challenge. He wanted to fight back, but Kane wielded tremendous power, even if he rarely flexed it.

"I'm sure you'll handle it appropriately" was the best answer Casey could muster.

# CHAPTER THREE

Jamison found the Thai restaurant at a little after one and doubted that Melissa would still be waiting, but it would probably be best if she wasn't. Meeting her for lunch was a mistake and he knew it. He might avoid crossing the line by being late, but if she were there waiting for him, he knew he'd do it anyway.

He parked a block away and jogged to the entrance. When he opened the door, he was smacked by sensory overload. All the restaurant's walls and tablecloths were red. The acoustical ceiling was painted black, and the floor was a checkerboard of black and white linoleum. The air was thick with smells of oil and spices. Melissa waved from her table and he went straight over to her.

He sat down on the leather seat beside her and she got close. "I was about to give up on you." She touched his forearm, squeezed it slightly, and pulled him toward her.

He nearly gave her a hug, wondering if that was what she'd expected. But he couldn't be sure and didn't want to screw up with her again, so he erred on the side of caution and stood his ground, his arm tingling at the spot her finger had pressed. He felt a little lost and couldn't really remember why he'd come, but he was very glad to be here with the woman he loved.

He put his hand on hers. "I thought you'd be gone. Sorry I'm late."

When she slid her hand away, he felt as though he'd been unplugged.

"That's okay," she said, taking a sip from her water glass. "Something happen at work?"

"Oh yeah, something definitely happened at work. Maybe we'll talk about it later." He swept his eyes around the restaurant but didn't see anyone he knew. "So, is the food any good here?"

Melissa leaned toward him and hesitated, then spoke in a low voice. "I know I shouldn't bring this up, but I heard about your project. I'm sorry."

He drew back from her. "How in the world did you find out?"

Melissa shook her head. "I'm just sorry, that's all. No questions, okay?"

He toyed with a menu while stumbling around for an easy question. He wanted to demand an answer but had to ease his way across the battle line. "This place is Thai, right? How hot is the food?"

She grinned. "Well, it depends. If you were Thai, they would make it very hot. Since you aren't, they'll calm it down and make it round-eye hot, unless you order it otherwise."

An Asian waitress, short, thin, and dark, came to the table. "Take your order now, Ms. Corley?"

"Yes, Pauranee. I'll have the Thai chicken again. Thai hot, please."

The waitress grinned, then turned to Jamison for his order, her pencil poised on the little green pad.

"I'll have the same." He shrugged and flipped his menu closed.

"Thai hot?" Her eyes widened. Melissa giggled.

"Jeez, yes. Thai hot, okay?"

Melissa's giggle turned into a laugh. Pauranee raised her hand and hid her mouth.

Jamison looked back and forth between them. "Make it double Thai hot, for crying out loud. Triple, okay? So hot you need asbestos plates."

As the waitress walked away, she whispered to another waitress and they giggled all the way to the kitchen.

"It would have killed you, I suppose, to order sweet and sour?"

Melissa hadn't laughed so loud that she offended him. She had the kind of laugh that made him want to hold her and laugh with her.

"You know me better than that, Peter. I *love* the hot stuff."

"Yeah." He looked around the restaurant, then leaned toward her cautiously. She leaned in too, her smile fading fast, her face getting serious.

"Melissa," he said, "I have to ask you something."

She cocked an ear toward him, her eyebrows close together. "Okay. I'll answer it if I can. No guarantees, though."

"Thanks."

"Sure."

"How hot is Thai hot?"

Her eyes filled with sympathy. "Oh, baby, it's hot. I mean, grab-your-ankles-and-hold-on hot."

"That hot, huh?"

"Hot. Very hot."

"Okay, I got it. Really, really hot chicken."

She kept it up, enjoying his worry and looking so natural with him, so happy, comfortable, and relaxed, as if she belonged there. He kept looking at her face, thinking there might be a way they could survive the damage she was causing Dillon, that there was a way to get her back. After all, they had survived other hard times, his stint overseas during a bad time in their relationship, and her brief affair with a disreputable congressman. Both had created problems, but dating the congressman was a real departure for Melissa. She usually avoided anyone of questionable integrity. Jamison had never understood the attraction and accepted the fact that he never would.

Her affair had ended when the congressman died on a D.C. street not far from the White House, murdered just outside the restaurant where he was to meet Melissa. She had watched him die from the window by her table. It was, of course, a bad break for the congressman, but Jamison had welcomed back the grieving Melissa, even though he was ashamed of himself for benefiting from the man's death.

"I understand," Melissa said, bringing him back.

He shook the memory. "I'm sorry, what?"

She reached over and pushed his hair away from his

face, her fingernails barely touching his forehead, electrifying him again. She was still grinning. "I said I understand why you ordered the same thing I did. You didn't want to back away from the challenge, right?"

His eyes were stuck to hers. "You call this food a challenge, a little hot pepper on chicken? Come on, Melissa, you're talking to a guy who still eats the occasional hot dog."

"And you think that's more of a challenge?"

"To eat? No. But try thinking about it while you eat one. Once when I was younger, I stopped by a slaughterhouse before going fishing, trying to get the parts of hog they don't use, for chum. Know what they told me?"

"Yuck. Can't imagine."

"They said there weren't any parts they didn't use."

She looked disgusted. "Oooo, hot dogs?"

Jamison licked his lips. "I doubt they're curing cancer with it. So, how about you? How do you keep busy these days? Aside from work, I mean."

She looked at the ceiling as if narrowing her choices. "Well, let's see. I'm still running a little, although I haven't competed since we ran the half-marathon. I'm keeping my times down, though. And I'm still fencing."

He rolled his eyes. "That is such an odd sport."

"You would love it. It improves your speed, reactions, and balance—all things that are important to you. Besides, it's fun to poke and stab at other people. I switched from foils to sabers a few months ago, so now it's all slashing and clanking, not just thrust and parry."

The waitress arrived and caught Melissa slicing the air with her knife. She chuckled as she set the meals down. The damned chicken was much hotter than Jamison expected. Hell, it was hotter than anything he'd ever eaten before, but he kept quiet about it, drank four glasses of water, and wiped about that much sweat off his face.

He finished when she did and paid the bill. When they stepped out onto the sidewalk, the sun was bright and the low buildings offered protection from the cool wind. It was almost pleasant, at least for December.

Jamison touched her arm. "Are you up for a walk? I'd like to talk a little before you go."

"Sure. That sounds nice."

They headed north, away from his car. The sidewalk wasn't crowded, only about twenty people were walking ahead of them and there wasn't much traffic in the street. They took a short stroll and stopped at the entrance of a jewelry store. Melissa looked at something in the window, but when she started to move on, Jamison didn't go with her.

She turned and walked back to him. He shuffled in front of her, then picked up her hands and held them low between them. "Melissa, I don't want to pick a fight here, but I'm really confused by the cancellation of my project. I think you know what happened and I would appreciate your help."

She smiled, but her lips stayed together. She reached up, adjusted his tie, then brushed her nails along his neck. "Peter, I can't help you. You know I can't."

"Sure you can. What's stopping you?"

She looked surprised. "Well, ethics, for one thing."

"Come on, Melissa. I know how you feel about ethics, but I also know how you hate to see people victimized. That's what's happening here. Seven of my people will lose their jobs unless I get the Wombat back on the hot sheet. Good people, Melissa. People with families who need your help. Give me something to go on. Really, that's all I'm asking, some direction."

She had a look on her face he couldn't quite decipher. Was it pity? Pain? Whatever it was, she didn't say anything.

"I'm not asking for Coalition secrets. Just point me in the right direction. I can take it from there."

"Peter, we shouldn't be having this conversation. Sure, I know some things about Dillon, but you know a whole lot more than I do. I think we should keep that knowledge separate."

"Well, I don't."

"You don't?"

"No."

She jerked her hands away and stared into the street. Then she snapped back. "Tough. I'm not doing this, Peter. This is so typical of you. We don't agree, so you want me to cave, even if I think I'm right."

"I want you to help me. That's all there is to it. I'm not trying to hurt you or the Coalition. I'm just trying to save jobs, damn it, and I need your help. As a friend, I'm asking for your advice."

She moved closer. "Okay, *friend,* here goes. Find another employer."

"Oh, that's great. Thanks a lot."

"You asked me as a friend, I'm talking like one. Get out of there."

He opened his mouth but didn't know what to say. He just stood there, looking at her. After a minute Melissa shook her head. "I'm sorry. Let's start over, okay?"

"Be glad to."

"I really can't say much, but if you tell me why you think your project was killed, I guess I can tell you if you're hot or cold. It might help a little."

"Except that I don't have a clue."

"They didn't give you a reason?"

"No. Hell, I can't even imagine a decent reason. It's too weird."

"No clues at all?"

"Not really. Although once, several months ago, I had lunch with our director of research, Ted Bronovich. He said the government still hadn't acknowledged the flaw in the current system, and our new system might not be cheap enough to justify replacing the old one. That was the only objection I ever heard."

"Was he right?"

"It was cheap enough. After our meeting, I spent a week pulling subcontractor bids for assemblage components. I added allowances for retooling, additional training, new distribution, and storage of spare parts. Then I amortized the new system's start-up costs over five years, which is about a third of the system's life."

"I'm impressed. Then what did you do?"

"I showed the costs and the prototype to Vice President Casey and demonstrated that our system was more accurate, more dependable, and far less expensive than the existing one."

A woman came out of the jewelry store and stared at Melissa as she walked past down the sidewalk. They waited until she was gone.

"Go on."

"I was cleared to go ahead, at least until last night." He looked across the street, then up and down the sidewalk. "What do you think?"

She buttoned her coat. "That we shouldn't be having this conversation."

"True enough. What else?"

"I really hate that you're doing this to me, putting me in this predicament."

"I know it, but if you can tell me a little, it might help."

"All I can say is, there are serious legal problems at Dillon. I can't be specific."

"Okay, thanks for that. Can you tell me how those problems might have affected the Wombat?"

"No, but . . . I suppose I could look at anything you have and give you my opinion. It'll just be between us, although I'd rather drop this right here and forget we ever had this conversation. You decide."

"Maybe you'll catch something I missed."

She shielded her eyes from the sun and shook her head. "Fine, no problem, I'll do it. Are you busy tonight?"

"No plans."

"Then come over to my house. Bring whatever you have. Now, if we're finished here I really need to get back to work."

Without waiting for an answer, she stepped out of the storefront's entrance and headed along the sidewalk toward her car. He fell in beside her and opened the car door when they got there. She stopped and stepped into him. "I've missed you, Peter. I've missed you a lot."

"Me too. You have no idea how much."

She slid into her car. He closed the door and headed back toward his car.

Jack Kane pulled into traffic as Jamison got close. He drove down the street and found a parking place that faced the sun and provided a concealing glare on the windshield. From there he had an easy view of Jamison and his car. He picked up his cell phone and pushed a speed-dial number. It rang once.

"Security."

He was busy watching Jamison and didn't answer right away.

"*Security,*" the man said again, his voice edgy with suspicion.

"This is Kane."

"Oh. Hello, Mr. Kane. What can I do for you, sir?"

"I'm working a case and need some help."

"Yes, sir. How many men do you want, sir?"

"You and two others. Individual cars. Right away. Head east on the Little River Turnpike. Call me in ten minutes."

"Roger that, Mr. Kane. We'll leave now. Be on the road in two minutes, tops."

Kane hung up and dialed again.

"Hello?" The voice on the other end was soft, but firm.

"Are you aware of the problem I'm trying to solve?"

"Yes."

Kane watched Jamison get into his car. "And my actions are approved, in advance?"

"Any measures you think necessary. This is too important, and there's no time to vacillate."

"Thank you. I'll take care of it. Good-bye."

Kane pulled out his map and picked locations for his men. He would start the tail of Jamison until the others got there to alternate with him. Whether Jamison had leaked information or not, he had met with the Corley woman twice and that made him dangerous to Dillon Aerospace. Kane's job was the elimination of any threat to the company, and he took his work very seriously.

# CHAPTER FOUR

Jamison parked in front of Melissa's Georgetown brownstone, lucky to find a spot on a Friday night. It was just after eight P.M. and the happy hour crowd had thinned out, but it was still a little early for the dinner and music set.

The darkness made it easy for him to sneak his box of data into her four-story building. Her apartment was on the third floor, accessed by an ornate wooden staircase with small chandeliers at each landing. His footsteps echoed off the paneled walls as he climbed the polished oak stairs. He could hear shuffling in the apartments he passed and saw peepholes go dark as people watched him from behind closed doors. He was glad when he got to her door and shifted the box onto his other hip and knocked.

Melissa swung open the door, holding a small stalk

of celery, wearing faded jeans and an oversized sweatshirt. No shoes or socks. She'd pulled back her hair and she wasn't wearing jewelry. His nerves kicked up when he saw her.

"Hi. Come in."

She leaned against the door as he passed. Her apartment was large, meticulously kept, and nicely decorated with an eclectic mix of pieces he recognized instantly. He set his box down on the floor by the couch and walked around, stepping slowly as though this were some kind of museum, trying to get his bearings and feel at home again. He gently touched some of the items but mostly kept his hands behind his back. He went slowly through the living and dining rooms without seeing any photos of another man.

She followed a step and a half behind him, looking where he did, keeping quiet for a minute or so. "How was your day?"

He picked up an antique dagger and examined it. "Okay, I guess. About what you'd expect. Better now that I've made it here with the data. You wouldn't believe the security at Dillon these days."

"I hear they're acting incredibly paranoid. Is this all the documentation on the Wombat? Everything?"

He looked at her suspiciously. "No. All of it would have filled a small pickup, a little awkward to carry past the guards. This is just the cost data."

He set the dagger down, walked over to the cardboard box, and kicked the lid off with his shoe. "I collected most of this stuff over the last six months, before Dillon cracked down so hard. But some of it is as recent as this afternoon." He turned away from the box and stared at a huge antique bookcase.

She stepped up beside him and looked at the book-case, too. "I'll never forget how surprised I was when you bought this for me."

His pulse fluttered. He hadn't heard her use that tone in a year. It was a beautiful sound, like a radiant angel calling him home.

"I'll never forget sneaking it up your stairs with my friends." He arched backward and feigned a bad back.

"Aren't you afraid that Dillon or the FBI suspects you? The newspaper says the agents have a short list of suspects. Won't you end up on it?"

Jamison shrugged. "I doubt it. I've never done any-thing wrong, at least not until now. The people they suspect have been on the list for some time, I imagine. Probably since the leaks began. Besides, I don't fit the profile." He thought about how fast she'd heard about the Wombat's cancellation. "But it seems likely the leak is someone who works with me, certainly in my depart-ment." He watched her carefully.

"Oh?"

"Yes, oh."

"Who do you think it is?"

He gave up and felt stupid trying to trap her. "I don't know. No one in particular."

She nodded, and her eyes were distant for a second. "What do you think will happen now?"

He didn't want to deal with this question. He'd spent the afternoon trying like hell to reverse Dillon's deci-sion, but finally concluded that nothing was going to change without a major fight. His motivation was sim-ple now. He was in a struggle for his team's survival and would use whatever tactics he could devise.

"If nothing changes, my team will get layoff notices

next week. Dillon can't carry people without current assignments."

"That's a shame. Will you lose your job, too?"

"No, it doesn't look like it. Dillon loves me because I do a good job."

"You do. No question."

"I keep hearing that the Coalition is threatening criminal charges against Dillon. You really think they're corrupt?"

She squirmed a little and pinched her ear as she walked off. "It's difficult for me to say anything about that. I'm too far over the line already."

"I suppose. But I'd like to know."

She walked back to him, took him straight on. "How much?"

"What?"

"I asked you how much. How much would you really like to know? How serious are you? Where does your comfort zone end?"

He took a step back to see more than her face. He needed to see her body signals. "Jeez, Melissa, what are you talking about?"

She put her hands behind her back. "Let me ask you something. Don't you think that Americans tend to just go along with whatever happens in government?"

"You mean that they don't bitch about the screwups?"

"Right. Low expectations are exactly what I'm talking about. Americans don't demand accountability for anything anymore. They've come to expect that everything's rigged, so why waste time trying to fight it?"

Jamison nodded and kept quiet. He was waiting to see what this had to do with the Wombat.

"This country needs accountability. Checks and balances, as originally intended, and people deserve it. The perverse incentives of Washington politics are wrecking this country, but all we do is get angry for a few minutes, shake our heads at the excesses and gridlock, then let it pass."

"You're right. We've all done it."

"Well, I don't. Companies like Dillon—who are only minor players in this game—are in my crosshairs because they're my best starting point. They're corrupt and I'll prove it before going another step up the ladder, then another."

"Hey, calm down. I've never seen this side of you before."

She closed her eyes and took a deep breath. "I'm sorry. I shouldn't have said all that. I passed your comfort zone, didn't I?"

"No, it's not that. It's just that it sounds . . . well, hopeless. You're taking on a monster. You can't seriously think you'll win."

She looked patient, as if she hadn't expected him to understand. "I'm not doing this alone. The Coalition believes we can do it."

"Well, good luck. Sounds like a one-way trip to me."

She wanted to argue, he knew that. He also knew she wouldn't. It wasn't her style. She'd fight, sure, but wouldn't waste time arguing.

"I'll get us some coffee. Make yourself at home and I'll be right back. Instant all right with you?"

He plucked her saber from beside a chair and chased her toward the kitchen, trying to break down the wall he'd just put between them. "Sure. Need a hand?"

She analyzed his bad form. "No, thanks, Sinbad, but

you can close the blinds. Some nosy people just moved into the building across the street."

"Sure." He tossed the saber onto the couch and went to the windows. They filled one entire wall of her apartment and looked down onto Thirty-third Street and across at an old building, which about a hundred years ago had been a warehouse. The new window frames reminded him of the remodeling Melissa had done two years ago. He wanted her to move in with him at the time to avoid the disruption but she refused. Typically, she had stubbornly held on to her independence. They had fought about it.

Now he wished she'd moved into his house. He wondered how different their lives might have been as he rotated the tilt wands of the blinds, incrementally concealing himself from the darkened building across the street. Melissa came back with his coffee.

"Ready to go to work?"

"Sure. Where do you want to start?"

She put her coffee on a table, grabbed a legal pad, and curled up like a cat on the matching love seat. "I guess at the beginning. Tell me about the Wombat project, right from the day you were assigned. We'll get into your data after we've identified the information we want to target."

He stalled for a second as he organized his thoughts. Her pen was poised over her pad, ready to write. She suddenly looked up at him.

"We don't have to do this, you know."

"What? Oh, I know. I was just thinking it through, that's all. I'm not having second thoughts."

"You're sure?"

"Yes," he said, trying to sound convincing. Then he began without any hesitation. He told the entire history of the project, including setbacks, successes, and management interferences. Melissa wrote quickly but never interrupted. Her head bounced gently as she wrote, her beautiful brown hair swinging with the rhythm of his words.

At one in the morning he finished his story and went into the kitchen for some water. When he returned, Melissa was throwing a sheet on the couch, maneuvering the linen as it floated down. He grabbed a corner and helped her tuck it under a cushion.

"Sleeping on the couch tonight?"

She grinned and slapped his arm, hard enough to hurt. "Not likely. Thought you might rather stay here than make the drive home. We can get a fresh start in the morning."

He tried to get a look at her eyes to see what she was thinking. But she turned away and fluffed a pillow. "Fine with me. Thanks."

She was grinning now. "Not quite like old times, but . . ."

"Uh, yeah. Not quite."

Melissa rubbed her hands together and looked around the living room. "You know where everything is. Help yourself to whatever you need. Use my bathroom, though. The guest bath is being remodeled. Take a shower in the morning if you like. The glass door is opaque, so don't worry. Besides, I've seen it all before."

He felt himself blush.

She rubbed her hands as if they were freezing cold. "Right. Well, I guess I'll see you in the morning."

He fidgeted in front of her, his feet desperate to take

the step that separated them but his heart telling him it wasn't right.

"Good night, Melissa."

Jack Kane used the key he'd been given and opened the door to a large, empty room. It was a storeroom of some kind or maybe an empty artist's loft. There were no interior walls except for a small room at the far end, probably a bath.

Directly ahead of him, about twenty feet away, was a wall of black plastic draped from ceiling to floor and end to end. It divided the huge room in half, lengthwise, allowing the area by the windows to stay dark.

A man with a nice smile, friendly eyes, and a big handgun walked up to him with a cup of coffee. "Good evening, Mr. Kane."

Kane took the coffee and sniffed at it before he sipped. "What are they doing over there, Corderman?"

Dan Corderman snickered. "Well, sir, they're getting ready for bed right now. We were in her apartment earlier, so Martin's got their entire evening on tape. We're betting they'll be bumping butts soon, so I left. You know I hate watching that stuff when I'm stuck on surveillance. It makes me miss my wife too much."

Kane chuckled. "I thought you hated your wife. I've never heard you do anything but complain about her."

"Doesn't matter, sir. You listen to enough of another couple's heavy action, and anyone would miss his wife." His eyes popped open and he stiffened. "Oh, jeez, Mr. Kane, I'm sorry. I didn't mean to say that."

Kane stood solid, turned his face to stone, and refused to give up any of the pain or sorrow or anger. He was saving it all for himself, feeling guilty that it had taken so long for the tragedy of his family's deaths to affect him.

He had been serving as a technical representative on cruise, the liaison between the navy and Dillon Aerospace, when tough problems came up with one of their planes. Aboard the carrier *Constellation*, the ship's captain called him to his quarters. "Mr. Kane," he began, trying not to hesitate. "I have some terrible news for you. Terrible news."

Kane remembered standing there, his eyes flicking back and forth as he waited quietly, terrified for the captain to finish.

"Your home was broken into last night, Mr. Kane. I'm sorry to say that your wife was killed. Both your children, too. You'll be launched stateside as soon as you're ready. I'm very sorry. If there's anything I can do . . ."

The captain's words couldn't be true. They didn't sound as if they could possibly be real, but then his family didn't seem real, either, not out here on a ship in the middle of the Mediterranean. He hadn't held them in his arms for six months. Six long months without hearing his wife's voice or her enthusiasm as she planned their future. If his family was gone now, it was hard to feel. He stood there knowing the captain was still talking and hated himself for not suffering more intensely, for not collapsing or crying the second he heard the news, totally unaware that the pain would settle in later.

By the time he got back to Washington the police had moved on to the next day's murders, leaving his family's deaths behind until someone jumped up and confessed. The detectives had to move on, they said. If they couldn't solve a murder within forty-eight hours, it might never be solved. They didn't have the man-hours to spend on something that might not end in an arrest. It was over, they'd told him. Try to forget about it.

Like hell. Kane worked the case himself and talked to everyone who knew anything. He pieced together tiny shreds of information until he had some leads and chased them down until he had suspects, then he chased the suspects until he had . . . nothing.

They were gone. His family's murderers were hiding, fearing the vengeful husband and father who was out to get them. The word of Kane's obsession had filtered back to them from the hundreds of people he'd interviewed.

That was when he found out about Dillon security. Two men approached him—not at the office but at the pistol range. Two men with FBI credentials, a piece of paper with an address, and two photos of the men who'd killed his family. Two men who said nothing except, "Dillon security wanted to help."

Kane accepted the photos and the addresses without speaking.

A few weeks later, after he'd gone to the addresses and killed the men, another man he did not know came to see him. He wanted to know if Kane was interested in shifting career paths at Dillon. They could use a man like him, he said. In security. Dillon's security.

And use him they had, with every one of his victims wearing the faces of his family's murderers. They'd gone down easily at first, then easier. It was his pleasure, and for nineteen years he had been venting his rage on whomever Dillon wanted dead, waiting for the meanness to drain out.

Kane shook the memory and tried to move past it, saving it for the right time. "What has Jamison been saying over there?"

"He's telling her all about his project and a bunch of other classified information. He has a pretty big stack of data with him to support it."

Kane stepped up to the black plastic and passed through the overlap. He walked to the spot where another man sat at a card table, monitoring video and audio recorders. Nothing else occupied the large room other than roaches.

"How's the signal, Martin?"

Samuel Martin shifted the headphones off one ear of his massive head. The thick fingers of his weightlifter's body were awkward but surprisingly gentle as he adjusted the small knobs of the equipment. "Good, Mr. Kane."

"Audio and video?"

"Yes, sir. You should hear the crap I'm taping. They sound like a couple of awkward teenagers over there. Know what I mean? Not understanding anything about love, yet absolutely certain they're in it."

"Really?"

"But they don't love each other, Mr. Kane. I know love and this ain't it."

"You're the expert, huh?"

Martin shifted his giant body around and pretended to pick up a microphone. "Yes, sir, and this is the *Love Connection*. Tonight we have Peter Jamison and Melissa Corley, two starcrossed—"

"Are all the rooms covered?"

Martin straightened up and set the pretend microphone on the card table. "Yes, sir. We've got a small blackout in the hallway, but that's all."

"Good. Stay on it."

"Mr. Kane, there's some Dillon material in there. You want me to go in and get it?" The huge man smiled, his big blue eyes looking like they belonged to a salesman who really needed a sale. He wanted to take Jamison down and pick up the bonus money for a killing. It was probably the right idea, too. Go ahead and do it, get Dillon's data back. Nice, simple, and clean.

But Jamison was an amateur. The Corley woman was, too. Kane could take them down whenever he wanted. He could wait a little while and not pay a price. Maybe, just maybe, there was a better way to use Jamison, stop the leaks, and retrieve the data without having to kill people. Kane watched Martin's massive body wiggle around in his seat. "Do you think we should, Martin?"

"No, sir. I mean, I don't know, sir. Just a thought, that's all."

"Thank you, Martin. If I decide to send Corderman in to get the data, you can stay here and guide him around Jamison and Corley."

A huge muscle bumped up on Martin's right shoulder and looked as if it might burst the seam of his shirt. "Yes, sir, Mr. Kane. Whatever you say."

Jamison slept until six. It was a very late start for him, but he knew how Melissa hated mornings and knew he'd still have time to get things organized before she woke up. He headed to her bathroom to shower, checking on her as he passed through her room. She was on her stomach, twisted in the sheets with her T-shirt up to her waist, revealing her black panties. He stood over her for several minutes wanting, more than anything else, to climb in bed with her, rub her back, and smell her hair. Nothing else mattered at that moment. He would give anything to wrap her up in his arms one more time.

He pulled himself away, climbed into the shower, and tried to forget that the woman he loved was half naked on the bed in the next room. He dried and dressed in the bathroom, then forced himself through her room without looking toward the bed. He made coffee and went to work in the living room. When she stumbled out an hour later, blurry-eyed and beautiful, he was standing beside five piles of data.

"How did you sleep?"

She shuffled up and hugged him, then hung on spaghetti-armed. "Good. You?"

He had trouble letting his arms go around her, afraid she would wake up fully and realize they were hugging. "I slept well. Care for some coffee?"

She nudged her head against his neck, then pulled herself away and rubbed her eyes. "That would be nice. Thanks."

"Be back in a minute."

She waved over her shoulder as she fell into the chair by the documents.

In the kitchen he stored all the pleasure of the hug, just in case it never happened again. He poured the coffee and returned. She held a piece of paper funneled in her hand. Her other hand clutched her robe closed. Delicate, wire-rimmed glasses added to her intense look of intelligence.

She reached for the coffee without looking up. "Hope you don't mind that I started."

"Don't mind at all. Why don't I make us some breakfast while you get up to speed?"

"Sounds wonderful."

She picked up some copies and went to her bedroom. Jamison headed to the kitchen and searched for a skillet. In fifteen minutes she was in the kitchen, toweling her hair, dressed in a T-shirt and jeans. She leaned against the counter, holding some of his documents.

"Why does Dillon use such old technology for the Wombat's targeting system? Microprocessor technology has advanced so much. I can't imagine where you get this old circuitry manufactured."

"That's a good question. Fact is, we pay a fortune for it." He waved a spatula in the direction of the living room. "Copies of the accounting invoices are in another stack out there. The savings from converting that item alone would more than offset the retooling expense and make the current system much safer for the pilots."

"I would think so. Hasn't anyone ever suggested that before?" She asked the question without looking up and went to another page.

"If someone did, they were about as successful as I was. You're going to find a whole lot of reasons to convert to a new system as you wade through that stuff. I can't be the first to ask about any of it."

He slid the omelettes onto plates. "How about grabbing silverware and the pitcher of orange juice?"

Melissa put down the documents. "Peter, I've already seen lots of things I'd like to check against the information in my computer. Would it be all right if I went over your stuff in my office? You can come along, or I could call you when I have a question."

"I'll pass, but you can do that. Just be careful about who you tell."

"I won't tell a soul. Anyway, hardly anyone works on Saturday, so the place will be quiet. The building has great security."

"Good. You'll call me later?"

"Sure."

Thirty minutes later he gathered his things to leave. Melissa approached him as he stepped to the door and looked around the room to make sure he had everything.

"What are your plans today?"

"To the gym and then out for a run. Maybe we can get together after you finish."

She picked up his hand and traced a finger across his palm. "Sounds nice. We'll set it up when I call."

"Great. Good luck today." He watched her finger working on his palm. It was driving him nuts, making him struggle to stay in control. His arms twitched to wrap her up in them.

She let go but didn't look up, then opened the door and leaned against the jamb. "Have a good workout."

She closed the door behind him. As he hit the stairs, he heard her bolt it.

Jamison spent most of the workout dealing with the pain and frustration of his friends' dying careers. At four o'clock he began to wonder when Melissa would call about their plans for tonight. He was counting on her. If anyone could find a way to save those jobs, she was the one.

He stopped in the kitchen on his way to the shower,

sweating from a ten-mile run. The phone rang and he answered it, dripping sweat all over the floor. "Hello?"

"It's me. Can you talk?"

He grabbed a roll of paper towels, snapping some off, and wiped the burning sweat from his eyes. "Sure. What's up?"

"I've been here all day going over your stuff, and I don't know how to tell you this without just blurting it out. It's really good news. Or really bad news, depending on your viewpoint."

He wiped sweat off his right shoulder and then switched the phone to that ear. "Go."

"I analyzed all of your information and came to the same conclusions you drew in your synopsis. But your Wombat project doesn't even matter anymore."

"What? Why? What do you mean?"

"Well, first let me admit that I haven't finished yet, so some of what I say might change slightly."

"Understood."

"Good. Remember those bids and invoices you had for the old system, the ones you got from accounting?"

"Sure."

"I cross-checked them with the information we have on file from those same subcontractors, most of it obtained through the Freedom of Information Act, tax returns, annual reports, and disclosure statements. We hacked into the Pentagon's computer to get some of it."

"And?"

"There's no question about it now. Dillon has been committing criminal fraud against the government for years. Decades. Just as we suspected, but honestly, it could have taken another year for us to prove it without your help. It looks like Dillon has defrauded American taxpayers out of . . . oh, I don't know exactly, but over a billion dollars since that weapons system first went into use. We can get criminal convictions with this information. Maybe restitution."

Sweat started running down his face again and he grabbed another towel. "You're sure?"

"I won't have the actual numbers finalized until tomorrow. But am I sure about the fraud? Yes, absolutely."

He wanted to ask again, maybe phrase his question differently. But he didn't. If Melissa said she was sure, she was sure. "All right, so what happens next?"

"Well," she started, and then interrupted herself. "I thought you might need to digest this a little first."

"No, I'm all right."

"Okay. But if you want me to clarify anything, just say so."

"What you're saying is pretty clear. What do we do now?"

She was excited and he could hear it. She was closing in on her prey and loving it.

"There are two ways to approach this. One, the Coalition could make a full disclosure and pursue prosecution, get the fraud out in the open, and put pressure on Dillon and the Defense Department administrators who must have gone along with them. The only problem is that it puts you in a bad spot. You could be charged criminally for passing along classified information, unless we get you some whistle-blower protection."

She paused and waited, but Jamison was not about to speak until he heard both options.

"I think the better choice is for me to give you the facts *we* have, and let you take it to the Hill. That would protect you because there'd be no proof you ever told us anything."

"Who would I take it to? I doubt there's a complaint department for this sort of thing."

"Senator Drummond, on the Senate Armed Services Committee. I've known him all my life and worked with him before. He's a real bulldog, always ready to jump down someone's throat. I can pretty much guarantee he'll open a Senate investigation and probably push for a special prosecutor."

Jamison didn't put much faith in politicians. Because of them, he'd fought McNamara's ridiculous war and had never forgotten how far removed they could be from real life. But he wanted to trust Melissa's advice. After all, this was her job, she was good at it, and he didn't have a better plan. "How soon can your guys have the facts detailed in a way that Drummond can understand?"

"I want to move quickly on this, so I'll call my people right now and bring them into work tomorrow. I'll call Drummond at home and set up your appointment for Monday. Are you ready to move that fast?"

"I guess so. Should I go into Dillon this weekend and look for anything else?"

"Absolutely not. This is dangerous enough already. There have been rumors for years about how ruthlessly Dillon retaliates. Don't cross them until we're ready. Promise?"

"Yes."

"We've got everything we need. Don't do anything else. I'll call Drummond right now."

Jamison hesitated long enough to think about his

team members. Would this help them? No, probably not. Could it hurt them anymore than they were already going to be hurt? No, again. They would be all right, or maybe not, regardless of what he did now. He would do the right thing and trust in that.

"That all sounds fine. Can we meet later to clear up some details?"

"Why don't you come over to my house? But think about this between now and then, Peter, because it'll get pretty ugly."

"Not much to think about."

"As long as you're sure."

"I'm sure."

Martin hadn't been comfortable since ten, when he got up to eat dinner. His muscular body wasn't designed for long hours sitting on a hard chair in a cold warehouse. He was too big and powerful, too used to pushing things around. Things like weights, people, and anything that annoyed him.

Right now Peter Jamison was annoying the hell out of him. Martin had sat on his ass all day waiting for the little prick to show up at Corley's apartment. He read magazines and played stupid mind games while he ate junk food he would normally avoid. It was all Jamison's fault. And Kane's. If Kane had given him his way, he would have finished last night and killed Jamison, maybe the Corley woman. He would have cut their throats and left with the stuff Jamison had stolen from Dillon. He could be out in the bars now, his favorite places on a Saturday night, using his raw power to impress young girls, and daring anyone to challenge his right to do it.

Jamison had come back to her apartment about six o'clock, right after dark, carrying a small suitcase as though he planned to stay for a while. Corley had arrived just after that. They'd sat on the floor of her living room since then, going over a bunch of damn receipts, talking about how incriminating those pieces of paper would be.

As if Martin found any of it interesting. Throughout the long evening, nothing those two lovebirds said had sparked anything in him except the desire to get out of this dark, roach-infested building, clean up, and go out drinking.

About midnight he tried to take things into his own hands by calling Kane, even though his instructions had been specific.

"Mr. Kane, this is Martin. Did you know that Jamison and that woman are planning an attack over there? He's definitely joined up with her. He's giving her lots more information for the Coalition to use against Dillon. I think I should do something, Mr. Kane."

"Martin?"

Martin cringed at the way Kane said his name. This wasn't going to be good.

"Yes, Mr. Kane?"

"Didn't you understand what I said earlier?"

"Yes, sir. Not to do anything unless it was absolutely necessary. But I just thought this might be—"

"Martin?"

"Yes, sir."

"Don't push me on this."

"Yes, sir, Mr. Kane. I understand."

"Are you sure?"

"Yes, sir."

"Good."

Kane hung up and Martin was glad to be rid of him. He checked and tweaked his monitors, then watched as Jamison laughed and gave the woman a hug. This was all Jamison's fault, the little bastard. Martin couldn't wait, was actually longing for the chance to even the score with him. Until then, he would have to keep sitting on his crappy metal chair, listening to the bugs scurrying across the floor in the dark, letting Saturday night slip away without him.

# CHAPTER FIVE

Jamison woke up Sunday morning on Melissa's couch, feeling much better than the other 382 mornings since their breakup. He spent the last two evenings close to her, roaming her apartment, sleeping one room away, and listening to her breathe throughout the night. He was thrilled to be so close.

Even more exciting was the fact that she enjoyed having him here. She'd given him a key again, and their relationship was beginning to give off some heat. Not much yet, but a little. If they kept it up, they had a decent chance of regaining the white-hot intensity of a year ago.

He pulled on his jeans and sat on the couch in the early morning light, fondling a headband she'd left on the coffee table, looking through her open bedroom door, watching her sleep. He was fascinated by every little movement of her body, knowing he was way over his head in love with her, far beyond the bounds of good sense. He was addicted to her. He had to have her and could barely think of anything else.

She rolled over in bed, twisting the sheets around her slender legs. Twice she pushed the hair out of her eyes without opening them, and then said something in her sleep that he couldn't make out. Mostly, though, she just lay there, still as could be, her chest rising and falling with a sensual, intoxicating rhythm.

He loved her too much and he knew it. More than she loved him. He couldn't imagine ever letting her go again and would do anything to win her back.

He was almost glad they'd killed the Wombat. The project's death had been the catalyst that rebonded them and gave their relationship new strength. Even if it didn't matter now, fighting the layoffs was the right thing to do: joining forces with her and fighting for his teammates. That was his original motive and it had been an honorable one, but nothing he did now would save his friends' jobs.

But Melissa would be proud of him if he helped her clean out Dillon, and that might make her feelings for him return. Why wouldn't they? She'd loved him once before, so it could happen again. There was no reason to believe she was in love with anyone else.

Until he believed she loved him back, he would keep his feelings to himself. He could scare her away if he wasn't careful.

She woke up about seven-thirty, which was early for her. She didn't like mornings, which was something else he found adorable about her. She staggered into the living room and sat down beside him, her T-shirt just covering her panties.

He didn't say anything at first, just sat there, watching her, not believing she was sitting so close. She opened those eyes that could make him do anything. "Hi" was all she said before she closed them again and leaned against his shoulder.

He wanted to put his arm around her and squeeze her shoulders, but he didn't. He did turn his face into her hair, though, and breathed in her scent. "Good morning. Sleep okay?"

She moved her head up and down against his shoulder.

"Hungry?"

She sat up slowly and rubbed her face with both hands. "Yes." Then, with a burst of energy, she scooted away from him and grabbed his arm, tugging her T-shirt down a little. "Peter, let's go out for bagels and coffee, like we used to. We could get the Sunday paper and spend a little time loafing over breakfast. What do you say?"

She was so excited, there was no way he could refuse, even if he wanted to.

"You're on. Get ready."

She jumped off the couch with so much enthusiasm that a stranger might have thought he was taking her to Cannes or Monaco. That was Melissa's way. It didn't take big things to thrill her, just the right things.

Thirty minutes later they were sitting at a front table of Einstein's Bagels, right under a poster that said, I WISH I WAS THE BAGEL BAKER. Melissa couldn't stop grinning as she split the newspaper the way she used to, taking the business section for herself, then giving him all the rest.

He sipped his coffee, took a bite of bagel, and tried like hell to sound unaffected by her presence. "This was a good idea."

"It feels good to be with you again."

He tucked that little gem away for safekeeping as he opened the *Washington Post* and glanced at it, trying very hard to notice something other than Melissa. "Sure does."

She hid her smile behind the paper. He did the same. Dillon's name was in the headline of the front page.

"Oh, shit."

"What?"

"There's a big article here about the leaks at Dillon Aerospace."

She lowered the business section but kept it in her hands. "What does it say?"

Jamison scanned the article, flipped to page A5, and read some more. "It gives a recap of all the information that's been leaked, the date it was first reported, and the criminal implications if the information is ever verified. And what they say is true. Damn. Whoever the leak is, he provided reliable information. The allegations appear completely accurate."

"I wish they'd stop," she said, "before someone gets hurt—or killed."

He folded up the article and put it in his pocket. "Come on, those are just wild rumors, circulated to keep people in line. I don't believe Dillon has a retaliation team or anything of the sort. You don't seriously think Dillon would ever go that far, do you?"

"You tell me. If you headed Dillon Aerospace, would there be a limit to what you'd do to protect your company?"

"Sure. But I wouldn't kill people or anything close to it."

"They would. They have."

"Go on. Killed people?"

"Yes."

"Who?"

Melissa looked away. "A few years back a woman helped another of the Coalition's investigators. We were sure Dillon killed her but we never found proof. At the time, it was a matter of survival for them. They survived. She didn't."

"And you think this article might get someone else killed?"

"It could. Every time the *Post* prints that stuff, they help someone at Dillon narrow down its list of suspects. One day the list will be down to one, and what will happen then?"

He saw the concern in her eyes and understood right then that she knew who the leak was. Not only did she know the leak, she cared about them.

"I don't know what will happen, but at least there are two of us attacking Dillon. Maybe that will confuse them a little, and one of us will take them down."

She grabbed his hand with a jerk. "Peter, I'm not asking you to provide a diversion for someone else's protection, and I sure don't want to sacrifice you over this."

"No argument there."

She stared at him, studying his face until he blushed. "We've got to go," she said. "I've got a ton of work to do before your meeting with Senator Drummond tomorrow. Are you ready?"

He looked at their bagels, only his one bite taken. Their coffee cups were still full. "Sure. Let's go."

* * *

Monday morning, 6:05. Jamison watched the clock flick to 6:06, and then threw his legs over the edge of Melissa's couch. He made himself do it, forced himself to move fast so he would get to work on time.

In that little slice of time he thought up a hundred reasons why he shouldn't go back to Dillon. Given any choice at all, he would never go back there again. He would prefer to stay away and wait for the war to begin, make his accusations loud and clear, then stand ready to defend them. But he had to go in and tell his teammates there was no hope. It would be cruel and cowardly to let them wait around until Friday.

Melissa had beaten him out of bed and was already in the shower. He entered her bathroom slowly and a little embarrassed, trying to shave without staring at the blurry image of her naked body through the misty glass.

"Peter," she said over the noise of the water. "Do you want to go over your presentation again this morning? We can take the time if you think it's necessary."

He finished shaving, washed off the excess lather, and turned around. He leaned against the sink and looked boldly at her body. "No, I feel good about it. A little nervous, but that will pass once I get started. We'll go over it at lunch. That'll be enough."

"Okay." She turned off the water, pulled her towel down over the door, wrapped it around her, and stepped out. She squeezed some water out of her hair and motioned him into the shower with a sweep of her hand. "All yours."

She started brushing her hair, and he suddenly felt

embarrassed to pull his boxers down in the bright light of the bathroom. When he finally did, she looked. It was just a quick glance at his reflection in the mirror, but he caught her. "Hey, what are you looking at?"

She turned around, crossed her hands over her chest, and stared right at him. "Nothing I haven't looked at before."

He did a weird sort of dance he couldn't quite stop, an embarrassing shuffle toward her, then a hop toward the shower, then a funny little squeeze of his knees, not knowing which way to go with this and not wanting to look any more stupid than he already did, flopping around indecisively in front of her, ready to go to her if she wanted him yet anxious to get out of her stare if she didn't. She seemed to enjoy his panic and watched with one eyebrow up and a tiny smile on her lips until he finally thought about the time, his team members, and Senator Drummond, and went for the shower. He knew he'd made the wrong choice when she wandered off to her bedroom.

When he came out of the bathroom she was ready for work. He dressed, reminding himself what an idiot he'd been and promising not to do it again. She walked with him to the front door, beautiful in a dark blue dress, looking almost as awkward as he felt.

"Maybe tonight," she said as she played with his shirt buttons. "I thought maybe you'd like to sleep in my room. I know that couch isn't very comfortable."

Blood rushed to his head and felt as if it might spout from his ears. He knew he was blushing but didn't care. He just wanted to keep his enthusiasm to himself so he wouldn't chase her off. "Sure," he said, giving in to the smile that fought to escape. "I think that would be . . . fun."

"Fun?" She tilted her head as if she hadn't heard correctly.

He wouldn't have thought it possible, but his blood pressure jumped another notch and percolated at the top of his head. He fidgeted in front of her. "You know what I'm trying to say. Not fun, but—"

"So it wouldn't be fun?"

"No, no, that's not it, either. Come on, Melissa, you know what I'm trying to say."

She rose up to his face and pressed her lips against his. They held each other for a minute before she stepped away. She turned him around, put her hand on his back, and pushed him through the door. "Good-bye, Fun Boy. See you at lunch."

He shuffled out the door, wondering if she would always be able to thrill him like that.

He parked in Dillon's huge lot, in the space with his name on it. Dillon was big on putting a good employee's name on things like doors, plaques, and parking places. Even tombstones, if what Melissa said was true. He stared at the sign, knowing it would be the last time he'd ever see it.

It felt reckless to hand his coded card to the guard, walk down the crowded hall, and then open his office door. He felt like a burglar prowling the darkness in someone's home, anxious to get out the door without taking a bullet before they woke up and discovered him.

At ten o'clock he quietly met with his team and told them to expect the end. This time none of them seemed caught off guard. They'd seen other engineers escorted out the door, their personal possessions jammed pathetically into old cardboard boxes. They wished each other well, promised to keep the news secret until Dillon made the announcement, then slipped out of the conference room one at a time. Steve Harrison was the last to leave. He stopped in front of Jamison and shook hands.

"It's been a pleasure, Peter."

"I'm sorry, Steve. If I could have done something—"

Harrison shook his head for Jamison to stop. "If anything could have been done, I know you would have. Believe me, I know. We all do."

Jamison stepped close and hugged him. "Take care."

"Will do." Then he peered into the hallway and left.

At eleven-thirty Jamison walked around his office, removed his personal pictures and certificates from the walls, and jigsawed them into his empty briefcase. He stopped at the door and looked back before heading to the secretarial pool to check out. Charlotte looked up when he approached.

"Hello, Mr. Jamison. Going somewhere?"

"Mark me out to lunch, please."

She changed screens and made the entry. "Yes, sir. Do you want me to enter a return time?"

He looked behind him to see if anyone was lurking there. "No, thanks. Don't know when I'll be back."

She'd caught a scent of something, he could tell, but she hardly betrayed it and made the entry without changing her tone. "No problem, Mr. Jamison. Have a nice day."

"You too, Charlotte."

She looked at him in a sad but understanding way.

He stared down the long corridor that seemed to stretch to Montana, maybe Oregon, with a hundred checkpoints along the way. He would never clear them all, could never summon enough strength to make that long trip down the hall and out the door on the way to his meeting with Senator Drummond, to his moment of defection.

He took a step and then another, all the way to the first checkpoint. The guard there only monitored travel from one secured area to another, so in the quirky world of security guards he wasn't too intimidating. Of course, all of Dillon's guards were former federal agents, most of them earning as much as an engineer and trained to notice anything that wasn't quite right. They were armed and deadly and looking for an excuse to prove it, so how could any one of them *not* be intimidating? It wasn't possible.

As he passed the first guard, Jamison's shoulder blades shifted, scrunching up as if they were about to stop a bullet. He forced his jumpy nerves into submission and walked away without tripping or dropping his briefcase or flooding the floor with sweat.

Two more checkpoints and two more successes, only a few standard questions and a hard stare from the last guard. Then he was out the door, the cold air feeling clean and fresh as he got in his car and drove away from Dillon for the last time.

Forty-five minutes later he was at the Chamber Restaurant, an old power-lunch place five blocks from the capitol. He saw Melissa sitting at a corner table, staring at the wall, waiting to go over the finer details with him one more time—a refresher before his meeting.

He didn't go to her. His senses were more active now than they'd been in a long time, flooding his brain with warning alarms and contingency battle plans. He'd heard too many rumors about Dillon in the past, and Melissa had convinced him that Dillon would kill him as soon as they found out what he was doing.

The restaurant was busy and could be dangerous; his attackers could conceal themselves in the crowd with ease. Was the man standing over there the same one he'd seen earlier on the street, a block or so away? He looked suspicious then, walking toward Jamison and then stopping short, turning into a store and pretending to look at something on the counter. It looked like the same man, but maybe not. Same type of blue suit, maybe the same shoes, but something about the jaw was different.

Jamison suddenly realized he'd been watching the man too long and had left his back completely unguarded. He turned as quickly as possible without attracting attention, then went to Melissa's table, reading her body language as he approached.

As he got within whispering distance he said, "What's wrong?"

He scooted his chair closer to her. She kept staring at the wall but didn't speak.

He asked again while he turned his head, still studying the man in the blue suit. "What's wrong, Melissa?"

She took a staggered breath as if she were struggling to keep from crying. She unlaced her fingers and reached for him, wrapping his hands up in hers, pulling the whole bundle of fingers up against her face.

"Peter, the leak at Dillon, the one you've been reading about, is . . . gone." She used the back of his hand to swipe at her wet cheeks. She stretched her eyes open and tilted back her head as if trying to call back the rest of the tears.

Jamison didn't want to say anything. He just sat there, trying to guess what she meant. Gone? He waited for a minute without an answer.

"You mean dead?"

"I mean gone, as in vanished. Maybe . . . maybe he's dead. His wife hasn't heard from him since he called from work last Thursday.

Jamison ran through faces and tried to remember who hadn't been at work Friday. "So you think someone figured out he was the leak?"

"He's been our primary source all along. As I told you, all those newspaper articles kept narrowing the field—"

She closed her eyes and breathed deeply.

"Someone finally found him. I knew it would happen, and I warned him, Peter, I really did. I told him to get some government protection but he refused. How could I make him?"

"Are you sure he's not just out of town for a few days? I've read the papers but I couldn't identify the leak, not for certain, anyway. Maybe the articles seem so close to home because you know him."

She rolled her eyes. "Oh, really? Who would you guess my informant was, if you had to, based on what you've read?"

He didn't want to get into this, didn't want to look across the battlefield again, and didn't really want to know who the leak was. He didn't need to know, and didn't want to be responsible for the knowledge. She kept waiting.

"Hell, I don't know. Based on the quality of the information, I guess they would be pretty high up, a grade-five engineer or higher, probably in the Development Division. It wasn't me—I just saw Harrison, so it wasn't him—and that just leaves Bronovich, if my assumptions are all correct."

She spooked and turned back to the wall when he said the name. She nodded her head, almost crying, as if she'd lost something important. A sudden shiver moved her in the cool restaurant.

"Peter, maybe we should stop what we're doing. We could destroy your files and act like this never happened. I can tell people at work you've decided not to cooperate, and then go after Dillon on my own. No one has to know you were involved."

Jamison listened to her, or at least tried to listen as he remembered Ted Bronovich asking him to get in touch with Rich Blevins. Was his death his fault for taking his time in talking to Blevins? Did Bronovich die because of Jamison's stupidity or laziness? He damned himself, already knowing he would drag this cross around with him for a long time, probably forever.

He tried to imagine how and when they might have taken him, if Bronovich struggled and maybe even hurt them a little bit. Had they killed the small engineer quickly, the way everyone wants to die, or did they make him pay slowly for what he'd done, recounting the specific information he'd leaked in tortured details?

Quick or slow, dead was dead. Only the length of the trip mattered. Maybe it was a car bomb like the one Jamison had looked for the other night. Not a particularly bad way to go. Maybe he started his car and blew a big damned chunk of D.C. asphalt into the cosmos.

Jamison felt guilty enough to want revenge, and

Melissa could help turn over the rock where Ted's killer lived. "No, Melissa. I'm not quitting and I won't run from this. I'm not made that way and you aren't either, so let's quit pretending we are and get down to work. We'll be more careful, but we're going after them. Agreed?"

She didn't answer.

"We'll think this through and take appropriate security measures. But we better get started because I'm about to meet Senator Drummond. All hell is going to break loose."

"Have they been following you, Peter?"

He nodded. "Yes, some, I think."

"Me too."

"When?"

"I'm not sure when or how many times. I couldn't really swear I've been followed, but Saturday when I went to the office to study your data, there was a car behind me all the way."

"Right behind you?"

"Back about half a block. As I said, I'm not positive, but it sure gave me a creepy feeling."

Jamison checked the room again, his senses crackling the way they had when he arrived. The man and woman two tables away were too loud to be a threat; but beyond them, angled off to the right, was a lone man in a booth, lean and hard and paying attention as if this were all business.

Or maybe it was someone in the small clutch of suits at the round table in the middle of the large room. Congressional staffers? Maybe, but weren't they looking over here an awful lot, and where was the other one, the one who'd stood and left a few minutes ago?

"Melissa, if Dillon got Bronovich we have to keep you safe until Drummond gives you protection." He checked the restaurant again and found the missing man returning with his wallet open. Lots of other people still seemed to be looking his way.

Melissa met his eyes when they came back to her. "The Coalition has excellent security. I could stay there, if necessary."

"That's a good idea, if you're sure you'll be safe."

"So many companies hate us that we really had to bolster security with a new system and armed guards. I'll go back there when I leave. You go there too after you meet with Senator Drummond."

"Depends on what happens, but I'll try." He pulled out a pen and snatched a paper coaster from under a glass. "Here's Rich Blevins's number at home, just in case something happens."

She gripped his arm as she took the napkin. "Nothing's going to happen. Promise?"

"I promise, but let's be careful anyway."

She looked around the room and never came back to his eyes. "Yes."

Senator Drummond's secretary led Jamison into his private office. The room was nearly as large as Jamison's condo, but messy and smelled of cigarettes. Files were stacked on several tables, set up in a haphazard maze running through the office. The only tidy area was the top of Drummond's desk, evidently the only place where the hardworking senator didn't do any work.

Drummond rose and limped awkwardly across the room to shake hands and help Jamison with the box he carried. After the data was on the desk, Drummond lowered himself into the chair next to Jamison—in front of his desk instead of behind it. It was a good gesture, Jamison thought, to sit so close. Probably not genuine, but a useful performance anyway, most likely perfected by years of practice.

Jamison had studied Drummond's media photo as he waited in the outer office, but now he had a little trouble recognizing the old man who sat next to him. The wrinkled face, bald head, and bony arms seemed an odd parody of the active senator portrayed in the campaign literature, but his eyes were definitely the same. Bright green, friendly eyes that were probably his best asset on the campaign trail.

"Mr. Jamison," Drummond began in a comfortable voice. "I want to thank you for coming by today. Since I received Miss Corley's call this weekend, I've been most anxious to hear what you have to say. Would you like some coffee before we start?"

"No, thank you."

Drummond rose and hobbled to a service bar while Jamison looked around his office. The walls were decorated with pictures of Drummond shaking hands with other political leaders from around the world. There was an honorable discharge from the marines and several pictures of a grown daughter on his desk—turned so that visitors would see them. It was nice imagery, Jamison thought, although it suffered for lack of a wife's photo.

"Now, how can I help you today?" Drummond sat down with a sigh, his words as polished and natural as an old priest offering absolution for the thousandth time. Jamison began with the leadoff sentence he'd practiced, and the facts rolled out smoothly. The documentation came out in perfect order and he sounded convincing: Dillon was corrupt. Several times he gave credit to Melissa.

Drummond listened to every word with an intense look on his face. The information obviously bothered him. His face flushed several times, but he never interrupted, never vented his anger or frustration. He just sat there and listened, his eyes almost hidden, his teeth grating together. When Jamison finished, Drummond stood up, hobbled to his desk, and picked up the phone.

"You just sit right there," he said as he dialed. "We're going to get some answers on this right now. There's no way I'm going to . . . Hello, Bostwick? What the hell are you guys doing over there?"

Jamison leaned forward and tried to hear the other half of the conversation, but couldn't. He was beginning to understand why Melissa trusted Drummond. He was fearless. It was a little scary.

"What do I mean? Hell, I'll tell you exactly what I mean. I have a nice young man in my office who says Dillon Aerospace has been defrauding you people for decades. I don't believe it's possible unless you or somebody who works for you is in on it. Yes, that's right. Uh-huh. Yeah, you're damned right it's illegal!"

Jamison cocked an ear and leaned in his chair, trying to hear the secretary of defense's response.

"Damn it, Bostwick, you'll be doing some big-time explaining if this information proves to be correct, so you'd better start digging around right now because I'm calling President Albright next and recommending a full FBI investigation."

Drummond slammed the phone down. "That son of a bitch. I never have trusted him."

"Are you going to call President Albright, Senator?"

Drummond grinned, hobbled over, and put a bony hand on Jamison's shoulder. "Yes. Give me a few minutes to cool down, though. It would be a bad idea for me to call him when I'm this angry. I can handle Bostwick, but I have to show Albright more respect. You know what I mean?"

"Yes, sir."

"Good." Drummond shuffled back around the desk, stopped at the pile of data, and reached for a cigarette. "Can I keep these documents, Mr. Jamison?"

"Those are yours, sir."

"I assume the originals are in a safe place?"

"They are."

"Sure?"

"Yes."

"Good. Well, Mr. Jamison, thanks for coming by today. If what you say is true, I'm going to tear the butts off a few people in this government. I probably don't have to tell you this situation will get dangerous, so I'd like to assign a security detail to protect you. I can do that, you know. It's not a problem."

Jamison smiled, stood up, and shook Drummond's hand. "I don't think that will be necessary, sir."

"Don't be too sure, son. I've been up on this Hill for a long time. It's a dangerous place, even for a nice old guy like me." He grinned as he lit his cigarette. "If you *are* right, you're going to be in danger, simple as that. I'd feel a whole lot better making sure you're safe."

"I'll be safe."

Drummond squinted one eye against the smoke and looked Jamison over carefully. "Yes, well, you young people always think you're bulletproof."

"Just careful, sir."

Drummond narrowed his squint. His other eye didn't close a bit. "All right, but I want you to stay in touch with me. Here's my card. Call me day or night. My home number's on the back, so let me know if you need anything. Be careful. Fraud against the government on this level is a very serious crime. Lots of people could go to jail, so they'll fight like hell to avoid it."

"Thanks for your concern, Senator."

"No problem. Give my best to Miss Corley."

"I will."

Jamison turned and left, feeling more confident than when he first arrived. In the lobby he called Melissa.

"How'd it go?" She sounded better than she had in the restaurant.

"Good, I guess. I don't know the guy like you do, but he sure got steamed. I think you were right, he's probably the best man to go after Dillon."

She laughed, still not anywhere near happy, but getting better. "That's why we call him a bulldog."

"I can see that."

"Did he give you any suggestions or instructions?"

"Not really. He made an excellent point about keeping the evidence in a safe place, though."

"Safer than here at the Coalition?"

"I think I've got a better place. I'd like Rich Blevins to keep it, if that's all right with you?"

"Sure, I'll trust Rich. In fact, that's a good idea because it keeps the Coalition further out of it, which helps protect you from charges of disclosing classified secrets."

"Then do me a favor. Put all of my research and all of your notes in a box. Seal it and leave it at the desk in the front lobby. Don't put my name on it, but tell the receptionist I'll get it shortly. Can you do that right away?"

"Sure."

"I'll call you after I've given it to Blevins."

# CHAPTER SIX

Jamison rushed out of Senator Drummond's building. He had passed some point of no return. Dillon would find out and come after him. It all seemed inevitable now.

Ted Bronovich flashed across his mind, their last meeting before he disappeared, the moment in his dark office when Bronovich asked for help. Now it was Jamison's turn in the line of fire. It was just a matter of time, and time was something Dillon didn't waste. Their retribution would be swift. He'd done the deed and the price had to be paid.

He did not intend to pay it without a fight.

Tourists in jeans and staffers in suits crowded the sidewalk in front of the Hart Senate Office Building. They parted for Jamison as he got close, used the good judgment God gave them, and got out of the running man's way. He stopped at the curb and scanned the street.

"Careful observation," he muttered to himself. "Memorize everything that pops up on radar."

He didn't see any danger, so double-timed it across the street. The other side had more cover. He kept looking around, constantly figuring where he'd go if there were trouble—making an escape and evasion plan if attacked. He got to his car and climbed in, still watching for an assault.

He pulled into traffic and stayed in the outside lane as he stopped at the light, the first car at the line. He sat there, looking everywhere while waiting for the light to change, wondering how long it would take them to find him.

A blue Ford pulled up beside him. Two men in suits—one fat, one ugly—sat in the front seat. The fat man must have felt Jamison's stare because he looked over and smiled, then turned to the Ford's driver. The driver leaned forward and both men grinned, looking at Jamison and bobbing their heads. Jamison watched the light, thinking maybe he'd seen them somewhere before, maybe in passing at work. That would be just his luck: The one time he'd see people he might know in this big-ass city would be right after he'd defected from Dillon. What were the odds? When the light turned green he looked back again, trying hard not to look like someone who'd just turned in his employer for committing a crime.

This time the passenger had a short-barreled assault rifle in his hand. The man's window was down and the gun was coming out in a hurry.

Jamison stomped on the gas and fired his car off the

line; he rolled a right turn and accelerated hard, watching the Ford cut off a car and do the same thing as the next light turned red. Traffic was stopping three hundred feet ahead and the guys in the Ford would pull alongside and shoot him. The oncoming traffic was slow, but there was a small gap in the inside lane coming at him. Jamison kept his foot nailed to the floor until he got parallel with the opening, then jumped on the brakes and started sliding; he arced a tight U-turn into the opposite lane just as the Ford finished jostling its way off Constitution Avenue.

The Ford skidded to a stop as Jamison finished his maneuver and passed them in the opposite direction. The driver glared at Jamison while his partner clambered into the backseat. Jamison laughed at their confusion, at the stupid look of failure, big and angry on the driver's face. Then the gun barrel poked out the backseat window into the crisp winter air. Jamison stopped laughing, felt the aim, and knew the flash was coming. He sped up and braked hard, then sped up again, trying to be the hardest target possible while stuck on a busy street.

He didn't hear the muzzle blast, but the metal of his car went *tang, tang* as two bullets struck the rear door and rattled into the dash. Round one had begun, just seconds after he'd left Drummond, and now, just as quickly, it was over.

Jamison turned back onto Constitution and made another U-turn, wanting to know if the Ford would come back for round two. He waited in a bus zone for twenty seconds, looking forward and back and all around, searching for people who might be planning to kill him. Enough time passed. He gunned his engine as the light turned red and shot through the intersection as the cross-traffic blew horns. At the next corner he turned again, then stopped and waited another minute before believing he'd lost them.

At the Citizen's Coalition Against Government Waste, he locked up his brakes and slid into the loading zone, jumped out, and charged up the steps. He ran through the lobby to the receptionist's desk, and although she was on the phone, she understood when he pointed to the box. She motioned him around to get it.

He put the box in his trunk and ran to a pay phone at the corner. His cell phone belonged to Dillon and he'd left it behind after clearing the phone book, so he had to dig around in his wallet to find Rich's card.

"FBI, Washington field office."

"Special Agent Blevins. Make it quick."

"Stand by."

He waited, checked the sidewalk, checked the street.

"This is Blevins. Who is this?"

"Rich, it's Peter."

Blevins's voice lost some of its growl. "How are you? You're not worried about me, are you? That little scratch over my eye isn't—"

"Rich, I'm in trouble. It's hard to explain quickly and I don't have time to tell you anyway." He rotated his body like a turret, checking his back, watching his car. "Could you meet me outside your building in ten minutes?"

Blevins started talking like an agent again, using the official government monotone. "Absolutely, but don't stop in front. Pull to the curb at the end of Half Street, the fire zone. I'll wait there for you and jump into your car. We'll talk while we ride."

Jamison felt someone closing in on his back and spun around to see a teenager walking toward him with a camera in one hand and change in the other.

"Ten minutes."

"I'll be there in four."

Jamison ran back to his car and stuck a quick finger in the two bullet holes. They were large-caliber rounds, and judging by the clean penetration, full metal jackets, a strange choice for urban warfare. They were the kind of round that could penetrate an engine block but only whistle a very clean hole through a man's body.

He rushed downtown, cursing the traffic and the men in the Ford, but mostly he cursed himself for not having his own cell to call Melissa. It was hard to guess what might happen next, but he didn't want to underestimate her chances of getting hurt. She was too important, too precious, and always had been.

Jamison slowed and Blevins stepped to the curb. His thick hands grabbed the door, and he flung his stocky body into the car before it stopped. "Drive, Peter. Go."

Jamison jerked back into traffic. He felt Blevins staring at him.

"So, how ya doing?" Blevins scraped his palm across his short crew cut.

"Damned if I know. You won't believe what I'm about to tell you."

Blevins didn't move a muscle. He just sat there with his back against the door, staring. "I think I might."

Jamison glanced over as he turned the corner. "What's that supposed to mean?"

Blevins glanced at the dash, then shifted around and caught the shredded backseat upholstery without comment. "My supervisor stopped me as I headed out to meet you. He wanted to tell me personally since you and I go way back."

"Tell you what?"

"The foreign counterintelligence squad just opened a case against you. They have a tip that you've been stealing government secrets, maybe for a foreign government."

"You've got to be kidding."

"Am I laughing?"

"No."

"Then I'm not kidding."

Jamison studied Blevins's eyes, turned to check the road, then came back and looked at Blevins. "So what does that mean? You gonna arrest me?"

"Hey, don't act like it couldn't happen. You know damn well our friendship wouldn't get in my way if you've crossed the line."

"You think I have?"

"I don't know. Tell me your story."

"Okay, quick and dirty. Dillon decided to scrap my project, and in building a case to keep it alive I uncovered some evidence of criminal fraud by Dillon. I have proof they've been defrauding the U.S. government for years. Decades."

"Have you shared this information with the press?"

"I'm not the leak, but I know who is. He's a guy in my department who's been missing since Thursday. Nobody's seen him."

"Ted Bronovich?"

"Jeez, yes. How did you know?"

"His wife came in today to ask for our help. She was pretty upset."

"That's tough. I'm the guy who's responsible if he's dead, too. He asked me for your help but didn't make it sound urgent." Jamison strangled the steering wheel.

"Don't beat yourself up until we find him. He may have run off with a woman or something."

"I doubt that. He's a family man."

"Back to your story, what have you been doing with your evidence?"

"I took it to Senator Drummond this morning, head of the Senate Armed Services Committee. He's going to look into my allegations."

Blevins pinched the bridge of his nose and squeezed his eyes closed. "Is that it?"

"Hell no, that's not it. Some yahoo just blew two rounds through my car and your foreign counterintelligence agents are out to arrest me. There. I think that pretty well covers it."

"You're not doing anything illegal, nothing that would give these charges some merit?"

"No. Damn, back off a little."

"Don't tell me to back off. You want my help, you got it, that simple and nothing else to it. But I've got to know what I'm dealing with here. If you're clean, I'll back you up a thousand percent. If you're dirty, I'll take you in, but either way I'll fight for you. So be straight with me. Every word. You read me?"

"Dillon is corrupt. I have a box of evidence in the trunk that proves it. Take it for safekeeping, look through it if you like, but right now I have to get going 'cause I'm worried about Melissa." Jamison rounded the block and turned into the curb at the Federal Building. He stopped, shifted in his seat, and squared up with his friend.

Blevins didn't look happy. "I should have known she was part of this."

Jamison tried to look cocky. "Think I could do this all by myself, get people mad enough to shoot at me?"

"I've seen it happen."

"Well, this time I had help. And I don't want to take chances with her."

"Then this is what we'll do. First, I'm going to open you as a 137—an informant. I'll file everything you tell me on an FD-302 as evidence for your defense if you end up on trial, but your identity will be extremely well protected, even by Bureau standards. After I've done that, I'll meet with the FCI supervisor and tell him you're a source for me and promise to bring you in next week."

"What should I be doing?"

"You'd better keep your head down or someone's going to blow it off. I'm not kidding. It looks like you've got some powerful people pulling strings here, and that makes me nervous, especially in this city. Don't go home or any place familiar. Check into a hotel under an alias, then let me know where you are. Do you have some cash?"

"About four hundred bucks."

"Let me know if you need more."

"You'll take that box out of the trunk?"

"Done. Call me tonight at home to let me know you're okay. Make the call from a remote location. Since the FBI knows we're friends, a wiretap on my phone would be a logical move."

"Maybe I shouldn't call."

"Don't worry about me; you've got your hands full already. Do you have any kind of weapon?"

"I brought my Beretta."

"Keep it close."

"Will do."

Blevins split his lips open and showed some teeth but couldn't seem to manage anything more. He was the smiling policeman, almost, all crew cut and clean-shaven and smiling because that's the way he did things. When trouble came, he smiled at it.

He went to the trunk and got the box, then came back to the open window. "Stay low, brother. We'll get you through this. Just don't go fugazi on me."

"Not to worry, I won't let the monster out of the box."

"Good. D.C. doesn't need the body count, and I don't need the paperwork. Now go, get out of here."

Jamison wheeled away from the curb, checked the mirror, and saw the blue Ford pull into traffic several cars back.

It was ten o'clock before Jamison could safely check into a Red Roof Inn near Ronald Reagan Washington Airport. He'd tried two other motels, but they'd insisted on seeing identification, so he went to the counter of the Red Roof, just before a crowd unloaded from a bus in the lot. He took his time with the clerk and let the long line pressure her into accepting cash payment and his story of a lost license and early departure.

He sat on the bed and thought about Melissa, trying to decide if he should call her, if Dillon or the FBI tapped her phone. He doubted it but wasn't sure, so he got in his car and drove to a convenience store ten miles away.

He dialed from the phone outside, knowing she'd be mad, hoping it wouldn't set their relationship back too far.

"Damn it, Peter, where are you?"

She sounded more concerned than angry, and the sound of her worry made him happy. But still, she was plenty sore.

"I've been waiting forever. This afternoon you said you'd call right back."

"Sorry, been busy. Some men were following me and I just lost them a little while ago."

"They just followed you around? That's all? You drove around all night and they didn't do anything?"

He felt a little stupid at the way she described it. "Yeah, that's all, just followed me. I tried to draw them close once to get another look at them, but even then they hung back. It was irritating."

"Well, at least they sound harmless."

"They do now. Earlier today they shot at me."

"They *shot* at you?"

"Can you believe that? Must not have liked the way I drove."

"Peter, this is too dangerous too soon. Did you talk to Rich?"

"Yes. He had good and bad news. I'll fill you in later."

"Where are you?"

"A pay phone. You okay, Melissa? Is anyone still there with you?"

"Security guys. Everyone else left hours ago."

"But you feel safe?"

"Yes."

"I was worried."

"Peter, the car that followed you wasn't dark blue, was it? A four-door Ford?"

Jamison felt muscles tighten all over his body. "How did you know?"

"It's parked outside. I noticed it a few minutes ago when the guard and I went out to get something from my car. There's a man sitting in it."

"Just one man?"

"I didn't actually walk up and take a head count, but yes, it looked like just one man. Someone else could have been lying down in the back, I suppose."

"Can I call you right back?"

"Why?"

"I need to find out whose car that is."

"Sure, okay, but *right* back, you understand? No more of this all-night bullshit."

"Promise."

He cut their connection and got a dial tone, then called Blevins at home.

"Hello?" The woman's voice was nice and fresh and easy. Jamison had so much energy coursing through him that she sounded sedated by comparison.

"Elaine, it's me, Peter. Is Rich home?"

"Yes, Peter, he's right here." He heard her pass the phone.

"I'm glad you called. Where are you?"

"Some place safe, but a blue Ford has been following me all afternoon. Know anything about it?"

"The one that shot at you after you left Drummond's office?"

"That's the one."

"When did it start again? How soon after we met?"

"Right after. They knew I was at your office, Rich. Damn it, they knew to find me there."

"Hey, I know what you're thinking, but it wasn't us. At least I don't see how it could be. FCI didn't move on you until after we talked. They sent agents to your home and office."

"I want to know who's in the Ford. It's important now."

"Maybe they're Dillon's security guys keeping tabs on you."

Two men, one black and one white, came out of the store and walked off in the other direction. Jamison lowered his voice and watched them until they got into their car and drove out of sight. "That's about what I was thinking."

"Where was the last place you saw them? Where can I find them?"

"They, or maybe just one of them, are over at Melissa's office. At least they were a minute ago."

"Do you want me to send someone over there? If you're worried about her we could pick her up and keep her safe until we identify those guys. She could spend the night on the boss's couch."

Jamison kept checking the street. "She feels safe right where she is. Why expose her to danger by moving her? Besides, I don't think she'd go for it."

"Your call, but we found your friend Bronovich this afternoon. It was a grisly sight. Somebody shattered his neck the same way the army trained us in Ranger school, but with a hell of a lot more power. Spun his head halfway around."

"Damn. Any idea who did it?"

"Nope. We know absolutely nothing, except that the hit was professional, European quality. If you'd seen Bronovich, you'd probably want to give my idea about

Melissa another run-through. I could call and try to talk her into it."

"You think these guys in the Ford killed Bronovich?"

"Don't know. Probably not."

"Why not? They shot at me."

"Earlier, sure, but not after you left me. Why the change?"

"Out of bullets?"

"Very funny. I think they have different orders now, only I can't guess why. If they are the same guys and they did pick up your tail again, I think they would have taken you down . . . unless they were just watching."

"Maybe they saw you take the box. Maybe that's what they're after."

"Could be. Maybe not. At any rate I don't think they'll bother Melissa. They're only watching her so they can pick you up again. I'd still like to bring her in, just to be safe."

Jamison ran his hand through his hair. "Go ahead and call her; see what she wants to do. She makes her own decisions. I'm sure you know that."

"Who doesn't?"

"Look, you and I have to meet. How about tomorrow morning, the Smithsonian, Museum of Natural History. Dinosaur exhibit. Ten o'clock? Be careful, just in case they're listening now."

"Sure."

"One last thing. The FCI supervisor refused to back off, even when I promised to bring you in. He wants his boys to arrest you, so we're going to have to develop plan B."

"We'll talk about it tomorrow. I want you to call Melissa."

* * *

Blevins hung up and speed-dialed the squad room. He wanted to get an agent moving Melissa's way before he called her.

"Okay, new Agent Davidson," he murmured as the phone rang. "You've wanted your chance to do something on your own. Out of the Academy a month and you haven't even checked out a car yet. This is your lucky night, pal. I'm calling you because you're new, you're green, and therefore, you're there. Just like all new agents, afraid they're going to miss the Big One. Don't ever want to leave or sleep. Can't get enough of the ego trip."

SA Davidson answered the phone as though he were responding to the crime of the century. "FBI Squad Seven, Special Agent Robert Davidson."

"Hey, Davidson, you keeping the world safe while I take it easy?"

"Yes, sir, Mr. Blevins. I'm in complete control and the world lies in obedient silence."

"Great, cowboy, that's great. You have no idea how good that makes me feel. Listen, I've got a little mission for you. Not much to it, I'm afraid. A little tame for a grizzled old veteran like yourself, but hell, a chance to burn some fuel. You want it?"

"Absolutely. What is it?"

"A woman named Melissa Corley is at her office, just a few minutes from you, at the Citizen's Coalition Against Government Waste. Some shit in a blue Ford is set up on the street in front, and I'm kind of thinking we should get her out of there."

"Should I take backup?"

"This is your mission, rookie, so it's up to you to decide if you need backup or not and how many. Don't they teach you fellas anything at Quantico anymore?"

"Has the guy in the Ford done anything to her?"

"No. He might have shot at someone earlier, but he's done nothing to her. Keep in mind, though, that this woman might have some association, and I mean way out on the tangent, with the body we identified today. I'm not sure about that, but maybe."

Davidson gasped at the nightmare of Bronovich's body that would haunt him for a while. Blevins gave him a quiet moment, some time for a quick appraisal of his courage and talents, as honest as possible.

"If it's just a taxi ride she needs, I think my sixteen hollow-point brothers and I can help her out."

Blevins laughed. He liked Davidson much better than other agents he'd trained. This guy understood that the job was mostly bullshit, bluster, and bravado. That's how they earned their pay, that and some deadly business on very rare occasions.

"You should have been a cowboy, cowboy. If that's your call, get on it. There's an alley behind her building. I'll phone her and ask her to meet you there. Leave now, Davidson, because I want you waiting the second her toes hit fresh air."

"Yes, sir."

"Go."

Blevins hung up and fumbled while he looked for Melissa's private office number. He had no reason to call her since she and Jamison broke up, so it had been a while.

"Melissa, it's Rich Blevins. Is everything okay there?"

"Rich, how nice to hear your voice. Yes, of course, everything's fine."

"It's great to hear you again, too. My heart flipped to a new year when Peter mentioned you earlier. I hope everything works out. Not, of course, that it's any of my business, but . . . ah, hell, Melissa, you know what I mean."

"I know what you mean."

"Look, Peter and I would like you to come down to my office, just until we find out what's going on with that Ford."

"That's ridiculous. They haven't done anything but watch my building."

Blevins thought about Bronovich's face, the thick, swollen tongue, and wide-awake eyes. He started to worry that he'd underassessed her danger. "We both know that, but I'm coming in early tomorrow and I was hoping we could go for breakfast. There's a great couch in the boss's office where you could sleep. What do you say?"

"You are too smooth, Rich."

"Yeah, I know. So great, go out the back of your building to the alley. I have an agent named Robert Davidson on his way, and he'll meet you there in a typical Bureau roadster. He's a good-looking guy like me, with short brown hair and brown eyes. And he'll be grinning, I believe, like he's just been promoted to top doggie. Ten minutes. Okay?"

"Is Peter all right? Why didn't he call me himself?"

Blevins was feeling it too, the same anxiety she had in her voice, the little fear nibbling a good-sized hole in his confidence. "He's fine. Get your stuff together. Ten minutes—the alley—got it?"

"Yes."

Blevins hung up but stared at the phone for half a

minute, then stood and walked over to where Elaine was reading a book. He bent over and kissed her cheek. "Got to go, honey. Make sure the boys finish their homework."

She stopped reading and looked at him with a thousand questions on her face. "I will, baby. Be careful. You know I love you."

"Love you too."

New Agent Robert Davidson was proud to have Blevins the Legend as his field-training agent, the man who'd dropped the top-ten fugitive with a long, clean head shot while a hostage struggled two inches away from impact. Tonight Davidson would make him proud.

On his second lap around the Coalition he jerked into the alley from the south end so that Melissa wouldn't have to walk around the car to get in. He screeched to a stop as she came out of the building, looked deep into his rearview mirror, and felt the butterflies flutter off with his stomach.

"Get in," he yelled. "Come on, get in!"

She jumped in, and when her butt hit the seat he flattened the accelerator, rocketed toward the other end of the alley as the blue Ford followed him into the alley and stopped a few hundred feet behind him.

He barreled down the narrow chasm, putting distance between him and the Ford as Melissa braced one hand against the dash and groped for a seat belt. They were halfway to the open street and building speed.

A brown Dodge sedan turned into the alley up ahead, bounced through the gutter, and blocked their exit. Davidson jammed on the brakes and slid to a stop, then cursed himself for not ramming the Dodge while he had the speed, pushing it into the street to escape.

He wanted to grab the mike and call for help but there was no time, he had to get away from these guys. What about that blue car? Still back there? Shit yes. Davidson's choices were down to two, merely a matter of which car to start with. "All right, you sons a bitches," he said as he dropped the car into reverse. "Want to play rough? Let's do it."

"Hold on to something," he yelled as he twisted around and blasted backward down the narrow alley.

The driver jumped out of the Ford and ran for a doorway. Another man, short and heavy in a loose-fitting suit, came from the passenger side and ran around in front of the Ford with an assault rifle in his hands.

"Lady, if you get a chance to run, go south, past this car we're about to smash into, away from the Dodge!"

He heard her say something but stopped listening when the fat man fired his weapon, blasting the rear window into shards of glass but missing both of them. It pissed Davidson off and he started yelling, his foot burying the gas, his car screaming through the chute, the tires churning up an acrid smoke that curled over the rear fenders and streamed through the hole where the rear window had been. "I'm going to get you for that, you shit! Stay right there, fatso, and catch the ass-end of this two-ton weapon."

The fat man understood, stopped aiming, and started to run as Davidson hit him, so hard his stubby body flew through the shattered back glass of the Bureau car with a surprised look on its just-dead face.

"That's one, where's the other guy? Lady, you see the other guy? He headed over to my side!"

"I don't see him! It's too dark. I don't!"

Davidson looked everywhere but didn't see the other man. "I'm going to barrel-ass out of here and launch into that other car like a big, bad bolt from hell. Ready? Let's go."

The transmission bucked as Davidson jammed it into drive and tromped on the gas. His eyes were still jumping around, still desperate to find the Ford's driver. He was barely moving when gunfire started again and more glass shattered. He raised his pistol, or at least struggled to, as bullets slammed into his body and burned their way through his flesh and muscle, ripping away big pieces of him. The wheel twisted out of his grip. He couldn't hold it anymore. He couldn't see, couldn't hear, couldn't . . . do . . . anything.

Melissa looked at Davidson when the shooting resumed and heard the sickening noise of bullets slamming into his body; she felt the car veer, and then idle into her building while the young man's body twitched and jumped from the trauma. She sat in concentrated horror as a large ugly man in a nicely tailored suit stepped from a doorway and walked toward the car, firing carefully aimed shots into Davidson's head with every step, splattering chunks of Davidson's skull all over her clothes and the inside of the car.

Someone pried her door open but she didn't turn, couldn't stop staring at the ugly man shooting Davidson. He walked slowly until he was beside the car, then reached in, took Davidson's pistol, and calmly checked the pockets of his blood-soaked clothes.

A hand grabbed Melissa's shoulder and dragged her out. Her mind was beginning to come back now, telling her to follow the man's orders until her feet hit the pavement. The second they did, she scraped her right heel against the man's shin, digging hard, going for oil, gouging as though she were jump-starting a motorcycle.

"Son of a bitch," he screamed, as he let go of her and fell away.

Melissa whipped around and pushed her hands into his face, raking deep furrows into his cheeks with her nails, then grabbing his head with her hands. She dug thumbnails hard into his closed eyes, the flesh of his upper eyelids stretching back into his head, much farther than she would have expected. But then the lids shredded open, making slits for her long-nailed thumbs to sink deeper into his head, gouging at the back of his eyeballs, not stopping until she'd completely buried them into the spongy material at the back of his sockets, his blood and tears squirting onto his face, the diluted red mixture pouring out of his head and running down her wrists, soaking the sleeves of her dress.

He screamed in a terrified voice and lurched backward. She pulled her thumbs out; the suction broke with a disgusting pop. He fell to the ground, whimpering and writhing, as she ran like hell for the street.

She screamed for help as she rushed down the alley, wiping her bloody thumbs on the front of her dress, heading toward the streetlight at the end of the alley, wide-eyed and watching carefully for potholes or slick spots. A man was chasing her. She could hear him, feel him. He was getting closer, gaining on her.

She burst into the spotty light of the street and made a hard right turn toward an all-night drugstore, hoping to open up enough of a lead to reach safety. Her shoes didn't hold the turn and she fell, the ugly man who killed Davidson crashing into her falling body and going down with her, giving her a whisper of a chance to get up and run again, at least until the ugly man did a quick parachute roll and landed on his feet in front of her, his gun back in his hand.

She collapsed onto the pavement, silent, planning to stay there and delay as long as possible. Maybe the police would come. Maybe someone had heard the noise and called them.

Above all else, she would not cower. She held her head up defiantly as the man walked to her. His steps seemed cautious, as if she frightened him a little, even as he aimed his pistol at her head. Three steps away, he reached into his coat pocket and pulled out a leather wallet.

"Melissa Corley, you are under arrest for espionage. You have the right . . ."

Melissa could barely hear the man, and she couldn't see him at all. Her eyes were stuck to the FBI credentials he held in his left hand.

# CHAPTER SEVEN

Jamison didn't sleep. He spent most of the night rattling around the Red Roof Inn and worrying about Melissa, hoping she wouldn't be angry that he'd asked Blevins to pick her up. She insisted on making her own decisions and didn't like being told what to do. If she thought he was trying to control her, she'd be gone, out of reach again. She was that independent.

During the few moments of that long night when he wasn't worrying about her, he'd tried to think through everything that happened since Thursday, hoping to tie it all together and figure out how to keep her safe. Assuming he hadn't pissed her off, he still hoped they could work through their problems after this was over and get back together where they belonged.

He started with Dillon's cancellation of his project, although that hardly seemed to matter anymore.

Melissa was positive that Dillon was evil, and Bronovich's death proved she was right. He'd been shot at after giving Senator Drummond his evidence, and Blevins was worried enough about the blue Ford to send an agent to get Melissa. It was pretty easy to buy her criminal corruption theory.

His project teammates were beginning to look like the lucky ones. They were only losing their jobs. As far as he knew, they weren't being followed or shot at or investigated. He tried to forget, at least for a while, that Bronovich's neck had been broken over this. He wished he didn't have to hold himself responsible, wished he'd told Blevins right away that Bronovich wanted to talk to him. Why hadn't he called Blevins at home? What had he been thinking? Several times during the night he thought about the way Blevins had described Bronovich's body, then immediately tried to forget what he'd heard. He didn't usually make those kinds of mistakes and wasn't used to failing people. If only he'd done what he'd promised and put Bronovich and Blevins together, maybe the engineer with the two sweet kids would still be alive.

He remembered the day Bronovich brought his girls to the office on Take Your Daughter to Work Day. It touched Jamison to see his proud friend roam the halls with them, introducing them to Jamison's team and everyone else they met. The little girls polite as debutantes, dressed in frilly Easter outfits and carrying patent leather purses.

Bronovich was gone now and his daughters were fatherless. Most of Jamison's team was gone now, too, or soon would be. It was just Melissa and him. He couldn't save Dillon from the penalty of its own crimes, but that was fine with him because he didn't care about Dillon. In truth, he didn't care about the corruption the way Melissa did. He was one of the ambivalent people she described Friday night, programmed to expect the government to act foolishly, or criminally. But pursuing them was important to her, so he would see it through. He would do anything to prove he loved her.

At five-thirty he gave up on sleep and showered, then dressed in some new clothes he'd bought after calling Blevins and Melissa. He walked to a diner for coffee and breakfast as the minutes crawled by, killing time before his ten o'clock meeting with Blevins. He didn't see how he could wait that long for answers. He wanted to know right now that Melissa was safe.

Was she at the FBI office, sleeping on the SAC's couch? Had everything gone okay, or had there been trouble? He thought about their last morning together—was it only yesterday?—sneaking glances at each other's naked body. He wanted to relive those few minutes again, travel back in time and disengage the safety catch from his feelings, forget his insecurities and press his bare body against her wet towel and see if she was as ready to pick up their relationship as he was.

He said a prayer that she was safe, even though he was lousy at praying. He'd never given it much of a try and never thought to pray for his own safety, but Melissa was different. For her, he would pray, make all the standard promises he'd heard his buddies say during the war with the very best intentions of keeping every one of them, respecting the possibility of a supreme being too much to take the obligation lightly.

He made no promises to God about killing, though, because trouble was coming. He was expecting it, could feel it. He'd danced on this deadly stage before and knew the choreography intimately. He understood the simple fact that Bronovich wouldn't be the last to die.

He was glad he saw the coming deaths. Expecting more people to die actually made it easier, helped him step up his defenses and switch his survival over to instincts and training. They were good tools that had saved him before.

Assistant Special Agent in Charge Leo Strick was filling in as the Squad Seven supervisor while the regular supervisor recovered from surgery. He was a weasely little prick with a ferret face and a woman's hand gestures, a fearful man who survived the dangers of being an agent by finding endless reasons for staying in the office. He deserved no respect from a street agent like Blevins.

Strick was a petty man with a scheming personality who made his career by stealing glory from other agents or successfully destroying the careers of agents ahead of him. Throughout the Bureau agents called him Strick the Prick. Blevins was sure his boss, SAC Sackett, distrusted Strick as much as he did. It was a normal reaction, the same wrench of the guts anyone felt when a cockroach raced across a dinner table.

It was too early in the morning for Blevins to be pushing this hard, but he stalked Strick anyway, backing him around the steel furniture and demanding more information. He wanted every single detail, wanted to know exactly how he'd gotten Special Agent Davidson killed.

"What were those other guys doing there anyway? And what about Melissa Corley?"

Strick backed away from Blevins and shrugged as

though he'd just spilled coffee. "It was just a mix-up. Those agents went to ask Corley some questions and Davidson overreacted, threatened them, I guess. It's not like they knew he was an agent."

Blevins kept advancing, glaring into Strick's face and wanting to kick his ass. But he was hurting, too. Hurting bad. He had gotten a young man killed, and no amount of ass-busting would change that.

"Davidson was gunned down by FBI agents? Is that what you're telling me? Who, Strick? Who was it?"

Strick rabbited to his desk and moved his pointy face away from Blevins's glare, his eyes searching for something else to home in on. "Don't start with me, Blevins. It was just a mistake. A horrible one, but a mistake nonetheless. That's all there is to it. It wasn't anyone's fault."

"When agents die in gun battles with fellow agents, it's someone's fault. Mostly mine, I know, but who else? Who dropped the hammer on him?"

Strick looked up as the squad secretary stepped silently to the door and watched for an opening. Strick greased his smile and focused on her. "Yes?"

Blevins turned to her, too. She fidgeted in his crosshairs.

"I . . . Gee, I'm sorry to interrupt, but Mr. Sackett wants Special Agent Blevins in his office right away."

"Good," Blevins said. "I'll get the story from him." He left Strick's office so fast, the secretary had to jump out of the doorway or he'd have knocked her down.

William Sackett was the Special Agent in Charge of the FBI's Washington field office. His was a political position, the powerful liaison between the FBI and the media, other law enforcement agencies, and the community. He didn't normally work cases, but Blevins expected him to be working this one.

All things considered, Sackett wasn't a bad investigator, at least not for a desk pilot. Unlike the fool Strick, Sackett had worked the streets hard while coming up and stayed out there in the line of fire longer than most. He'd made some good arrests and obtained solid convictions of a slew of organized crime figures. That gave him honor in Blevins's eyes.

Blevins charged past Sackett's secretary without breaking speed, opened the door, and stormed in. He tried to catch his boss off guard and tilt the advantage in his favor. Two other agents were in the room, quietly standing near the far wall. Blevins had met one of them before, a big, ugly bastard named Pate.

Sackett sat at his desk with his family's pictures on the bookshelf behind him—a wife, son, and daughter, both the kids nearly grown, about college age. Blevins figured Sackett to be about fifty-one, maybe fifty-three. A little softer now, sure, but still showing plenty of physical power. His brown eyes were steady and calm, framed by silver wire glasses and a gray mustache.

He was reading a file but rose as Blevins kept coming. He walked around and intercepted him. "Morning, Blevins. How are you?"

Blevins went right into it, animating a short countdown with two fingers. "Well, let's see. One: An agent I was training is dead. Fresh and green and dead, right out of Quantico. Two: I don't know who killed him, but I'm told it was our guys. I'll tell you what, Sackett, I'll feel a whole lot better when I find out who shot him and why."

Blevins pivoted on the balls of his feet until he faced

the other men. Pate held most of their power; it was obvious by the easy shift of his ugly face as he followed Blevins's movements and the squint that studied Blevins's hands when he moved close. Blevins chose him as contestant number one, stepped up to him, and jammed a hard finger into his chest. "Was it you? Did you kill Robert Davidson?"

Pate rocked back from the impact, looked down slowly, and stared at Blevins's finger with cold eyes.

Sackett stayed back and kept quiet, allowing Pate time for his own defense. When Pate's head came up like a snarling dog's, pushing emotions more toward critical mass, Sackett hurried over and stepped between them. "Ease up a little, Blevins. Nothing we do here can bring Davidson back. It was just a damned awful mistake."

"So I've been told."

"And it's the truth. Hell, you contributed to it by sending him there without backup."

"I know it's my mistake but I want to know who killed him."

Pate took a little step toward Blevins. He was meaner looking than most agents and genuinely ugly. Not just bad-skin, bad-features ugly, but warped and twisted so badly that his face had a burned-in look of evil. He almost looked as though he'd been scarred in a fire. Blevins would normally find him hard to look at, but right now he was staring.

"I'm sorry about your partner," Pate said, looking down into Blevins's eyes. "I know exactly how you feel. Davidson killed my partner first, while we were attempting our routine traffic stop. New agent. Guess he just overreacted and took us by surprise. I barely got off my shots before he tried to run me down the same way he ran down my partner. We didn't know he was an agent until later." He took a step back.

Sackett spoke to Pate and his partner. "Please wait outside."

The two of them hesitated, then walked out slowly, showing they hadn't been thrown out but were moving on their own, leaving Blevins to decide how things stood with them. They headed toward the door while Blevins stayed balanced, knowing that one more push, the slightest error by him or Pate, might start a game of bleeding.

Sackett picked up a file and slipped on his glasses. "Blevins, come over here. I've got more bad news for you."

Blevins looked at the departing men, and then crossed to Sackett's desk, leaned on it, and hovered over the file.

"Have a seat."

"I'll stand."

Sackett glared up at him, waited ten or fifteen seconds. Blevins didn't budge, so Sackett stood up, his eyes even with Blevins's. "I've opened another administrative inquiry on you regarding your association with this fellow Jamison. Apparently you two are good friends, old war buddies and all that. Since he's the subject of a national security case, I have to make sure you haven't acted criminally with him. If he turns out to be a foreign agent, this could end your career."

Blevins threw up his hands. Sackett jumped, started to go defensive.

"He's no more a foreign agent than you are, Sackett. It's ridiculous that FCI would even call him a suspect."

Sackett's glasses came off. "Dillon's a high-profile case, and if Jamison's part of it and selling secrets, it would be a terrible embarrassment to the FBI. Regardless of what you say, I'm reassigning your cases until we accurately gauge your criminal involvement, if any, with Jamison. As of right now you are on administrative leave, pending the outcome of my investigation."

Blevins said nothing. He looked at his watch and saw Sackett do the same. "I'll be gone by eight-thirty, but I want last night's shooting covered in absolute detail. I'll take every dose of my blame and know I've got a lot coming. But I want to know the hows and the whys. Everything that went wrong."

Sackett replaced his glasses, seemed to shift off ready-alert. "Will do, Blevins. You have my word on it. And I'll keep you updated on the inquiry, as much as possible."

Blevins turned and left. In the secretary's office he stopped in front of Special Agent Pate and memorized the hard look of his face. Then he stepped into him, eye to eye and toe to toe, his clothing brushing against Pate's, his nose locking in the scent of the man who'd killed his young partner. He stayed there, staring, waiting for Pate to take a step back. It took a long, long time.

By the time Blevins got back to his squad room, a black agent was already removing Blevins's files. Every other agent was rushing for Strick's office.

"Thomas," Blevins said to the agent at his desk. "What's going on with Strick?"

Thomas didn't look up. He spoke quietly and didn't

give away anything by his eye or body movements. "While you were in Sackett's office some agents brought your buddy's girlfriend through here, the one involved in that firefight at the Coalition."

"Was she all right?"

"She looked okay to me. Pretty lady. It must have been shit for the fan, though, because now we're all assigned to the case. Nobody's exempt. We're going to prosecute her, arrest your friend, and save the planet. All the normal jerk-off things but in double time."

"Sorry I won't be here to help and that you're stuck with my cases."

"That's cool, but this whole process aggravates the shit out of me. If you work for the FBI and one of your friends gets in trouble, well, it's whoops, sorry, and bend over, chump. They'll drag you through months of mud just to prove you're clean, in case someone should ever ask. It's degrading and insulting."

"I know what you mean."

"I'm sure you do. They've probably autographed a copy of that playbook for you."

"If they haven't, they should. This is my third inquiry."

Thomas dropped another stack of files on the desk. "That's a crock, man. You're the best man here. If you're not clean, no one is."

"They feel they've got to check."

"It's still a crock."

As Blevins filled in his three-card, he whispered to Thomas, "One other thing. I was going to do an FD-302 today but obviously won't have time. There's some evidence in the locker I promised a guy I'd release. The case is weak and ready to close. It's a white, file-sized storage box. Can you take care of it?"

Thomas played it coy, made no movement that might attract Strick's attention. "I don't know. Strick and Sackett will want access to everything you've been working on."

Blevins straightened up and bobbed his head as he checked what he'd written on his card. "You're right. I just didn't want to screw this guy if I didn't have to. He didn't want to part with the stuff but decided to be a cooperative citizen. I hate making it hard on good guys like that."

Thomas leaned over and looked all the way to the back of the file drawer, then slammed it shut. "If I can shake it free for him I will."

"Thanks, but be cool about it. I don't want you to end up like me."

"What do you mean, brother? Ending up like you is my career goal."

Blevins picked up his briefcase and looked around one last time. "Thanks."

"Don't mention it. I'll see you around."

"Be back when the ice melts."

Jamison sat in the diner until the hardware store opened up across the street, then walked over and bought a roll of duct tape, a standard telephone with an RJ11 plug, and a multipurpose tool with pliers, a knife, and an assortment of screwdrivers. By eight-thirty he was back in his room, dumping everything out of his gym bag, then refilling it with the items he expected to need: some deodorant, a razor, a change of underwear and socks, the stuff from the hardware store, a roll of quarters he'd picked up at the diner, a box of nine-millimeter ammunition from his trunk, and his Beretta. When he finished packing, he stuck the gym bag along with the suit he'd worn yesterday into the trunk of his car, then caught a cab for a twenty-minute ride downtown.

He made the driver go down every street within ten blocks of the Museum of Natural History, keeping a keen lookout for the blue Ford or anything else that looked like a threat. But he saw nothing and started feeling silly, thinking his imagination might be over-stimulated. He paid the driver and got out four blocks from the museum, walked a few blocks, then stopped in the chilly shadows of the post office depot. He watched the museum's entrance and every car that passed in front of it.

At nine-thirty he entered the museum from the north side and rode the escalator up to the main hallway. He stayed at the edges of the rotunda and kept his distance from the African elephant in the center of the huge round room because people couldn't help but look in the direction of that big-eared beast. He edged toward the dinosaur exhibit, his eyes and ears set at highest sensitivity, his hands open, his fingers together and rigid. He was creeping through a minor hall—a series of displays depicting ancient hunting techniques—when he heard a squeak of a shoe. The noise had come from behind him, a little to the right and closing fast.

Jamison whipped around, guts up, ready for what-ever level of threat awaited him. He recognized Blevins immediately but couldn't abandon his attack and only managed to decelerate to a ridiculous-looking slow motion.

Blevins stepped back and put a hand to his chin, his

raised eyebrow bending the butterfly strips that held his ripped flesh together.

"Pretty slow there," he said. "I could have paid you back for this eye. Are you on medication or something?"

Jamison dug his hands into his pockets and looked up and down the hall. "Anybody ever tell you what a funny guy you are? Come on, let's get someplace safer." He led him down a smaller hallway and stopped as soon as they were alone.

"Is Melissa all right?"

"I knew that would be your first question. Yes, she's all right. At least she was earlier this morning. I don't know what's happened since then, because I'm on the bricks again. But she was in the office today. Some FCI guys picked her up last night."

"I thought *you* sent an agent to get her. Isn't the FCI trying to arrest me?"

"I sent my new partner. Apparently the FCI guys went there to question her." Blevins lowered his eyes a little. "In the confusion, my partner got gunned down. Another agent was killed, too."

"Man, I'm sorry."

"Yeah."

"But Melissa's all right?"

"Yes."

Jamison squeezed Blevins's shoulder, checked his eyes, and remembered seeing that same look the day he'd led their squad into the ambush, a mistake that cost five lives and gave birth to the crazy man. "That sucks about your partner."

"Yeah."

"I caught the morning news but didn't hear anything about it."

"Maybe the media didn't get the story yet."

"You think?"

"I don't know, it's a little strange. We usually hit the news right after a muzzle flash."

"Even in Washington, FBI agents killing each other should be a big story, shouldn't it?"

"You'd think so."

"What do you know about the dead agent?"

Blevins glanced around, seemed to answer without thinking. "Theirs or ours?"

"Huh? What the hell does that mean? Aren't all of you guys on the same side?"

Blevins looked puzzled for a second, then seemed to understand what Jamison was asking. "Sure. Of course we are. It's just that I met two agents this morning who were, well . . . different. They're still on my mind. That's all."

"Different in what way?"

"Don't know exactly, but all agents are a little different in how they work. Organized crime guys work differently than white-collar crime guys. Reactive agents handle things differently than drug guys. Differences are kind of expected and come with the territory, but these guys had an entirely different set of marching orders."

"No kidding?"

Blevins narrowed his eyes. "No kidding. Sometimes it happens. I've seen it. A few guys work together awhile as a team, develop their own, oh, I guess you could call it consciousness or direction. Whatever. Sometimes they forget about the law. They just become more careful, less open."

"Like what happened in Houston?"

Jamison watched the pain streak across Blevins's face, but he had to know if this situation was similar. Melissa was involved.

"You said you'd never bring that up."

Jamison kept his eyes steady, even though he ached to drop them. "Sorry. But I still want an answer. Those agents set out to kill a man, gunned him down in cold blood, and you went along with their story."

"It's real easy to stand here all safe and snug and judge me for what I did. You weren't there. You couldn't possibly gauge the pucker factor when it takes a high-speed chase to catch your suspect. It was late, dark, and scary. The guy was supposed to be A and D. They said he went for a gun and that forced them to shoot him. Case closed."

Jamison bit his lip, then looked away from Blevins. "Uh-huh. If you say so."

"Damn you, I just said so!"

Blevins's eyes squinted and his lips pinched tight, warning signals that Peter knew to heed. "Sorry, buddy. I'm upset and pissed off. Didn't mean to make it personal."

Blevins took a deep breath, then exhaled and wrenched a kink out of his neck. "Ah, hell, you're right, anyway. About Houston. I wish you weren't, but there wasn't a reason in the world for us to kill that guy. We had him easy. Man, they just gave that poor bastard a quick vote and decided he was a blight on society. And he was."

"Even so, I'm surprised you went along with it."

Blevins raised his eyebrows. "The other agents were convincing with their story, swore they thought the man went for a weapon. I never saw it and it turned out no gun or knife was there, but they stuck to their story and I backed them up. More correctly, I didn't dispute them. It was wrong, I know. Would I do it today? No."

"Good."

"It sucks, but that's the very best and worst part of my character, definitely the part that causes the most problems in my work. I trust people too damn much. When they said they saw a gun, I wanted to believe them. I've always had trouble believing that people lie as often as they do."

"Strange problem for a criminal investigator."

"I fight it all the time. Can't tell you how many times I'm disappointed by people."

"And you think the guys that got Melissa might be like the agents in Houston?"

"Did I say that? No, I did not say that. I said they were different, that's all."

"What do you know about them?"

"Not much. As I said, I think they were FCI types, and that makes them a different breed right off the bat. I've seen one of them before, at Quantico. He's a big, ugly guy that might have been on the SOAR team."

"Sore team?"

"Special Operations and Rescue. Kind of like SWAT but a notch up. I've barely even spoken to him until today."

Three men in suits headed down the hall. Jamison split from Blevins, giving the interlopers harder targets if they were looking for trouble. There were no straps from shoulder holsters bending the men's jackets, no bulges around their waists, and the cuffs of their pants wrapped smoothly around their calves as they stepped, so no ankle holsters. There wasn't an indication of any weapons, but he stayed on guard until the intruders passed.

"How often do you think agents cross the line?"

"What kind of question is that? And how should I know anyway?"

"But you think it does happen?"

"There's temptation out there, fueled mostly by frustration. Once in a while, sure, somebody goes over to the other side."

"Could there be more than one, more than just a couple?"

"What are you getting at?"

"I'm just wondering. It seems strange to me that a dozen FBI agents have been ripping Dillon apart for months, looking everywhere for the person leaking classified secrets. They never could find him, at least as far as I know."

"So?"

"Melissa told me the leak was Bronovich. He was murdered, and I'm trying to figure out how the FBI with all its resources, couldn't finger him while someone else managed to do it secretly."

Blevins grew about an inch. "Are you thinking *we* killed Bronovich?"

"I don't know. Maybe your guys sold the results of their investigation to someone at Dillon. But—and this is where it gets scary—it would have to be all of them, all of the agents assigned to Dillon would have to be involved. Otherwise, the honest agents would have jumped up and made some noise when their suspect died. Don't you think?"

"Makes sense."

"And what about your partner getting gunned down?"

"Very unusual, of course, but those things happen. It was my fault."

"But why were those other agents there to pick up Melissa? What could they have wanted from her unless they were working with the guys from Dillon? Maybe they knew your partner was going to get Melissa and followed him there. Maybe they were afraid she still had more data from Bronovich. Did anyone check to see if her apartment had been searched?"

"Some agents are executing a search warrant at the Coalition. Makes sense it would be her office."

"Can they do that? Do they have the right? She hasn't done anything."

"They can do it all right. All they have to do is convince some judge to sign off on the warrant, and that's not hard to do. Once they get the evidence out of there, even if they never use it in a trial, it could get, you know, lost. And Bronovich certainly couldn't provide it again, so—"

"So the case he was helping her build goes right down the drain."

"What about your stuff, Peter, the data you gave Senator Drummond? Wouldn't they need to get that, too?"

"They'd need all three sets. Melissa's, Drummond's, and the copies I gave you."

Blevins rubbed his chin. "I might need to get Drummond some extra protection, before he ends up on someone's list, too."

"Good idea."

Blevins looked him over, as if sizing up Peter's chance

of survival. "If your suspicions are even partially correct, this mess is going to turn into a downhill shit ball,
fast. I know our guys are serious about arresting your
ass. I'd expect them to stake out your car, Melissa's
apartment, your condo, your office . . . The whole
stinking office was called in on this."

"Should I be flattered?"

"You should be scared to death. Let's just assume for
a moment you're right, that FBI agents had something
to do with Bronovich's death. That means you're pissing off the same people who killed him. Whoever they
are, they're very well connected. They got us working a
full-blown case against you in a matter of hours, and
we're the good guys, at least as far as I know. Have you
wondered who else may be after you?"

"No."

"I'd start thinking along those lines, while I was still
breathing."

"If we're right, who's going to protect Melissa?
Those agents who arrested her are probably part of the
corruption."

"She should be all right. Try not to worry about her."

"You know better than to expect me to wait and see
if you're right, unless you can absolutely guarantee her
safety."

Blevins looked around, came back shaking his head.
"There are no guarantees, Peter. But I'm sure she'll be
safe."

A family was walking toward them, so Jamison
pulled Blevins against the wall and spoke in low tones.
"Don't expect me to stand around and watch her get
hurt, Rich. You have no way of making sure she's safe,
probably don't even know where she is right now. If

I'm in danger, I have to think she is too, so I'm going after her."

"You can't. I'm already under investigation because of you. Don't make things worse. I'll make sure she's protected."

"And just how are you going to do that? People are dying because of Melissa's charges against Dillon. I'm not about to stand around and let some asshole put Melissa's name on that list. I'm going to get her."

"You're going to turn your world to shit, Peter."

"It's going to happen regardless of what I do. I'm not the cause. I'm just getting ready."

"Getting ready to get killed."

Jamison cut his eyes over to the family walking by, the parents and three kids smiling and laughing, living proof that he was already missing the best parts of life. Without the hope of winning Melissa back, there wouldn't be much left anyway. "I wouldn't bet against you, but I wouldn't bet against me, either. I'll get her back and keep her safe. If I die trying, that's just the way things work out sometimes. It's not a tough choice."

Blevins's pug face made another weird contortion, half grimace and half grin. "You're an ass."

"Thanks for noticing."

Blevins pushed his hand against Jamison's chest, a friendly way of moving him out of his way. "I've got to go, want to start checking this out. Call me at this number, three o'clock sharp." He handed Jamison a piece of paper.

"Will do. Have some answers when I call."

# CHAPTER EIGHT

Kane's call to John Butler had come before dawn while Butler was out running the ridgeline with a pack full of rocks, a challenge he loved because a misstep in the dark or an unexpected shift of the pack's weight could send him over the edge of a sheer rock wall. It was one of many things he did to stay in shape and ready between assignments.

He played the tape twice, dripping sweat and watching the sun climb into the sky, listening for an underlying meaning, hating Kane's voice and surprised to hear it again. He recognized it instantly, knew it belonged to one of the few killers who could best him. Maybe the only one. He hated to admit it, but in his line of work it paid to be brutally honest with yourself about where you stood with your enemies.

"So, you need me again. Well, screw you. You should

know better. What are you thinking, that maybe I'd forgotten that last time you refused to pay me? Your age must be making you stupid."

He slid out of his climbing shorts and stood naked at the mirror. The desert sun, already intense as it began its path across New Mexico's sky, threw harsh light on his scars. He touched them with respect, ran his fingers along the jagged healing, and remembered: the horizontal scar across the center of his face where a Namibian bushman in the civil war had sliced through his nose, the ragged patch on his chest where the Khmer Rouge had tried to skin him, and the one on his stomach that had healed with his skin folded over, leaving a lump of flesh on his left side he'd pierced and hung through with earrings. Each scar was a tribute, a medal for beating circumstances that should have killed him. The injuries were hideous because he'd never sought medical care, but he wouldn't trade them for anything and looked forward to getting more. He gloried in his defects and felt proud as he headed to the shower. He was addicted to the challenge of killing people. The adventure. The rush. He was a danger junky, and bloodshed was his fix.

Butler was the very best: the one most often called and the highest priced. He had done this kind of work since his savage role in Vietnam, a bloody war he would always miss. After three tours and the fall of Saigon, he'd slipped over to Cambodia in order to stay in a killing environment. In 1976 that wound down enough to get boring, so he hired out to the Rhodesians to fight in their civil war, and he stayed there perfecting his craft until Zimbabwe statehood ended the strife in 1979. He liked the Dark Continent, with its harsh pockets of isolation, and returned there often. Recently he'd helped the last vestiges of Boers stir up trouble in South Africa but quit when the proud heritage of the AWB demanded its soldiers to work for the glory of the Volkstaat instead of a paycheck.

He now lived in a simple and remote two-room shack far out in the dusty bumps thirty miles north of Roswell, New Mexico. He could relax there, the isolation providing his most basic need. The millions of dollars he'd earned over the last twenty years were buried in jars around his property, but he couldn't remember where he'd stashed most of it. Money didn't matter much to him, except as a way to measure his worth to the people who employed him. As long as no one ever visited him and his only calls were about work, he was content. He didn't need anything else.

The shower water was so cold it hurt. Water was the only thing in the desert that stayed cold without refrigeration. It came from deep in the earth, unspoiled by the sunlight that bleached everything else. He washed his legs, scrubbing hard to get off the sweat and desert dust, watching the dirty water swirl down the drain and onto the sand below his shack, not even noticing when his fingernails snagged the scab of last week's wound— the stab of a knife that had passed through his calf. Before he could stop, his nails peeled back the skin flap and tore the healed edges loose, sending the white puss of infection running down his leg.

Butler hardened to the pain, hating its power and refusing to give in to it. He grabbed the big stainless steel knife that always hung in the shower and took a wild, arcing swipe at his leg, just missing the calf and slashing off the loose chunk of meat. He threw down the knife and the chunk of meat, then jammed his thumb into the wound until it poked out the other side of his leg—a simple matter of honor over enemies. He screamed. It was a war cry, not a whimper.

He twisted his thumb around in the wound, made the nerves tingle and twitch, and then popped it out in a quick movement that produced a loud, sucking sound. He screamed louder, enjoying the pure sound that pain produced, even if it was his own.

Once out of the shower, he wrapped his leg with a dirty T-shirt in a halfhearted effort to slow the bleeding. His curiosity forced him to pick up the cell phone he'd leased under a series of credible aliases, then, while the hot breeze dried his naked body and his leg gushed blood onto his raw pine floor, he poured a glass of water and returned Kane's call, leaving a thick trail of blood as he moved to the chrome and plastic dinette table for a pen and paper.

There it was, the voice that kept coming back to challenge and aggravate him. "Hello," Kane said.

Butler was silent for more than a minute, but he knew Kane would let the silence last forever. Finally, he spoke. "What do you want?"

More silence now, pissing him off even more, tilting the power away and making him do the asking, again. "I *said,* what do you want?"

Kane's gentle voice was chilling, and reminded Butler that Kane could kill him whenever he wanted. "Don't be a shit to me. Do you understand?"

More time lost to bravado that could turn deadly. Butler would normally rush to a plane and fly straight to anyone who said that to him, go for all the marbles, life or death, over an insult like that. But with Kane, he knew he would lose. He squeezed his water glass until it shattered, driving a sharp glass wedge deep into the meat of his left palm. "Yes. I understand."

"Good."

A few seconds of silence passed, giving Butler time to challenge or accept that Kane ruled the battlefield.

"I've got some exigent circumstances and would like you here as soon as possible. Your standard fee, two hundred thousand."

Butler tried to mimic and sound calm and unhurried. "All right. Same drop zone as last time. Same signal. Nine o'clock tonight, your time. Agreed?"

"Agreed."

Butler hung up and stepped over to the full-length mirror. He admired his naked body until he began to feel better. Then he combed his hair precisely and dressed.


Kane hung up and looked at Ross Casey before he re-dialed.

"How soon before he's here?" Casey asked.

"Nine o'clock. I have a lot of work to do before then, but at least this should finish it. Jamison won't be a problem after tomorrow."

"Do you think it will work this time, as well as before?"

Kane held up his hand to silence Casey as he pressed the phone to his ear. Someone had answered, and he needed to make sure he was talking to the right person.

He nodded to Casey. It was the right voice. "It's me again," he said into the phone while glancing at his watch. "Twenty-four hours. No more."

Casey watched with his mouth open. He never knew who Kane called for authorization or to update at times like this, but he'd long ago stopped asking.

"Yes, sir," Kane said, then hung up.

Casey leaned back into his power pose, hands behind his head. "You're sure Butler will come through for us and kill Jamison."

"Butler's a good man and a tough predator. He'll get the job done, and he'll recover the evidence, if that's possible, assuming our guys don't get Jamison first."

"How many have you assigned?"

"Five of our men. Butler makes six. I'll send more if necessary, but right now I've got to get going."

"Good luck, Jack."

Kane ignored that and walked out of the office. He needed to sort through all the information he'd collected on Jamison for significance and accuracy.

He knew he was shirking his responsibilities by hiring Butler. He should be the one to kill Jamison, but it was getting so much harder now. Bronovich's eyes—the panic, the terror, the frantic glance toward his family's picture as he died—stoked the loss of Kane's own family. Kane was having trouble carrying the load.

He would have to work on it from this side, sorting and selecting information about Jamison as if putting together a puzzle, forgetting, at least for the moment, that another life would end when the puzzle was complete.

SAC Sackett wasn't taking any chances this time. Too many times the FBI had earned a black eye for allowing spies to operate with impunity, and he wasn't about to let that happen on his watch.

So he'd detailed two hundred agents, sent them out to arrest Peter Jamison, and would assign more if they didn't bring him in soon. Dead or alive, he wanted Jamison off the streets. His days of selling secrets had to come to an end.

Catching Jamison was proving to be difficult, even with the emergency wiretaps and mail covers. Jamison hadn't used a credit card, tried to buy a weapon, been involved in a traffic stop, rented a car, bought an airline, bus, or train ticket, charged a phone call, or been seen anywhere. He'd vanished. There were no clues out there. His disappearance was compelling evidence that the FCI supervisor was right: Jamison was a highly trained foreign agent.

Sackett worked all through Monday night. He'd poured so much coffee down his throat that the burnt smell was coming out his pores. His head hurt, his eyes ached, and his stomach felt as if gasoline sloshed around inside it, burning the lining and sending bitter fumes up his throat. But he ignored it as he closed his door and stalked the White House counsel who'd arrived at ten-thirty this morning, insisting they meet right away.

"Aughton, I'm up to my sphincter in this manhunt for Jamison, and now you want me to call it off? It was just yesterday afternoon that the U.S. Attorney stormed in here with the FCI supervisor twitching like a cat. He said President Albright was demanding that I pursue this case, so I don't really give a tinker's damn what Albright wants today."

Aughton didn't move, but just sat there dressed as though he'd come straight from a country club, too comfortable in a golf shirt and sport coat, soft-skinned but tan. He sat quietly in a leather chair opposite Sackett's desk, glancing around the office as if expecting trouble to jump out from under the desk. His sharp, lean face had a natural urgency to it. He nodded at Sackett, then smiled with only one corner of his mouth.

"That's right, Sackett. I want you to call it off."

Sackett looked out his window and watched Aughton's reflection in the glass. "I told you earlier and now I'm telling you again, unless the attorney general closes this case, it's staying open until Jamison goes down. Hell, two agents have died already and another was totally blinded by that crazy Corley woman, who right this minute is screaming about unlawful arrest. I've had to put my very best agent under an administrative inquiry and divert agents from other cases this office is working. With all due respect, counselor, if you think I'm going to let a political appointee like yourself close down this investigation before I get some solid answers, you're pissing up a drainpipe."

"This case should never have been opened. Clearly, President Albright overreacted to Senator Drummond's information. He worried too much about Jamison and didn't want to take a chance that he'd sell our military secrets to the world. No question, the president prematurely labeled Jamison as a threat to our national security. He was just afraid—"

Sackett got up and walked around his desk.

"Afraid? Now we're getting somewhere. Tell me what scared Albright."

The attorney stretched out his thin neck. "He was just . . . concerned. That's all."

"And that made him quick on the trigger?"

"I wouldn't say that. Between you and me, I think President Albright was perfectly justified in demanding Jamison's arrest. The information was too highly classified to allow Jamison to run all over town with it. Considering the number of military secrets that have leaked out of Dillon, I think he acted prudently. But now it's gone too far. The president wants you to back off before other people get hurt."

Sackett sat down next to Aughton. He hoped Aughton had more than simple marching orders. "Come on," he said in a low, easy voice, "tell me what's really going on here. If I knew the truth I might be inclined to cooperate."

The lawyer shifted in his chair. "It's just as I said. Although President Albright made his decision in good faith, in retrospect it appears to have been a mistake. We're simply trying to remedy it."

Sackett got out of his chair and went for the door. "That's a load of crap and we both know it. This case is still under investigation. "I'll let *you* know when it's ready to close." He snatched the door open.

Aughton stood, and for a moment he looked like a failure. But the look was soon gone, replaced by the confidence of one who believed he was untouchable. Sackett had seen the look before and worried about it. Nixon had it, so had Alexander Haig. Clinton had his own look of invincibility. Bush Senior tried to get the hang of it during investigations into his relationship with Saddam Hussein before the first Gulf War but never quite managed to pull it off. George W. Bush's was tainted with confusion, but all the looks said the same thing as Aughton's: The White House is untouchable.

Sackett stepped to his secretary's desk as the lawyer cleared security. "I need an update from the case agent on Peter Jamison. Get him in here right away. I also want Pate and the other agents who arrested Melissa Corley to stay in the area until the arraignment. They can go back to Quantico but no farther. Make sure they know these are my orders. I also need complete service jackets on all of them, including the one killed this morning by Robert Davidson."

"Yes, sir."

Sackett went back into his office and picked up the White House lawyer's affidavit that was still on his desk. He sat down and reread it, worried about what it might really mean. He thought about the way things used to be done, and the agents he suspected were still doing things that way. He knew it went on, but he usually turned away without looking for evidence, hoping that somehow he was wrong. But there were times when special assignments were just too political, and the agents who worked them somewhat insulated from FBI guidelines. He knew he should start looking harder at them, but as long as justice was done in the end, he didn't really want to interfere.

So where did that put him? Was he culpable for turning a blind eye, even if the country was probably better off for what was done? Had he been an accomplice to conspiracy simply because he'd allowed his agents to do the job they were paid to do? Would his career end when the truth, if such a thing really existed, came out?

He read the affidavit once more, certain that this was one of those times he should worry about, but less certain about what he should do.

\* \* \*

Kane examined the stack one last time before he left, checking for anything that could be traced back to him. He'd cut off every letterhead and removed all references to anyone but Jamison. On his way to interview the Corley woman, he stopped in to see Casey.

Casey looked worn down and almost out. "Jack, I've just found out the FBI won't close their case against Jamison. Damn, Kane, it was stupid of you to bring in the Bureau. Stupid."

Kane wouldn't apologize. He would just explain it calmly, again. "We thought Jamison would be an easier target, Casey. Our guys from Quantico thought he was picking up the Corley woman. They had no way of knowing the guy at the Coalition was an agent."

"Well, he was. And killing an FBI agent is kind of bad business, don't you think?"

Kane strolled over to Casey and parked his big frame right in front of him. "You just hold up your end, Casey, and I'll take care of mine. Jamison is a little smarter, maybe a little better than I expected, but Butler will be here tonight, and Jamison isn't that smart or that good or that lucky."

"I hope you're right, Kane. I sincerely hope you are."

Melissa's prison wasn't what she'd expected. When the federal marshals had come to transport her from the FBI office, she thought she would be going to jail. Jail meant bars, dingy bunks, and filthy toilets.

There were no bars here. The walls were concrete, white, and freshly painted. She had a small, clean toilet/sink combination and a clean bed. All of it was in good shape. The door was solid steel with a small window of wire-embedded glass. A person on the outside could take in her whole room from that window.

She sat on the bed and thought about the shooting of Special Agent Davidson. It broke her heart that she couldn't remember his first name. A young man had died last night for her. At the very least, she should know his full name and the name of the man who killed him. She couldn't recall if the shooter identified himself or not, but she could remember him without a name. Even the darkness of the alley couldn't hide his ugly features. She would remember him forever, stepping carefully toward Davidson and firing into his young face, the blood and tissue spraying all over the car and covering her dress.

She could not remember anything about Davidson's face before it was totally destroyed, so she wanted his name. Wanted it desperately.

A stranger looked through the window of her cell door, but she caught herself before she showed any fear. A key clanged as it twisted the lock open. Two men stepped inside, then locked the door behind them. The ugly man was not one of them. She was glad for that.

One of the men was hyperactive, his deranged-looking eyes wide open and shooting around the room, his head twitching and his hands moving constantly, messing with his thin, curly red hair. He was lean, but strong-looking in a stringy sort of way. His face was thin with sharp angles. His razor-sharp lips hardly moved when he said to his partner, ". . . and that's all she's told them so far."

The second man was almost the exact opposite, big and fluid, but with sharp lines in his face, too. Sad gray eyes. Intelligent, you could see that a mile away. Both of them smart—no undergrads in this room. She wanted to know, right away, how smart they were.

The big man responded, "That certainly isn't much. Maybe we won't have a problem with her after all."

She started right in on them, challenging the skinny man with the twitch, the man she would call Jitters. She'd been denied her rights, but there were still plenty of safeguards in the legal system to protect her.

"You should learn what the Miranda warning means, moron. I asked for an attorney during the last questioning. I am demanding one now. If you don't—"

Jitters's hands had been moving since he entered, so it was a little hard to tell exactly when he struck, blasting at her head like some old-style interrogator. But she saw it in time to snap her head back from the danger, understanding instantly that this was going to be a different game than she'd expected.

His hand flashed by her face, close enough to make her mad. She was not going to be victimized by a violent man, so with the speed and accuracy she'd learned in fencing, she reached out and grabbed a handful of his thinning hair, knotted it into her fingers, then jerked that scarecrow close to her. She spun him around with her other hand as she backed into the corner with him, reaching under his coat as fast as a saber slash and grabbing . . . nothing. His holster was empty.

Jitters grunted and tried to untangle his hair from her hand, but when their bodies smacked into the wall, he backed into her and slammed his elbow into her ribs. She held on to his hair as he knocked the wind out of her, her weight dragging both of them toward the floor. He jammed his elbow into her ribs again, and then again. Six times, fast as the snap of a rattrap. She heard some ribs crack on her left side and felt the muscles deflate in that arm.

He struggled against her grip until the hair ripped out of his head. Then he spun around to face her from five feet away. Drops of blood formed a connect-the-dots pattern on his scalp where the hair had been. His eyes were wet, and tears were streaming down his outraged face. She stayed on her feet, cornered, but managing to smile as she reached out slowly and dropped the handful of red hair on the floor.

She looked straight into his eyes and laughed as the hair fell. It almost killed her to do it, her ribs screaming with every breath, but she wanted both men to be uncertain about her and was willing to pay for it. She wasn't going to be anyone's easy victim again.

Jitters went into motion before the hair hit the ground. Her laughing had done it, she could see that. She had leaned toward him and laughed at his falling clump of hair, and he'd gone nuts. Jitters wanted his revenge. He was coming, and she had nothing left.

"Stop it." The big man intercepted Jitters's lunge and held him back easily, like a grown man with a small child.

Jitters had exploded, but Big Man had stopped it. Stopped it in a second.

"Yeah, that's right, Jitters," Melissa said, enjoying the chance to use the moniker out loud. "You'd better stop, like your friend says. It's anybody's guess what I'll rip off and throw away next time."

Big Man shot her a dirty look, then pushed Jitters past her while both men watched her carefully. She started for the door when Big Man opened it, but he was too fast and too ready. He shoved Jitters out of the cell, then locked the door and backed into the opposite corner, near her bed. He sat down slowly.

"You should get the prison doctor to look at your ribs, Miss Corley. My friend—what did you call him, Jitters?—is good at his work and might have done some internal damage. It could be serious."

She sat down on her bed, watching him, knowing he still had the key. She was waiting for her chance. "Next time I'll play rougher," she said, "do some serious damage to him."

Big Man seemed to like that. His eyes opened up as he gave an avuncular smile. "My, my, Melissa. You are everything I expected, absolutely everything."

"Based on what?"

"On who you are." His smile faded a little. "I knew your father."

What little strength she had spilled out, emptying her for a minute of everything except grief. And guilt. And anger. She wouldn't let it control her for long; she had learned to deal with it years ago.

"My father was an important man. Lots of people knew him. You think that makes you special?"

He leaned back and pushed down on the bed as if checking the springs. "No, Melissa, I think that makes *you* special. My question for today is, how special? How much do you know?"

The muscles around her ribs spasmed and pulled at the cracked pieces, but she allowed no sound of pain to come from her mouth. "I know what I was taught in school. There's a lot of stuff I've learned since. Some things I've known since birth. You want to be a little more specific?"

He laughed and stood up.

She wrapped an arm around her ribs and stood up with him, almost as tall as his chin. He took a small, slow lap around his end of the cell and then sat back down, a little closer to her but still out of easy range. "What do you know about your father's profession, what he did for a living?"

"He was an engineer. If you'd known him you wouldn't be asking."

"Yes, of course. He was an engineer, an excellent one. Do you recall how rapidly he was promoted, the great fortune he amassed?"

"He worked hard and was appreciated for it. It's not a big mystery."

Big Man was losing patience. It showed up first in his eyes, then his hands started moving, too.

"What do you know?"

"About what?"

"I want to know how much you've found out."

Melissa suddenly jerked in his direction, not attacking, but testing to see if she should.

It was a bad idea. Big Man was lightning, way too fast and much too smart, too good at reading her mind. She could never come close to matching his speed, much less beating it.

"Whatever I know is staying with me. You must be an idiot to think I'm going to sit here and chat with you about my father's business."

He shifted on the bed and got a little closer to her. He wasn't worried. She'd shown her speed and he'd done the same. She had nothing for a man like him to worry about.

"I may be trying to help you or I may be your worst

enemy. You'll have to decide that for yourself, then follow my suggestion or not."

She moved closer, just to keep him in doubt, maybe. He did not move away. "And what is your suggestion?"

"Keep what you know about your father private. I've been watching you for years, thinking you might be out for some kind of revenge. So far I haven't seen you use what you might know. I suggest you do not start now."

She stared at him, thinking about his face. Maybe she'd seen it somewhere before? In a store, or a congressman's office, or her father's living room. Maybe not.

"Is that all?"

He stood up and kept his distance as he moved toward the door. "One last thing. Has your investigation, or your heritage, made you aware of anyone trying to take control of your father's business? I'm sure you know that rumors have circulated for years."

She took two steps in his direction, two of the five steps necessary to cross the distance.

"If I knew anything, do you think I'd tell you?"

"No."

"You're not stupid, then. You may even be smart enough to understand that I'm going to destroy you and all those despicable people like you. There won't be anything left of my father's business when I'm done, so if I were you I wouldn't lose any sleep over someone else taking power."

He smiled at her. It was a nice face. "Pretty big talk."

"Can I go now?"

Big Man opened the door all the way, an invitation to leave. "No." He stepped out and started to close it, but stopped and looked back as though he expected her to beg.

Melissa turned away and looked at the wall. Could he possibly think that she was the begging type?

Jack Kane caught up to Jitters outside the men's room. He'd dried his eyes and combed some hair over his scabbing scalp. He was still twitching, though, over-flowing with explosive vengeance.

"Step in here a minute, Jitters."

Kane smiled when he said it. Jitters followed him into the bathroom.

"Don't *you* start calling me that, and don't you ever, ever touch me like that again. I don't care who you are. If you put your hands on me again, I'll—"

Kane turned and grabbed Jitters. He twisted him just the way he wanted, then uncupped his fingers from his knife and buried it deep into the side of Jitters's sinewy body while covering his mouth with his free hand. Jitters's eyes went still and stared up at him as his whole body went rigid. A first time for everything.

Kane moved his hand, like always, to hear his victim's last words.

"Why," Jitters gurgled. "Why, Jack?"

Kane knew why, even though Jitters would never understand. He was making his own decisions now. Who was good and who wasn't. They weren't based on assignment, or Dillon's worries, or a politician's paranoia. It was strictly his call.

"Because it's your time, Jitters."

Jitters slid off the knife and slumped to the floor. Kane stepped away and washed his hands. He washed the specks of blood off his sleeve, then called Dillon security from his cell phone and waited twenty seconds before stepping out into the hall. Two uniformed prison guards were running toward him with their guns drawn. Kane waited until they were close.

"Put those weapons away. Do not enter this room. There'll be an emergency unit here soon. Let no one else in. Do you understand?"

They didn't, Kane knew that. He didn't really want them to understand. He just wanted them to stand in front of the door, doing what they'd been told, guarding the crime scene until experts arrived.

"Yes, sir."

"Thank you."

He left and walked to the exit of the Federal Detention Center. At the sign-in desk he picked up Jitters's FBI credentials and gun, along with his own weapon.

# CHAPTER NINE

Jamison held back and stayed in the Smithsonian another hour. He wandered around and set up ambushes for anyone who might have intercepted his phone call to Blevins last night or followed Blevins this morning. Kids with cheap cameras walked through his kill zone along with fat-bellied men in sweatshirts and overweight moms in running shoes and fanny packs. None of them triggered his warning sensors, and the display of out-of-shape humanity tempted him to drop his defenses and wonder again if he was exaggerating the potential for danger. So far, he hadn't seen anyone who could make him worry.

But that was how people got killed and he knew it. Just let your guard down a little, boy, and that's when you tripped the wire or missed the small warning detail that could have saved your life.

He rode down the escalator and walked out onto Constitution Avenue, joining the Tuesday crush of tourists and federal workers. He ignored their presence and took no comfort in being among the living because he was spiraling into some kind of war, as surely as he had years before. He knew intuitively that war meant casualties. The city's buildings were big and concrete instead of squatty and bamboo, but his role was the same. He was armed, edgy, confused, and ready to kill whoever hoped to kill him. It was war wherever it occurred, and the innocent people around him were nothing but incidental soft targets for the sniper who might lie ahead or the bomber who could be across the street with a transmitter.

He'd hid last night, caught up in the escape, baffled by what was happening around him, and waiting to see which way this was going to play out. But they'd taken Melissa and that was a step too far. FBI agents, maybe the same men who'd killed Bronovich, had arrested her and killed Blevins's partner. There was no way he would assume the best and pretend she was safe just because the Bureau had custody of her. He wanted her back. He kept thinking about yesterday morning, her coming out of the shower with wet hair and a sexy smile, looking him over and driving him nuts.

That meant he was hunting humans, searching for whoever might keep her from him and not caring what badge or uniform or alias they used for hiding. He walked big down the street after leaving the museum, looking for trouble. He would beat the answers out of his victims once the fight was over, so he made himself an easy target, hoping they'd crack one off at him.

The walking increased his anger and it pissed him off

that no one was coming. Where were they? He crossed streets against the lights, walked at the edge of the gutter, did everything he could to attract attention. All the while he ground his teeth, almost to the point of shattering. He was mad, but not crazy. He still had the crazy man by the tail, holding him back. Twice before, he'd seen the uncontrollable fury of the crazy man, and he never wanted to see it again.

Melissa, thank God, had never seen the crazy man, even though she'd been nearby the one time he'd escaped on American soil. But Blevins had. He'd seen what that wild animal could do and Jamison was sure he hadn't forgotten. Who could?

They had been out on patrol. It had been another hot, smelly, rain-soaked day in southeast Asia and they were humping far out in the boonies, through a tangle of vines with all of their gear and all of their fears, carrying forty pounds of deadly tools that intimidated them with their own destructive power, carrying letters from home and photos and bug spray and smokes and water and grenades, humping foot powder and dry socks and a sidearm and knife and an M16. Pushing through dense bamboo and wanting badly to live through this day but knowing that some of them probably would not.

It wasn't anything like the movies. There was no soundtrack, no John Wayne, and no sweet endings, just land leeches and itching and sweating and worrying that your next step through the brush might pick up a wire and drag an armed grenade out of a tin can nailed to a tree across the path.

In some sense, though, it was boring. Walking alongside the trails and daydreaming about home, about eating with clean hands and sleeping in a dry bed. Or kissing a girl and touching her breast. Starting the day with a hot breakfast. Going to a job where you didn't have to kill strangers to earn your pay. Simple things like that.

How many times had they humped their way through this jungle to attract enemy fire? And why didn't the army just let them go kill the Viet Cong? Hell, every grunt was sure he knew where to find them. Only the REMFs back at Headquarters seemed to be in the dark.

But they crept along in split columns, staying off the trail for safety reasons but close enough to it to find their way. Rich Blevins was their new second lieutenant, a nugget who'd just arrived from the World, given the assignment after Lieutenant Trask diddy-bopped into some VC tangle-foot and was shot to pieces as he struggled against the thorny wire. Jamison's squad fired back at the VC, emptying magazine after magazine while Trask's shredded body danced hideously between them and the enemy.

No one trusted Blevins. He was a new guy, and FNGs knew nothing. Especially the officers. Where were they supposed to have learned, anyway, college? OCS? No way, man, you learned the rules of this game by playing it and this was Second Lieutenant Blevins's first time at bat. But they would walk his patrol and follow his orders, as long as Blevins's commands followed their own formula for survival.

Jamison was nineteen. He'd spent the first part of his life bouncing around America with his parents, his father a pioneer in the consulting business, city management type of stuff with six months to a year per location. There had been lots of schools, missed lessons, and lots of trouble. They'd settled in Virginia Beach long enough for him to finish high school, but he was far behind his classmates and barely made it through.

After graduation, the army requested his attendance at his first real chance to be a part of something permanent. He was thinking about that now, and thinking he would try to write his parents tonight if he lived that long. Where were they living? Portland? No, that contract had ended. Maybe—

Blevins didn't do anything wrong, but it was just one of those days when bad things happened in the Zoo. He led them as well as anyone, using all the training he'd been given and looking pretty sharp up there in his newly pressed uniform, giving perfect hand signals. Jamison and a couple of others had just finished laughing at how worried he looked pushing away the giant leaves of the banana plants and peering into the wall of jungle, looking for a hole big enough to allow a patrol of men to pass through. Blevins was the first one hit by rifle fire—it looked like two rounds in the stomach—but he turned, grabbed his guts, and signaled his men toward their target before he went down.

Automatic weapons began popping at them from the trees. Five or six of them, Jamison figured, with all the advantages—high ground, cover, concealment, and surprise. He was the very last man, covering the rear, and was barely in the VC's kill zone.

Everyone blasted away with whatever weapon they had in their hands: shotguns, M79 grenade launchers, M16s, and the ubiquitous M60. A jet could have screamed by and no one would have heard it over the high-tech chatter of their M16s laying down good fire against the mechanical stutter of the communists'

AK-47s. You could tell from the sounds how many were shooting: how many GIs and how many VC. They were scary statistics. Lieutenant Blevins's squad was already down by half, maybe more. It had been less than a minute. Hell, less than half a minute and they were down by 50 percent.

Once the primary kill zone had been worked over, the fire began raking in Jamison's direction. Up until now he had been taking carefully aimed shots into the overgrowth, shooting at targets just behind the dancing leaves, but now all the leaves were flipping toward him. It was going to be bad, real bad. There was very little fire from the M16s anymore; maybe just him and one other GI shooting back, but still lots of it from the Kalashnikovs. Had anyone called in air support? Artillery? Was help coming?

He listened for aircraft, longing for the bittersweet smell of Napalm dropped Danger Close by some clean-shaven, God-love-you, A-4 driver. But all he heard were the screams and crying of the men in his squad, gruesome proof that you really could die out here.

And that's when his water broke and Jamison felt another person born inside him. A person so powerful that he was barely controllable, recklessly powerful, crazy. Crazy Man didn't care about anything. He was fearless and frightening as he jumped up from the jungle floor, taking Jamison with him. There was a second of absolute silence in the steamy heat of the jungle, as if the whole world stopped and said, "Oh, shit. Do you see the look in that guy's eyes?"

Then the AKs starting clacking at him again.

Crazy Man walled over Jamison's face. He could feel it changing, toughening, and could feel the change all over his body—the jump in blood pressure, the cotton spit in his mouth, the swelling of his muscles, and his mind's new obsession with brutality. He became unstoppable and murderous. He jumped up and ran straight into the brush line, firing his weapon, flipping the clip, firing some more, running hard and fast and . . . couldn't wait. What a strange feeling. Crazy Man was absolutely exhilarated by the near future, by the chance to run straight into the foliage and right up to the damned Gooks, smashing their pumpkins with the butt of his weapon and hearing the ripe thump of a shattered skull.

He angled across the trail and moved into the brush at a trot. He was shot right away, and then hit again, but Crazy Man didn't care—paid absolutely no attention. Couldn't even tell for sure where the bullets had entered his body. Crazy Man was screaming, scaring the shit out of Jamison and scaring the shit out of the VC, too, because *look, there goes one now,* right in front of him. Crazy Man wished for a bayonet so he could stab the little bastard right through the back, but he had to settle for a quick burst to the man's head, his VC noggin ripped apart like a paper target while his wobbly legs kept his body moving.

Crazy Man had not broken stride yet, hadn't even staggered when he'd been hit. He was a bullet himself and could not be hurt by them. Terrain didn't matter. Thick vegetation didn't matter. He would fly over it, through it, straight to his enemies, straight for their hearts.

There was gunfire behind him now. Crazy Man spun around, arms first, so close to the other muzzle that Jamison wanted to jump back to get away from it. But Crazy

Man would not allow it. He stepped into his enemy, inside the tip of the AK's barrel, and pressed his weapon against the forehead of the communist's face and fired a short burst, then turned and fired again, bringing down another one who had jumped up and run.

Jamison was hit again but so what? *Who's next? Which one of you little bastards goes on my list?*

The jungle suddenly went quiet. He started noticing his own sounds for the first time, loud as a battle tank crashing through the jungle.

*No. Please, God, no.* Crazy Man shattered the silence as though it were glass. "Noooo! Get back here, you sons of bitches!"

But the enemy was moving out, so Crazy Man had to settle for long shots at the last of them, the two VC who'd seen the crazy man, had heard the crazy man, and didn't want to fight him. They'd seen up close what he could do. Saw firsthand that they lacked the power to stop him.

Jamison tucked himself into the jungle for a long time after that, as long as it took to learn how to lock the crazy man away. He wanted to hurry, to get back to his squad, and give first aid, but he didn't want the crazy man to lead the way. Not again. Not twice in one day.

He waited to be the last man medivaced from the firefight, so he listened for the thump of the last chopper. After two Dust-Offs, he walked to where they'd been ambushed and sat down beside Blevins, who looked shocked to see him. The lieutenant was holding his guts but showing little pain. Morphine, probably.

"What's your name, again?"

Jamison didn't want to talk. He was still coming back, trying to be ready to recognize normality when it hit. He figured he'd know he was there when his wounds started to hurt. "Jamison, Peter."

"Well, Jamison, that was really something. You're one brave mother."

"It was stupid."

Blevins grimaced but fought it back and didn't say anything about it. "I'm too green to really know. I can tell you one thing, I'm putting you in for a citation."

"Don't."

Blevins flung his chest and head forward, and threw up a smelly mixture of blood and food. Jamison supported his lieutenant's head until the retching stopped.

Blevins leaned back against the tree. "You deserve a medal. They would have killed us all. We'd be in body bags, every last one of us."

"Just don't. Okay? I don't ever want to hear about it again."

Blevins kept staring, but Jamison had learned in that brief slice of time what it was like to live with the crazy man. It was going to be hard, and would be almost impossible back in the World. He didn't need people honoring the guy. That much he knew for sure.

This D.C. street was no place for the crazy man. Still, even without him taking charge, Jamison was ready to go at it, right here, right now, thinking a little bit about torture and a place to administer it. He'd take any odds as long as they offered close-in fighting. No long shots that could drop him or his enemy. Up close and personal where the answers would be found. Answers that would get Melissa back and rescue her life from the fire.

\* \* \*

Dillon security man Samuel Martin had his orders. Kane had not been very specific that night in the warehouse by Melissa Corley's apartment, but they were orders all the same: Watch Peter Jamison, but don't kill him unless it becomes necessary.

Martin's problem was a simple one. Although he liked security work, he loathed being on surveillance. He preferred things face-to-face. Rough and tumble. Bloodied knuckles and broken noses.

He was a pugilist. His huge body was perfect for it. He loved to hurt people more than anything else in the world, except maybe getting teenage girls out of their silky panties. Even that would be a tough choice.

His propensity for violence had cost him his job on the Metro Police Department, and probably would have kept him off Dillon's force except for that big favor they owed him. He had killed one of their traitors when he was a cop and made it look like self-defense. There was the routine traffic stop, followed by his frantic radio call for backup, but by the time other cops showed up, he'd shot the suspect four times in the face and stuck a freshly fired throw-down weapon in his hand. Martin's story held, even against the gentle backdrop of the traitor's peaceful reputation.

That job had been easy, a short hunt, then straight to the kill, just the way Martin liked it. This bullshit going on now was cat and mouse, the kind of thing that really hacked at his nerves. Because of Peter Jamison, Martin had spent an entire night in a dark, roach-infested warehouse, spying on Corley's apartment. Then he'd spent long hours in his car, glaring at curious pedestrians while he kept a surveillance log and shot rolls and rolls of pictures. Both were things he hated to do, things he could stop doing as soon as Jamison was dead.

He'd followed Jamison to the museum, wondering how Kane knew he'd go there. Kane was truly amazing and had informants everywhere. They enabled him to maintain his status as the organization's ultimate enforcer. Martin fantasized sometimes—not often, but in the middle of the night, maybe, alone in some car—fantasized about being like Kane: intelligent, efficient, quick and silent, and deadly.

Martin didn't idolize him, of course. He had no idols because he was his own. Kane was just an inspiration, nothing more.

Jamison left the museum and walked down the street in Martin's direction. "Not very smart," he muttered to no one. "You came out the same way you entered. I'd have gone out the back or a window. Ain't showing me nothing; I could take you down anytime and get off this lousy detail."

All of a sudden that seemed like a good idea. He'd been up all night drinking coffee, and most of the previous night and day, too, so he knew his thinking might not be perfect. What were his orders again? Don't kill Jamison unless it was necessary?

He heaved his weightlifter's body out of the company car and started down the sidewalk. He was about a half block behind, but damn if Jamison didn't already have him. Martin had seen him turn around and take in all faces for half a second. Martin was caught. He felt Jamison's stare for a long time, a very long time in the context of hunting. Maybe two seconds. Long enough and bold enough to show that the terms of their meeting, whatever they might be, were perfectly acceptable to Jamison.

Martin was surprised, actually impressed by Jamison's bravery. Excited. If he was lucky this might be an actual contest. Not another boring mismatch between him and some pencil neck, but a fair fight, if such a thing existed for him, between him and a guy who was as ready as he was. Jamison sure looked ready, so Martin would get his chance to show off a little. It would be fun.

"What the hell? Has Jamison lost his mind? What was he doing?"

Jamison had no idea who the big bastard was but figured he was on the other team and, therefore, might have the other team's playbook. He would take the man down and beat out whatever answers he could, then use them to get Melissa free.

The guy was huge, that's why he'd been so easy to spot. Six feet seven, eight maybe, and pushing three hundred pounds. A giant by most standards, but Jamison thought he could take him with no help from the crazy man. Take him straight on, but careful as a surgeon.

In the middle of the crowded sidewalk, Jamison turned around and stopped at a noisy spot where workers tore down a brick building. People muttered and scowled as they squeezed around him and quickly formed a flow, like a fast-moving stream around a large rock. He waited.

The giant stopped and flashed a stupid look when Jamison stared at him. He glared back as the two of them held their ground, separated by a hundred feet and several hundred people, jackhammers and car horns filling out the soundtrack. Finally, the man's stupid look lifted, replaced by something else, something mean and simple. The giant started coming for him.

Jamison waited, watched the man's hands and his walk, looked for any kind of weapon or weakness, but saw neither. He came close, then closer. The giant slowed. Ten feet away, the stupid look—or was it surprise?—tried to work its way back onto the giant's face as Jamison stood his ground. Slower now, eight feet, six, four. The giant stopped three feet away, an arm's throw—big arms. His biceps had to measure twenty-five inches, maybe thirty. Hell, it didn't matter because a full blow from those arms could kill Jamison. So he did the only logical thing and stepped into the man, almost against his chest, and closed the gap to less than a foot.

The look—definitely surprise now, not stupidity— was big on the giant's face. His chest was as large as a reclining chair and sucked air like a huge pump that seemed to rob half the block of oxygen.

Jamison was on his tiptoes, trying to stay balanced as he rose up to the giant, trying to get close to eye level. "Where's Melissa?"

The giant must have spent one of his past lives as a chameleon; his face was changing from surprised to stupid and back again. Now it was set on stupid. "Huh?"

"Don't 'huh' me, dumb-ass. Where's Melissa?"

The giant smiled, and damn if he wasn't fast for such a big man. He threw his right leg back, found his range, snapped up his fists, and started to swing.

Jamison didn't let it happen. Like a shadow, he stepped with the guy and stayed within a foot, then smashed his right elbow across the bridge of the giant's nose, sharp and hard and quick as electricity—*crack!*

Then he came back with his elbow from the opposite direction, not wanting to leave his ribs open for long. *Crack* again.

The giant's nose squirted blood and the crowd shoved back. Giant was hurt a little but didn't seem to mind. He smiled, then took a slow swipe across his face with his monster hand, smeared blood all over his fingers, and left four clean streaks along his bloody cheek. Then he came like a bear, those huge arms closing around Jamison like a clamp.

Jamison shoved his open palm up at the big face, driving hard, hoping to cram the giant's broken nose deep into his head, but he missed and the clamping arms closed around him, pinning his own arms by his sides, dragging his face into the giant's smelly shirt. It wouldn't take long now that the big arms had him, so he had to do something quick. His lungs gave up air, and his organs shifted higher into his chest as the giant squeezed them out of position with his powerful grip.

He raised his right foot and then drove it hard onto the giant's size-sixteen shoe, or whatever, smashing his toes. He ground in his heel and felt as if he were standing on five large mice.

Giant's arms stopped closing, but Jamison knew he wasn't hurt. He had a curious look on his face, as if he wanted to look down and see what had happened. He let Jamison slip, just a little, so he could see his foot.

As soon as he had room, Jamison fired his fist like a rocket, launched from way down low and close. It traveled the straight path from the giant's belt to the bottom of his massive chin, hitting home, rocking the big bony jaw skyward and throwing the giant a little off balance. Jamison swept his right leg behind the giant's calf and drove himself against the hardened chest. The man was unbelievably solid. Even with the giant leaning back, it was like ramming an elephant's rump. Jamison pushed as hard as he could, kept his right leg locked behind the giant to keep him from stepping back. Gradually, Big Boy began to fall.

Jamison jumped on him as he hit the pavement, grabbing his head and banging it onto the concrete, pummeling it with his fist, smashing the nose so many times that it became unrecognizable, a flattened slab of bloody mush. But it wasn't enough. He tried to crack the giant's head on the concrete and break it open, but the neck muscles were too strong to allow him a good blow.

Giant pulled his hands up and covered his face. He seemed confused; things were going so wrong so fast. He looked as if he'd never been on the losing side before.

Jamison heard sirens several blocks away, making their way through the workday traffic. No time to question this guy, but time enough to put him away for a few days. People screamed and construction workers yelled at each other to stop the fight. Jamison jumped off the giant, who was bleeding from his nose and ears and eyes but still not badly injured. Jamison knew he would see him again if he left him like this. He knew the giant would be more careful next time. More deadly.

Crazy Man started screaming in Jamison's head, the only voice he could hear now, shouting that the giant must have a gun and that Jamison should grab it and shoot him. Shoot him now, before the police came. There was still time.

Jamison flipped open the giant's jacket and reached for the big handgun, but as his fingers touched the grips he stopped and begged the crazy man not to kill this man, screamed that it was way too much. Crazy Man hesitated, and Jamison did the same, his fingers wrapped around the butt of the weapon but not pulling it from the holster. Crazy Man stunned Jamison by agreeing, as long as the giant was hurt badly enough. He backed down but stayed very close.

There were loose bricks from the construction area twenty feet away. Jamison ran and grabbed one, then came back to the giant—who had watched through the cracks in his fingers—and started breaking ribs, two of them there, now a couple more over here. He listened to them snap as the giant's massive body twitched on the sidewalk. One more wild swing at his sternum. Ugh, that was a good one. *Okay, that's all the time.*

He jumped up, held the brick like a football, and threatened the crowd opposite the sirens. They immediately split apart, couldn't seem to do it fast enough to suit themselves. He threw the brick down and ran through the hole, turned the corner, and slowed down and started walking, one of hundreds of people in the Tuesday crush, heading back to work.

# CHAPTER TEN

At three o'clock, Jamison walked into the Grand Hyatt Hotel to call Blevins. The lobby was busy with guests checking in, a few sitting in chairs, and two Japanese waiting for the concierge. None of them seemed threatening, just people going about their day in a world far distant to Jamison's. The only people who were suspicious at all were a man and a woman who seemed to be having an affair, both dressed in business suits and standing too close while acting like strangers as they waited for the elevator. The man looked away when he talked to her; she looked down when she giggled. But they weren't a threat to Jamison, so they stayed on his radar screen less than two seconds.

He walked past the cocktail lounge to the phones in the back, looking away from the lounge because there were too many faces to scrutinize at once, any of which could have recognized him in a second. He ignored the clink of glasses and sound of laughter because they reminded him of his meeting Melissa in Jonah's Bar, the night that changed his life. Now she was in custody, an agent assigned to her was murdered, she was probably in as much danger as he was, and he was unemployed and on the run. For all their troubles since then, they were good changes because Melissa was back in his life. At least she would be if he could just find her.

He called Blevins at the number he'd given him, sure that it would belong to a pay phone. Blevins liked to be in a busy area when he talked secrets.

Blevins was out of breath when he answered. "Hello."

Jamison looked around to make sure he was still alone. "Is everything all right?"

"Yeah, yeah, I'm fine. Just tired from dodging the Bureau's surveillance teams."

"What? They're following you?"

"Don't sound so surprised. I'm a suspect now, just like you. Why shouldn't they follow me?"

"I guess. Did you find Melissa? Is she safe?"

"Yes, the Bureau turned her over to the marshals. They'll be responsible for her until the arraignment."

"You sound like that's supposed to make me feel better."

"It's good news, under the circumstances. She'll be fine. I'm sure of it."

"Yeah. Right. She's under arrest and facing trial. Excuse me if I don't share your confidence."

"Have faith in the system, Peter. They don't have much on her. Maybe a little disclosure violation, some computer hacking, but nothing they'll spend much time on."

"What's she told them so far?"

"From what I hear, the same stuff you told me. About Dillon. But the agents didn't buy a word of it."

"Why not?"

"They're just words, Peter. She has no evidence. I'm sure her charges of high-level corruption sounded ridiculous."

"Why wouldn't they check out her story? They could have called Drummond."

"I can't answer that. What's interesting, though, is that a guy from the National Security Agency was there when agents questioned her. He warned them not to disseminate her information in any form. Not one word. Even though Melissa's allegations couldn't possibly be true, he said they were of a highly sensitive nature."

"Is it normal for the NSA to show up like that?"

"Actually, it's weird, and set my mind to thinking in strange ways. So I visited a friend of mine at Langley, a middle-echelon guy. We crabbed for a while about old times, talked about things that affected both the FBI and the CIA, just to get the conversation rolling. Then I asked him your question, is there a rogue element in the FBI?"

"That was bold. What did he say?"

"He was reluctant to talk at first. Very, but I kept breaking down walls until he eventually told me some pretty strange things. It was funny, but he didn't seem bothered at all about what he was telling me."

"What kind of things?"

"Some pretty way-out stuff. Apparently, a long time

ago—I have no idea when it started—some rich Belt-way bandit with a big scheme and connections formed a select group of politicians and warriors, then armed them with the power to do things secretly without a lot of fuss or fanfare. They had some kind of secret fund."

"What are you saying, that America uses mercenar-ies?"

"Jeez, Peter, I don't really know. I'm just thinking this through myself, based on the examples my CIA guy used."

"Which were? Any specifics?"

"Not at first. But I've known him a long time, and once he started talking it was like opening a tap. One story led to another. These guys go all their lives with secrets jammed into their brains but they like to brag when they can."

"So what did he say?"

"Ready for this? He said those guys with the cash kept our hostages held in Iran until it turned the presi-dential election. Then they funded the Contras after North got his hand slapped, bought the cooperation of criminals like Noriega and Ferdinand Marcos, and shipped arms to Iran."

"Wow, what did you say?"

"I said nothing. Man, the guy was starting to per-form, telling me about those weapons shipped to Sad-dam Hussein before he invaded Kuwait. They never showed up on any government balance sheet, and George Bush always denied sending them, even after George W. sent troops back to face them. He asked where I thought the money came from to pull that off."

"He said all that?"

"Yeah, and more. Hell, he talked for an hour or so,

detailing crap like the windfall channeled into this fund. The DOD scrapped all one hundred and ten of the military's Atlas missile sites after just three years instead of the scheduled fifteen. That program was fully funded at the front end, so the early shutdown meant—"

"Big dollars to work with."

"Bingo. But here's the kicker. When I asked him about the Wombat, he said companies like Dillon were what Eisenhower meant when he talked about the military/industrial complex."

Three men came out of the bathroom and Jamison memorized all of their faces, then compared them to the other faces he'd logged into his brain today. "What's he talking about, this military and industrial complex?"

"Not sure. I guess some kind of illegal cooperation between the military and American business. From what he said, I would probably define business pretty narrowly. He probably just meant defense contractors."

"They would have the motivation."

"You bet. He said that between 1980 and 1990, contractors subverted ten billion, *billion* dollars in navy funding for aircraft they'll never use. The F-14D, the ADVCAP, the A-12 Avenger, the A-6F."

"I wondered how those programs survived. So you believe this guy?"

"I think I do, although I hate to admit it. I'll tell you something else, too. He seemed to think this fund was a very good thing, the one and only way for this country to stay powerful. He was a flaming zealot."

"You're kidding."

"Not at all. You have to remember those guys in Spookville get very cynical about public opinion. It hinders their range of options. They'd prefer to conduct their slice of America's business without any oversight at all. That's why they'd support just about anyone in any endeavor they could pull off to further their goals."

"Can you go back and get more out of this guy?"

"Doubt it. When he stopped, he knew he'd gone too far. But he did mention one other thing, and feel free to take this personally. He said that anyone who was thinking about confronting these fund guys had better be well informed, ruthless, and invincible."

"Great. I love it when people use hyperbole where my life is concerned."

"He didn't say it to insult your abilities, Peter. I never told him anything about you. He believed one hundred percent that anyone challenging these guys should expect to be dead within a few days. Less than that if he wasn't professionally trained. There have been rumors for years about someone trying to organize a takeover of this cozy little group by getting rid of the top layer of leaders, and it's made the current regime paranoid and dangerous. They feel threatened by Melissa and the Coalition, so there's another good reason for you to expect them to be deadly."

"I'm not challenging these guys. I'm not interested in their little fraternity. I tried to save some jobs, that's all, and now I'm trying to get Melissa back. It's as simple as that." He sounded weak and hated that. "But if it's a fight they want, I'll sure give them one."

"You may have to. Here's the last thing he said. He told me the FBI has been pretty clean, whatever that means. Your guess is as good as mine. But at one time he did know of a group of dirty agents working around D.C. I guess that would mean Washington Field Office, Headquarters, Baltimore Field Office—"

"And Quantico! You said you recognized the agent in Sackett's office yesterday. He was from Quantico, the SOAR team, remember? Do you have any idea why he was assigned to this case?"

"Not yet, but I'm thinking like you. I'm calling Headquarters as soon as we hang up to find out the whole story about him and the dead agent. It's not unusual for an agent to show up at an office for a brief special assignment, but it's usually at the SAC's request or because the case relates to something he's already working on. I don't see how that could apply here. You and Melissa weren't even a case until yesterday. Maybe you two dovetailed into something he already had open."

"Either that, or Sackett's in on it, too. No matter how you slice it, I still hate that the government has Melissa."

"Try not to worry. If they wanted to kill her she would have died in the shootout behind her office. Since they brought her in she's pretty much out of harm's way, at least that's the way I see it. My guess is they want to use her to catch you, either by piecing together the information she supplies trying to defend you or, if they let her go, by following her. Either way, your play is to back off until this is over, for her sake."

"Probably good advice, but it sucks and I won't do it. I'm going to get her back. Help me if you can, but I'm going after her."

"I knew you'd say that but I had to try. Sure, I'll help. Got a plan of what you're going to do?"

"There's not a lot I can do, short of marching into the federal building with a ransom note and a bomb."

"You're kidding, right? About the bomb?"

"Just barely. Actually, there's a secretary named Charlotte who might be willing to monitor activities around Casey's office, if I can still get to her. I'd like to find out what Dillon's security men are doing, then pick them off one at a time and get a little information from each of them."

"Not a bad idea. Where will you be staying?"

Jamison's warning lights popped on. A familiar face of a man nearby just matched up with one in his brain's data bank. It had taken a couple of seconds to make the match and now the face was gone. Where was he?

"Got to go, Rich. Remember the hotel where you and Elaine stayed New Year's Eve three or four years ago? I'll be there if they have room, using the name . . . using your cat's name."

"Okay, I'll call you at eleven tonight. Be there, damn it, or I'll assume you're dead and take over responsibility for Melissa."

"Thanks."

SAC Sackett was talking out loud, just as he'd done through lunch and dinner, telling himself that it was way past time to figure out what was really going on.

"Okay," he said, "one more time through these personnel files. First the dead agent from Quantico, then his ugly partner, Pate. What's wrong with this dead guy's service record? Something at the most basic level, where simple things can be so elusive. Slow down, Sackett. Concentrate."

The agent's file was not impressive, and Sackett was hard-pressed to see any reason why Headquarters had been reluctant to release it. But they'd kept it locked down until he'd shown up personally and shoved his demands down a clerk's throat. He'd been plenty pissed by that time and his anger had sent all but one of them scurrying for cover. The slow mover had finally gotten him the file he wanted.

It contained all of the information he expected: background checks, grade increases, a couple of "aw, shit" letters offset by several "atta boys." Eight years in the Bureau and all of them at Quantico. It was weird that he'd stayed there after his sixteen weeks of New Agents Training, all of his other field assignments being TDY, temporary. In Sackett's twenty-six years he'd never seen anyone permanently assigned, but it was a new FBI these days and things like that surprised him less and less.

Toward the end of his third pass the snake jumped up and bit him, just the way he hoped it would. The file contained no mention of case assignments. There wasn't a single arrest or conviction statistic. No case numbers cross-referenced by the indices clerk. Nothing. It was as if the man had served eight years as an FBI agent without ever enforcing a law or investigating a crime. Sackett was shaking his head as he picked up the phone and called the Academy.

"Get me Special Agent Warden."

Sackett waited, thinking about Amos Warden, looking forward to hearing his old friend's voice again, hoping he would learn something from him. They had shared a dorm room during New Agents Class 71-9, then been assigned to WFO together. Five years ago, Warden had been gut shot during a raid at a bikers' clubhouse outside of Houston. He had recovered pretty well and now lived at Quantico, training the SWAT teams that cycled through from the various offices.

His voice boomed out of the phone. "Warden."

"Jeez, take it easy on my ears."

"Bill! How the hell you doing?"

"I'm good. You?"

"Me? Damn, I'm exhausted from this hard work down here."

Sackett leaned back in his chair. "Sure, Amos. Don't forget I spent some time at Quantico, too. I've got a pretty good idea how hard you're working. Were you in the bar?"

Warden didn't let up on the volume. "Absolutely not. There's a bunch of National Academy guys up there tonight, so I passed. Even this early in the evening, there's too much tension up there for a guy like me to have any fun."

"Hasn't changed much, has it?"

"Never will. Those cops think they know all there is about police work, while our boys are on home turf and a little smug about their advanced degrees and higher salaries. Mixing those two in a small barroom with discounted booze has always been a bad idea."

"You're right."

"Of course I'm right."

Sackett leaned toward his desk, turned the file sideways so he could read the agent's complete name off the tab. "Look, Amos, I've got a dead agent here—"

"Yeah, I know. I was briefed right after it happened. Hell of a tragedy, but at least there isn't any family, no grieving widow."

"You knew him?"

"Hell yes, I knew him. Trained him. A good trooper, too. Not as good as his partner, Pate, but still a great agent. Skillful, intelligent, resourceful—"

"And dead."

"That's right."

"What was his job at Quantico? Hostage Rescue Team?"

Warden laughed, way too loud for a guy in his line of work. "No way. He was way too independent for HRT, too individual in the way he worked. Not a team player at all. He didn't even like having Pate as a partner until they got to be friends."

"So what did he do?"

There was a little silence on the line, an unusual element when talking with Warden. "Sorry, Bill. Can't tell you."

"Don't bullshit me. I'm not in the mood."

"Then get in the mood, or go ask your question someplace else, 'cause I can't help you. By now you probably know those guys were working under a Group-I status. After the shooting, security clamped down even harder. I can't tell you more than that."

"Who directed the increased security? At least tell me that much. I'll go to him with my questions."

Warden cleared his throat. "Ah, hell, it was an assistant director, but I won't tell you which one. Why are you bothering me? Who put the gerbil up your drainpipe anyway?"

"Who put the gerbil—damn you, Warden! Something illegal is going on around here and I'm in charge of finding answers."

"Then I really can't help. And while I'm at it I might as well tell you something else to piss you off."

"Which is?"

"The other agents involved in Corley's arrest have been prohibited from talking to you. Or anyone else."

"They *what*? They damn well better talk to me! I'll

have their credentials if they don't. Hell, I'll prosecute them for obstruction of a criminal investigation. I don't give a damn if they are agents."

Warden chuckled, as though someone had told a dirty joke in mixed company. "I know you would if you could, but the simple truth is you can't. The orders came down from above. Top floor. My boss, their boss . . . your boss, so you won't override them. Besides, they're dropping the espionage charges against Peter Jamison, so there's no investigation for the agents to obstruct. There'll be no arraignment of the Corley woman and no prosecution of either of them. You'll probably get word in the morning."

"How come you know so much?"

"Come on, Bill, don't act high and mighty with me."

"What?"

"You've played along before and done your share, so don't pretend you haven't, at least not with me. You went with me on my first time, remember? What's it been, twenty years? Twenty-five?"

"I didn't know it was wrong at the time."

"Liar."

Sackett squirmed in his seat and checked to make sure he was on his private line. "Why are you doing this?"

"I'm trying to save your life, that's why. Don't make me destroy you. You know too much to let you roll over."

There was a crack, and then the phone went dead. Sackett sat there for a long time, confused and a little worried. Finally, his frustration drove his fingers back to the phone. He called Blevins's home number, left a message, then paged him.

* * *

Blevins got the page as he rolled down his own street, heading home for the first time since he sent Robert Davidson to pick up Melissa and got him killed. Had that only been last night? It seemed like a week ago. Maybe more.

He waited until he got inside the house to call. "This is Blevins. Let me talk to Sackett."

The perfect silence on the line reminded Blevins that a large spool recorder was turning slowly in a back room, taping every word of incoming calls. Its presence had never bothered him, but he never forgot it either.

Sackett sounded like he already had a head of steam going when he got on the line. "Blevins, I'm going to be working late this evening, going over your administrative inquiry, Jamison's espionage case, and, hell, just about everything that revolves around them. You and I should talk. How soon can you be here?"

Blevins had spent most of the afternoon sneaking in and out of Headquarters, and he knew they were closing the case against Jamison. He was glad to hear it, even though it wouldn't be the end of Jamison's problems. It might even make things worse if it caused Jamison to drop his guard.

"I'm an hour away. Soon enough?"

"Get here earlier if you can. Expect it to be a long night."

Blevins hung up and headed for a quick shower and a change of clothes, thinking about what he'd found out today and wondering how much of it Sackett already knew.

He had called in every favor he was owed by anyone who might be helpful. He learned that at least one contract was out on Jamison but he didn't know any of the details. Jamison was still alive, though, at least a few hours ago. The agent who killed Davidson had returned to Quantico, and Melissa was doing all right at the Federal Detention Center. Things could be a lot worse.

He dressed, then picked up his nine-millimeter pistol, released the magazine, and snapped the action open, sending an unspent round somersaulting onto the bed. He checked the breech, counted the rounds in the magazine, and then slipped it into the handle. To reload, he pulled back on the slide and let it slam forward, seating a new round. Then he flipped the decocking lever, dumped the magazine, and topped it off. This was the procedure he had established back in the war and it never varied. Whenever the weapon had been out of his sight he would empty, check, and reload it before holstering. With all the other uncertainties in the world, he wanted no doubts about the readiness of his personal firepower.

The District Drugstore, near the corner of Fourteenth and K Streets, had always worked out well for Kane. The copier was in a back corner and out of easy view. But it was still a public copier, muddling the usefulness of any clues from paper type or toner analysis if the copies were ever discovered and tied to the crime.

Kane dropped in his quarters and copied all the material for John Butler. He made two sets, just in case Butler somehow failed and another man had to be assigned. He doubted it could happen, but it was a possibility. He wasn't going to underestimate Peter Jamison a second time and look as foolish as the men who tried to shoot him after his meeting with Senator Drummond.

He wore driving gloves as he bought a large envelope

and tape, and then drove to Ronald Reagan Washington Airport and went directly to Delta ticketing. He found the bench they'd used before, unoccupied as usual in this little stretch of hallway. There was no long view to this place, so there was no way to set up surveillance from a safe distance away. Someone would have to be close to see him, and that's what made it a good drop zone.

The envelope was held in the center of his briefcase by a wad of putty. Kane slipped a gloved hand under it, then pushed it up under the bench and stuck it to the bottom. Now to signal that he'd filled the drop.

Kane headed down the main corridor and followed the crowd to a small incline in the hall. As he started up the grade he slipped his hand into his pocket and squeezed a slick of petroleum jelly out of a tube and onto the tips of his fingers. He glided the palm of his hand along the rail until he reached the designated spot, directly under the overhead sign. At that point he curled his greasy fingertips around to the bottom of the aluminum handrail and lubricated a foot of it with a thin streak of gel.

Butler's plane arrived at eighteen minutes after eight and he'd been the first passenger off. It was a convenience of first class that there were usually seats available for last-minute ticketing. The short flight to Albuquerque in his own helicopter had made the schedule easy to keep.

The pressing crowds of the airport reminded him of why he lived where he did and how. Almost everyone coming toward him stared at his face. Some turned away when he looked at them. Others couldn't seem to do it, although it looked like they were trying hard. His scars and ugliness made him special and he liked the feeling. Some of those same people bumped into him and stepped rudely in front of him. He didn't like that. Their assaults made his fingers twitch, but he was a professional and could control himself. He walked through the terminal, looking for the ramp he'd used once before, a little uneasy at the idea of using the same signal and drop zone twice.

Butler shifted the shoulder strap of his canvas carry-on bag as he headed up the incline. The bag was his only luggage and contained everything he might need. He was quirky about firearms and condemned them as noisy, sloppy devices that were laden with evidence, used by amateurs who couldn't differentiate between a killing and an assassination. His weapons were no less deadly, but silent, and perfectly legal to carry on board a commercial aircraft.

He slid his fingers along the bottom of the handrail for the entire length, not trusting in anyone's accuracy but his own. They hit the slick of gel right where it should be, a greasy skid of goo. At one time in his life he would have turned around suddenly, or at least looked around to see if anyone noticed him or who might have left this signal. But that curiosity had been cut away years ago, thrown into the scrap heap of weak parts that didn't fit his profession.

He went to the bench near Delta ticketing and recovered the envelope, rented a car, and was out of the airport in fifteen minutes.

# CHAPTER ELEVEN

Jamison stretched out on the bed at One Washington Circle, a wonderfully private hotel with lots of comforts he wouldn't use. He hated leaving the hunt and couldn't wait to talk to Blevins, then get back on the street. A few more minutes. Blevins was a man of accuracy and would call at eleven o'clock.

He closed his eyes and tried to rest, tried to make good use of the downtime, but his mind wouldn't relax. There were too many unsolvable questions washing around in it, too much that would not compute until his brain's program was upgraded. He hoped Blevins would provide the information he needed to get Melissa back.

He'd called Senator Drummond after his street fight, hoping for help in identifying the giant. Drummond was furious with him for putting himself at risk and demanded he come in immediately and accept the protection his office could provide. He wanted Jamison alive, at least long enough to testify at a Senate hearing. Jamison tried to explain that it was impossible. He couldn't do that now. When he was sure Melissa was safe, then maybe. They might even come in together. But not before he had her out of danger. He'd failed the last time she counted on him, and he would never forget her tortured plea. He had no intention of spending the rest of his life with another failure like that.

It had happened two years ago. They had gone down the coast together on a golden fall weekend, hoping to work out the hurt they'd caused each other and forget the painful things they'd done to their relationship. They spent two days longer than planned because it had been a wonderful time, a healing time. He had never wanted to leave.

It happened on their last night, a starry evening cold enough for a jacket but warm enough for bare feet, a perfect night for an easy stroll along the Delaware beach. They had seen the men coming but there was no reason to suspect them, although in hundreds of shameful replays Jamison *had* suspected them and watched them carefully, ready. After all, he was bigger, stronger, and better trained. They were just a couple of local toughs out for a thrill. When they made their move he would make them regret it.

But the reality was entirely different, and time stubbornly refused to rewrite it.

The men had come up while he and Melissa were walking slowly, sharing secrets and good feelings on the isolated beach just south of the Cape Lewes ferry. The men were easy and friendly in their approach, said something nice and polite, and then hosed Jamison's face with pepper spray. Instantly, his eyes turned to flames and his face heated up.

Through the itching and burning he heard Melissa scream, "Peter, help, please help!" It was a terrifying, shrieking sentence that ended in a muffled garble. Jamison went right to attack, hastily dragged the crazy man out of his dark cell, and threw him into action, allowed him to burst out blindly with everything he had, even as Jamison felt the knife slip through the ribs of his lower back. Then one of the men clubbed the side of his head and sent him toward the sand, but the crazy man caught his attacker's hand and wrenched it around, snapped it back, and broke it at the wrist. He twisted the limp thing a few times, listening to the man scream and liking the sound of it. He still couldn't see and had no idea where Melissa was anymore.

He grabbed the man's forearm with his other hand, then yanked the dangling hand back toward the man's body. His attacker's horrible scream almost deafened him with its pitiful plea for mercy. "Please, mister, don't! I'm sorry!"

But the crazy man wasn't finished. Even without eyes, Jamison could feel the man dropping. He followed the man's arm to the ground, then stomped down with his foot, braced himself against the man's body, and gave the arm a violent twist, rotated it until the shoulder separated and the arm rolled out of the socket. Then he cranked it again while the man twitched around, crying and screaming and swearing. The floppy appendage led Jamison to the man's neck, which he grabbed and broke with a Ranger's twist.

No more than thirty seconds could have passed. Not much time, but at least ten seconds longer than it should have taken. Ten extra seconds that might have cost Melissa her life. Where was she? *Calm down. Stop. Listen. Where?*

There! He heard a scream over the dunes—away from the sound of the breakers. It was high-pitched and terrified, but it wasn't Melissa. It had to be the second man. He must have pulled Melissa away and now, God bless her, she was hurting him.

He started running but there weren't any more noises. He ran blindly all over the beach, blocking the pain of the wound in his back. He ran and fell. More time passed. How long had it been? Ten minutes? Twelve, maybe? He stopped and listened, then ran some more, falling and bleeding, then running—the crazy man loose the whole time and wanting a victim. Wanting to get his hands on the son of a bitch who'd taken her.

Finally, he heard crying, and this time he knew it was Melissa. It was the only time he would ever hear her cry. He followed the sound and worked his way to her. He forced his burning eyes to open and sat down to hold her, the crazy man having no idea what to do now but sticking around just in case he got his turn on the animal who had done this.

Her jeans and panties were stripped off. Her blouse was ripped and her bra was loose. She was lying in the sand with her knees together, her arm covering her eyes. She was sobbing.

He wanted to pick her up, carry her off, and call an ambulance. He wanted the police to arrest her assailant. He waited for some sign that she was ready.

She stifled her crying, as if locking away her suffering and forcing herself to talk.

"Peter," she said as she sat up and reached her left

hand for the sandy panties, her right arm across her naked breasts. "I . . . I want to forget this, okay? Will you help me? Please? Don't call the police. I don't want to relive this just so the cops can get their jollies. I feel so dirty already."

He closed his eyes and bit his lip, hating that the bastard would get away with what he'd done. "Shouldn't you see a doctor?"

She shuddered. "I can't. The thought of another strange man inside me—"

"I understand," he said quickly, then held out her jeans and looked away. He didn't really understand, but he wanted to stop her because he couldn't bear to hear any more. He knew she was strong enough to live with this. He'd watched her carry her father's suicide for years without the slightest stumble. She had an enormous capacity for suffering, so he would respect her wishes and keep her secret, understanding that some people preferred to suffer quietly, and alone. He would learn to do the same.

They walked back to their hotel. She took a shower and insisted they never talk about it again. Forget it had ever happened.

He had never forgotten. He heard her begging for help all the time and never forgave himself for letting the man take her. He should have been ready for the attack. He should have been quicker to kill his attacker and quicker to get to Melissa. Why had he taken so long, wasted those ten extra seconds and given her rapist extra time to drag her away? Was it fear? Had it entered his mind, even for a second, that he might get hurt helping her? Had he been less anxious to get to her than he pretended? It hurt him to wonder, preferring to believe that it wasn't possible. But he'd wasted precious time, and he'd spent the last two years trying to figure out why.

He despised himself for the possibility, regardless of how remote, that fear might have held him back or slowed him down. He was conscious of fear all the time now and would never again give it a toehold on his actions. It was why he'd fought so hard for his coworkers' futures. It was the reason he would do anything, and kill anyone, to get Melissa back. He was never going to shame himself again. And this motivation, he knew, was selfishness. He hadn't really been out to save his coworkers' jobs. Even today, right now, he was only trying to preserve himself, wasn't really trying to save Melissa. Everything he did was selfish because every action created a personal record, for better or worse, which he would later *scrutinize* harshly. He could not live a life that might shame him later.

He stared at the ceiling of the hotel room, remembering Vietnam and his murderous run through the jungle. But he couldn't take pride in what he'd done there either. A thousand times he'd looked back and tried to convince himself that he'd been completely unselfish, that it was loyalty to his squad that had sent him dashing into the deadly foliage. He tried to believe it was the one pure act of his life, but he knew he couldn't take credit for what he'd done, so there was no way to take pride in it. The crazy man had saved those men. Jamison had just gone along for the ride, and hadn't even done it willingly.

He sat up on the bed and rubbed the sides of his head, struggled to think about something else. He began to wonder if Charlotte would actually be able to help him. He met her earlier at a small coffee shop, and she told him everyone at Dillon was jumpy; Jamison's name was spoken in the same hushed tones as Ted Bronovich. She liked him, though, and for that reason she would help him, even though he told her he loved Melissa.

The phone rang and he caught it instantly. "Yes?"

"Mr. Caligo?"

Jamison shook his head, felt himself blush. It was a stupid cat's name, assigned to the poor beast before Blevins's sons were old enough to say calico. "Yeah. How you doing, Rich?"

"Good, buddy. You?"

"Confused, but alive and kicking. Small favors, you know. Where are you, anyway, a bomb shelter?"

"Almost. I'm down in the FBI garage, calling from my cell phone. I've been upstairs with Sackett for the last few hours. He called me in."

"Did you ask him about Melissa?"

"I demanded he tell me about Melissa."

"And?"

"Nothing new. She's still under the marshals' custody, doing okay."

"I guess that's good."

"Sackett and I have been working out our differences, getting closer to trusting each other. He had a question he wanted me to ask you. Obviously I didn't want to call on his phone."

Jamison moved to the table in front of the sliding glass doors. He looked out and saw his reflection in the glass, then the statue of George Washington on horseback in the traffic circle beyond. There was nothing else in the darkness. He picked up a pen and pad and got ready to write. "What's the question?"

"It's off the wall."

"Perfect. It'll fit right in with the rest of my day."

"That's true enough. Ready for this? He wants to talk to you."

Jamison flipped the pen in the air and watched it pinwheel to the floor. "Oh, sure, that sounds like fun. Let's see, a little polite conversation, a few minutes of kid and giggle, and then, oh yeah . . . my arrest! Sorry, Rich. No can do."

"Kind of thought you'd say that."

"I'm kind of surprised you'd even ask."

"It does sound stupid, doesn't it? The entire FBI is looking to take you down and I want to bring the boss by for a visit."

"I'm glad you didn't miss the irony. It was the best part."

"No. Here's the best part. I think it's a good idea."

"You do? Well, I don't. And since it's my life that'll slide down the drain, I'll pass if you don't mind."

"I don't mind. But Sackett is starting to have some doubts about what's happening around here. He's a smart guy, Peter, and this case looks funky to him. He took me off administrative leave to help him sort through it. Things aren't adding up in his book and he's not accepting anything he doesn't check out himself."

"What will keep him from trying to arrest me?"

"He's promised to talk only. If he tries to arrest you, I'll restrain him myself."

"I'll stop him before you ever get the chance."

"Fair enough. Can we come by?"

Jamison kept staring at George Washington on horseback. Something in the statue's beleaguered look of determination made him realize how far he really was from Melissa.

"I don't like this, Rich."

"I know. But if you can convince him you're clean, that's a big step. He'll probably assume Melissa's clean, too. That gets you a lot closer to getting her back."

Jamison looked around the hotel room, trying to size it up for an interview, or a fight.

"Okay. I'm trusting your judgment here. Room 318. Warn him that he might get hurt."

"I will. Good-bye."

John Butler hid in the shadows of the FBI garage. Although he listened hard, he hadn't heard anything clearly. But he was willing to bet that Blevins was talking to Peter Jamison or making plans that involved him. The short biography Kane provided on Blevins identified him as Jamison's best friend. Kane even suggested that Blevins might lead Butler to his victim. Kane might be right, as usual.

He kept silent, watching as Blevins hung up and tossed the phone back into his car. All of a sudden Blevins looked edgy, as if his senses had missed something lethal in the dark recesses of the underground garage. Blevins slid into the shadows and started moving among the concrete columns. Butler watched him pull out his pistol and probe around the parked cars, making hilarious lunges and quick steps.

Butler had to work like hell to keep from laughing. This was just too damn funny. He always wanted to laugh when he held the trump card. And he held it now, with that stupid FBI agent bumping around in the dark, afraid of something he couldn't see and hadn't heard.

Special Agent Blevins could *feel* his presence. He felt it pushing against his chest like the bony finger of Satan. Felt the spiritual presence and knew it could kill him whenever it wanted.

But Butler wouldn't, at least not now. He had a mission for him first. He needed Blevins to take him to Jamison. Then, maybe he would kill him.

"Go on now, Blevins," he whispered in the dark as Blevins started to leave. "Go to the elevator with your gun drawn, stand there in the light like an easy target waiting for the doors to close and take you out of here. Point your weapon into these shadows if it makes you feel better. I won't hurt you now. You'll live through this engagement, but I make no promises about next time."

The elevator doors closed and Blevins was gone. Butler bent down over the dead guard. He cut off his left ear, put it in a plastic bag, and admired it. A nice addition to his collection.

Thirty-six minutes after Blevins's call, Jamison heard the stairwell door shut quietly with a rub and a click. It was alarming because it hadn't slammed like a dozen other times tonight. The noise switched on his instincts and sent him flying.

He launched out of bed, grabbed his Beretta, and got prone on the floor, listening carefully to footsteps in the hall. Two pairs, light. The hotel walls were hiding nothing. Jamison had his Beretta up, the hammer back, his kill zone selected. He was ready to light this place up and cut down anyone who smashed open his door.

There was a gentle knock.

"Who is it?"

He was far enough back in the room. Any shots through the door would probably not hit him.

"It's me, Rich," he said a loud whisper. "I've got Sackett."

Jamison rose and crept slowly, noiselessly, toward the door. He wrapped his left hand silently around the doorknob, then flung it open and flashed through the doorway, sticking his Beretta right into Sackett's face.

"Don't move a muscle."

Sackett's eyes crossed as they followed the muzzle to the tip of his nose. "You kidding? You think I'm stupid?"

"You are if you think you're going to breeze in here with a weapon."

Sackett was lifting his arms in slow-motion surrender. "I left it in the car. Blevins made me."

Blevins raised his hands, too, just about halfway. "That's the truth, Peter. He's unarmed. I searched him before we came up."

Jamison didn't say anything as he stepped back, his pistol still trained on Sackett as the two FBI agents entered the room. Blevins closed the door and the three of them stood there as if none of them knew what to do next. There was a small table by the sliding glass doors. Jamison motioned Sackett to sit.

"Can I put my hands down?"

"As long as I can see them. In the air or on the table. Your choice. Nowhere else."

"Thank you."

Jamison leaned against the dresser, his pistol low but both hands holding it, ready to do some quick combat shooting if Sackett came up with a weapon.

"Let's get on with it. What do you want?"

Sackett eased into a chair and made a dry smile. "I just want to ask you a few questions, Mr. Jamison."

"About?"

Sackett chuckled, as though it was a private matter he was embarrassed to reveal. "I've got a problem."

"That makes two of us."

"It does, doesn't it?"

Blevins wiggled uncomfortably and glanced at Jamison's pistol.

"Peter, Mr. Sackett would like to know what you discovered in your research of the Wombat."

Jamison shot a look at Blevins: He didn't like the question. Even if he decided to answer it, how much should he tell? Sure, he could let this guy into his room and make nice with him. But they—the government—had Melissa, and Sackett was one of them. Blevins, too, although it was Sackett's turn under Jamison's microscope.

He decided to give up a little information. He would tell Sackett some of what he wanted to know: a little about his research, the meeting with Senator Drummond, the shots at his car, and the giant on the sidewalk. Then he'd ask about the agents who arrested Melissa, and where was she now?

He started talking, cautiously turning over his part of the deal. Sackett interrupted with questions, always asking Jamison to clarify more than he wanted. When he finished, Sackett stood up.

"Where's your evidence, Jamison?"

Jamison was standing at least a second before Sackett.

"Where's Melissa?"

"She's safe."

"I bet. So is my evidence."

"I'll need to see it."

"Tough. Get it from Senator Drummond."

"That's helpful."

"Listen, Sackett, Rich says I should trust you, so I'm trying. But right now you're just a big question mark in my book. Your men arrested Melissa and came after me. I'm not giving you any more of an advantage."

Sackett lowered himself back into his chair. He glanced over at Blevins.

"Drummond's a hothead, Mr. Jamison. If he thinks something criminal's going on, he'll suspect everyone and tear this city apart. He won't even trust the FBI. I doubt he'll give me copies of your data."

"Then you're out of luck."

"Not so fast. How about if I had Melissa brought over here? Would that make you more cooperative?"

Could it possibly be that easy to get her back? He looked at Blevins.

"What do you think?"

"It's worth a try. I'll go get her myself. I can have her back here in an hour."

"I won't be here. Sackett knows I'm here, so I have to leave after he does."

"I think you can trust him."

"It's not your life if you're wrong. It's mine. And Melissa's. Besides, what's to keep him from having agents pick us up right after he gets what he wants?"

Sackett nodded, as if it was a logical concern.

"I'll tell you what, Jamison. How about I let Blevins send some men up here, men he trusts completely, operating strictly under his orders to keep you and her safe? Would that do it? Remember, you have to think about Melissa, too. How would you feel if she got hurt while you two were on the run?"

"We can take care of ourselves."

"Maybe. But I'll need you to testify. I need you both alive."

Jamison turned to Blevins. "Rich, call the odds. Good or bad?"

Blevins stood up and stretched, then spoke easily.

"I've told you before, Peter. Agents build up loyalties to each other. I've sure got my share of brothers who are loyal to me. You can trust them, I'm sure. Good odds."

Melissa, just an hour away. This whole ugly thing could be over tonight. Blevins could give Sackett the data, and Jamison could slip off with Melissa someplace and start over.

Or maybe this was a trap. What was the additional risk? His life? Hell, Melissa's neck was already on the block, so this was a chance worth taking.

"Okay, Sackett, the data for Melissa. I'll give it up after Blevins brings her here."

Sackett spun toward Blevins and took command. "Pick any six agents you trust, any office close by. Use my authority to get them here on the double. Use our planes if you need them. I want that information right away." He turned back to Jamison. "Does anyone else know you're here?"

"No."

"Are you sure? Because I'm about to turn up the heat, maybe scald a few people in high places. You're going to be right in the thick of it, so I'll ask you again, does anyone else know you're here? Sure you don't want us to move you?"

"I'm sure. As long as you didn't tell anyone and weren't followed."

Sackett ignored him and didn't answer. He kept

staring at Jamison, looking for doubt to creep across his face.

"All right, then. Blevins, how long before your men get here?"

Blevins was just hanging up the phone. "Fifty minutes."

Sackett smiled. "There you have it, Mr. Jamison. Fifty minutes. Try to stay alive until then."

"I wish you wouldn't say it like that."

Sackett laughed, touched him on the arm, then walked out. Blevins lagged behind and whispered to Jamison, "My guys will identify themselves by asking if you ordered champagne."

"Thanks."

Jamison followed as far as the elevators, then watched the doors shut before heading back to his room. He closed and locked the door, then headed to the bathroom. He wanted to clean up before he saw Melissa.

# CHAPTER TWELVE

John Butler followed the two agents to the hotel and to the elevators. He waited to see where their elevator stopped, then took the stairs to their floor and waited in the stairwell, listening for men's voices in the hall. A door opened, and through the wire-embedded glass of the stairwell door he watched the agents walk out to the elevators and leave. Jamison went back to his hotel room and closed the door.

He decided to give the agents a few minutes to leave the hotel before he struck, just in case they planned on circling back. After ten minutes he walked out of the stairwell and crept down the hall, then worked Jamison's lock with his pick and rake. He cracked the door open but stopped when he heard the gentle creak of its hinges and stood absolutely still, ready to fly into the room and start the bleeding.

He heard water running in the bathroom but no other sounds. He slipped in, ready, just in case Jamison was still undressing, and searched the room thoroughly but didn't find the box of evidence Kane was looking for. He knew it wouldn't be that easy to earn the bonus money. If this guy were that much of an amateur, Kane would have used one of his own men to take him down.

Butler decided to wait before starting the game. If Jamison didn't take too long, he would allow him to come out of the bathroom and get dressed before he killed him. There was no need to do it in the shower, torturing Jamison's naked body to find out where he'd hidden the evidence, getting himself soaked. He'd done that before and hated it, slopping around afterward as if he'd fallen into a fountain. No, he would let Jamison get some clothes on and give him a chance to cooperate, then let him die with a little dignity. Maybe earn the same privilege when his turn to die came around.

He removed the magazine from Jamison's pistol and emptied out the cartridges, putting them in his bag along with the extra magazines he'd found. Then he placed Jamison's Beretta back on the dresser where he'd found it. He was ready.

Jamison stepped out of the bathroom, naked. He dried quickly, then combed his wet hair straight back and walked over to the bed. He dragged the socks and clean underwear out of his gym bag, dressed, then checked himself in the mirror, hoping he would look okay for Melissa. The mirror's reflection was shocking. His eyes had become hard, painful-looking disks. Until last Monday, they still held some of the luster from his youth, but now there was nothing of that innocent glow from when a new car or a peek at a girl's bra made them shine. That was all replaced by a dull flatness. He stood there and stared at himself, wondering if it would be possible to find the lights again when this was over.

He was still looking in the mirror when he noticed the small movement of the closet door. It was almost imperceptible, but riveted his attention. He whirled around, grabbing his gun and aiming it in the same motion, knowing he should have expected this. It had been stupid to trust Sackett.

The door swung open with a bold sweep. Jamison focused on his pistol's front sight, anxious to train it on whoever stepped out of the dark closet.

"Who's there?"

He was shocked to see the face that emerged. He knew and understood it, recognized it so suddenly it stunned him. God, it was the ravaged face of his crazy man, fleshed out and scabbed over, no longer a specter of his conscience but a low-order life form standing across the room. Jamison gawked at the face. He always wondered what it would look like but never expected evil to look this terrible. It sickened him that this same creature lived in him, an alien eating his insides, always trying to gnaw its way out.

The face looked like a burned marshmallow except it was smiling, all quiet and calm but threatening as hell. Relaxed, but moving with deadly precision. The jagged mouth spoke without any emotion.

"Mr. Jamison, I'm John Butler."

Butler grinned as he said his name, as though the mere mention of it should intimidate him.

"I'm sorry to intrude on you like this, but we have a little business to conduct. You have some papers, I believe. Your copies of the documents you gave Senator Drummond. I've been sent to get them, so please tell me where they are."

Jamison was dead-on ready with a head shot but his finger was stuck in uncertainty. Not that he was afraid to kill. Hell no, he had done his share of killing. More than his share, but it had never been like this. Every other time there had been a clear-cut reason for pulling the trigger. Uniforms, flags, battle lines, or self-defense had spotlighted the enemy, making the decision to kill an automatic one. But this man showed no weapon and made no overt threat. Was he even a threat? And wasn't he really, in some strange way, family?

Jamison was stuck briefly in this doubt, but then he decided and lined up the sights of his Beretta. He squeezed the double-action trigger, feeling the smooth movements of the pistol, engaging the case-hardened parts that would cause the weapon to fire. He aimed directly at Butler's gnarled head as the butt-ugly thing took a step toward him.

The hammer extended fully, then slammed down with a powerful snap. Jamison steadied his aim, allowed himself no distraction while waiting for the explosion and the messy spectacle of bloody tissue spraying across the room.

*Click.*

The simple mechanical sound was terrifying. Butler was only five feet away now, stalled in the Beretta's sights. Jamison threw down his gun and charged, his eyes searching for a gun to muzzle up or a knife to flash.

Butler fell onto his back, out of range, his feet pointing at Jamison. He scissored his legs around Jamison's shins, one in front and one behind. The foot that snuck behind Jamison jammed into the back of his knee joint and shoved it forward. The leg in front kept him locked in place, unable to move and compensate. He fell hard and landed on the floor next to Butler, who was already on his way up.

Jamison jinked around, trying to get out from under the mountain boot that hovered over him. But in less time than it took to flinch, Butler launched his right foot at Jamison's head, smashing it against the floor and grinding the boot into the flesh above his right cheek. Then Butler kicked him, a full, well-trained blow to the chest, then one to the stomach, and finally the groin, each kick harder than the one that preceded it.

Jamison was stunned, but that didn't keep his body from convulsing. His stomach heaved a big wad of bloody juice out of his mouth and onto the carpet. He couldn't see very well because his right eye had filled with blood and his head whirled from being stomped and crushed. A paralyzing fear had done something to the crazy man, and Jamison felt alone.

He struggled to his knees, his stomach still pitching bloody phlegm balls, his testicles swelling in his clean drawers. He caught a glance of Butler strolling around the room and watched for an opening, knowing he had to find one soon or die, recognizing that he was dealing with a crazy man. He struggled to his feet, protecting his organs with his arms, expecting Butler's mule kicks to knock him down again.

Butler leaned against the dresser, spoke calmly, and almost sounded kind. "Mr. Jamison, please don't attack

me again. I cannot continue to be patient unless you cooperate. Do you understand?"

Jamison made it to his feet, briefly celebrating the
fact that he and Butler were at eye level again. But his
brain had lost its gyro and he had trouble standing. He
could feel blood flooding into his ear and down his
neck. How bad had he been hurt? Did it matter? He
would die if he wasted time thinking about it. He used
his free hand to cover his blood-soaked eye, struggling
to focus on the blurry image pacing the room.

"The evidence isn't here."

Butler slipped into an eerie, conversational tone. "I
know it's not here. Don't take me for a fool, because
I'm not one. I do, however, tend to run a little short on
patience." He moved to Jamison's blind side and disappeared. "Where is it?"

"Who hired you? What are you going to do with the
evidence?"

"Are you stalling?"

"Just trying to figure out what's happening."

"Does it really make any difference?"

Jamison knew Butler was close, most likely within
his striking range. Fear held Jamison back and kept the
crazy man from attacking. There was no way to win if
he had to guess where Butler was. It would be hard
enough if he could see him.

But it was fear, nevertheless, that kept his hands by
his side. Jamison recognized it and hated it. If he lived
through this, he would chalk his hesitation up to his
crazy man's terror and good judgment when coming
face-to-face with himself. Try to live with that excuse.

"Probably doesn't make a difference to you, freak,

but it's important to me. So humor me, and maybe you'll get what you want."

"I'll get what I want regardless, Mr. Jamison."

"You're going to kill me?"

Butler stepped in front of him, just out of range, and grinned. He seemed to like the idea.

"Yes."

"Then screw you, scab-man. I'm not telling you anything."

Butler disappeared behind him, then snuck up on Jamison's blind side. He patted his back as he passed and made Jamison jump. He wished he'd known Butler was coming.

"Foolish of you, Mr. Jamison, but if that's your wish . . . ready?"

"Go to hell."

"Maybe later. Right now, here is the way our little story will go. In a few minutes, you'll be dead. Sad, isn't it? But as unfortunate as that news is, you need to remember that the data I seek will do you absolutely no good afterward. It could, however, have done Melissa Corley quite a bit of good because your cooperation would have allowed her to avoid this same line of questioning."

He cracked his chapped lips into a smile.

Jamison didn't move. He just stared, not afraid anymore. Angry, though, and getting worse. It was building from his deep guts, from the place he usually locked up the crazy man, and flushing through him like bad medicine.

Butler sauntered around the room.

"I must admit, Mr. Jamison, that I am stimulated by the idea of having that beautiful woman to myself.

With a face like mine, I get very few opportunities to be intimate with beautiful women. I could have quite a time with her." He grinned as he rubbed his left hand up and down his crotch.

Jamison straightened up. After the attack on Melissa, he swore it would never happen again. He had never, ever broken a promise to her, and the thought of failing made him snap all of his senses into alignment, focus everything he had on killing Butler. He was sure he could do it but had no earthly idea how.

"You are some piece of work, freak. She hasn't done anything."

"Of course not. Give me your research data. This is your last chance. Where is it?"

A film of Melissa suffering at Butler's scarred hands jumped right to the center of his mind's eye, but strangely, it didn't hurt. Not even a little. And the crazy man—where was he?—didn't even seem to notice. What the film did, though, was splice his hatred of Butler's threat with his love for Melissa, giving him a sharp image of what he had to do.

"Tell me who hired you. I'll give you the data."

"I'm bored with this game, Mr. Jamison, I've already—"

Jamison lurched forward so quickly that Butler's reflexes snatched him back and out of range.

"Who hired you? Answer me!"

Butler stiffened. His face seemed to jump off his skull as he narrowed his focus on Jamison. Just for a second, his jaw muscles chiseled anger onto his face, but then, just as quickly, he smiled. It was a hideous look on him.

"Kane sent me."

"Jack Kane?"

"How many Kanes do you know? Where is your data?"

Jamison started making plans for Kane. He just needed to get rid of this guy first. "I buried it. I'll draw you a map, but you've got to promise not to hurt Melissa."

"Fine. There's no money in it anyway. A bonus for the data, but nothing for killing her."

Jamison tried not to listen. He didn't want to hear the economic considerations of the killing business.

"There's a pen and some paper on the table by the patio doors. Can I go over there?"

Butler slid along the dresser until he was close to the table, never looking away from Jamison and never giving him an opening. Once there, he motioned Jamison over.

Jamison had stabilized and his mind had reset the controls. His balance was returning and his movements were more fluid. Butler studied him as he hobbled to the table, leaned over, and began to write, but he was too far away to attack.

"It's buried, like I said. By the boathouse on the west side of the Key Bridge, the Georgetown side of the river. As you go down this little private road, look left, toward the bridge."

Butler moved a step closer. Jamison could see the man's reflection in the patio doors. Butler's face looked intent, as though he was trying to catch all of the details Jamison was giving, certain that a buried object would be difficult to find, even with directions. His eyes strained at the paper from a distance.

Jamison watched his reflection in the glass but kept his body turned so Butler couldn't see him. Twice Butler checked the glass, too, but Jamison looked back to the paper in time.

He slid his fingers along the plastic pen until his thumb corked the end of it, then pointed his left hand at the map while he checked their reflections once more. This was as close as Butler would get but it wasn't close enough. There was more than an arm's length separating them and it was clear that Butler's interest had not dissolved his caution. Butler kept his hands open, like a wrestler.

"You'll have to watch very carefully or you'll miss the marker. There's a fallen tree right about here. . . ."

Butler leaned a little closer. Only two inches, maybe three, but close enough.

Jamison exploded. He pivoted his left foot around and rotated his body like a discus thrower. His right arm, the last thing to take flight, absorbed all the speed and momentum, racing around in a wide arc toward Butler's head.

Butler quickly struck Jamison twice in his bad eye and once across the throat. Then he casually stepped back, heading out of Jamison's range with mild disappointment on his face.

Jamison ignored the pain, although his windpipe felt crushed and his bad eye throbbed from the pounding. He boxed away the hurt, he would not succumb. His arm was still in flight. He still had his good eye. He still had a chance.

Butler had taken a step back and began to take a second when he jerked to a stop. The bed blocked his retreat. Suddenly his face lit up with an interesting look. Perhaps it was fear. He raised his hands again.

Jamison's right arm had incredible speed, his hand

holding the pen like a knife, flying it sideways through the air. He grimaced as the last second ticked off, no variables left to either of them in the piece of time that remained. The pen would hit its mark, and there was nothing to do now but watch.

Butler stopped moving. He just stopped and waited for impact: He recognized destiny when he saw it coming. He looked queerly at Jamison and relaxed his hands, all in a tenth of a second. So quickly, yet with plenty of time to see it and understand. Surrender. It was almost as if Butler wanted to.

The point of the pen struck Butler on the left side of his neck, almost directly below the ear. It slid through tissue and muscle and slurped its way into Butler's skull with much more ease than Jamison expected. The exposed meat of his palm screamed as he jammed the pen into the lower part of Butler's head, the pressure driving through the soft skin of his hand as he kept pushing, giving his arm all the gas he had.

Butler cried out, a mixture of gurgling air and bloody blockage. He reached for Jamison's throat with his right hand while his left grabbed the wrist that drove the punishing instrument. He smiled as Jamison watched the point of the pen come out the other side of his neck.

Jamison tripped Butler with his feet, then pushed the short end of the pen toward the carpet, using it as a tiny lever to crank Butler's head around to the floor. He let go, jumped on Butler's back, and reached for his chin. He yanked Butler's ugly head backward until his neck reached full extension, so far back he could see Butler's eyes looking up and watching him, far enough to keep Butler's skull from catching on his Atlas vertebrae. Then he snapped the head sideways with every bit of strength God had given him. The sickening pop, coupled with a fleshy, tearing sound, made Jamison's wrenching stomach puke more of the bloody juice, which landed on Butler's back. It was the first time he'd ever gotten sick killing. Was this a good sign? He savored the taste of the vomit, realizing he'd never killed without the crazy man before. He was disgusted by what he'd done but willing to do it all over again to save Melissa.

He climbed onto the bed and stayed there a minute, ventilating. Then he started moving, gaining speed with each action. He searched Butler's pockets for a weapon or identification but found nothing. He walked over to the closet and snatched the bag lying on the floor. It contained a large assortment of small, peculiar items: a man's ear in a plastic bag, two full magazines for his Beretta, an empty magazine, and a bunch of loose nine-millimeter rounds that Jamison knew were his own. He scooped them up, lifted his pistol from the floor, and reloaded it.

Should he wait for Melissa? Hell, was she even coming? Had Sackett told Kane where Butler could find him? Why had he stepped into this trap, and how could he avoid the next one?

He thought it all through quickly, knowing from the very start that he couldn't stay here and wait. If Sackett actually did let Blevins bring Melissa here, Blevins would read the scene and get her away. He would trust his friend to do that.

He washed the blood off his face and Butler's blood off his hands. Then he slipped into the hallway and left, down the stairwell and out into the late night. Hunting.

# CHAPTER THIRTEEN

Rich Blevins sweated the entire twenty-eight minutes it took to drop off Sackett and race to the Federal Detention Center, hauling ass down deserted streets in the middle of the night, wanting to get back to Jamison's hotel as soon as possible. He squealed into the parking lot and skidded into a space marked RESERVED FOR LAW ENFORCEMENT PERSONNEL TRANSPORTING PRISONERS. He jumped out of his car and ran into the three-story building through the prisoners' entrance.

Once inside, several sets of security checkpoints slowed him to a frustrating pace, and then forced him to stand around and wait for an escort to take his weapon and lead him to the transfer pen. He was completely out of patience by the time a buzzer opened the last two sets of doors that separated him from the processing officers.

Blevins charged to the counter and pounded on the bulletproof glass, making enough racket to wake up the prisoners in the first cell block. Two uniformed guards, isolated behind the counter, jumped out of their seats and one of them dumped coffee on the broad beam of his belly. He cussed as he flicked the hot brown liquid from his fingers but stopped the instant he saw Blevins glaring at him.

"I'm Special Agent Blevins, FBI, here to pick up a prisoner." He stuck his credentials against the inch-thick glass, steadied them while the other guard wrote down his number. The guard finished writing and stepped away to make room for the other guard to pass by. "Okay, Special Agent Blevins, I guess I can help you with that. Where's your paperwork?"

"It's being processed. You'll have it within an hour."

The guard did a slow roll of his head, looked at his partner as if in love, and gave Blevins a stupid grin.

"Well, don't that beat all, Sam? Another one of them hotshot agents come to get one of our guests without the proper paperwork."

He bent over and dug his right elbow on the counter to support his head.

"I suppose you know, Special Agent Blevins, that we don't go around handing out prisoners to every agent who asks for one. They ain't free, you know."

He smiled as he looked at Sam for congratulations.

"I'm afraid you'll need to run on along, Mr. Blevins. Go back to your office and get the proper forms filled out. Then, shoot, I'll be more'n happy to give you your prisoner." He stepped back and smiled, folding his arms across his chest.

Blevins knew the guard was right, so he'd kept quiet

as long as he could and let the man play his silly game. But enough was enough. He leaned toward the glass with such force that both guards reeled back a little.

"Look, pal, I really don't care how this goes down, but I'm out of time. I'm going to walk around the corner and order your boss to open this door. Then I'm going to beat on your stupid skull until my arms get tired. You've still got a choice, I'll give you five seconds. Call the paramedics or get my prisoner, but decide right now." Blevins lined his watch up with the guard's face and studied them both closely.

A short silence followed, and then Blevins moved, just a little. The guard wasted three seconds conjuring up his toughest look, but it withered. He snatched a couple of forms and dropped them into the slot.

"You've got to fill these out, Special Agent Blevins. It's the very minimum. I'd lose my job if I released someone without these forms in the file. Court's orders."

Blevins took the forms as he yanked a pen from his pocket. "Fine. How about getting my prisoner while I write?"

The second guard was all elbows, moving quickly to the computer keyboard, then looking up at Blevins with cooperation written all over his face.

"What's the prisoner's name, sir? I'll locate him and have him brought down right away."

"A woman," Blevins said, without looking up from the papers. "Melissa Corley."

Both of the guards' heads snapped, drawing Blevins's attention.

"What? What's the problem?"

The guards looked at each other in silence. Then the smaller guard at the terminal said, "She's not here, sir.

One of your agents came for her earlier. She left about . . . let's see . . ." He scrolled down the screen. "An hour, well, almost two hours ago."

Blevins pressed his face against the thick glass and tried to see the screen.

"Who came for her? Give me a name."

The guard jumped to the file cabinet. "Here it is, right on top. Brewer, Special Agent Phillip Brewer. Credential number 1282. Paperwork is . . . yeah, it all looks in order." The guard stuffed the forms into the slot.

Blevins didn't recognize the agent's name, and he should if the guy was working this case. He flipped open his cell phone and called Sackett, studying Brewer's paperwork while he waited.

"Yes, Blevins, what is it?"

"Melissa Corley's gone, taken from the Detention Center by an agent named Phillip Brewer. Credential number 1282. They left about two hours ago."

"Brewer? You know him?"

"Never heard of him. How about calling Headquarters and getting his office assignment?"

"Good as done. There's something else, too."

"What?"

"One of our security men was killed in the garage tonight, about the time you called Jamison from your car. Very professional. No bleeding at all, except for a little bit where his ear was cut off."

"His ear was missing?"

"Mean something to you?"

"Nothing good. Go on."

"It's just a guess, but I'm thinking it had something to do with you and your relationship with Jamison. Whoever killed the guard might have put a positioning transmitter on your car or followed us to the hotel. Are you going back there?"

"Got a better idea?"

"No. I'll send some agents to guard the room until you get there."

"Don't. My men should be there any minute. If Jamison's still alive, they won't let anything happen to him."

"What do you want me to do?"

"Tell the switchboard to route all of my calls to you, in case he calls the office for me."

"Done. After you clear from the hotel I want you to hook up with the SWAT team. With any luck, we're going to serve some warrants later. You'll want first look at any evidence seized."

"Got it."

"Go."

"One last thing. If Jamison does call, expect him to be suspicious of you. He told you what you wanted and a killer came knocking. Now Melissa's gone. You're not looking good to him."

"I can understand that. How about you, Rich? You suspicious of me?"

"Trying not to be, boss, but not sure. If you turn out to be dirty, you and I will spend some time talking about it. Got to go."

Melissa Corley sized up Special Agent Phillip Brewer as he led her up the back stairs of a two-story building and into a nicely furnished apartment. He was a regular-looking guy, about five feet eleven. Medium build, but strong. Brown eyes with a goofy sort of look, as though they were focused on two different things.

Her wristwatch was still in the property envelope so

she had no idea what time it was. Maybe two A.M. Maybe three. It didn't really matter. But she did wish she had some idea of where she was. She tried to get her bearings after leaving the jail but Brewer had been too careful and kept her down on the floor. He hadn't let her see anything that could serve as a landmark, and they hadn't spoken since they left the Detention Center. But she watched him, waiting for her chance. It would come, she was sure, and she would take it. She wouldn't even think about this guy, whose side he was on, whether he was good or bad. He had the power to abuse her and that made him bad.

Then there was Big Man. She worried he would come back: the big man who had sat down in her cell and spoken with gentle words and a killer's movements, the one who probably suspected what she was going to do and had given her something else to think about, the one who had her visiting the ghost of her father.

Her damaged ribs flared up and she tightened, but she was not about to show Brewer she was hurt. It would give him an advantage when the music started and the dance began. She hid the pain while watching for her chance, praying it would come quickly.

Rich Blevins met his agents in Jamison's room, then quickly assigned most of them to guard all the hotel's entrances. They did as they were told, protecting the crime scene as best they could while groping around for any information about the dead man in Jamison's room.

When Blevins came down from the room he went over to one of his agents and spoke casually as he headed to his car.

"What do you think, Roland?"

Roland straightened his lanky frame, then rubbed his big hand over his mouth to wipe away a frown. His sharkish black eyes scanned the area as he grabbed Blevins by the arm, bringing him to an abrupt stop.

"Rich, your man lived through this one, don't you think? We didn't find any evidence that his wounds were life threatening. Did you?"

Mostly Blevins's mind was on Melissa, part of it was trying to remember an agent named Phillip Brewer. The rest was celebrating the fact that Jamison had killed the assassin in his hotel room. His friend could still take care of himself.

"No."

Roland went to a whisper. "You want my opinion here, Rich? Because I've sure got one."

"Let's have it."

Roland glanced around and lowered his voice another notch. "Okay. I hate to say it, but I think another assassin might already be hunting your friend."

Blevins pushed Special Agent Brewer out of his brain and gave Jamison's situation his total concentration.

"What makes you think so? It's only been an hour."

"You're right, it would be pretty quick. But if that dead guy is any indication, he was being hunted by experts. You see the stuff in that bag of his?"

He nodded. "He was a pro."

"And professionals usually have access to police information, right? Maybe the police themselves?"

Blevins looked around, then stepped closer.

"Maybe. I don't know. What's your point?"

Roland's eyes swept the area again, then he leaned close to Blevins's ear.

"A hotel guest saw the hitter working Jamison's lock.

The guest was in a room down the hall, some kind of insomniac. He called the Metro PD."

"That's right."

"So the cops arrived before we did and worked the room pretty thoroughly. They found the dead man and his bag. That the way you see it?"

"Yeah. So?"

"Well, I'm not sure, but I think the police department knows who the dead guy is and has a positive ID. Of course, *we* haven't got a clue who he was. There's no record of the guy anywhere, based on what we know about him."

"Did you ask the PD for an ident?"

"They stonewalled me."

"What makes you think so? Maybe they honestly don't know."

"It's possible, but listen to this before you believe it. Somebody called the hotel right after the first patrol unit arrived here. The desk clerk switched the call up to the police officers at the crime scene because the caller asked for Jamison's room. He used Jamison's real name."

"So, somebody knew he was here. Maybe it was someone from the precinct."

"I think it's worse than that. Ask yourself how the desk clerk knew Jamison's name. How did *he* know what room the caller was asking for? I would have expected him to check his computer, and then tell the caller there was no one registered by the name of Jamison. But he didn't."

"Damn, you're right. Wasn't thinking."

"Neither was I at first, but I just couldn't figure out how he could have known, so I asked him. Know what he said?"

"That he's psychic?"

"No, something even more unbelievable. He said the police told him about Jamison when they arrived. They told him Jamison's name, if you can believe that. Well, at first I thought, fair enough, they just did something stupid, that's all. We've all made mistakes like that. But—"

"There's no way the police should have known Jamison's name. He signed in under the name of Caligo. Paid cash, didn't use a phone card or anything else dumb. What little evidence he left—fingerprints, some blood, hairs, and fibers—are still being collected, and hours away from processing."

"That's my point. If the PD knew who he was, they had the information before they arrived. There's nothing here that would have enlightened them, so that makes me think some of them are playing from the other end of the field. Assuming that, I have to conclude that the caller was another assassin, scrambling to pick up Jamison's trail. He called here hoping the PD would save him time."

"If you're right, Roland . . . damn! Any idea who the caller was?"

"No. The clerk remembers the call and the approximate time, but nothing else."

"Shit!"

"You can say that twice if we don't find Jamison pretty quick."

"Okay, clear the PD from the scene, now! It'll probably mean a fight, but throw their asses out. Have the SWAT team roll over them if they won't leave peacefully. Then get the hitter examined, head to toe, fingertip to fingertip. Analyze everything he had with him. Get the lab running laser tests. I want an ID and I want it soon. Maybe we can track this guy back to whoever hired him, then work the trail in both directions to find the caller."

"I'm on it."

Roland waved for six other agents to join him, then headed into the building.

Blevins stood there watching while they ran into the lobby, their pistols in hands. He waited another four minutes without hearing gunfire and began to believe the PD might leave without a fight. He ran to his car and took off.

Jamison kept his head cocked so he could use his good eye. He saw Blevins run out of the hotel, stop and talk to another man for a few minutes, then run to his car and leave. He wished he could have gotten his attention, spoken with him for a moment or two, but it just wasn't possible.

He watched the cops and agents from across Washington Circle, hunkered down at the edge of a cold-ass alley, his feet in a half-frozen puddle. His head and body ached, and the damage Butler had done was intensified by his uncontrollable shaking for more than an hour.

He suffered through it, standing in his frozen puddle and memorizing it all: faces, vehicles, uniforms, gestures, everything. It was always good to know your enemy, and what better place to see a whole bunch of them than right here? Only Sackett and Kane were missing.

He was also looking for someone in particular; he just didn't know who it was yet. Jack Kane was at the very top of Jamison's suspect list, but it could just as easily be someone from the Coalition. Or it might be someone who had passed through his field of vision once too often to be a coincidence. Whatever the circumstances, if the mystery person showed up he could turn this frosty vigil into a chance to get some real answers, the tools to pry Melissa away from their enemies.

But so far, nothing.

Four hours passed, slow and icy. The activity in front of the hotel had slowed considerably once the body was carted off and there wasn't much left to watch. He walked to the other end of the alley and checked the sidewalks of L Street before stepping out of the alley's shadows. The sun's light was just making its move and a few pedestrians were in the street. Jamison walked down to a coffee shop he knew near the corner.

The little shop was hardly more than a counter with stools on one side, a grill on the other, and an old man staring at Jamison's bloody face. Bagels and donuts were in a glass case beside the register. The smell of hot coffee was overwhelming, and he ordered a cup and a bagel. As he paid, he bought one of the phone cards for sale behind the counter and took his coffee with him to the pay phone in the back.

He was trying to remember how he'd seen Blevins do it, once at the gym and once at his condo. He'd only watched those two times, but if he could at least get most of the words right, maybe that would be enough to cover up some of his nervousness. He practiced his lines to himself several times, then looked around before whispering them out loud. He got the number from long-distance information and dialed.

A woman answered and sounded all business.

"FBI, Houston field office."

Jamison's hands started to sweat. Probably the coffee. He set it down on top of the pay phone.

"This is Special Agent Forbus," Jamison began. "I'm here in Houston on a special assignment. I need an FTS line to WFO."

The phone was quiet. He fought the desire to hang up. If the operator in Houston was at all suspicious, she could be tracing him right now. He turned, took in all the cars and all the faces he could see on the street, and locked them into memory. He held his ground and waited and worried. Thirty seconds. A minute. He had hoped to be done already.

Suddenly, she was back.

"I'm sorry for the delay, Agent Forbus. I was waiting for an FTS line to clear. I'll connect you now." There was a click, then another, then a ring.

"FBI, Washington field office."

He was in. As long as they didn't check back down the line, he was safe.

"I need to speak to Sackett, your SAC."

"Who's calling, please?"

"I'm a friend. It's personal."

The operator asked nothing else.

Jamison took a quick sip of his coffee as Sackett picked up his phone. He sounded angry.

"Who is this?"

"You set me up."

Sackett's voice turned to feathers, all soft and fluffy. "Jamison, jeez, are you all right? Where are you?"

"No chance, Sackett. I don't trust you anymore."

"Guess I can't blame you. I probably wouldn't either."

"There's a nice answer."

"It's the truth. In your situation you can't afford to trust anyone."

"I still want Melissa, Sackett. Do you still want my research data?"

"Yes."

"Then let's stop bullshitting and trade. You give me Melissa and—"

"I can't."

"Then you'll never get—"

"I'd like to, Jamison, really, but I can't. Someone took her from the Detention Center a couple of hours before Blevins got there. We're doing our best to find her, but so far we've come up empty."

"That's just great, you lying bastard. We're finished talking."

"Wait, don't hang up. I may not be able to give you Melissa, but you and I both know that whoever is holding her is acting out of fear or self-preservation. They're afraid of you and whatever evidence you have against them. Give me your data, Jamison. Let me use it. I promise I'll find her."

"Forget it."

"It's not doing you one bit of good. Use your head, give it to me!"

"It's the only leverage I've got."

"On who?"

"On you. And people like you."

"Listen, you jerk, I'm trying to help you. But you're making my job—"

"You want to help me? Give me Jack Kane's home address."

"What did you say? Who?"

"Jack Kane. He's a security man at Dillon. I want his home address. It's not in any public records."

"What good do you think it will do you?"

"I don't think you want to know."

"You'll trade for the data?"

"Yes. You give me Kane's address, I'll give you the data. But no agents go to his house, Sackett. I'll kill any of your men I find there. I won't think twice about it."

Sackett didn't say anything. Was he really thinking about giving up the address or just stalling for time? Jamison was about to hang up when he heard Sackett talk to someone on a speaker, asking for the address. In less than a minute, the voice on the speaker came back with the information and confirmed it was reliable.

"You get that, Jamison?"

Jamison didn't answer until he had the address scribbled down.

"Yeah."

"Good luck. Try not to do anything I'll have to arrest you for."

"Can't guarantee anything."

"And your data?"

Jamison reread Kane's address just to be sure it made sense. He tried to remember if he'd heard of the street before.

"Blevins locked it in your evidence vault. I hope it helps you. Be careful, it's the last set of copies."

"I'll be careful with it. I guess I'll see you around."

"I plan on being around."


Sackett initiated the trace the second he heard Jamison's voice and called WFO's communications room immediately after hanging up.

"Where did he call from?"

"Houston, sir. Our field office there."

"That's impossible."

The sound tech didn't say anything or waste his breath defending himself.

"Are you sure?"

"Yes, sir, I'm sure. His signal came in on our FTS system."

"Well, I'll be damned. Jamison is either a very smart guy or he's been well trained in this business."

"Or he's both, a smart guy who's been well trained in this business."

"Contact Headquarters. For the next seventy-two hours I want a trap and trace on every FTS call, Bureau-wide, effective now. I want all the logs on my desk, up-dated every ten minutes. Got it?"

"Yes, sir."

Sackett hung up the phone and stared at it. "I'll be damned," he said again. Then he hurried to the evidence vault, wondering how much Jamison knew about Jack Kane and where he learned it.

# CHAPTER FOURTEEN

The sun was up when Sackett brought Jamison's data from the evidence locker. He set it on his desk and reached for his coffee. It was probably his fifteenth cup since he'd eaten anything that hadn't dropped from a vending machine. The bitter Bureau coffee made his stomach grind, motivating him to work faster so he could get this mess behind him. He'd been careless. He'd overstepped himself by giving Jamison the address he wanted. If Jamison went over there and killed Kane, or Kane killed him, his career could be over.

Sackett had called the U.S. Attorney's office, right after Blevins said Melissa Corley was gone, and left a message for him to come down the instant he got to work. He wasn't sure exactly what he would ask the U.S. Attorney to do, but he knew he had to make some decisions and arrests in order to earn his pay. Since

Monday, the situation had deteriorated steadily, and he didn't want to sit around waiting for it to get disastrous.

He decided to start with Special Agent Pate, the man who'd killed Robert Davidson. No part of his sworn statement held up under scrutiny, so he was Sackett's chief target. The fact that Amos Warden and assistant directors were covering for him made Sackett want him even more.

Oscar Riley, United States Attorney for the District of Columbia, popped through the door just as Sackett's lips touched the rim of his cup. Riley leaned into the room, his hands hooking onto the door's frame and his body hanging forty-five degrees to the floor.

Riley was young, in his mid-thirties, with brilliant, flashing features. His hair was dark and cut like a model's, the top just a little too long and the sides cut short, and his tailored clothes went well with the look. There was no way to mistake this guy for normal. He was much too young, way too powerful, and far too good-looking.

"I got your message, Sackett, so here I am, first case this morning. What have you got? I'm on a real tight schedule with lots to do before lunch." He grinned like a kid and chewed gum.

Sackett waved him in. "Sit down. I'll make it brief."

Riley fidgeted his way into the room and dropped into a seat, stretching and twisting a rubber band around his fingers. His assistant, a tall woman with gangly legs and a long print dress, followed him in and sat down next to Riley, her pen poised over a legal pad.

"I need an arrest warrant for one of our agents," Sackett said. "And search warrants for three locations at Quantico."

Riley tipped back his chair and brought the front legs a couple of inches off the floor. He stretched his arms behind his head.

"No kidding. What are the charges?"

"Murder, and conspiracy to commit murder. Here's my complaint detailing the probable cause."

Sackett slid the affidavit across the desk but Riley stayed put as his assistant leaned forward and picked it up. She adjusted her round glasses on her narrow nose and studied it.

Riley ignored the document. He leaned farther back in his chair, right to the balancing point, and continued chewing gum with a cocky smile on his face.

"I might be able to do something with a conspiracy charge, Sackett. But murder isn't even a violation of federal law, so we don't typically have jurisdiction unless it happened on federal property."

"It didn't."

Riley pounded the front legs of the chair onto the floor and leaped out of it. "Then I guess we're finished. Nice seeing you again."

"Wait a minute, Riley. One of my agents was killed, a nice young man named Robert Davidson who had a constitutional right *not* to be gunned down. Call it a violation of his civil rights, if you want. That's federal. I want his killer arrested today. I don't want to trust local jurisdiction with it, because the overriding case is federal."

Riley gave a sly smile and started pacing, plucking the rubber band in his hand. "Okay, I'll work something out on the arrest. What about the search warrants? What's your probable cause there?"

"That's a little tougher."

"Yeah, it usually is. Are you working with information provided by an informed source, something that would sound credible?" He turned so his assistant couldn't see his face, then narrowed his eyes and cut them to Sackett.

"Uh, yes. I have an allegation made by an informed but confidential source in the CIA regarding the conspiracy. He told Special Agent Rich Blevins about unlawful activities conducted by a group of agents assigned to Quantico. Blevins confirmed these facts, to the best of his ability, by cross-checking the allegations with another source, a 137 informant who, until Monday, was an engineer at Dillon Aerospace." Sackett stated the information in a way he hoped would be upheld as probable cause in a trial that wouldn't take place for months or years, if ever. He watched to see if Riley's assistant looked convinced.

"Sounds weak to me, Sackett. Anything else?"

"Nothing I can disclose at this time."

Riley stopped pacing and turned with a big smile on his thin lips, as though he and Sackett were planning a practical joke on the legal system.

"Are you looking for a conviction based on the evidence gathered during these searches, or are you willing to have any seized evidence thrown out once you get a chance to look at it? If the search is deemed unlawful because of insufficient probable cause, do you understand that none of the resulting evidence can be used as grounds for any other arrests or in any related trial? A separate, legal search would be required or evidence would have to be obtained through the confession of a suspect legally arrested without using the fruits of the illegal search."

Riley popped his gum and blinked. He seemed to love the sound of his own voice.

"The charge against Pate for Davidson's death has to stick. That's important. As far as the search goes, I have other information that won't be tainted if the resulting evidence is thrown out. I can live without the search warrants being upheld. At least the search will confirm the suspicions I already have."

"Hold on, Sackett, not so fast. Would a sharp defense attorney be able to show that your other information, without the confirmations obtained through the tainted search, would have been too vague or broad to uphold the final arrest warrants?"

"I don't think so."

"Sure?"

"Pretty confident."

"Okay." Riley worked the floor again, snapping the rubber band frantically. He stopped behind his assistant and looked over her bony shoulder at Sackett's document.

"How's the complaint look?"

The assistant frowned, then shrugged. "Not great, but it should stand up all right."

Riley seemed satisfied and didn't read the affidavit. "All right, Sackett, you know how it works from here. Do you swear that the information you are providing in this affidavit is the truth, to the best of your knowledge?"

"I do."

Riley spun around and headed for the door. The assistant scribbled as he spoke to her over his shoulder.

"Give Sackett his arrest warrant. Carefully identify the three locations for the searches and give him those warrants, too. Good luck, Sackett. Tell me the rest of the story when you can." And then he was gone.

The assistant sighed. "You can have these in thirty minutes, Mr. Sackett. I just need the locations at Quantico."

Sackett sat down, closed his eyes, and couldn't believe what he was about to do.

"The SOAR's office, FBI Academy, Quantico, Virginia. The living quarters of the arrestee, Pate, and the living quarters of Special Agent Amos Warden. Both their addresses are FBI Academy, Quantico, Virginia."

She was still writing as she rose and headed out the door. Sackett reached for his coffee, which was stone-cold, but he drank it anyway. He heard Blevins on the radio, telling the dispatcher he was signing off at the office, so he picked up the phone and asked his secretary to send him in.

"I just got back from Jamison's hotel room," Blevins said as he rushed into the room. He sat on the arm of a chair but looked ready to fly out again.

"Any word from the crime scene guys?"

"No, boss, nothing."

Sackett walked over and stood behind him, put a hand on his shoulder. "Well, I've got some good news for you. Jamison is still alive. He called me about twenty minutes ago, an FTS call from our Houston office, if you can believe that. Wonder where he learned that trick."

"What did you talk about?"

Sackett turned away. "I can't tell you. I promised Jamison he could go somewhere without us hassling him. If I told you, someone may end up following him out there, and I don't need another dead agent."

"Sounds like you're breaking the law."

Sackett kept his back to Blevins. "I did what I had to. Let's move on."

"Whatever you say."

Sackett sat down at his desk but didn't look Blevins in the eye.

"I'm about to hand you a live grenade with a missing pin, so try not to let it blow up in your face."

"Sounds like a plan."

Sackett slid a personnel file to Blevins, a credential photo of Special Agent Pate clipped to the top. "You remember this man from yesterday?"

"You're kidding, right? Of course I do."

"Good. The U.S. Attorney has just issued an arrest warrant for him. I want this ugly bastard taken down this morning, at Quantico, if possible. You'll also have a search warrant for his domicile, as well as Amos Warden's domicile and the SOAR's office. But if you arrest Pate somewhere else, search that location for evidence, too. As thoroughly as possible without exceeding the legal standard."

"Evidence of what?"

"I believe he killed Davidson as part of a conspiracy. I'm looking for evidence to support that charge."

"It takes more than one person for a conspiracy, boss. Who else am I going to take down, this Warden fellow?"

"To be honest with you, I don't really know. Depends on what you find searching his room. By the way, has Jamison ever mentioned a man named Kane?"

"Kane? Not that I recall."

"Well, get going then. Be careful. As you can imagine, most agents at Quantico will be acting like your favorite brother. Sort through them carefully. Anyone who acts like he might get in your way is probably part of the conspiracy, so react accordingly."

"Is that it?"

"For now. Try not to get any of your guys hurt. You'll need them later when we arrest Phillip Brewer. Assuming we ever find him."

Blevins's eyes brightened up. "Can't wait for that."

"I'm sure. Especially if he still has the Corley woman. Questions?"

"None."

"Then that's it. I'm assigning this whole mess to you. You'll be the overall case agent and will have responsibility for every other case that spins off from here. I'm closing your administrative inquiry and transferring all the files on my desk to you."

Blevins looked at the stacks of files. "Thanks, I think."

"Good luck. Be careful."

"No other way."

Blevins started out of the office but stopped and turned when he got to the door. "You all right, boss? You seem a little jumpy. Anything else we should talk about?"

"I'm fine. Too much coffee."

Sackett walked over and closed the door of his office, then sat down on the couch. He covered his face with his hands and thought about his career swirling down the drain. Amos Warden had been right. Sackett had done his share of going along, and now it was judgment day.

Had he fooled Jamison on the phone, or had the sound of Kane's name made his voice falter?

Jack Kane. Twenty years ago, when Sackett was a nugget agent, he had no idea Kane was going to be so powerful. Kane was just a sad, broken, and hateful man whose family had been murdered. A supervisory agent friend of Kane's had sent Sackett and Warden on their first real assignment after new agents' training. They checked out a Bureau car and drove to a gun range in northern Virginia to look for Jack Kane. They found him and gave him an envelope, then said their lines carefully: "The FBI and Dillon Security wanted to help." It was simple at the time, almost innocent. For all Sackett knew, he might have been handing Kane a subpoena or a job application.

After Kane killed the two men who'd murdered his family, the Metro PD asked Sackett why he'd gone to the gun range that day, and how had Kane managed to find the killers when they couldn't? They didn't buy his story, and Sackett—young and cornered and alone in an interrogation room—lied about who sent him to meet Kane, and why. When the supervisory agent had first assigned Sackett, he said it sometimes worked that way between law enforcement agencies and Sackett hadn't questioned further. It was a blip on his radar screen, an assignment completed and forgotten.

His career took off from there. He worked hard and made more arrests than anyone else, but the supervisory agent who sent him to deliver the envelope always kept a helpful hand in his promotions. Sackett could never be sure of his reasons.

Warden had been wandering back and forth across the line ever since, but Sackett didn't do anything to stop him. In truth, Sackett had crossed the line with him a few times, though not in any big way, and certainly not like Warden. Nothing that got anyone hurt, incarcerated, or killed. He'd merely passed along some information from time to time, provided valuable assistance to high-powered people who could advance his career. It didn't seem so bad at the time, but now that it looked as if he might get caught, he wished he hadn't done it. Just like every criminal he'd ever arrested, he was experiencing the Pragmatic Repentance, as he liked to call it—regretting bad actions only because they caused troubles later.

All of his justification for past violations of the law evaporated the second he assigned Blevins to arrest Warden. Warden knew the truth and could bring Sackett down, could dime him out if he decided to make a deal with U.S. Attorney Riley. Sackett had sacrificed his honor for his career, and now he might lose that, too.

Jamison rushed out of the coffee shop after getting Kane's address and left his coffee sitting on top of the pay phone. Several cabs were at the corner, so he ran down and climbed into one, gave the driver an address a few blocks from Kane's house, then slumped into the backseat for the twenty-minute ride.

He rubbed his tired eyes and flinched when he hit the bloody scrape on his right cheek and sore spots on his neck. He had forgotten all about the injuries, but the cabdriver must have seen them, which was probably why he kept checking his mirror.

In less than forty-eight hours, from Monday afternoon until this early on Wednesday morning, he'd taken a long, long slide from aerospace engineer to killer. No wonder people looked at him funny. It was impossible to make that kind of trip without it showing on his face, even if he didn't have scabs from a recent conflict. And it wasn't over yet. How much further would he slip? Why was he doing this to himself?

The cab hit a pothole and took a bad bounce. Jamison's sore muscles tightened, and his body stiffened all the way up to his neck. It made him think about poor Ted Bronovich. His skinny little neck must have hurt, too. Not even allowing for fear and terror, it must have been agonizing when the killer grabbed his tiny head, angled it just right, then twisted his head until the neck and skull separated, the spinal cord stretched until it ripped apart like hard taffy. That poor, honest bastard. Who would have thought he had the courage to take on Dillon?

Jamison might have been able to save Bronovich. He didn't have to die, but Jamison, being the lazy bastard he was, hadn't done the one simple favor his friend asked of him. He put off telling Blevins about Bronovich until it was convenient, the only problem being that Bronovich didn't have the time.

Jamison had to redeem himself now, kill someone who had a hand in Bronovich's murder, and make some attempt to settle the score. This whole ugly deal was decaying into a simple, bloody math problem. Would one John Butler and one Jack Kane equal one Ted Bronovich? What would one Sackett be worth in trade?

He had no idea, would have to wait to find out, all the time knowing that Melissa was an unfathomable number. Nothing equaled her value. He would kill as many people as necessary to get her back. There was an infinity sign in the equation of her worth.

He slumped down in the cab and closed his eyes,

vowed again—for the hundredth time since the FBI arrested her—that he would not fail her again. He would not let anything else bad happen to her, would go the whole distance, do anything and everything to make up for what he failed to stop before.

The cab careened around a corner, a tight turn that almost threw Jamison across the seat. He kept his eyes shut and found that he was staring at himself, seeing the real reasons for what he was doing right now. For the first time he was looking at a part of his soul he had never wanted to examine, a little cell of truth, a filthy dungeon where honesty reigned as pure and unencumbered as a Tibetan monk, only a door or two away from the crazy man's cell. The door to this intimidating room was marked with the question: Was he really doing this for her?

He jerked his closed eyes away from the dingy room and didn't even want to think about looking inside, afraid, suddenly so afraid. His hands shook and his throat clogged up, but the truth kept calling him, louder and louder like a siren's song, telling him he had to understand, someday, what his motives were. Why not today?

He floated into the room and felt pain immediately, as if God had reached a big hand into his chest and squeezed his heart like a wet sponge. Melissa was in the room, waiting for him, lying with her clothes shredded and her legs squeezed together at her knees, watching as he approached. He looked at her, and . . . God, what was he feeling now? Something entirely different from ever before, something terribly wrong but so natural and understandable, too. Something unspeakable, but honest. Was it hate? It was so intense that he wanted to spit the bitter taste out of his mouth. It was definitely hate, he was sure now. Nothing else tasted that foul.

How was it possible? How could he ever hate Melissa for what had happened? She was a victim and had been completely powerless to stop the attack. It was irrational to feel otherwise, to hate her for letting it happen, but he did hate her. God help him, he was actually holding her responsible for the attack, for letting something happen that would destroy their relationship. He had lied, pretending they'd split up over their careers, a convenient excuse for their friends and themselves, but it was obvious to him now that the rape was the reason. He hadn't been able to live with it and couldn't accept the fact that he'd been worthless when she'd really needed him. He couldn't get past the pain of failing her.

The terrifying room had more to tell and wouldn't let him go. He tried to open his eyes, tried to get away, but he was trapped in a web, the silken strands trembling as the truth crawled to get him. He was crying now, his shoulders lurching up and down in a staggered rhythm with his sobbing. He thought briefly about where his body was, and about the cabby who had to regret picking him up. But he hardly felt the cab around him anymore, and he surely didn't care about the driver.

Guilt was his worst enemy, he saw that now. It had been for two years. It wasn't the guilt of allowing the rape, either. It was the guilt he felt about his own feelings, the ones he could repress no longer.

He had stayed strong for her after the attack. He'd been patient and loving and understanding because that was what she had asked of him. He held her while she cried, tried not to treat her any differently than he had before, and reminded her over and over again that she deserved none of the responsibility for what had happened. He stood by her quietly, trying to remain patient and understanding.

But he wasn't patient about finding her attacker, and he sure as hell didn't understand why he had to contain his vengeance. He was mad as hell, and wanted to move to Delaware and hunt that animal down.

But she'd said no. She was worried that she might have to confront the man herself someday, if the opportunity ever arose, and that Jamison would be victimizing her again if he eliminated that option. So he hadn't said anything more about it and did nothing to heal his own pain. As he wore the mask of a patient lover he began to hate her. Because he loved her so much, he was willing to do what she asked even if it cut him off from his own emotions. Whenever he thought about his own needs, he felt ashamed and self-indulgent, and that completed a nasty circuit that made him hate her even more.

As he bumped along in the cab, he finally understood that he wasn't out to save Melissa. Not really. The truth from the scary room was that he had to prove something to himself. Prove that he had the power to help her. Prove that she could count on him, and that he would not fail her.

His feelings for Melissa changed that very second. He saw her as a timid, frightened woman who needed his help. His love for her shook him as suddenly as a lightning strike, and it occurred to him that maybe he really had saved her after all. If nothing else, he'd done a lot to help her save herself. He failed her on the beach, but in the months and months that followed, he had been her soldier, her strength. He sacrificed for her, sacrificed his good, natural feelings about sex, sacrificed the chance ever to make love again without thinking of that night. He did the things she needed and put her healing far ahead of his own sanity, suffered for her in ways she would never understand, did more for her than he'd ever done for anyone else in his life. Right now, for the first time, he felt pretty good about all that.

The cab slid to a stop and the door to the room slammed shut, locking him out. He opened his eyes and blinked. Somehow, everything seemed a little different.

He paid and jumped out, feeling lighter and faster than he had in years. He still felt like crying, but he didn't have much trouble holding back the tears. He was nearly happy. For the first time since Delaware he realized how much he really did love Melissa, a love unfettered by guilt for a past mistake.

He headed down the sidewalk, about four blocks from Kane's address, almost breaking into a run. He was forgiving himself, and enjoying atonement. Forgiving himself for letting the rape happen, and for the shame he'd felt about his self-centered whining, but most of all, he was forgiving himself for the guilt that drove her away. While he was at it, he forgave himself for Ted Bronovich, for being a normal human being who made a very bad mistake by not asking Blevins for help.

His motives were pure now and he understood them completely. He loved Melissa Corley more than anything else on this earth. God have mercy on anyone who stood between them.

# CHAPTER FIFTEEN

Melissa sat across from Special Agent Brewer and waited. Neither of them had left the living room of the second-floor apartment since they arrived. Brewer had sat there since the middle of last night but said hardly anything; he hadn't moved, hadn't even gotten up to make coffee when the sun rose an hour ago. They'd been staring at each other for several hours, separated by a dozen feet of hardwood floor and the silent suspicions of two enemies.

Any time now, she figured, it wouldn't be long. He was waiting for someone, she was certain. Probably the big man who'd come with Jitters to her cell at the Detention Center. Her chances of getting away from Brewer were slim but would never be better. She wouldn't have any chance once Big Man arrived. If only Brewer would come closer, then maybe she could do something. He had to be tired of sitting there, staring at her legs. *Come on, let's get on with it.*

She'd tried getting him to adjust the cuffs that chained her right hand to the arm of the couch, but he said he'd left her plenty of room, and that was that. So what now? She waited and planned and thought about Peter. He had no idea of what he was up against, no concept of the power of the organization her father had started, the power he was pitting himself against.

When she was a little girl, she overheard her father's quiet conversations, sometimes on the phone, sometimes with the important men who came to their home. They were sharing secrets. They talked about money, sources, and necessary actions. *Necessary,* they said it a lot. Whatever her father and these men decided to do, they did because it was necessary. It was all very strange talk for an aeronautical engineer.

In her second year of law school, one of her professors, a sixties radical who still wore his frizzy hair a little too long, lectured on the illegal influence of big business on the policies of American government. He was an intelligent man who seemed to have all the answers, so after she got to know him better she asked him about some shreds of information she'd carried from childhood, things she'd overhead her father say, things that had never made sense to her but refused to be forgotten. What did he think they meant?

The professor thought a moment before answering, and watched her carefully as he told her he could only speculate. He answered delicately, and barely skirted the issue of corruption and fraud while making vague allegations. She could still remember his look, the suspicious way he eyed her as if she'd read a very rare book that made her smarter than him. A book he would never be able to get his own hands on but would give up his tenure to possess. As they finished he said she shouldn't discuss this with anyone else unless she was willing to testify against her father. He walked away without explaining further.

That weekend she went home and talked to her father, quietly, while her mother was out. She confronted him with the professor's allegations, respecting her dad too much to do otherwise. Had he committed crimes against the United States government? She waited for his answer, positive he would deny it and clear away her doubts. When he did not, she knew her face showed disappointment and shame, feelings she'd never felt toward her father or even considered as a possibility.

He looked hurt, but did not say a word in his own defense. Instead he walked over to her and slowly put his hand on her head, very gently. Then he looked up, the same way he often looked into a starry sky on a clear night, and stroked her long hair.

"You are a very smart woman," he said, "and I am extremely proud of you. I'm sorry, and hope you're not too ashamed of me. You know how much I love you, don't you?"

"Yes."

"Good. I'm glad."

Then he kissed the top of her head, wandered to his bedroom, and shot himself in the head.

Melissa's body shuddered as she shook herself out of her past, and her sudden movement attracted Brewer's attention. Her father was gone—God, how she missed him—but a man from his organization was standing in front of her now, stretching. If she was ever going to accomplish the goal she set for herself the night her father died, she might as well start with him.

"So, who's in charge of you guys now?"

Brewer looked a little shocked. "What do you mean?"

"What part didn't you understand? It was a simple question. I asked who's pulling your strings these days. President Albright would be my guess. I know it was once the Speaker of the House because nobody trusted Carter with the power, but Albright is probably playing along just fine with you guys."

Brewer had a kid's look on his face, as if he wanted to stick out his tongue and call her stupid. Melissa studied his face and tried to decide how much ridicule she could put into her voice without sending him over the edge.

"What's wrong, Brewer? Afraid you might say something you shouldn't and get yourself in trouble with the big boys?"

He glared at her.

"You are afraid, aren't you?"

She laughed to try and convince him that he was playing the fool.

"How does it feel, being a grown man who can't think for himself? You're stumped because no one's told you how to answer a simple question. I'd feel ashamed."

"Shut up."

She wanted to make him talk or drive him nuts. Either way it went, he would try to kill her afterward. She understood that, but she would make the deal. She had to be sure who was in charge of the fund, who sat at the pinnacle. She wanted to take him down and anyone else who could ascend to power, assuming she got out of this apartment alive.

"It is President Albright, isn't it? Come on, little boy, you can tell me."

Brewer lurched toward her and she flinched, just a little, but not enough for him to see. His face was angry as he hovered over her.

"You want to know who's got the power? No problem, but it's a trade between us, and after that I kill you. We'll wait a few more hours, just to be sure they don't change my orders. Then I'll take what I want and give you your answer."

She rose as far as she could into his face and looked right back at him.

"Deal."


The address for Jack Kane did not exist. It was an alley between two row houses, a set of missing digits, a worthless trip, and a waste of time. Jamison had traded his data for nothing and was now shivering in the shade of Ross Casey's mansion. The stabbing wind couldn't dull his anger toward Sackett. That bastard had tricked him again.

Although his target was Kane, his best play was here, huddled under a window of Casey's home, hidden by shrubs as he kneeled by the telephone interface mounted on the brick wall. He wished the device was on the sunny side where nice, warming sunshine could beat down on his frozen body. But he was all alone out in the cold, following his own orders, doing everything he could to get Melissa back.

His plan was to break into Casey's home and go through his closets, desk, and dresser, find anything that would lead him to Kane, then see if Kane would lead him to Melissa. If not, he would go after that lying prick, Sackett, then go wherever that led him, taking his suspects in order, going straight up the list without looking back. Nothing was unthinkable. There were absolutely no limits.

Casey's house was impressive, a huge home on a large estate surrounded by lush landscaping. A tight line of evergreens concealed Jamison from the neighbors, a thousand feet away. He was sure no one saw him sneak up to the house through the backyard, an acre or more of perfectly manicured winter grass. If someone had seen him, the cops would have been there by now.

He saw only one person moving inside the house, an attractive blonde about his age. He'd watched her through the window for half an hour, waiting for her to leave so he could go in. She was going out soon, he could tell by the way she'd dressed. He would wait a little longer. The cold wouldn't kill him but bad timing might.

He dabbed a finger at his swollen, scabbing eye, and ran today's plan through his head once again. It wasn't much, a flimsy scheme based on the hope that he could trust his secretary, Charlotte. She seemed trustworthy when they'd met on an obscure sidewalk last night, a little before Blevins and Sackett had come to his hotel room. She said she would keep her ear to the ground and let him know what was going on at Dillon.

He was having trouble trusting anyone now. Sackett had tricked him twice, so he could be wrong about Charlotte, too. She could also be the enemy.

The woman he assumed to be Casey's wife put on her coat, set the alarm, then left. He saw the alarm code and was pretty sure he'd gotten it correct, 9407#. He stayed in the bushes until she pulled away.

Time to go to work.

He dug into his gym bag for his multitool and used it to open the interface box. He unplugged the house phone line from the jack, then plugged in the portable phone he'd brought with him. He dialed Dillon Aerospace and asked for Charlotte.

"Good morning," she said, "Dillon Aerospace, Research and Development."

Jamison could hear her fingers dancing on the keyboard.

"Hi, it's me." He listened closely, wanting to hear her recognize the sound of his voice. Not wanting to hear surprise or nervousness.

Her voice didn't carry anything but words. Some happiness, maybe, but nothing really measurable.

"Yes, sir. How are you?"

"Fine. Can you talk?"

"Yes. Wait a minute."

The keyboard went silent, Charlotte giving him all of her attention, probably shifting away from the other women in the secretarial pool.

"Okay, go ahead."

"Have you found out anything? Heard them say anything about me?"

"Nothing." Her voice dropped to a whisper. "I checked the computer when I came in this morning. You're still down as being on vacation."

"Who made the entry?"

"Don't know. There's no record."

"That's all?"

"Sorry, yes. Haven't heard a whisper about you. I think, with the way things are going around here now, people suspect you're in trouble but don't want to mention your name. I'm sure that's what everybody's guessing."

"I'll let you go before anyone gets suspicious. Can I call again? You're still ready to help?"

"Anytime. Yes, of course."

"Be careful, Charlotte. Don't take any chances on my account."

"Don't worry." Her fingers shifted over to her word processor, her voice moving back to normal as the rhythm of her keystrokes picked up.

"Thanks for calling, sir. I'll make sure he gets the message."

"Good-bye."

Now it was time to wait and see if the police showed up. If they didn't, then Charlotte was good. He would go into Casey's house, find Kane's address, then call Charlotte and put his plan into action.

Jack Kane felt good today. He walked briskly down the long corridor, watching Charlotte at the other end take off her headset and place it in her lap, expecting him. He walked right up to her desk and stepped close. He kept his voice low.

"You did a nice job, Charlotte. Remember, this is strictly between us."

"I will." She dropped her head toward her chest.

"I know you will."

Kane turned away and headed toward Casey's office. He walked in without knocking and caught Casey pouring scotch.

"A little early in the day, isn't it?"

Casey tossed back the scotch without setting down the bottle, refilled the glass but didn't drink it. He set the bottle and the full glass on the bar, took two steps toward Kane.

"It's none of your business. Did you trace the call?"

"I did."

"And? Find out where he is?"

"Yes."

"Well, don't just stand there, send someone after him. I've got to get rid of Jamison today. You have no idea the pressure I'm under."

"Sure, Casey, sure, we'll get right on it. As it turns out, we have some men near there. Right across the street, in fact."

"You're kidding. How is that possible?"

"Lucky, I guess. After he killed Butler, I realized how badly I'd underestimated Jamison. He's really quite good, a professional if he wanted to be. Since I couldn't figure out what to expect from him, I hired several more independent contractors and upped the reward to seven hundred and fifty thousand dollars. Our security men are set up at every place he might go: Dillon offices, favorite company bars, executives' homes, places like that."

"And Jamison called from one of them?"

"Yes."

"Which one?"

Kane smiled, turned to walk out the door. "He called from your house, Ross." He spun around quickly to catch Casey's reaction.

Casey was at the bar raising the shot glass and stopped with his drink halfway. He turned around and looked at Kane.

"Oh, shit."

Kane laughed. It slipped out and felt strange, his first real laugh in years. He tried to choke it back but couldn't. He had forgotten what it was like to feel something funny deep down and how hard it was to keep laughter from forcing its way out. His life was beginning to seem a little more enjoyable these days, even with the disaster he faced over Jamison. His blood was warming, melting the ice in his veins. The watered-down fuel was barely sufficient to power his hatred, and he worried what his wife would have thought if she'd seen him laugh like that.

He always kept his last glimpse of her and their daughters on one side of his scale. They deserved that place of their own, away from the savages he'd killed and piled haphazardly on the other side.

But weren't they all starting to look like victims now? What about the families of the men he'd killed? Didn't they suffer? Had those men's deaths done one damned thing to help his own suffering or brought his family closer to him? Were all these years of vengeance helping him, or killing him?

Dillon security man Richard Murray led his partner, Hamel, up Casey's porch, then smashed open the front door. They'd been across the street, surveilling the house from the home of a neighbor who wintered in the islands. Dillon's data sheet provided them with Casey's alarm code and keypad locations, but no key. After busting open the door, they turned off the alarm during the thirty-second delay.

How had they missed Jamison's approach? The sun was shining and the streets were quiet; anything should have caught their attention, certainly the approach of the man they'd been told to kill with extreme prejudice.

Was Jamison really that good? Had he been in the house with Mrs. Casey all along, hiding in some unused room, or had he gone in and made the call after she left? Why was the alarm still on when they smashed in the door?

It didn't matter. Their job was to find Jamison right now and kill him or pay Kane his pound of flesh for letting him slip away. Kane's price for failure was steep.

Murray was the older of the two men. He'd joined Dillon after freelancing for too many years. At forty-one, the strain of independent contracting had almost caught up with him. As good as he was—and some told him he was the closest thing around to Kane—he'd gotten tired of the bullshit of self-employment. It was much easier working for Dillon as a team player with others on his side. He liked the regular paycheck, the occasional bonus, and having someone else worrying about expenses and payments. He'd started wearing suits then, Armani suits, and having his hair cut once a week. Those were his only diversions. He concentrated everything else on his missions.

Hamel was much younger, maybe twenty-eight. A kid, really. Murray always suspected that Hamel knew someone high up at Dillon security, otherwise he wouldn't have been hired. He was too fast and too messy. Of course, no one learned the finer points of this job in his twenties. It couldn't be done. At Hamel's age, it was still a fun game. Catch the guy, then whack him. Hamel didn't seem to worry about evidence left behind or getting hurt himself. For him, it was just a deadly game of tag.

As they crashed open the door, Murray crouched low, just inside, and aimed his pistol down the hallway that went through the center of the house. Hamel strolled past him, standing straight up, moving easily with a big smile on his face and an automatic weapon in his hands.

Jamison hoped he could trust Charlotte because he really needed someone inside Dillon to help him. He hoped for the best but expected the worst and hid in Casey's shrubbery waiting to write down plates if anyone showed up. He hoped it wouldn't happen, but part of him wanted the street to fill with Dillon cars. One of them might be Kane's.

Then two men came running from across the street and broke into Casey's house. He worked his way to the porch and stayed low, listening as the two men hesitated at the broken door. When they entered the house he crept up the steps, just behind them, quiet as a ghost. He didn't want to be left outside where he'd have to open the door and go through it once they were inside. Besides, he needed to know where they were in the big house. He pressed himself against the wall outside the front door, listened hard, and waited for the two men to move away from it.

He heard them split up. Neither of them closed the door. The younger man headed upstairs while the older guy whispered that he would search the first floor. Jamison decided to go after the guy on the first floor because the young guy was just too hard to read.

The man stepped slowly away but Jamison waited, wanting him out of the hallway. It would be bad news to be caught in the foyer where the young gun could look down from the balcony and shoot him.

Finally, Jamison stepped through the foyer with his eyes going up the stairs, then back to the lobby straight ahead, then again up the stairs. He stopped at the living room, peeked in, and advanced. In the dining room, he waited for the man to come out of the kitchen.

He didn't have to wait long. The man came out quickly and strolled back into the dining room as if it were familiar ground. Jamison was standing right beside the door and stuck his gun against the man's head, so hard the man nearly fell over sideways.

"Shhh."

The man started to swing around, but Jamison kept the gun to his head and pulled back the hammer of his double-action Beretta. It was unnecessary, the pistol would have fired without cocking, but the sound sent a clear message. The man stopped instantly, as though his life had been one long study in good judgment.

Jamison reached over and took the gun from the man's hand. Second chance was written all over the guy's face, like, "Okay, I'm not dead yet. This isn't over yet."

Jamison concentrated on not giving the man any advantage. "Over here," he whispered, "and you know I'll kill you if you make noise. I'll need you dead so I can concentrate on the guy upstairs. Don't force my hand."

The man seemed to understand; it all made perfect sense. Jamison pointed to a dining room chair that faced the hall, then pushed the man over to it. The man started to sit down.

"Wait a minute." Jamison was still whispering, even though he could hear the young man clomping around upstairs at the far end of the house. He still had time. He grabbed the man's coat at the collar and pulled it down to his waist, leaving the man's arms in the holes, a kind of makeshift straitjacket. "Now sit."

The man sat.

Jamison stood behind him, facing out toward the hall. He checked to make sure the man's hands hadn't wriggled out and that the coat had them pinned behind him.

"I want two things from you. One, the location of a friend of mine named Melissa Corley. Two, where to find Jack Kane. Start talking."

"I—"

"Shh. Keep your voice down."

The man tried again, low, and gave Jamison an earnest look.

"I don't know."

Jamison got his whiskers right against the man's face and whispered into his ear.

"All right. I knew you would say that, and you knew you would say that, but now that game is over and we get to start a new one. Where's Melissa?"

Jamison pulled the multitool from his pocket and flipped out the scratch awl. He stuck it into the man's ear canal and pushed. The man's head made a violent jerk when the point hit his eardrum. It punctured, and a stream of blood ran down the side of the man's head. Jamison moved to the other side, still watching the doorway, his hand reaching around his victim's head and pushing hard on the tool.

He spoke into the man's good ear, the one that didn't have a sharp instrument buried two inches into it. "If you don't tell me where she is, I'm going to drive this blade right into your brain. I don't want to, but I'll need to move on to contestant number two. You understand? You've got five seconds."

The man was going to answer. His face lit up like a pinball game, lights flashing and bells ringing. The truth was coming, and Jamison wouldn't have to kill him for it. Surprisingly, even the crazy man seemed satisfied with that, just watching from the bleachers with bored disinterest.

Then it happened. That damned kid from upstairs jumped into the doorway, spraying the room with gunfire. Jamison caught a round in his side. His skin ripped and blood gushed but it didn't feel serious. If he could avoid the rest of the kid's bullets, he'd be all right.

Jamison had barely heard him coming, or maybe he hadn't heard him at all. Maybe he'd seen it in the other man's face. Either way, his reactions took over and threw him toward the doorway, right at the kid with the automatic weapon. Jamison hit the floor and rolled forward while the kid rushed backward, trying to get Jamison in his sights but unable to move the long-barreled weapon fast enough.

Jamison was at the kid's feet now, at least a foot inside of the barrel's tip, the silenced rounds tapping into the floor behind him, each one just missing his head and going past his ear with a *pffft* and a *crack*. He raised his Beretta, jammed it into the kid's stomach, and fired. The blast lifted the kid off his feet and sent him backward. Jamison fired twice more before the kid's body hit the floor.

Now, quick, where was the other man? Jamison couldn't see him from where he was, lying on the floor. Had he gotten away, or worse, taken a position of advantage? Jamison jumped up just as the man came charging at him, empty-handed.

"Stop!"

The man kept charging. Jamison hesitated, didn't want to kill the man, wanted him alive to answer questions, but the man kept coming, almost on top of him now.

"Stop, damn you!"

No change. The man sprang off the floor and flew through the air toward him.

Jamison fired twice at the man's head and watched it snap back as his body went down. The polished wood floor shuddered as it caught the man's dead weight.

The gunshots sounded like cannons going off but Jamison convinced himself that no one had heard. Expensive neighborhood. Big open spaces between houses. *Calm down. Make the call.*

He picked up the phone in Casey's kitchen and dialed the office number that was taped to it.

"Hey," Casey said, as if he expected a friend, or maybe his wife, someone close enough to know his direct number.

"They're both dead, Casey. Are you next?"

"What? Who is this?"

Then Jamison heard him gasp. There was a little stagger to it.

"Oh my God. Is that you, Peter?"

"You got it. I had no choice out here, but you're a different story. It's your fault Melissa's gone, so tell me where she is or I'm coming for you next."

"I don't know."

"Don't even start with that. You want me to ask you these questions in person?"

"No, but it's the truth. I honestly don't know. Kane had her picked up. Kane sent those men to kill you. This whole operation is Kane's. He hasn't told me anything."

"Where can I find him? Where does he live?"

"He's gone. He left right after you called your secretary. And he's never said where he lives. I'm not sure anyone knows."

"Don't dick with me, Casey."

"I wouldn't. Honest. It's the truth, and that's all I know."

"You tell him I'm going to find him, Casey. Tell him I'm going to take Melissa from him. Tell him!"

"I will. I hope you do get her back. Really."

"Go to hell."

# CHAPTER SIXTEEN

Blevins returned to his office from the Quantico raids with Pate's blood on his hands. Pate had taken a hostage, a new agent working her way through the obstacle course in the woods, and hurt her pretty badly. He tried to ransom his way out with her, but the negotiations were cut short when a sniper's .223 round whistled through the tip of Pate's nose. The small, high-velocity projectile rattled around in Pate's skull until it shredded his brain into rice and ran out of gas.

They almost spilled more blood when they raided the office of the SOAR team, a nasty group of men who weren't used to being ordered around. The black-suited SOAR agents made a short stand. They refused to leave their building or give up their weapons until they added up the odds, counted the number of gunmen with

Blevins, and realized they were outnumbered. Doing the mathematics of life, they finally decided to cooperate.

Blevins next led his men into the main complex by way of the armory. They ran through the tunnels to attack the living quarters, rushing past agents-in-training and instructors and support staff who probably thought it was just another training exercise, at least until the gunfire erupted.

Amos Warden rushed into his room while Blevins's agents were tossing it. Blevins was working security for the search, so when Warden pulled his weapon and started to fire, he'd had no choice but to give Warden a quick double-tap, two fast rounds fired into the K5 area of his upper chest.

Warden died slowly, writhing on the floor, talking about a diary and telling Blevins he wanted him to understand. Blevins used his fingers to plug the holes in his chest while Warden demanded that Blevins respect him for what he'd done for his country, even if he didn't understand the reasons.

Agents found the diary in a small personal safe and handed it to Blevins as if it were the silver chalice, all of them speculating about what it might reveal. Blevins skimmed it quickly, learning just enough to know that Warden and some other agents were dirty. He wondered how it could happen, how the Bureau became so corrupt that his men needed to get a SWAT van, drive an hour to Quantico, then kill two of their own agents. Was the line between good and bad that poorly drawn? If so, was he one of the good guys? Hell, he was just a grunt following Sackett's orders, so how would he know which side of the fence he was on?

Now he was back in the office, huddled in a corner of the squad room with Warden's diary, like a boy with his daddy's *Playboy*. He read it carefully and started feeling ashamed of himself and the FBI. According to the diary, Sackett had allowed Warden's crimes to go on under his nose and even conspired with Warden at times. But others had to have known, too. Were there that many bad agents?

Sackett walked into the squad room and strolled in his direction. Blevins set down the diary and wondered what kind of a man he really was.

Sackett sat down beside him, nodded at the diary, then reached over and picked it up.

"Anything good in here?"

Blevins took the small book out of Sackett's hands. "No. Enough covert crime to bring down a government, but nothing I would call good."

Sackett put his hands on his knees and stared at them. "Did Warden mention me?"

Blevins breathed deeply and took a hard look at the side of Sackett's head. He made sure no one could hear them, then looked away as he spoke. "You want an attorney, boss? It might be a good idea."

Sackett gave a nervous laugh. "You think I need one?"

Blevins offered the diary to him. "I think you might."

Sackett turned his head enough to see the small book in Blevins's hand. "Thanks, but I don't need to read what's in there. I don't want an attorney, either."

Blevins set it down and put his hands in his lap. There was lots of hustle farther away in the squad room. Agents kept glancing their way, but no one stepped closer than twenty feet. Blevins kept quiet for a long time, pissed off, lost in some kind of trance as he and Sackett sat like stones while the rest of the agents bounced off the walls.

"Peter Jamison saved my life once," Blevins said. "A bunch of other men's lives, too. Now he's out there fighting to save Melissa and not giving two shits about his own survival. The last time I spoke to him, he said he wouldn't fail her. It was a threat and a promise, so I wouldn't want to stand in his way."

"Neither would I."

Blevins still didn't look at him and kept his voice down. "Maybe not, but it might be too late for that. While he's been out there catching fire, you've sent me on bullshit details that haven't helped him one bit. I've wasted time at the Detention Center and in running the raids at Quantico. Now I'm sitting here like an idiot, out of ideas. What I want from you right now is one good lead. Something solid. I'm a good investigator, boss. Just give me something worth a damn."

"You think I'm tied in with Warden, don't you, privy to information you don't have?"

Blevins didn't answer.

"Do you think I'm part of the corruption Jamison and Corley were uncovering?"

"A lead, boss. One lead, that's all I'm asking, so I can help my friend. Right now, I don't care about anything else."

Sackett stood and paced, doing small laps. He stopped and looked down at Blevins.

"Jack Kane."

Blevins wanted to jump up and shake Sackett for more information, but he didn't. He kept his mouth shut and waited for more.

"Jack Kane is the man in charge of killing Jamison. He probably has Melissa, too, or knows where she is. If Jamison's as good as I believe he is, he'll be getting close to Kane by now. You'll probably find them in the same vicinity. But keep something in mind, Blevins."

Blevins didn't realize he was staring at Sackett until he heard his name.

"Yes?"

"If Jamison gets too close, Kane will kill him. He hasn't got a chance, not against Kane. I doubt anyone does."

Blevins thought about a day long ago on a jungle trail. He remembered Jamison performing the most savage acts Blevins had ever witnessed and caught himself praying that Jamison still had what it took to do that kind of work.

"We'll see. My money's on Jamison."

Sackett didn't say anything, just stood there waiting for more. Blevins went to a computer, thinking of every possible spelling of the name Kane.

"Blevins?"

He turned around. Sackett looked lost, frightened. Blevins really didn't care.

"You going to arrest me, Blevins? I would if I were you."

Blevins had thought about it, but he still didn't know who was good or who was bad. All he knew was that the body count of agents was rising and that Phillip Brewer was still out there, waiting to become dead agent number five.

"Pick a team, Sackett. I can't waste any more time on you. Just let me know where you stand."

Sackett glanced at the spot where he'd said Kane's name, then stepped in front of Blevins. "I just did."

The other agents were twitching around the room but keeping their distance. Blevins hoped none of them knew what was happening as he made the call.

"All right, Sackett, I'll take your sworn statement later. Do you have an address on Kane?"

Sackett smiled a little, sighed, and put a hand on Blevins's shoulder.

"That's something I can help you with. I can take you there. I'm probably the only person around who can. I had to go there once when he'd been hurt. I took one of our doctors to do some confidential work, remove a bullet from his chest."

Blevins didn't care and he didn't smile back. "Yeah? Well, how about Phillip Brewer? You know where I can find him, too?"

"No. Sorry. I was telling the truth when I said I didn't know him."

Blevins started walking away, switching back to combat status. Then he stopped, turned back to Sackett, and grinned, just a little. "Get the SWAT team ready, then meet me in the assembly area. I want Kane."

Blevins left to lock the diary in a security vault before anyone else read it, passing the lobby on his way. Reporters were elbow to elbow and cameramen held their bulky equipment over their heads in the crowded room. Their numbers had increased exponentially since the evening news broke the story that FBI agents were still killing each other. It hadn't ended with the shoot-out at the Coalition. It looked as if every newsperson in Washington was in the lobby, trying to jump on the lead. Blevins glanced at the crowd through the bulletproof glass and turned away when the cameramen snapped on their floodlights.

Leo Strick stepped out of the SAC's office, his pocked
and pointy face smiling at the cameras. He held up his
hands like a preacher, waiting for Blevins to move
through, but Blevins grabbed him in front of everyone,
dragged him back into Sackett's office, and slammed
the door closed.

Blevins threw him against the wall, taking his frustration out on Strick the Prick.

"Before you do your Hollywood celebrity thing, I
want to tell you something. Listening?"

Strick did his best to look mean, but his hands were
pressed together in front of his chest protecting himself.
He looked like a small, cornered animal, overmatched
and hoping to get away.

Blevins wanted to thunk him on the head, disgusted
that the FBI had actually promoted this rodent to ASAC.

"I've got twenty agents looking for Melissa Corley
and Special Agent Brewer. I'm going to be gone for a
while, Strick, but I want continued updates on their
progress. Every thirty minutes, then an immediate call
when they find either one. Understand?"

Strick muttered something, then sniffed and went
back to rehearsing his lines.

Blevins was close to his limit. He slammed Strick into
the wall again. "You hear me, Strick? I want an update
on Melissa Corley every thirty minutes! No excuses."

Strick looked at the door.

"Right, Blevins. Corley. Sure, sure, I got it. Let go of
me."

Strick squirmed in Blevins's grip and finally pulled
away. He walked out, smiling and talking to the reporters. Blevins didn't stick around to hear whatever
stupidity came from his mouth. He locked the diary in

the gun vault, then ran down the hall to the main assembly area. It was a large room, almost fifty by sixty feet, but it felt like a five-by-six closet. Agents were crammed into every inch of it, talking and breaking down their weapons and rechecking their gear. The unity of their voices mixed well with the mechanized clicks and snaps of magazines being loaded.

The room went silent when he entered and everyone turned to listen. Sackett stared at Blevins, too, one question lighting up his face, something he seemed to want answered before anything else happened. Was he a leader, a follower, or a suspect?

Blevins nodded to show he would wait for him to get started.

Sackett nodded back, and hurried to the center of the room. "Okay, men, real quick, here's the deal, all down and dirty. We're going to the residence of a man named Jack Kane. You all have his picture. We will arrest Mr. Kane if he's there, search the premises either way. If he's not there, some of you will head to Dillon Aerospace to search for him there. If anyone gets in our way, we will arrest him. If anyone fires on us, we will kill him. Questions?"

No one spoke. The crowded room was so quiet that when someone shuffled a boot, half of them flinched and reached for their weapons.

"Blevins will be the team leader. I will coordinate and control the search. You've all been briefed on what we're looking for, so grab anything that looks like it might tie into this corruption. We'll deal with any sticky legal issues later. Expect resistance, men. Respond with deadly force. And, gentlemen, you may not like some of what you find tonight. You may discover some traitors among us, people you know very well. Be ready for that." He looked at Blevins, gave it a second, then shrugged. "Ready? Let's go."

Blevins headed toward the stairwell with his men, sneaking out to avoid most of the media. They stomped down the stairs to the garage, heavily armed and ready to fight a small war. They carried fully automatic weapons, shotguns, night-vision equipment, gas masks, and M79 grenade launchers with high-explosive rounds. Blevins carried extra CN tear gas. There was no way they were going to be caught unprepared or out-gunned tonight. It was the FBI way, a long tradition of using overwhelming force.

Jamison headed to Melissa's Georgetown apartment for a chance to recharge, to be around her things and in her home. It was also a chance to think up some new strategy while he sewed up his bullet wound.

That damned kid at Casey's house had sent one round burning through him. The bullet had passed through his side, slightly below the tip of his lower ribs. It hadn't done any real damage, considering that a few inches over might have killed him. No organs were hit, but the bullet had torn a two-inch gap between his ribs and his pelvis and ripped the flesh wide open. No guts were squeezing out and there was surprisingly little pain, but the damned thing would not stop bleeding. It had soaked the dish towel he'd taken from Casey's kitchen and stuck in the hole, his shirt, and the inside of his jacket. It was still running down his leg in a sticky stream. It wouldn't be long before people would start pointing and staring as he walked among them.

He knew there was a chance that his enemies would

be at Melissa's, waiting for him to show up, and paid to kill him if he did. If Jamison was in charge of the other team, he would have stationed someone there. He hoped Kane was thinking the same way. He wanted a chance to capture an opponent and interrogate him in the quiet solitude of her apartment. He'd take his time, torture him as long as necessary to get the answers he wanted, and find out where Melissa was.

He hobbled down the street, holding his side, glad that it got dark early in the winter. He was light-headed from the loss of blood so he focused on simple things, testing his judgment and acumen in small ways. *What day is it? Wednesday. When's Melissa's birthday? April second. How many rounds does my Beretta hold? Sixteen, including one in the pipe.* Each right answer made him stronger and gave him the confidence to keep going, through the front door of her building and up the stairs, stumbling a little and making a racket, not even trying to surprise someone behind the door, suspecting now that if they were here he would die. The trip here had cost him too much and left him little with which to fight.

If he died here, it would be as close as he could hope to dying in her arms. He would be glad for that. It would offset some of the sadness of knowing he'd failed her miserably both times she needed him.

He banged up the last flight of steps, somehow keeping himself from falling back down as he passed the last door, then wrestled his Beretta out of his waistband. He unlocked her door with the key she'd given him, flung it back, and stood smack in the middle of the opening and waited for the flash of light that would blow him away.

It didn't happen. The room stayed dark, with no light at all inside. He kept his Beretta in his hand, parallel with the floor, and waited some more, listening like hell for a sound in the darkness, not afraid to hear it. He wanted to hear it, wanted someone to be there, needing to get information from them, and then take another enemy out of the game.

He stepped in, kicked the door closed with his foot, and leaned back against it, realizing how exhausted he really was. He started slumping down the door, wanting to fold into a neat little puddle on the hardwood floor, sit there and close his eyes, pass out and sleep. But he didn't. He pushed himself away from the door and turned on a light.

Melissa's apartment was destroyed. He stood there with his fingers on the light switch, looking around her apartment, thinking an earthquake couldn't have caused more damage. He wandered through the debris, wondering how someone could have done all this without alerting the neighbors. Or had they told the neighbors, given them a good story that convinced them? Maybe showed them some credentials and a warrant?

Nothing had been overlooked. Every item on the shelves had been flung down and broken. The furniture had been dumped over and gutted, the stuffing shredded and the drawers emptied into several piles. The antique bookcase he'd humped up the stairs as a birthday surprise was smashed to pieces. Holes were punched in the walls as if someone was looking for a hidden safe. Boards had been pried up from the hardwood floor.

As Jamison picked his way through the rooms, his strength began to come back, chasing away the weak resignation he'd felt a few moments earlier. His anger returned with his strength, or maybe it was the other way around. Either way, he was building power he needed to keep moving, to do more than he believed was still possible when he'd first arrived.

He walked to her bathroom, trying to avoid the piles of her clothes on the bedroom floor that had already been trampled by an army of dirty shoes. He picked up some of the cleaner items and laid them over a chair, hoping Melissa would live here again and need them.

He lifted the dress she wore last Thursday at Jonah's Bar. The silky blue dress still carried the scent of Il Bacio, which worked its way into his nose and forced him to press the dress against his face.

Everything in Melissa's medicine cabinet had been swept out by the flick of a hurried hand. He found her small sewing kit on the vanity, half buried under the fallout that covered every flat surface. Jamison picked it up and took out a large needle, selected white thread because it looked clean, and sat down on the commode. He wrapped a towel over his hip above his jeans, just below the jagged edges of his flesh.

He wasn't going to sew up the wound; hell, he had no idea how to do that. He just needed to close it a little, bring four edges together in the middle to give him a solid foundation for a field dressing, which would stop the bleeding. The loss of blood was making him too weak, and too obvious. He had to bring it under control.

He studied the hole for a minute, picked around it with his fingers, and found four skin flaps that would stretch the distance. He punched the needle through the piece of ragged skin farthest away, came in from the outside so the knot would rest against the epidermis, and stretched the skin as far as it would go to determine where the four pieces of flesh would meet.

He felt only a mild tingle as the silver needle and white thread passed through the meat. When the knot snugged up against his skin he jerked it tight, tugged on it several times, and checked to make sure it wouldn't pull through the hole. Then he came straight up with the needle through the underside of the flesh under the rib and pulled the thread tight before stretching the two pieces together. They fit pretty well, and made him sort of proud of his sewing. He pulled six more stitches to hold these pieces together, then knotted the thread off, cut and retied it, and repeated the same procedure with pieces from his front and back.

The patch slowed the bleeding to a trickle, but Jamison didn't kid himself. He knew infection would set in. Blood might pool inside him. He could die without proper medical care. He had to go to a hospital, but knew he wouldn't take the time to do it. He had to get Melissa back first. He would ignore every twitch of agony, every signal of pain that tried to work its way into his brain. He would pretend he was dead already, or at least sentenced to death. With that attitude, it would be easy to ignore anything else.

He searched around for an antiseptic. Something, anything. Alcohol, peroxide, iodine. When he couldn't find any, he remembered the army teaching him that urine was sterile and could be used in an emergency. He hated the idea of doing that and searched some more. He held his side and went to the kitchen where he found a bottle of antibiotics. He took four, and they gave him hope. The hope gave rise to pain, which he quickly converted into anger that he would unleash on Jack Kane.

He pressed a hand towel against his patch job and tied it in place with one of Melissa's stockings, then changed into some clothes he'd left there. He felt pretty good actually, relieved as much as recharged. His anger had been energized by the sight of her apartment. The touch of her clothes had fueled his determination and the smell of her perfume had refreshed his senses. It was the closest he'd been to her since Monday.

He'd called Drummond earlier and said he needed help in finding a very elusive man named Jack Kane. Drummond begged Jamison to come into his office, hide behind a security detail, and let the trained professionals get Melissa back. Drummond said he'd known Melissa all her life and loved her as much as Jamison did. He understood his motives completely. The FBI would get her back, he said. Jamison didn't have to get himself killed in the process.

Drummond must have heard the pain in Jamison's voice. Not the pain of injuries but the pain of panic, of knowing he had a loved one out there needing his help. He sounded like a hysterical parent whose child had been kidnapped.

Drummond agreed to help. Both of them valued Melissa's life, so Jamison tried to sneak into Drummond's building an hour ago, straight from Casey's house. There were too many Secret Service agents camped out for a bleeding man with a handgun to get near the building, so now he searched her apartment for an address book or Christmas card list, and found one under a kitchen drawer that had been dumped on the floor. He opened it to D, wrote down Drummond's home address, took one more look around Melissa's apartment, then left. Back to work.

# CHAPTER SEVENTEEN

Jack Kane turned off all the lights except for a small brass lamp his wife had given him the last Christmas she was alive. The lamp wasn't an antique, but it had the worn look of one. He had rewired it twice over the years, polished it a dozen times, and replaced the switch. He would keep the inexpensive gift working until he took it to his grave.

By the fragile light of its little bulb he pulled the spindled envelope from his bottom desk drawer. He held it gently in his hands, stared at it for a long, long time. All of Dillon's offices were quiet this late in the evening, and quiet times were never good times for Kane. Silence always took him back to when the lady in the envelope was real, a beautiful, graceful lady who had shared his life, raised his children, and loved him like he would never be loved again.

He pulled out her picture and held it in one of his big hands, and the pictures of his two sweet daughters in the other. Suddenly, without any warning, he started to cry. The tears came immediately and surprised him terribly. Not one drop had ever leaked out before, much less flooded out like this. They had never been strong enough to penetrate his barrier of hate.

But he was crying now, like a small child. His lower lip quivered as he remembered her sweetness, the way she loved everyone and worried about every person on earth except herself. Knowing her the way he did, he suspected she'd been nice to the men who'd killed her and their children that night, concerned about them getting into such serious trouble and making a genuine offer to help them if they allowed her family to live.

He savored her memory as long as he could before pulling out her killers' pictures. He always waited like this, holding on to his family as long as his anger would allow, shutting off the venom until its pressure became overwhelming, his big hands snatching the killers' pictures as he remembered the sounds of their painful deaths.

Something strange happened tonight, an aberration, a miracle. His anger did not come. He held on to the pictures of his wife and daughters longer than he'd ever managed before, and the anger still did not come. He was still crying, even worse than before, yet somehow better. The sobs made him ache and drew him into a knot, curled him up in his big leather chair with his hands fidgeting over his mouth, shaking in staggered rhythm with the rest of his body.

Some of their personal things were in the envelope. Kane hadn't been able to touch them in twenty years, but now he gently tipped the envelope over and let the sacred items spill onto his desk. Her wedding ring, and the inexpensive charms he'd given his daughters to wear around their wrists. He picked them up and caressed them, held them against his face and stained them with his tears.

He could not stop trembling. His lips, hands, and legs twitched with the rest of his body. The shaking was uncontrollable, like his sobbing.

He saw his family alive for the first time since they'd been murdered. Saw them laughing and giggling and rolling on the floor with him, playing games and tickling each other. Having more fun than he could believe had ever been possible. The haunting, full-color morgue photos began to fade from his mind, and he heard their laughter. He heard his daughters teasing him about his clothes, for being out of style. Heard his beautiful wife join them as she put an arm around each of his girls in loving solidarity. He watched himself chase them out the door of their comfortable home and take them to McDonald's, then miniature golf.

Kane was afraid to move. He wanted to live in the past as long as the ghosts would stay with him, to enjoy his memories like rare old movies rescued from some dusty shelf. Gradually he began to understand that the pleasant ghosts were not going to leave, that his family was back to live with him again. Even if they were confined to his mind and heart, he was happier than he could describe and felt as though he'd come out of a long, dark coma.

He saw his life as something entirely different than what it was a week ago and couldn't wait to get on with it. He had no desire to look at the men who'd taken his family away. He picked up their photos and dropped them into the garbage.

He hurried down the hall but moved slowly into Casey's office, not wanting to scare him in the darkness. Casey jumped anyway, although Kane didn't actually see it. Casey snapped to attention while Kane located him and analyzed his changing position, all from the sound of a flinch. That sort of thing came automatically to Kane, a sadly normal part of his day-to-day life, as natural as breathing.

He flipped on the lights and watched Casey squint, his eyes streaked with red from booze or crying. Kane imagined a wicked combination of the two.

"What, Jack? What have you found out? What's the FBI doing? Are they coming here?"

Kane sat down and smoothed the crease of his trousers. "I received another call from one of our men inside. He said FBI agents have gone to my home. Sackett has rolled over and is leading the way. They'll be coming here next."

Casey's hand went to his lips and made a fist. He jerked his eyes around the room in no particular direction. They ended up back on Kane.

"Okay, Jack. We're still okay, I think. They won't find much at your place, will they?"

"No. Nothing."

Casey slumped in his seat, probably the position he was in when Kane entered.

"But they won't stop there, Casey. They've got Jamison's data. That friend of his, Blevins, has copies of all the stuff Corley and Jamison put together."

"That shouldn't be a problem once they're dead. But how far will they go? That's the real question."

"Frankly, Casey, I don't think they'll quit until they find everything. We're not going to dodge this one. It's over."

"All the stuff in the storage vault, Kane? Is that what you mean? I've never seen it, but you have. What's in there?"

Kane walked to his spot at the window, wondering where Casey had even heard about the vault. Casey stood up and followed him, trailing like a kid begging for candy.

"Yes, I think there's a decent chance they'll find it, and it's all there, Casey. Everything. It's a big walk-in safe built for military secrets sixty years ago. It's jammed with records of everything our group has ever done, back to the beginning of the Vietnam War. By tomorrow the FBI could know what's there, which will justify search warrants for hundreds of locations. Maybe thousands."

Casey's eyes and mouth were wide open, staring as if Kane's head had just spun around.

"Then . . . then we're finished, Kane. All of us. After all this time, why does it have to end now?"

Kane checked his nails. "It's probably just as well."

Casey slammed his hands against Kane's chest. "What's that supposed to mean?" He quickly jumped back with a terrified look and stood there for a second. Then he came at him again and hit him with a clenched fist.

Kane took it, let Casey get some of it out, let it continue until Casey started to rage. At that point he stepped back and gave him The Look, but had a little trouble getting it onto his face.

Casey stopped, then came again with a panicky kind of terror in his eyes. Kane waited until he got close, then grabbed his arms and twisted him around. He pinned him against the glass and spoke quietly in his ear. "Listen, Casey, you need to cool down."

Casey struggled. He wriggled and squirmed in Kane's big embrace, but he couldn't work anything loose so he calmed down. Kane let him go.

"Sorry, Jack. Really. I'm just . . . Shit, they're going to find out everything, and I'm the one that's going to take the fall for Dillon."

"Maybe."

"But you'll go down, too! Hey, at least I haven't been going around killing people. I might have contributed to a little corruption, but jeez, you *killed* people!"

Kane was losing his good feeling. If Casey kept it up he might actually hurt him, just to shut him up, to preserve the pleasure he felt for his family.

"You're right, Casey. But it doesn't matter. If all the FBI has is Jamison's evidence, we could get past that. Pay a fine, get cut off from contracts for a year. But to go any further with that evidence, the Justice Department would just be wasting time, chasing vapors. Once they open the safe, though, our world is going to cave in. America is going to come down hard on people like us."

"We're not the ones who started this cozy little relationship, so I'm going to take all of them down with me. You hear me? I won't look so bad if I drag a long parade of corrupt politicians and corporate leaders into court behind me."

Kane laughed because Casey was right. Richard Corley had married the defense industry to the Hill long before he and Casey had come along. He'd shown the way to finance their missions through cost overruns, and it was a tribute to his genius that they'd lasted this long. Except for a couple of small issues that blew up in their faces—six-hundred-dollar hammers and thousand-dollar toilet seats—they'd managed to divert billions of dollars with nobody the wiser. And that was just Dillon's contribution.

Casey paced to the window and looked out, then walked back to Kane. "Well, it never had to end. You should have killed Jamison when I told you to. But you said no, just kill the project. Lay off the whole division and that would stop the leaks. Well, guess what, pal. You failed. Failed Dillon and all of us. You're the reason this is happening."

"I suppose you're right. I guess that would have ended it, at least for the time being. But we all knew it would end someday. We couldn't last forever. Eventually, someone would have caught on. If it hadn't been Jamison, it would have been someone else. Anyway, I'm about finished with it."

Casey looked up quickly, as though this sounded pretty good, an option he hadn't known existed. He wanted to be finished with it, too. "What do you mean?"

Kane was at the service bar, pouring himself a cola. "I'm going to turn myself in to the FBI and make a full confession. I've got a few things to do first, but I'm heading there in the morning. If you can make it out of this, fine, but you better start moving."

Casey stared at the drink fizzing in the glass. "Why, Kane? Why would you do that? We're not really criminals, neither of us. Sure, some things have gone on that we participated in, but we can say it was blackmail. It was those guys controlling the fund. They made us cooperate and would have cut us off from government contracts otherwise. The FBI will believe that. Our attorneys can make us out to be victims. You know that."

"You're probably right. Problem is, if I don't confess to hiring those men to kill Jamison, no one will try to stop them. Hell, *I* can't even find them, so I know the FBI won't without my help. As you can see, I'm not holding much of a hand."

"Why would you care about Jamison? Hell, he's the cause of all this. Let him get picked off, I say. I sure wouldn't lose any sleep over it."

Kane stretched out his big, dangerous hand, held it in front of Casey's stomach. "I know you wouldn't. Listen, good luck to you." He squeezed Casey's hand, then turned to leave.

"Yeah. Same to you, Jack. Same right back to you."

Special Agent Brewer had stayed calm and struggled with his temper every time Melissa Corley taunted him and spent the entire day waiting for orders to kill her or move her or release her. But no orders came, and her words were really starting to bug him, creating some genuine fear about what he'd done. The darkness outside made him feel more alone than he'd felt during the day.

He knew the FBI assistant director who assigned him would quash any criminal charges filed against him for taking her. Hell, all of them would probably avoid prosecution, just as they had in the past. But Brewer had never been so blatant before, signing out a prisoner with his own credentials, and that was the part that really worried him.

"What are you waiting for, Brewer? What are you going to do with me?"

She hadn't spoken in more than two hours. Her voice startled him a little.

"I'm sure they know you have me. What do you think will happen when they find us?"

Brewer peered out of the safe house window, then walked to where she sat on the couch. He already had plenty of worries and didn't need her antagonizing him again. He checked to make sure her right hand was still cuffed to the couch, then sat down beside her and looked at her. He let her see that he'd crossed the line once, years ago, and decided to stay on the wrong side. Just in case she wondered where it stood with them.

"They won't find you, Corley, so I don't have to worry about what happens. You and Jamison have no idea what we're doing. But to answer your first question, you are going to die, as I told you this morning. I've waited as long as I was supposed to and no one called to rescind or amend the orders. Your time is up. Sorry."

He hoped the news would make her beg. It certainly would have made him beg if the roles were reversed. He watched her closely but was disappointed. She gave back nothing, looked absolutely fearless. That pissed him off.

"Second, I don't think anything will happen when they find out I've killed you. It's the way we do things. You, obviously, should know that."

Corley's free hand reached for her forehead, as if rubbing away a headache.

"Tell me about your work, okay? Tell me some details."

"I think you already know how our government really works."

"Only the way it's supposed to work."

He chuckled but didn't smile. "Oh, I see. All that investigative work with the Coalition hasn't enlightened you at all?"

"Enlightened? In what respect?"

He moved closer and tried to make her squirm. She was stalling for time and he knew it, but it didn't matter. He could give up the time. Nothing was going to change.

"Come on, you expect me to believe that the daughter of Richard Corley doesn't know how we operate?"

"I didn't say that. I know you don't mind distorting the system of justice we have in America. You don't care about rights or laws."

"See, I knew you understood. Surely, then, you understand that we only work this way because our legal system is so badly busted. If people like your father and others like us didn't work outside of the system, who would defend the regular honest guy? How else can citizens' rights be protected when courts are obsessing over the rights of criminals?"

Brewer felt his engine building pressure, straining his control, but he would kill her shortly so he could afford some indiscretion.

"Do you know, Corley, jeez, do you have any idea how hard it is to bring someone to trial in America, let

alone get a conviction? The defense attorneys manipu-
late the law, and the prosecutors have no choice but to
plea-bargain everything they can. The ACLU wants
every single right—never mind the cost to past and future victims—protected with a vengeance. The criminal
breezes in and out of court like a celebrity."

"It's American justice, Brewer. It's not perfect, but
it's the best thing going."

"It stinks! Everyone is afraid of incarcerating an innocent man, worried to death about the possibility of
making him a victim. Well, lady, they're right, there's
always a chance an innocent man might go to jail. But
there's a war going on in our streets. There have to be
victims! If one innocent guy goes to prison along with a
thousand criminals, sure, he's a victim, and it's a damn
shame, no question. But the justice system is so afraid
of that happening that they let a thousand criminals go
free with him, just to avoid the risk. So what happens
then? Huh?"

Melissa was staring at him. She looked like a
teenager being lectured about cleaning her room.

"I'll tell you what happens then. The criminals who
*weren't* sent to jail go out and create their own pool of
victims. Maybe hundreds of them. Maybe thousands.
Thousands of victims instead of one. Now, you tell me,
where's the justice in that? Who protected the rights of
all of those victims?"

Corley shook her head, she didn't seem to get it. "A
criminal's rights have to be protected, Brewer. I suppose the ACLU would argue that all of our rights are
protected along with the criminal's."

Brewer had heard that argument hundreds of times
but still couldn't believe the stupidity of it.

"That's bullshit and you know it. The fact is that honest, law-abiding Americans don't even need or want most of those rights. Why? Because they're not breaking the law! They've got nothing to be afraid of and they're not hiding anything. You stop an honest man and ask him to open his trunk, you know what he says? He says, 'Sure, Mr. Policeman. What's the problem?' So you take a quick look inside his trunk, thank him, then go on to the next guy who matches the description and drives a similar car.

"But try stopping a criminal and the story is big-time different. He knows his rights 'cause he's some kind of a half-ass jailbird lawyer and he says, 'Screw you, get a warrant.' Drives off laughing, with maybe a dead body or a kilo of heroin back there. Those, lady, are the rights the courts are protecting. I think those great men who wrote the Bill of Rights were brilliant, no question, but they'd never want to see the protection of individual rights lead to the collapse of this nation."

"And so that's where you guys come in, huh? You level the playing field?"

Brewer was going good now, he couldn't even get his hands unclenched.

"You bet your sweet ass we do. We didn't take this job to be judge, jury, and executioner, but no one else seems willing to do it. The courts, hell, they aren't any kind of deterrent to crime. Ask anyone, any of those career criminals who've been through the revolving door. They laugh their heads off and couldn't care less what the law says. But you can take it to the bank that I'm a deterrent. And others like me. We deter crime by eliminating the criminals who perpetrate the majority of it, the ones who would already be in prison if they'd done their crimes in any other country in the world. And I don't mean just harsh, Third World countries, either. *Any* other country."

Corley checked her nails but had a little trouble seeing them with the handcuffs. "Does President Albright authorize all of your actions? Is he your leader?"

Brewer was up and pacing now, feeling the inspiration of the truly converted. "You're shitting me, right? You don't know, really?"

"Don't know what?"

Brewer shook his head as if this was just too funny. "President Albright is just a figurehead, like the queen of England. He's not smart enough or tough enough to handle this kind of power. We're running this country from the background, and Albright is just fancy scenery that—"

Corley laughed, damn her. But it made her breasts move and he liked seeing that. He felt a twinge in his groin.

"You're kidding," she said, still laughing. "You're telling me that someone with more power than the president spends his days worrying about petty criminals?"

Brewer hit his head, hard enough to hurt, sort of liking the feel of it.

"No, damn, of course not. He hardly has time to worry about our justice system at all. He's far too busy with world affairs. But don't you see? The same types of problems exist in world politics. Just think about it, some second-rate shit running a Third World nation starts creating problems for America, and everybody talks about using sanctions to weaken his power or diplomacy to placate him. But what we really should do is smack the crap out of the little bastard. Know what I mean?" He slammed his right fist into his left palm, then looked at her for some signal of understanding.

"Oh, sure," she said. "I guess it makes sense. I can believe that some of the leaders around the world are just, well . . . plain old criminals."

Brewer made a hallelujah with his arms. "Well, thank you, ma'am, and you're exactly right. So all we're really trying to do, to the very best of our abilities, is . . . our jobs. Exactly what we're paid to do. Protect this country from all enemies, foreign and domestic, just like we promised when we took the oath of office."

Corley looked at her dress, smoothed it out a little with her free left hand. "I see. And how many people in the Bureau and on Capitol Hill understand and support your efforts?"

Brewer's stop sign went up. His zeal had not overtaken his FBI training.

"You wouldn't be playing me for stupid, would you?"

She turned her hands up and shrugged her shoulders.

Melissa held on to her nerve and waited with what she hoped was a fearless look while Brewer hovered over her. A second later he lunged at her and grabbed her shoulders. She struggled, but he held her tight with his left hand and ripped her blouse down with his right. One of her bra straps got tangled in his grip and he jerked it down with her blouse, exposing her breast. The nipple must have gassed his jets because he climbed onto her and straddled her legs, his heavy weight pinning her down as he kissed the side of her neck. Then he slid off her legs, kept kissing her neck while he pinched her nipple and groped around under her dress, moving up her legs until he reached her panties. The ribs that

Jitters had injured were screaming for him to get off, but she fought the pain.

She didn't struggle, not even a little. She waited, thinking, planning. After all, this was what she'd wanted. His rough face was grating her skin but she didn't resist. He was too close and too strong to push away with her one free hand, so she gasped lightly, as if this were something she hated herself for enjoying but didn't want to stop. Then she slid her left arm around his head and pulled him in, close and tight like a lover's embrace.

He followed her lead, grinding his body up and down on hers, pinching her nipple harder, squeezing her breast too hard. He slid down her and licked her nipple, then started sucking her breast, hard enough to hurt. He kept rubbing his body against hers, grinding his crotch against her hip, faster and faster, the blood pumping up the veins of his neck as his hand slipped under her panties and into her body, his mouth moving back to her neck as she squeezed her legs together and locked his hand in her crotch.

When her teeth first penetrated the skin of his neck he went rigid, just for a second. Then he screamed, a frantic, desperate, hopeless scream, the agonized cry of one human being eaten alive by another. The horrible screams grew worse, then turned pathetic as she sank her teeth all the way into the left side of his neck, as far as they could go, so deep that jaws hurt from the strain. Then she clamped down hard, ripping and tearing the flesh, shaking her head like a hungry shark trying to shred away the loose meat. The bite was too big and wouldn't come away in one piece, but Brewer's carotid artery popped and gushed blood all over both of them. She almost gagged when Brewer's blood filled her mouth and flooded her throat, but she swallowed it, gulped it down with the rhythm of his heart, holding on to him with her teeth and left arm while her stomach engorged.

Brewer rocked and jumped but she'd clamped down hard, held him in this awkward position, and gave him little leverage, knowing the end would come quickly. She just had to hold on. She kept his right hand jammed so tight against her breast that it wasn't any help, and her strong legs locked down on his left hand like a vise. She kept his feet off the floor and his head scissored in the crook of her arm until the gushing stream of blood slowed to a trickle and he whimpered his way to death.

Brewer's blood was already turning sticky by the time she dug the handcuff key out of his pants pocket and unlocked herself. She grabbed his gun as she threw up his blood, then stepped toward the kitchen to wash up. She had just moved out of the living room when the front door shattered and a pistol whipped into the apartment.

She raised Brewer's pistol to fire at whoever was on the other side of the door. But she didn't. There was something wrong here, something weird. Somehow, she didn't feel threatened. Then the big man moved into the room and aimed his pistol past her, took in the bloody scene behind her without ever aiming in her direction.

"Are you all right?"

She kept her aim pinned on him and followed his movements precisely. "Yes."

"Anyone else in here with Brewer?"

"No."

The big man closed what remained of the door and walked past her pistol without even glancing at it. He checked Brewer, then holstered his own pistol and walked straight into her aim.

"You need to get out of here, go someplace safe. I can help you if you want. Actually, I might be able to help you find Jamison."

She stared at him and recognized him, but didn't know him. He was acting too different from the way he did in her cell. She lowered her pistol, just a little.

"Who are you?"

"My name is Kane. Jack Kane."

"Whose side are you on?"

His mouth went a little crooked. "My own, I guess. I'll help you if you'll trust me."

Brewer's big handgun was getting heavy. She lowered it a little, wondering what this guy's story was. Wasn't he the enemy? Sure he was. But then, he'd protected her from Jitters back at the Detention Center, so maybe not. And besides, what were her choices? Who else might know where Peter was, assuming he was even alive? Who else knew where the next act of this play might be performed?

"Okay, Mr. Kane. We'll try it awhile and see how it goes. But I keep my gun."

Kane picked up the phone and dialed, turned his back to her.

"Do you know how to use it?"

"Yes. Absolutely."

"Good. I may need the help."

# CHAPTER EIGHTEEN

It was raining and cold and dark as a nightmare. Jamison was angry and calloused, hard and desperate. The scent from Melissa's dress was still in his nostrils, driving him toward trouble, blocking the pain of his wounds, keeping his body's warning signals from reaching his brain.

The cold could not bother him in this condition and didn't deserve more than a passing observation. It was freezing, so what? He was killing again, had lined himself up at the gates of hell and killed three men in twelve hours. Three more people added to his personal body count. There would be more, he was sure, and there was no way to forget any of them. Especially the one who got away. The one who had raped Melissa.

He watched for the crazy man as he marched through

the scary forest of rage, never wanting to give in to wholesale slaughter again. His fight with Butler had intimidated the crazy man, but Jamison still stayed on guard. He was determined to fight him as he'd always done and kill only when absolutely necessary, let logic and clear thinking pick his targets. He killed Butler, and two men at Casey's house, without the crazy man. He hated doing it, but liked the strange feeling of doing it alone, a justifiable approach to killing.

He wouldn't kid himself. He knew the truth, even as he denied it. He was playing the crazy man's game, a game of unspeakable violence where he would do barbaric things to other human beings, heinous acts he normally wouldn't be able to think about without shuddering. But there was no other option if he wanted to survive and get Melissa back. It had become a very simple business.

Smithson Lane was a quiet street lined with beautiful houses of distinguished character. Each home was unique, yet true to the Tudor theme of the area. Large porches, steep rooflines, and exposed beams. A very upscale neighborhood. Jamison logged in several places to hide as he trod along the sidewalk, just in case he'd brought his troubles with him—killers who might have followed him to Senator Drummond's house and might hurt Drummond if he got in their way. He hoped it would only take a minute to pick up the information and be gone, leaving the old man to his rest.

He turned into Drummond's driveway, keeping close to a hedge that ran toward the garage in the rear, checking behind him often, keeping a careful vigil against being followed. He passed some windows and peered in, and saw Drummond and another man through the sheer drapes. Drummond sat at a table strewn with papers, as though he had just cleaned out his office. He looked very relaxed, sipping from a brandy glass as he picked through the clutter.

The other man was strong-looking and clean cut, a bodyguard of some kind. Maybe Secret Service, assigned to protect Senator Drummond as he went after those corrupt bastards at Dillon. The bodyguard was pacing the floor. There was a holster on his belt with a large-frame, stainless steel revolver stuck in it.

What the hell? In the bodyguard's right hand was the paper coaster Jamison had given Melissa at the Chamber Restaurant, the one with Blevins's phone number on it.

Jamison looked closer at the papers on the table. There were some Coalition letters there, along with files and disks and the picture of him with Melissa that she'd kept on her desk, the two of them standing knee deep in snow at Sugarloaf. All the items appeared to be from Melissa's office. Drummond had her things spread out on his dining room table, picking through them like garbage. It took five or six seconds for it all to make sense.

His stomach was grinding and his arms were twitching as he whipped his Beretta from his belt, rechecked for a round in the chamber, then ran toward the rear porch. He was going fast, almost running, his side straining his patch job, Melissa's stocking slipping down. He covered the three steps in a single leap, then smashed the door with his foot. The glass shattered and the jamb splintered. Somewhere nearby a dog barked, but not in the house.

He rushed into the kitchen, his pistol cocked and ready at eye level. He was halfway through the kitchen when Drummond's bodyguard jumped into the doorway that separated the dining room. As the guard drew his revolver and raised it to fire, Jamison aimed straight at his head and rushed him. He paid no attention to the guard's weapon, but concentrated on his own aim as his trigger began to travel, his legs still hurtling his body toward the man.

Three blasts were separated by the smallest margin of time. Jamison felt the second recoil of his Beretta a split whisper before the impact of the other man's bullet. It burned its way into the meaty biceps of Jamison's left arm, then punched a hole out the back and exited. He shut off the searing pain like a faucet.

His two shots found their mark and smacked the bodyguard in the face, one below and one just above his right eye. The bullets flattened out on impact and ripped the flesh away from his face before they tore off the top of his head. The bodyguard crumpled to the floor and didn't move.

Jamison shifted his aim to Drummond, who was still sitting at the table, looking nice and relaxed with his brandy glass still in his hand. Jamison was short on time—there was no chance those blasts had gone unnoticed by the neighbors.

He dropped his pistol on the table and charged at Drummond, his good right arm leading the way. In the two seconds it took to cross the room, Jamison's anger went to the very edge of sanity. Without a thought he crashed the back of his right hand across Drummond's face, cracking some bones somewhere and opening an ugly gash across the senator's aging hide. But the old man reset himself and remained still, unflinching.

Jamison lunged deep into the old man's face, his spit spraying Drummond's wrinkled skin.

"You son of a bitch! Where's Melissa?"

Drummond dabbed at the bloody gash with his fingers, then held them out and examined them curiously. His face twisted into a toothy smile.

"Who?"

Jamison smashed Drummond's face a second time, not realizing what he was doing until he witnessed it.

"Where is she?"

Drummond tried to stand as a show of authority, or fearlessness, but Jamison wouldn't have it. He spread his right hand into a V and drove it hard across Drummond's neck. He lifted Drummond out of his chair and slammed him against the wall. A picture fell and the china cupboard rocked. Jamison bore down hard, compressed the wrinkled neck until all of his fingertips were touching the wall.

"Where's Melissa?"

Drummond stayed calm as he dangled there. His throat strained against Jamison's hand, squeaking in casual gasps as though this whole discussion bored him. Jamison loosened his grip a little, watched how far the old man sank before his feet touched the floor.

Drummond swallowed through the pinch in his throat. "The hell with you, Jamison. And the hell with Melissa Corley."

Jamison crushed the neck again, cracked it around until the skull flopped back and forth.

"Tell me where she is. I'm willing to trade lives here. Yours for Melissa's, that's the deal and it's on the table. But the clock's running. Decide."

He threw Drummond on the floor and watched him huddle by a chair.

"Don't hesitate on my behalf, Jamison. You want to kill me, go ahead. But keep in mind that if you destroy me, you destroy my work."

"Good."

"Oh? You think so? You think we should go back to the way things used to be?"

"I hate what you're doing!"

"Then who will protect America if not me? The American people? Do you really think those people who don't read papers, don't vote, and don't care can adequately decide how this country should handle itself in domestic and foreign policy? Listen to me, Jamison, they're not interested, and wouldn't know what to do if they were."

Jamison went to the window and looked outside to check for cops without looking away from Drummond for more than two seconds.

"So you do their thinking for them?"

"Someone has to. They deserve to have *somebody* protecting them and their possessions. Someone who doesn't give a shit about the hows and the whys. You know, Mr. Jamison, Americans only pretend to care if something is legal or illegal. In truth, all they really want to know is that they'll be safe, along with their families and their fortunes."

"I think you're wrong. I don't think they want your vision of this country. You're a criminal, and they don't want criminals running their government."

"I'm a revolutionary, Mr. Jamison. All revolutionaries start out as criminals, it's part of the definition.

Look at our history, look at Washington, Jefferson, Adams. Weren't they, in most ways, criminals, too? Certainly the British thought so."

Jamison reached down and snatched Drummond off the floor. His side ripped open and spilled more blood down his leg.

"I'm not going to argue history with you. Let's go, you're coming with me."

"Listen, Jamison, you're a smart man. Aren't you tired of seeing every policy and law of this nation bickered over and used as political leverage by two houses and a president?"

Jamison pushed him toward the kitchen but Drummond's feet stuck to the floor.

"Aren't you tired of that kind of gridlock? Of course you are. And why? Because Americans are people of action. They hate that their government has become moribund because of idiotic political posturing."

Jamison pushed him again, a hard shove in the back, and Drummond moved this time. Jamison picked his gym bag off the kitchen floor, took out the roll of duct tape, and strapped Drummond's hands.

"We've done all right so far, old man. You're not the savior you think you are."

"You don't think so now, but just wait until the straitjackets that Congress and the president have put on each other prevent America from acting decisively in a national emergency. And it will happen. Hell, it already *has* happened. Everyone's afraid, and unable to act in a crisis. As a country, we are very, very vulnerable. It's terrifying. If my organization hadn't been there to act in America's best interest, our enemies would have destabilized our nation already. There's not any-one else to stop them."

Jamison finished taping Drummond's hands, watch-ing for lights outside, knowing he'd taken too long.

"Let's go for a ride, old man."

"Huh?"

Jamison picked a ring of keys off the counter, pushed Drummond out of the house and over to the garage. He opened the trunk of Drummond's Lincoln, forced him in, and taped his legs together while he listened to the sirens in the near distance.

Jamison ripped off one last piece of tape, about eight inches long. "This is for your mouth. You'll have to breathe through your nose, you old goat."

Drummond looked panicked for the first time since Jamison had crashed through the door.

"I can't do that, Jamison. I'll die."

"I hope so."

It was almost midnight when they got to the under-ground garage. It was completely quiet as Jamison pulled in and stopped at the vacant spot for unit 213. The other parking place for that condo had a new white BMW parked in it.

He backed Drummond's car into the extra space, leaving plenty of room behind it. He got out and opened the trunk, and pulled Drummond's shoulders erect.

"Recognize this place, old man?"

The bumpy trip had taken some of the swagger out of Drummond. He had a dazed look as he shook his head from side to side.

Jamison was too tired to go easy on him. His mind hurt and his body ached too much to ignore the pain any longer. He'd tied one of his socks over the hole Drummond's bodyguard had shot through his arm and it had stopped leaking, but he was more light-headed than ever. Coupled with his lack of sleep, too much worrying about Melissa, and too much time in the line of fire, and he could already believe he was a dead man. Being dead was actually beginning to sound like a good thing, an inviting change of pace.

He wrestled Drummond higher out of the trunk, twisted him around, and gave him a better view.

"Really? Maybe you didn't get a good look. Let's try again."

Drummond actually managed to look dangerous as Jamison bent him around. Right up until the second he spotted the white BMW. At that instant his eyes bulged open and he looked back at Jamison with something else, something new, on his face. It was hope, maybe, or desperation.

"You know where you're at now, don't you? You recognize your daughter's car?"

Drummond nodded slowly, as if his neck were in a brace.

"Can we leave now or do I have to go through with it? I'm really hoping you don't make me, 'cause it's not something I want to do, but it's your call, she's just upstairs. If I have to torture your daughter to get Melissa back, I'll damn sure do it. Won't like it one bit and will hate myself forever, but I'll do it just the same. After you watch her suffer for a while, I'm sure you'll help me. Any father would. So what's it going to be? Tell me now 'cause I'm tired and fussy and short on time."

\* \* \*

Drummond had already decided to tell him. The hard ride had done a good job of convincing him. He was too old to be rolling around in the trunk of a car, and hadn't Jamison gone out of his way to find all the damned bumps in the road?

Why shouldn't he release the Corley woman? She meant nothing to him anymore. He had Kane's men pick her up to quiet her and to flush out Jamison, but her silence hadn't saved his organization, and Jamison wasn't exactly a hard man to find, at least not anymore. Why not give her up? He'd only been waiting for a decent reason, his lifetime in politics telling him to trade only when you want something. This seemed to fit the bill.

Besides, he could use this. He'd become a senator by exploiting tough situations like this and turning them to his own advantage. He could do it now by giving her to Jamison. Get Jack Kane to bring Melissa out, nice and easy. Trade her for his own freedom, then let Kane kill both of them. Kane could do that. Sure, it would be easy for a man like him. He and Kane could use this as an opportunity to end their problems with Peter Jamison.

The evidence, well, the evidence would be another story. He'd already been told of the plan to get that back from the FBI and was confident it would work. The organization that Richard Corley had built would survive this attack, even as it had survived so many others.

He thought about Richard, and how they used to meet at his home when Drummond was a freshman congressman. Melissa was just a little girl on her father's lap, sitting there until the meetings turned serious and her father scooted her out of his library. Richard was a brilliant man, a patriot who'd seen the uncertainty in his country's future and decided to protect

America from itself. Drummond wondered what Richard would think if he knew his precious daughter had to die in order to protect his organization.

Drummond dragged his stare away from his daughter's car and took Jamison's look straight on. He nodded his head yes, and sincerely meant it.

Jamison pulled him out and let him drop to the ground. He cut the tape from his feet and hands, then pulled it away from his mouth and helped him stand.

"There's a pay phone over there. If you make any kind of sound I don't like, anything at all, we're upstairs. You'll get to watch. Understand?"

Drummond nodded again as he picked sticky tape residue from his wrists. Jamison prodded him in the back, aimed him toward the phone, poked him several more times as they crossed the garage.

"Local or long distance?"

"Just local, Mr. Jamison."

Jamison dropped some change into the slot and Drummond dialed. He didn't even try to conceal the number, even as he saw Jamison writing it down. Jamison got in close, put his ear next to Drummond's and his hand against his throat, making it a little hard for Drummond to speak.

The phone was picked up after four rings.

"Yes?"

Jamison recognized Kane's voice, it was obvious by the way his hand tightened around Drummond's throat and his body twitched with fearful energy. Drummond choked, said nothing more until Jamison worked some of the rigor mortis from his hand. Then he bent out a few kinks and went back to his phone call.

"Do you know where the Corley woman is?"

"Yes."

"Good. I need you to bring her to me."

"All right, sir. I can do that. Where and when?"

Jamison turned Drummond around to face him and covered the phone. "Harborplace, in Baltimore. The northwest building. First thing in the morning. Seven o'clock. Make sure that's enough time, 'cause I don't want to wait. No one else comes or you die there, Drummond, and I'll come back for your daughter."

Drummond spoke carefully. "I think Baltimore might be a very nice spot. How about Harborplace? Say, seven sharp? Northwest building?"

"Fine."

"Just you and Miss Corley, please. I think there are going to be some trade negotiations. If you bring more of your staff, they would only complicate things. Understand?"

"I understand, sir. I assume our missing engineer will be negotiating for the other side?"

"Yes. He's a skillful negotiator, too. You would be wise to come alert and prepared."

Drummond was suddenly thrown away from the phone and down onto the concrete. He stayed down and didn't move, watching Jamison race for the phone as it dangled by the cord. He held it for a few seconds and listened, then hung up without speaking. He was tempted to kick Drummond's head.

# CHAPTER NINETEEN

Blevins stood in the middle of Kane's living room, staring at his walkie-talkie while his agents tore the place apart. They found little evidence and none of it was worth a flip. Now the dispatcher was playing some stupid game with him, providing another perfect little annoyance to an aggravating day.

"Say again, dispatcher."

"I have a message for you, 705, and the caller insisted that I shouldn't put it over the airwaves, either radio or cell phone. Call me on a land line right away, ten-four?"

"Yeah, roger that. I'll call right now."

He moved away from Sackett and picked up the phone in the study, an elaborately furnished room in Kane's northern Virginia mansion. The phone was a complex piece of equipment that Blevins had never seen

before. After looking it over for a minute, he understood that the high-tech contraption monitored Kane's
phone line for traces, pen registers, recorders, or multi-
ple connections. There was also a control unit plugged
into the status monitor, which operated a signal-
scrambling device, an integrated recorder, and an in-
coming/outgoing call register. Blevins almost didn't
want to use the damn thing, afraid he might acciden-
tally destroy some evidence. But he wanted the dispatcher's message and, truthfully, wanted to play with
the phone a little. So he took the risk.

"This is Blevins."

The telephone's status monitor flashed on and off,
the alphanumeric display signaling that the call was being taped by the FBI office. The damned thing worked.

"Sorry to bother you in the middle of a search, but I
just received a weird call. Since you're Jamison's case
agent, I thought you'd want to know about it."

"Go."

"It was a man who called here a few minutes ago. He
didn't identify himself, but told me where we could find
Special Agent Brewer. He said he'd just left the location
and that Brewer was dead. He also warned that he had
assigned several other killers to get Peter Jamison, and
that we should find him soon and get him under
wraps."

"I wish I could."

"I know. Anyway, this guy said he'd come in tomorrow morning and tell us more."

"That's weird all right."

"Gets weirder. This guy seemed to know every one of
our procedures and was emphatic that we not broad-

cast any part of his message over the airways. He even said I shouldn't use our burst transmitter. It was almost like talking to an agent, but I don't think he was one."

"What's the phone number, and did you run it?"

"Just did. It's local, 555-0090. Assigned to a business with no phone book listing, no records in indices, no phone calls—and I mean zero—originating from the number during the last six months. At least not until tonight."

"Not much of a business. Anything else?"

"Just this. The billing address is a mail drop. It's picked up and brought here twice a month."

Blevins snapped to attention, looked around the room, and lowered his voice. "Shit, so this guy called from one of our safe houses."

"It looks that way, yes."

"Okay, thanks a lot." Blevins hung up, surprised at the status monitor's light show, displaying a message stating that someone at the FBI office had attempted to trace the call, which the device had successfully blocked.

Sackett walked into the study, came over with his head low and his hands in his pants pockets.

"Trouble?"

Blevins took a deep breath and exhaled.

"I hope not. It was just someone worried about Peter Jamison. Said Brewer's dead, killed in one of our safe houses."

"Then the caller must have been Jack Kane. If he killed Brewer, then he might have taken Melissa from him."

"Would he kill her, too?"

"Don't know. He's cold enough, but he's also very

smart. There's no way to predict, but I'm guessing he wants the evidence back, the stuff Jamison gave you that provided probable cause for this search. I know Kane, so I expect he'll get it. He probably plans to barter with Corley."

"Even if he gets our data, Drummond still has copies."

Sackett looked away. He seemed very interested in what the agents were doing in the living room.

"I don't know, Blevins. Wouldn't count on it."

"You want to tell me what that means?"

"I wouldn't count on Drummond's material doing you any good."

Blevins looked around for something he could kick to the moon, a sacrificial target for some of his evil spirit. A trash can would work just fine. Or a wall, in a pinch. The ass-end of an agent bending over Kane's desk tempted him, but also made him realize he couldn't do a damn thing and forced himself to give up on the idea.

"Then I'd better buy some insurance because Jamison's evidence provided the probable cause for the three searches at Quantico, too. Without it, everything we've seen will be subject to suppression. It will all be fruit from a poisonous tree."

Sackett came back around, looking strange. He wasn't smiling, but he didn't look sad either.

"You're right. Everyone you've accused, including me, will be able to walk. You won't even be able to talk about this without risking a slander suit."

Blevins wanted to grab Sackett by the front of his shirt, twist the fabric in his grip, and lift until his boss was standing on tippy-toes. But he didn't because his men wouldn't understand. Or worse, they would understand, and that would mean they knew about Sackett, making them the enemy.

"Is that what you want? To walk? I thought you chose a side earlier."

"I did, that's why I'm telling you to be careful. If Kane is after the evidence, you'd better be a step ahead of him."

Blevins picked Kane's phone up again, redialed WFO, asked for the evidence clerk.

"Yes, sir. This is Cunningham, evidence tech."

"Listen, Cunningham. I need some clerks and agents to start making copies. Make sure they have plenty of paper because I need thousands of documents."

"Yes, sir."

"I want you to copy the entire contents of a white file box in the evidence locker. I checked it in on Monday."

The line was silent.

"What, Cunningham? What is it?"

"Sir, that box isn't here. I did an evidence check when my shift began two hours ago, and it was gone then. I've filed an affidavit for the SAC, according to the manual."

"Are you sure, maybe it's—"

"Agent Blevins, I'm telling you it's not here. I know my job, sir. Someone took it."

Blevins let the trash can have it, sent it flying across the room. "Shit!"

Jamison needed to rest before Kane and Melissa showed up at Harborplace, the final meeting where he would get Melissa back, then kill Kane for what he'd done to both of them. His body was desperate for sleep.

It didn't have enough energy to keep going or heal. His head and eye still ached from his fight with John Butler, he'd hurt his neck rolling into the young gunman at Casey's house, half of his stitching had ripped out of the makeshift patch on his side, and infection was spreading through his left arm, radiating out from the bullet hole he'd gotten at Drummond's but had never disinfected.

But pain wasn't the problem. He could ignore it easily, and wouldn't let it distract him until he was finished. The fear of death didn't bother him either, even as he wondered which of several things would cause it: loss of blood, infection, Jack Kane, the FBI, or some other adversary he hadn't yet identified.

Exhaustion was the real enemy, a very dangerous one. He worried about it more than everything else combined, and wanted this to end before his body quit completely and collapsed.

He parked Drummond's car in an automated lot ten blocks from Harborplace. It was nearly empty this early in the morning, and he hoped the five-dollar cost would cut down on the number of cars and police that entered. He wouldn't get any sleep there, but at least he could give his body a little rest. He wouldn't even be able to do that if cars were cruising around.

Drummond was completely quiet in the trunk, maybe dead. Jamison thought about what that would mean, and how it might create a problem for him and Melissa. But it wouldn't stop him. He would just trade Drummond's keys for Melissa, then tell Kane where the car was parked. Kane would have no choice but to make the deal. If there was a problem, he would kill Kane, then take Melissa. It was a simple decision. He would know what to do if Kane acted dissatisfied with the arrangement.

Worry would not let him relax, and kept reminding him of all the things that could go wrong, things he hadn't thought of, dozens of little setbacks, some of them bound to happen and cause problems. Kane might not have Melissa with him, because he might be planning a similar trick on him. He might not show up at all. There might be other people there, forcing Jamison to take on more than he could handle. The FBI might be on to him and secure the whole area around Harborplace once he entered their trap. The worst possibility was that Melissa might already be dead.

But deep down, he knew exactly what would happen. In less than two hours he would get Melissa back or he would die trying.

He pulled out of the lot at six A.M., wanting to drive by the exchange point and survey the area before anyone else arrived. It took only a few minutes to get to Harborplace, dimly lit in the early morning hour.

All of the bordering streets were empty as he drove by at five miles an hour over the speed limit. Soon the cars of the early arrivals—the deliverymen, bakers, and first-shift workers—would start filling the streets, and he would be able to drive more slowly without looking too suspicious.

He searched for a good place to park, a spot that was not very open, somewhere he wouldn't be accosted by delivery drivers or shop owners. A place where he could drag a taped-up old man out of his trunk without being noticed.

It couldn't be far away, either. When the time came he would have to control Drummond on a public street in the bright light of morning while he hobbled along in bloodstained clothes. He didn't want to do that any longer than necessary. It could be trouble if the old man started screaming, or if someone recognized him as a U.S. senator, or if he tried to twist away and forced Jamison to manhandle him, or someone noticed the mixture of wet and dry blood on his pants.

He cruised the city's waterfront a second time, noting the side streets and the high ground and the places of good cover, seeing all of it with a sort of bored concentration. The first employees were beginning to arrive, adding sparks of life to the waking street scene. It was getting safer to stop, only twenty minutes to go, not much chance of being harassed by the cops or employees now. He drove around the corner and backed the car in between two delivery vans with frost on their windshields, got out, and opened the trunk. He looked all around for witnesses but saw none, and strained his wounds as he lifted Drummond out of the trunk and shoved him up against the wall of the building, his hands and feet still taped together.

Jamison snatched the tape from Drummond's mouth, the old man's skin stretching long and loose, following the tape a little before letting go.

"You have a nice ride?"

The old man had suffered back there. Hours stuffed in the trunk like a bag of laundry had completely effaced his mask of power.

"No, damn you, it was hard."

"Good." Jamison took the tape off Drummond's ankles and then his hands, ready to hurt the old boy if he so much as twitched.

"We need to talk, old man."

"Is it time to meet Kane?"

Jamison looked around. He thought he heard someone walking around the trucks. "Yeah. Almost."

"Then our business is nearly finished. What could we possibly have to talk about?"

Jamison leaned toward him and caught the foul stench of Drummond's body odor. "Just this. I have no choice but to take you out into public, out where you could cause trouble for me. I want you to understand what I'll do if that happens."

Drummond massaged his wrists where they'd been bound.

"You will kill me, Mr. Jamison, then get the Corley woman if you can. If you don't succeed, you'll use my daughter as leverage to get Melissa, assuming you can find someone besides me that values her enough to trade. Do I understand you correctly?"

"You do."

Drummond shivered a little in the cold morning air and crossed his chest with his bony hands. "I won't give you any trouble."

Jamison looked at him and almost felt sorry for him. It was over for Drummond, no matter how the pie was sliced. He was going down, shamed and humbled, if Jamison lived long enough to tell what he knew. But Drummond was still responsible. Jamison would not forget that Drummond was one of the men who had caused his problems. He deserved whatever he had coming to him.

Jamison turned away, listened to Drummond's erratic breathing, and wondered how close Melissa was to him now. Could he feel her presence? Maybe catch a glimpse of her? Only twelve minutes to go.

He waited, checking his watch a hundred times to make sure it hadn't stopped. He wished he could have been here earlier, hours ago, and had the chance to set up someplace safe and watch all the approaches, make sure everything went down nice and clean. But he was stuck dragging Drummond around and didn't want to have him out in the open for too long. He had no choice but to walk into an unknown area held by the enemy.

At three minutes before seven he headed toward Harborplace, knowing that being on time was the same thing as being late if things were screwed up. He kept Drummond a little in front as they moved down the street. He could watch him there, and use him as a shield if the balloon went up.

Dan Corderman liked to believe he was Kane's friend, or at least the closest thing Kane had to one. They'd worked together at Dillon Security for more than a decade. Kane had never showed him any favoritism, but Corderman was pretty sure Kane liked him. He didn't think anyone else would have gotten away with the stupid crack he made the other night on surveillance, telling Kane how any man would miss his wife while watching Martin record Jamison and Corley in her apartment. Kane must have liked him to let that go.

Corderman had just returned to Dillon when he got Casey's call. Casey had fumbled security procedures badly, but was very explicit in what he wanted. Kane was changing sides, he said, and was just leaving his office. Corderman had to stop him. His career, and his own life, depended on it. The price was two million dollars, split with anyone Corderman included, however Corderman decided. Plus seven hundred and fifty thousand if he got Jamison. Casey seemed to think it might happen that way.

So he'd followed Kane as he left Dillon's lot, lucky enough to get to the safe house without Kane spotting him. He called for help along the way, but they didn't get there before Kane left with the Corley woman. Corderman hadn't been stupid enough to take Kane on alone.

Now Corderman crouched down in a thicket of holly bushes, shivering in the morning air that drifted off the harbor, knowing that his chances of success sucked. Hell, squaring off with Jack Kane was the last thing on earth he'd ever wanted to do. Even with the three professionals he brought with him, he was worried. Kane could come alone and still have a good chance of killing them. Corderman should have brought more men. A dozen more. Twenty, just to be sure.

He was a lot less comfortable now that the sun had come up. He was close to the entrance of Harborplace and ran the risk of being spotted. He glanced along the hedge, gave his second man a thumbs-up. The man grinned, as if he'd forgotten who they were about to tangle with, and returned the signal. Then he shifted around and passed it on to the third man, another fifty feet away, who signaled it to the end assassin. They were ready. Kane was standing on the corner with the Corley woman and Jamison was walking toward them with Senator Drummond. They had a clear field of fire from here. Corderman was trembling.

Jamison and Drummond moved slowly down the sidewalk, which was still nearly empty on this chilly morning. A few people approached them, then passed. None of them paid much attention.

Then he saw Kane and Melissa standing near the corner on the opposite side of the street. But Kane wasn't watching him or hadn't seen him yet. Why? He had to be better than that. If not, Jamison had really overestimated him, and that gave him a lot of worry because he'd based every plan on the assumption that Kane was a professional. He had no idea how an amateur might act but wanted to change his game plan if that was the case. He kept watching Kane, trying to decide which was correct. Kane was glancing up at the high ground, looking very edgy as he moved his eyes along the building, not paying any attention to him or Drummond.

A trap? Maybe. Jamison stopped, pushed Drummond down beside two parked cars, and scanned the area carefully. This looked way too easy. Something had to be wrong. He reached behind him, wiggled the Beretta out of his belt with his right hand, and felt the bullet wound burning his left arm as he touched the two magazines in his pocket.

"Let's go, Drummond. Stand up and cross the street. It's open from here on in, so if there's going to be a problem, this is where it'll happen. If I die, you die. Move."

They crossed without a shot being fired, even though they were easy targets on the empty street. Kane was watching them now, eyeing their approach warily. Melissa was watching, too. Fifty feet away, Jamison reached forward with his bloody left hand, grabbed Drummond's shoulder, and slowed him down.

Melissa started to shout to him, but Kane hushed her with a quiet word and a gentle touch to her shoulder. Jamison wanted to yell at him to keep his hands off her but didn't. He would go slow. Walk easy. Quietly. Getting closer all the time. He would wait for his turn. A few more seconds now.

Kane spoke as they came within easy range. His hands were empty but his jacket was open. Jamison saw the butt of an automatic pistol hanging under his coat in a long shoulder holster.

Kane nodded, then glanced up toward the high ground near the building and made it very obvious to everyone.

"Good morning, Mr. Jamison. Mr. Drummond. Everyone okay here?"

Drummond started to talk, the politician's ways coming right back to him.

"Hello, Jack. Nice of you to come this morning."

Jamison would not look at Melissa, not even a glance. God, how he wanted to look her over and check for injuries, but he knew Kane would be watching for it, waiting for the second he looked over to check on her, maybe say something to her. Kane would use that lapse of concentration to kill him.

He glued his eyes to Kane and settled for her blurry image at the edge of his focus, her dark features offset by a tan overcoat, which was probably Kane's. Then he spoke quietly, watching Kane's eyes, knowing they would give him the first warning that the fight was about to start.

"There's not much for us to talk about, Kane," he said. "Drummond for Melissa. I'm prepared to trade and walk away. Are you?"

Kane stepped from behind Melissa and left her alone as he walked over to Jamison and stood still, right in front of him, his arms loose and hanging all the way down. Kane had no protection at all, but didn't act as if that bothered him. It was a damn gutsy move.

"I can understand your hurry, Mr. Jamison, so let's call it a deal. Good luck to you both." He backed away, one step toward the street as if it was all over now. He nodded for Melissa to go to Jamison.

Slowly, she shifted sides, taking her time, carefully avoiding Jamison's line of fire. He was proud of her for thinking like that and a little surprised. She stepped beside him and turned around.

Drummond moved next, took his first step toward Kane. It was an awkward swap of prisoners, agonizingly slow, pregnant with the seeds of treachery. And this was just the exchange. Jamison still had to get out of here with Melissa alive. He looked up toward the high ground, the same place Kane kept glancing, and checked for shooters but didn't see any.

Kane held up his big left hand, the palm facing Drummond.

"Don't bother coming to me, Senator. I'm afraid you're on your own. I want nothing more to do with you."

Drummond stopped halfway between the two men and looked confused. Jamison looked at him, then at Kane, suddenly very worried and growing more so by the second. If Kane didn't want Drummond, why the trade? What was going on here? Was this just a ploy to get them here so Kane could kill them?

He wouldn't wait for the answer, but whipped his pistol up and aimed it at Kane to shoot him in the face, suddenly feeling terribly alone. He pulled back on the trigger, hoping that something made sense before he started popping caps.

Kane just stood there, staring back, gazing into the bore of Jamison's Beretta as the trigger traveled and drew the hammer back. Melissa screamed while Jamison watched for the crazy man, wanting to make sure the decision to kill Kane was his own. The crazy man seemed to be gone, maybe for good. It was just Jamison now, aiming down his sights at the middle of Kane's big face, trying to decide, knowing it was time to kill or be killed.

If he died here, Melissa would be on her own, alone and unprotected, vulnerable to being victimized once again. It didn't take much in that way of thinking before he squeezed the trigger harder and increased the speed of its travel. Kane watched him with an interested curiosity in his eyes.

The muscles in Kane's face suddenly jumped, made Jamison flinch and almost finish his draw of the trigger. Kane shouted something as he reached over and pushed Melissa toward the protection of a concrete retaining wall. He was still an easy target for Jamison and not much of a threat.

"Get down!" Kane yelled. "Get down!"

Kane drew his pistol while Jamison fell over Melissa, protecting her with his body. He kept his Beretta pointed at Kane but waited to see where the big man would aim, still ready to kill him if the barrel of his weapon swung anywhere near their direction.

Kane jumped up and beaded his weapon on something Jamison could not see. He fired two shots. The pistol's noise suppresser made the shots nearly silent, but pedestrians in the area saw what he was doing and panicked. Chaos took over and people screamed. It sounded like hundreds of people. Where had they all come from?

Then the background noises faded and Jamison began to hear selectively. A splattering thud up near the building. Kane's weapon seating another round. His own Beretta scraping against the concrete as he hugged the wall. Kane's feet scurrying away, giving the shooters two different target areas.

Jamison popped up and took a quick glance over the wall. He saw Kane's target rise a hundred feet away, screaming, his bloody hands covering his face as he fell into the bushes. Then all hell broke loose.

Drummond started running, tottering away from the wall and into the street with a wobbly, old man's gait. Automatic weapons fire sputtered down from the high ground and stitched a neat line up his back, from his waist to his skull.

Jamison took his aim off Kane, uncomfortable doing it, but having to decide. He peered over the wall and looked for a target, hoping for the chance to start blasting. Gunfire rained down as soon as he did and kept him pinned against the short wall, crouched low over Melissa. He saw Kane catch a burst of rounds high in his right arm and spin around, then muscle his way back against the wall.

One of the gunmen stopped shooting, and Jamison used the opportunity to pop up and fire. As soon as he did Melissa started crawling along the wall toward Kane, distracting Jamison's aim and making him drop back down again. What was she doing? Hell, what was Kane doing? Were they all on the same side now? Was

Jamison safe working from that assumption? Was there really any option? He leaped to his feet and fired six quick rounds for effect, just enough to keep the shooters' heads down until Melissa covered the forty feet of kill zone.

Jamison shouted to Kane, feeling strange in their new alliance but trusting Melissa completely. It was her life he was here to save, so if she wanted to team up with Kane, he would too.

"I'm thinking there are three of them left! They're firing alternately, Kane, so we'll have to rise into their guns no matter how long we wait! Can you still shoot?"

Much of the muscle of Kane's right arm had been blasted away, bloody pieces of meat dotting the sidewalk. His hand and forearm dangled from the denuded bone like a weight on a string. Every time it swung around him, Kane's eyes pinched tight, even as he dropped his pistol and used his left hand to stuff the lifeless right into his waistband. His face was contorted but he didn't make a sound. He picked up his pistol with his left hand and shouted back.

"Yes."

"Okay, let's watch the spray at the next shift of gunfire. Whoever is getting it, the other pop up and unload! Got it?"

Kane nodded, just as Jamison came under heavy fire. Kane jumped up and fired three times with his left hand. Jamison heard one of the shooters cry out as Kane stood there, wide open for a long, long time as if nothing could hurt him, his pistol ready for the next target. Then the high ground fell briefly silent, so Kane crouched back down beside Melissa.

As soon as he did, Kane and Melissa started arguing,

shouting at each other. The gunfire erupted again and Jamison couldn't hear over it. He had no idea what was going on until Melissa jumped up and started running in the direction of Drummond's body. Jamison heard sirens coming and thought maybe she was running to them, but they were still far away and coming from the opposite direction.

"Damn it, Melissa, get down! Get down!"

She looked back at Jamison with a sad smile, as if this were the last time she would see him, then turned and kept running.

Jamison scrambled off the sidewalk, jumped up, and blasted away at the bushes. He emptied his weapon. Store windows shattered and set off the alarms but he stood his ground. He dumped his spent magazine and slammed a fresh one home, started blasting again, five rounds, ten, twelve, fifteen rounds, as fast as he could sight in and shoot.

Kane was up and blasting with him. Then Jamison saw him get hit, then hit again. He was out in the open and took three or four more hits in the chest before he got back against the wall and collapsed in the middle of a huge red puddle.

Melissa was gone. Thank God, she'd made it out alive. Jamison dropped back below the wall, slammed his last magazine home, and hunkered down as the rain of firepower splattered him with shards of chipped and broken concrete. The police were close now. This would all be over soon. He started thinking about ways to get away without having to kill cops. He was proud of Melissa for escaping. Deep-down happy that she was free.

As he sat there listening to the gunfire that couldn't quite hit him, he looked up and saw a gray Chrysler weaving down the street, going fifty or sixty miles an hour. It slid ninety degrees when it got to Jamison, bounced over the curb and onto the sidewalk before it slammed into the wall right beside him. He whipped his pistol around to shoot the driver but stopped when he saw it was Melissa.

"Get in, Peter!"

Jamison ran to the passenger door and started in, catching fire the whole way. He stopped partway into the car and shot twice, then looked down the sidewalk at Kane, who was pinned down and hurt bad, maybe dead, fifty feet away. It might as well have been a mile.

Jamison fired two more shots at the bushes, shouting over the gunfire.

"You alive, Kane? Can you make it?"

Kane was lying on his side with blood pumping from his chest like a natural spring bubbling up out of the ground. He wiggled a little, proved he was still alive by stretching his hand up over the planter wall and firing with his eyes closed.

"No. Get out of here."

Automatic weapons fire shattered the car's windshield and sprayed across the roof. Jamison fired again as he checked on Melissa. She was under the dash and pretty safe, all things considered.

"He's not going to make it, Peter," she shouted, her eyes big and desperate and locked onto his. "Come on, get in. Leave him!"

Jamison looked at her face, then looked back at Kane and fired five shots up the steps. What should he do, hotfoot it through this shit after that guy? It would be suicide, and who was Kane to deserve that kind of sacrifice? He should throw himself into the car and let Melissa haul his ass out of there.

But something made him want to get Kane. He found himself lost in time, staring at another victim who lay on the ground, hurt and scared. It was Kane, all right, no question about it, but all Jamison could see was a memory of Melissa, raped and beaten and left to suffer on a Delaware beach. The memory made him feel dirty and helpless.

But this time he didn't have to live with the feeling. This time he could stop it. This time he would not fail.

It wasn't the crazy man telling him to do it, either. It was something as powerful as the crazy man, except completely different. Something that gave Jamison the choice. Go, or don't go, entirely his decision.

Peace washed away the dirt and shame and poured energy and confidence into him. Then he was running. By God, running like nature's finest athlete. He felt happy and good and honest, running through the firefight, making each and every decision himself. When to shoot, who to shoot, when to slow. No crazy man dragging him along, no, sir, this was all his own doing. Going back to save someone who needed him, someone who had just helped him save Melissa. Absolutely determined not to fail again.

He got to Kane and knelt down, saw a sniper working his way down through the bushes, fired once, and got him.

"Let's go, Kane! Help me get you out of here."

Kane's bloody hand was stretched wide open, trying to cover three holes in his chest. The blood was pumping through his fingers, gushing out in a thick, frothy foam. He tried to struggle to his knees but couldn't.

"I can't do it. Go."

Jamison jumped into the open and waited, knowing there were still two shooters left. Then he saw one of them. Just a little of his head, checking Kane's Chrysler. Jamison took careful aim and fired. The shooter rocked back, his body lifted up by the impact, his entire torso a target. Jamison fired again and now there was only one left, dug in deep at the far end, near the entrance to Harborplace.

"We're going together, Kane. Let's move."

Jamison had all the strength now. Much more strength than normal. Crazy Man strength, but without the crazy man. He sat Kane up and shoved his left hand under his armpit, the pain of his infected bullet wound blistering its way through his mind and forcing him to scream in Kane's ear.

He dragged Kane sideways so he could keep shooting with his gun hand, firing at the last sniper once every three seconds, just enough to keep his head down. He helped Kane struggle his way into the car, then dove in on top of him while Melissa climbed up behind the wheel, put it in reverse, and stomped on the gas. The tires spun and the smoke rose and for an instant they just sat there as hundreds of horses failed to produce an inch of movement. When the tires finally stuck, the Chrysler shot out into the street, screeching and leaning wildly as Melissa whipped the wheel around and dropped the gearshift into drive.

And then they were gone.

# CHAPTER TWENTY

The emergency room doctors treated Jamison's wounds in less than two hours. He would heal fairly well, they said, after a few days of observation and several weeks of recovery. Jamison wandered away while they filled out the admitting forms and was now leaning against the wall outside Kane's hospital room, wondering what was wrong with Melissa.

He understood why they hadn't talked on the way to the hospital. Her top priority had been his wounds, Kane's life, and their own survival. But they were safe now. Melissa had smuggled his pistol in under her coat. He'd checked every room of the entire floor and pissed off all the nurses in the pre-op area, then watched the elevators and stairwells with the concealed Beretta ready and loaded with shells he'd found in Kane's glove compartment.

She sat on the bench near him but didn't move, just looked down, cradling her head in her hands. Maybe the stress of the shoot-out had been too much for her, or maybe it was the relief of being free, that overwhelming feeling of deliverance. In either case, Jamison knew she wanted time alone, and though he wasn't sure of her reasons, he understood the need. He would give her all the time she wanted. He was anxious for her to feel better so he could sit down beside her, stroke her fingers, look into her brown eyes, and tell her their breakup had been his fault. He understood that clearly now, and was glad to have a second chance.

The elevator rang. Jamison reached under the jacket that hung off his right shoulder and wrapped his fingers around his pistol, prepared to yank it out and start blasting. Maybe it wasn't over yet after all. Maybe there was more dying left ahead.

The elevator doors popped open and Blevins burst out and ran toward Jamison, his men crashing down the bright white corridor in dark uniforms like an invading army. Blevins led the pack, staring at the sling on Jamison's arm and the bandages wrapped around his middle. As he got close the other agents dropped out of the herd, one by one, and stationed themselves along the hall. Most of the nurses stopped what they were doing and watched while a head nurse made a mad grab for each passing soldier and demanded to know what was going on.

Blevins ran all the way, then stopped in front of Jamison and set down a briefcase he'd been swinging along the hall.

"What the hell happened, Peter? I just got your message that you were here. Damn, are you all right?"

He poked a finger at Jamison's arm, hit the bullet hole hard, and made him jerk away. Melissa rose from the bench and stepped up beside Jamison. A bewildered look crossed Blevins's face and stayed there as he leaned over and gave her a hug. He backed away, looked at the huge bloodstains all over her blue dress, then snuggled up and hugged her again, his bulky body armor and weapons making the maneuver awkward and comical.

"You, Melissa, are a sight for sore eyes."

She smiled and looked shyly at Blevins. "So are you, Rich. Been a long time."

"You're not kidding. You okay?" He lifted her hands and spread them apart, leaned left and right, looked her up and down.

She rose up on her toes and kissed his cheek. "I'm fine. Thanks for worrying about me."

"Sure." He turned back to Jamison, still looking confused but quite a bit calmer. "I heard about the shootout and Drummond getting killed. The dispatcher said two men and a woman got away. I figured the woman to be Melissa. Hoped one of the men was you, that you'd stayed alive long enough to cause that kind of trouble. Who was the other man?"

Jamison lifted his right thumb like a hitchhiker back at Kane's room. "Jack Kane."

"The security man from Dillon? I searched his house earlier."

"He brought Melissa to me."

"No shit? Man, I should've picked up a program when this show started so I'd know who the players were. It would have made everything a whole lot easier."

"No doubt about it."

"He really brought her to you? Got shot up during the exchange, I guess?"

"Yes."

Blevins couldn't keep his hands away from Jamison's arm, prodding around, seeing how badly it really hurt, making Jamison flinch and eye him suspiciously.

"Well, good for him. Was he badly wounded, or was that just a lot of noise over nothing, like this little thing?" He stopped prodding and his grin grew bigger. "Through and through?"

Jamison swiveled around to move his bad arm out of Blevins's reach. "Yes. The bullet went right on through, no problem. Drummond's bodyguard did it last night, okay, so will you leave it alone now?"

"What's with the mummy wrap around your stomach?"

"Do you really care, or are you just morbidly curious?"

Blevins laughed and banged his fist into Jamison's good shoulder.

"Just curious."

Jamison groaned, feeling all of his pain now, but also feeling some of the relief that was making Blevins so giddy.

"Give me a break. I ache in places I didn't know I had."

"How bad did Kane get it?"

"Took several hits and was barely alive when we got here."

"Will he live?"

"He's in bad shape. Doctors were amazed he's alive at all."

Blevins lowered his eyes. "Shame."

"He's a strong man. He might make it."

"And Drummond is definitely dead?"

Jamison tried to lift an eyebrow, but even it hurt. Hurt so bad he thought about laughing, glad to be noticing pain again. It amazed him that he'd been able to shut it off and keep going. He thought about sewing himself together last night and could not imagine how he'd done it. Remembering the feel of the thread drawn through his skin made his knees weak.

"Drummond looked dead to me, Rich, but I didn't hang around long enough to check." He massaged the itchy bullet hole of his swollen arm. "He has to be dead, though. Took way too many rounds to survive."

"Well, the hell with him, anyway. Did he tell you what he'd been doing, the crimes he'd been pulling?"

"Some. Do you think you can stop the others who went along with him?"

"We hope to."

"Do you still have my data?"

Blevins shifted to his other leg, looked at Melissa again, and smiled big. "Man, she sure looks great."

"Yes, she does. Do you have my research data?"

Blevins looked at the floor and dug at it a little with his boot. "Well, that's a problem. I'm afraid your stuff is missing."

Jamison pushed off the wall, banged his swollen arm in the process.

"Ouch! What happened?"

"It was stolen from our safe. I tried to get copies made earlier, as a precaution against something like this, but it was already gone."

"Then it must have been an agent."

"No other way. A clerk, maybe, but definitely FBI."

Melissa nudged in between them. "Will the FBI still be able to prosecute those politicians and corporations who worked with Drummond?"

"Well . . . sure. Yeah, I can still build a case against them, at least the guys at the top, the ones who controlled everyone else. There'll be a lot of low-level guys we'll never get, but I can put the head men in jail and leave their organization without any leadership. It should crumble pretty quickly after that."

"Good," Melissa said, then slumped a little and sighed. "It would be nice to get the soldiers, too."

"I think we're screwed on that score. Warden's diary identified a lot of them, but we can't use it because your data was part of the probable cause for that search. And that, my friends, is the law."

"There has to be some way to arrest everyone involved."

"Sorry, works out that way sometimes. It's American justice, Peter. You can't fight the system."

Jamison pushed hair off his forehead. "Drummond did."

"You want to be like Drummond?"

"Course not."

"Neither do I. If that means letting some small potatoes get away, then that's the price I'll pay. I have faith in the system. Although the wheels of justice grind slowly, they do grind. Sometimes it just takes those big ol' wheels a while to be effective." He turned to Melissa.

"Don't worry though, even if we can't arrest the army that followed Drummond, and even if someone takes Drummond's place and keeps the corruption going, eventually we'll stop it. It's our job. We take that kind of thing pretty seriously."

Melissa stepped into Blevins's face. "What do you mean, if someone takes Drummond's place? You think someone else will take over?"

"Don't know, really." He looked at Jamison and locked up with him. "You didn't tell her?"

Jamison leaned back and grimaced as he shook his head, then looked away. "Haven't had a chance."

Blevins frowned.

"Well, for several years now a rumor's been going around that someone was building a power base, planning to topple the current leadership of that criminal enterprise. It may or may not be true, but my guess is that if the rumor is circulating, the chances are good that someone will make a move. It depends on how well connected they are. With Drummond dead, there will be a huge power vacuum that someone will try to fill. You know the old saying, nature abhors a vacuum? Well, it's not much different in criminal organizations. The good news is that the person angling for the top spot is probably near the top already and should go down with the rest of the leaders we arrest."

Melissa tossed her hair back. It moved as a clump, Brewer's dried blood still matting it together. "It's unbelievable that you can't be sure you'll destroy them."

"How about your friend in there, Kane? Think he might have a lead on your data? Like I said, it would be nice evidence to have."

Jamison didn't answer until he'd caught Melissa's eye, saw how she'd taken Blevins's news. "Let's try to ask him. Melissa, you coming?"

Melissa picked at her hair and tried to separate the

strands from the blood. "In a minute. I want to get this awful stuff off me first."

Jamison watched her walk toward the bathroom, then told Blevins a little more about Kane, speaking with respect and admiration, almost as if Kane were already dead. Even though the nurses were monitoring him at their stations, he knew they already figured him for dead. It was obvious by the way they treated him. Special and gentle, as if giving him some kind of Hippocratic last rites. Kane had buzzed for a nurse about an hour ago for her help in making a short phone call to say good-bye to his family. Jamison helped the nurse prop the phone against Kane's ear and dial the number, then walked out with her. She was sniffling as she left, already giving up.

Kane's eyes were open when Jamison entered with Blevins but he couldn't tell if he was awake or dead. He didn't seem to be breathing. There were tubes and bandages all over his chest and arms, and monitors beeping around his head. Then Kane blinked, waved them in with his left hand by making little circles in the air.

"How you feeling, Jack?"

Kane coughed, whispered. "Pretty good, actually."

Jamison looked along Kane's body, saw the destruction of countless bullet wounds, and knew he had to be lying. "Good," he said. "I'm glad."

Kane tried to smile. Somehow he actually managed to do it.

"I'm really sorry to bother you, but we need to find a white box of evidence, the stuff I discovered at Dillon."

Kane coughed again, deep down in his chest and sticky wet. "I know about it."

Jamison leaned closer. "Who stole it?"

Kane coughed some more. This time his body went into convulsions and his monitors went off, buzzing steady tones. Two nurses rushed in and shoved Jamison aside, started fidgeting with the machine and examining Kane until Kane amazed them by getting himself under control, lying there with a feeble grin on his pale face, staying perfectly still while the nurses asked each other questions. After a few minutes they backed out of the room, looking at Kane as if they couldn't imagine how he'd done it.

"Yes," he whispered. "I know who has it."

Jamison moved in very close, tried not to sound excited. "Who?"

Kane shifted in the bed, squeezed his eyes shut, and kept them that way for ten or twelve seconds, his face screwed up in a painful grimace. After he settled down he opened his eyes and looked right at Blevins, who was just coming over from setting his briefcase on a nearby tray table.

"I recognize you," Kane said. "You're the FBI agent, Blevins."

"Guilty."

Kane smiled with clenched teeth. "There's an agent in your office named Strick." Kane coughed some more. A big bubble of thick blood formed on his lips, popped, rolled off his mouth and onto the pillow. Neither Jamison nor Blevins wiped it away.

"Strick was instructed to take the evidence from the vault, then hold on to it until he heard from me. I'm sure he still has it."

Blevins's face tightened into stone. "That bastard, I'm going to crush his balls." He marched to the door and opened it. Jamison could see chaos in the hall.

Someone was screaming off in the distance and Jamison panicked for the second it took to be sure the voice wasn't Melissa's. Agents were running to new positions, pushing people out of their way as they crashed down the hall toward the screaming woman. Jamison watched the turmoil as the nurse gave Blevins directions to a phone, kept watching for several more seconds. Blevins made a quick glance back into the room from the doorway to let Jamison know he'd just been appointed to guard Kane.

Kane was smiling and seemed to like Blevins's threat toward Strick. He was still chuckling about it when his chest went into a spasm. More blood rolled out of his mouth. He grabbed Jamison's sleeve and held on to his arm with a gorilla's strength until he finished coughing. Then he composed himself again, acting like a man who had some unfinished business he needed to wrap up before leaving. Jamison looked at the blood oozing from a half dozen bullet wounds, then at the smile on Kane's face. He couldn't begin to understand the reservoir from which Kane drew that much strength and control.

"Jamison, several men were assigned to kill you. Some are from Dillon, some are freelancers. Some are the FBI's. It will be hard for you to get away, maybe impossible, but it's your only chance. You need to get out of the States and lie low for a long time."

"What if I don't? What if I stay and make a stand?" Jamison was hovering closer now, trying to hear every word. Blevins muttered his way back into the room, bitching and moaning about whatever had happened outside, then joining Jamison beside Kane's bed.

"Then you'll die over this," Kane said, glancing at

Blevins as he said it. "You've done very well so far, but they'll find you and kill you. My bet is you'll die right here in this room, along with me. I'm sure they know I'm here and they can't allow me to live, not after this morning. They will be here soon, could be any minute now, and you'll be killed in the bargain."

Blevins raised his walkie-talkie and held it in front of his mouth but hesitated before he keyed the mike. "They may be here already, guys. Someone just killed the nurse in charge of the medication cart, stole a syringe and some succinylcholine, or however the hell you say it. Some kind of a paralyzing drug used in anesthesia."

Melissa rushed in and spun around, pushed the door shut, then held it closed, bracing herself against it to hold back an army. Jamison watched her, his hand on his pistol, waiting for someone to force the door. Twenty seconds later she relaxed and straightened up, looked a little embarrassed as she walked to him, grabbed his good arm, and squeezed it hard. He looked her over and noticed that she hadn't gotten much of the blood out of her hair. He also saw that she was angry. Or was it worry? She threw another panicked glance toward the door as if she wanted to warn him about what was going on outside. He closed his eyes and nodded that he already knew about the dead nurse.

"I'm not running," Jamison said. "I've got a job to finish."

Kane's body convulsed again. He closed his eyes, squeezed them very hard for about a minute before he opened them again. A tear rolled from the corner of his left eye and tracked into his ear.

"That's too bad."

Blevins motioned for Jamison to step away with him. The two of them left Kane with Melissa beside his bed and met near the windows. Blevins put his hand on Jamison's shoulder.

"Don't be an idiot, Peter. You're not staying around here and that's all there is to it."

Jamison whispered, tried to keep Melissa from hearing. "You know Melissa won't let this go after coming this far. You heard her, she wants all of those people prosecuted. If she's staying, I'm staying. There's no choice here for me."

"I need you alive. Hell, I need Melissa alive, too. You guys are my witnesses. You'll have to validate the evidence when I get it back. I can't let you hang around here and get yourselves killed. Too many people have died already."

Melissa walked over as Blevins finished, probably heard most of what he said. "He's right, Peter. I hate it, but he is. We've done what we can for now. If the FBI can make a case, they'll need us alive to help them. If they can't make it, well, we wouldn't be able to make one either. We'd just get killed for nothing."

Blevins kept watching the door. Jamison noticed that his hand was wrapped around the grip of the MP5, which hung on a strap from his shoulder, his finger resting on the trigger, his aim following his eyes. It was clear that Blevins was expecting trouble any minute now. Jamison touched the butt of his own pistol, just for the assurance.

"We'll make the case," Blevins said. "It's just a question of how deep we'll be able to penetrate. We'll shave off the top few layers with or without your data, and that should destroy the organization. It's pointless to die now, no matter how you look at it."

Jamison looked at Kane lying in the bed across the room, thinking how he'd been ready to kill him just a few hours ago. Then he thought about the men who had already died on both sides. The good ones and the bad ones. Ted Bronovich. Two agents at the Coalition. That ugly animal Butler. The two killers at Casey's house. Three men at Harborplace. Drummond and his bodyguard. Kane, maybe. And how many had Blevins killed since Monday?

Then he thought about how many more would die. This was shaping up into a war, surely, and war meant casualties. If he was going to do any more to help his side win, he and Melissa could not be among those killed in action.

"Okay, Rich. Let's talk about what you have in mind."

"It's real simple. The Justice Department wants to take away your old lives and give you new ones. They've got a million bucks to carry you two through to old age, assuming you'll testify. So all I want is for you to take the money and get your ass . . . Melissa's, too . . . to Costa Rica. Hide out there under our protection for six months, a year maybe. Live like sheiks, have a great time. By then everything will be cool and you can come back. If I need you, I'll know where to find you. We have a legal attaché there who will be your contact. I know the guy well, which is why I picked Costa Rica. You can trust him."

Melissa stuck her hands underneath Blevins's bulletproof vest, grabbed his shoulders, and gave him a hard squeeze. "Rich, you swear you'll get the leaders, the top levels of corruption. I don't care about the followers. As you said, they'll fade away without leadership. But you have to promise me you'll get the leaders, get them all, leave no one capable of running that organization."

Blevins had to think about this. It was obvious by the way he raised his hand to his mouth and held it there. Jamison knew from that simple action that whatever he said next would be sacred.

"I promise. I've got enough evidence, even without the data you guys collected. Sackett, the SAC of my office, was in on the corruption, and he's already made a sworn statement to U.S. Attorney Riley and has agreed to testify. He said the organization was highly fragmented but that he knows a few people at the top. Almost none below him, though. At least his testimony will help me pry the door open and from there I can keep moving up the list. If Kane makes it, I'm sure he can feed me a lot of information that will allow me to work in both directions and pick off most of the soldiers who did Drummond's work; but even if he doesn't make it, yeah, I'll get the top layer. I'm sure. I promise."

"What's going to happen to Sackett?"

"He's out. After he testifies in closed court, he'll be out of the FBI. I'm not going to prosecute him, though. In fact, I'm going to let him keep his secret, even from his family. As far as anyone at the office knows, he's still the SAC and will be until this all shakes out."

"That's good for our side, I guess. Doesn't seem right, though. Kane's dying and Sackett gets to walk?"

"I need his testimony, it's as simple as that, but don't think he's not being punished. Sackett's worked for the Bureau since he was twenty. Started as a clerk, then

went to college and retreaded through as an agent.
Now he'll be without a pension, respect, or money. I'd
say that's pretty severe punishment."

"I see your point."

Melissa picked up Jamison's hand and caressed it
without looking at him. "I'm willing to hide out if that's
what you think best."

Jamison shrugged, couldn't think much beyond his
fingers being stroked by Melissa's hand. "I guess."

Blevins sighed as if he'd expected this to be much
harder. "Good, let's go. There's already a dead surgical
nurse down the hall. If her death is related to Kane, I
don't want you guys here any longer than necessary."

Jamison stepped over to Kane's bed and stood there a
few seconds, waiting until Kane opened his eyes.

"I've got to go. Thanks for bringing Melissa back to
me. I owe you." He touched him on the shoulder.

Kane looked up and grinned with his teeth locked together. "Call it even. That was really something, seeing
you trot down the sidewalk through that rain of gunfire
to help me." He closed his eyes and his body tightened
all over. Then he slumped down, deflated, and grinning.
"It was really dumb, but amazing. Thanks."

Jamison smiled with him and shook his head. He felt
good about himself. Then he turned to Blevins.

"Ready?"

"Yeah," he said, and then spoke to Kane. "Don't
worry, big guy, we'll keep you safe. I have men stationed right outside your door. They won't let any
strangers in here."

He headed to the door and Jamison followed, walking with Melissa. When Blevins opened the door

Melissa stopped and turned. She gave Kane a sad look, then squeezed Jamison's arm.

"Peter, give me a few minutes alone with him, please. I want to thank him for helping me and for bringing us back together. It won't take long."

Jamison understood, even though he didn't know the story between her and Kane and couldn't guess what Kane might have done for her. For all he knew, she might owe him her life. He walked out into the hall with Blevins, closed the door and waited, and watched the body of the dead nurse being moved to another room.

# CHAPTER TWENTY-ONE

Melissa walked the few steps to Kane's bed, stood over him, and stroked his forehead. She looked into his eyes and loved the way they looked back at her with complete understanding. They were nice eyes, gentle and peaceful, with absolutely no doubt in them. No fear and no wonder. He seemed to know everything about her, even her deepest secrets. He had acted like that since the first time she'd met the great Jack Kane, face-to-face in an eight-by-nine prison cell.

He struggled to lift his hand and held it in the air about four inches from the bed. He was so sweet, waiting for her to hold it. She picked it up, took the strain of its weight, and caressed his fingers. She stroked them, marveling at the strong muscles in his thick fingers, feeling an odd, wonderful kinship with this big man.

Kane gave her a loving look, the same favorite-uncle

kind of look he gave her in prison after he'd pushed Jitters out of her cell. He licked his lips, cleared his throat, and squeezed her hand very gently.

"You're going to kill me now, aren't you?"

She stroked his forehead again, gently pushed the hair in front into a neat line.

"Shh, it will be all right. You won't feel anything."

"I don't feel much of anything now."

She smiled. "I'm glad. You're not in too much pain?"

"No. The drugs."

"They've given you a lot?"

He glanced away for a second without moving his head, then came back to meet her eyes.

"Melissa, do you really think you can run the organization?"

She looked around the room, then came back to him with quiet confidence. "Of course. Who better than me? After all, I am Richard Corley's daughter. I've spent my life learning how the organization works. I know all the players now. When the FBI eliminates the current leaders, I'll be the only one who knows everything, the only person who knows how to keep the machinery running. It will be easy for me to take over. No one will know it's me, at least not for a while. I'll do a good job, Kane, I promise. I'll make my father proud."

Kane frothed out some blood and Melissa dabbed it off his mouth.

"I don't think so, Melissa. In the end, your father regretted what he'd done. He would be impressed by the way you orchestrated this whole thing, though, getting the FBI to eliminate your competition."

Kane's body trembled, but he gritted his teeth and let none of the pain show in his eyes.

She pinched his cheek. "My, my, aren't you the clever one? How long have you known?"

"Been suspicious for years, ever since you went to work for the Coalition and started digging around. Every time I heard the rumor that someone was trying to take over, I thought of you, but you hid your plan well, and I wasn't really convinced until I saw you meet Jamison at Jonah's Bar last week. I knew—" He closed his eyes and stiffened his body for ten seconds but kept talking through the pain. "I knew you didn't love him, that you were just going to use him. The same way you used Senator Armstrong, dating him and then killing him after he gave you the names he knew. Do I have that about right?"

She adjusted his pillow, trying to make him comfortable as she spoke.

"It's funny, you know. I tried to kill Peter once, too, had some men attack us on a Delaware Beach. But he really surprised me by killing one of the men I'd hired and scaring the other one so badly he ran away." She giggled and glanced away for a second, then shook her head as if not believing her own memory.

"I tried to stop the man from running but couldn't, so I stripped down and acted like I'd been raped. You should have seen me, tearing at my clothes on the sandy beach, trying to get my tight jeans off before he came over the dune. I tell you, it was a surprise to hear him coming to help me."

"He's a good man. I'm not surprised by him anymore. I was once, but not now."

She felt some pain in her heart and stopped talking long enough to figure out why. She hoped it wasn't for Peter, at least not just for him alone. Maybe it was for all men like him, men who left themselves wide open to being hurt, used and abused, over and over again, for love.

"Jack, you know I don't really want to kill you, but you crossed the line and went back to the other side. Are you really serious about helping Blevins and the FBI?"

"Yes."

"Then I'm truly sorry to do this, but it does me no good to take over the power and then allow you and Blevins to destroy my army. I've spent too long figuring out how to eliminate the leaders without hurting the forces they control. There's no way I can let you live."

"I know."

She pulled the syringe out of her pocket, picked up the IV tube, and gave Kane a silly grin.

"There's a dead nurse down the hall who didn't need this anymore."

Kane watched her, almost looked amused. "What about Jamison? Are you going to kill him too?"

She stopped with the syringe inserted into the Y-site injection port, her thumb resting on the plunger but not pushing it.

"Now, that's a good question. Truth is, I've grown fond of him, of the way he treats me. I guess, if he'll go along with what I'm doing, I won't. I'm not an animal, you know. I don't kill because I like it. Besides, I need love, too, and Peter's a very nice man. He wouldn't be a bad person to grow old with."

"The Jamison I've seen the last couple of days won't go along with you. You know that as well as I do."

She flipped her hair away from her face. "He might. He loves me."

She pushed the plunger of the syringe and the muscle

relaxant swept into the IV, then into Kane's arm. She watched the fluid enter his body, then put the syringe back in her pocket.

"Good-bye," he said as his hand fell to his stomach. She ran her fingers through his hair once more and fixed it neatly. "Give my love to Daddy when you see him."

Kane's eyes rolled back and the alarms went off. She raced to the door and threw it open, then shrieked as loudly as she could. "Get a doctor in here, quick! He's dying, he's dying!"

She stood in the doorway and watched to see what would happen. The corridor was plenty chaotic already with frightened-looking nurses watching their backs while FBI agents milled around with their weapons ready. Several nurses and two doctors raced toward Kane's room and pushed past Melissa. It took less than a minute to pronounce Kane dead.

She went back into Kane's room with them and stood there crying, waiting for Blevins and Jamison to shoulder their way into the crowd, expecting Jamison to put his arm around her, pull her into his chest, and say something comforting, tell her it would be all right, that Kane was going to die anyway.

Jamison didn't come into the room, neither did Blevins. She watched the door, looking out into the hall each time someone opened it until curiosity moved her feet in that direction.

Jamison kept staring at the four-inch screen in Blevins's palm, even after Melissa walked out of the frame and headed toward the door. He knew he would be able to see her in a second if he would just look up and over the heads of a dozen agents. She would be standing at the other end of the long hall, right at Kane's door, looking for him. But he didn't want to see her.

Blevins pulled the headphones off his head, reached over, and pulled the other pair off Jamison's ears and let them drop around his neck.

"You okay, Peter? Man, I'm real sorry."

Jamison couldn't take his eyes off the screen. He kept them glued onto Kane's body, hoping and praying that Kane wasn't really dead, that Melissa hadn't really killed him. If Kane would just move a little, maybe Jamison would wake up from this nightmare and everything would be okay again.

Blevins let him stare for another minute before he snapped the lid over the small screen, wound up the wire that connected it to the receiver of the video recorder. He was cussing, quietly.

Jamison stared at the spot where Blevins had held the video screen, scared to death that if he looked up he would see Melissa walking down the hallway toward him. His heart was already breaking so deeply he couldn't feel any other parts of his body, even the shot-up parts. He was absolutely sure it would kill him to look into her eyes.

He turned in Blevins's direction but didn't look at him. "You need me anymore or can I go?"

Blevins put his hand on Jamison's back and rubbed it as a father might.

"You want to say anything to Melissa before I arrest her?"

Jamison kept his eyes down. He still hadn't looked at anyone since he watched her kill Kane.

"I don't know what I'd say, Rich." He sighed, and his lip quivered. He bit it so hard that blood squirted into his mouth.

"I understand. If you're ready to take off, I'll assign some agents to go with you. I want you out of here."

Jamison raised his eyes, but lifted them past everyone around him and looked at the ceiling. He fluttered his eyelids a few times.

"I guess I'm ready, but I'd like to know how you knew she would do that. How did you know she was the one trying to take over the organization?"

"I didn't. Didn't even suspect her until Kane called me."

"Kane called you? When?"

"About an hour ago. A nurse helped him place it. I was almost here when I got the call, just a couple blocks away. He told me everything, all about the men he'd hired to kill you and that Melissa was probably going to kill him. She was the only one who could take over the fund. He suspected her of orchestrating this whole thing. He knew he was going to die, Peter, but he promised to convince her he wasn't so she would have to do something about him. That's why it took me so long to get here. I had to go back to the office and get the briefcase camera and recorder."

"Damn you, Rich! You let a man die just so you could put Melissa in prison?"

Blevins didn't look away, just stood there and took everything Jamison's look was saying. "It was hard to do. Man, you know I care about Melissa, almost as much as you do. I had to stand here and watch her kill a man, knowing I could run down the hall and stop it, keep him alive, and keep her out of jail. It was about the hardest thing I've ever done. Kane wanted it this way. He wanted to end his life doing the right thing, and I wanted to stop the corruption." He paused for a few seconds. "So did you. Remember?"

Jamison took a few paces, then pointed to the recorder. "I bet that tape won't be admissible. Even if it is, her attorney will make you look like an animal for standing by and allowing her to do it. What you've done is despicable."

"You're right, her attorney will have a field day with it but it will be admissible, Peter, and lead to a conviction. I'm sorry, but that's the way it'll go. I had no choice. I hope you'll understand one day."

Jamison snapped onto him and thought about hitting him with his good right arm. "You realize you're talking about the woman I love?"

"Hey, don't forget that she tried to have you killed on that beach in Delaware."

"I never said she loved me. Hell, for all I know she still might want to kill me. I can't help that, any more than I can help the way I feel about her. Damn you, Rich, people overlook the sins of people they love. You're a parent. Could your sons ever do anything bad enough to make you stop loving them?"

Blevins bit his top lip, then sighed. "No."

"Then don't hold your breath hoping I'll understand someday. I hate you for what you've done and I'll always hate you for it." Jamison spun on his heels and headed toward the elevator.

"Wait a minute, where are you going? You need protection, someone to keep you safe so you can testify. My men found Strick and recovered your evidence, but without you it's worthless. Where can I find you?"

Jamison jammed his finger into the elevator button and turned to Blevins as he waited for the doors to open.

"Go to hell, Rich. You just go to hell."

The doors opened and Jamison stepped in, turned around, and watched Blevins staring back. As the doors began to close Blevins turned an angry face to some other agents and pointed at Melissa. "Put her under arrest for murder. Do it!"

# CHAPTER TWENTY-TWO

Jamison rode the elevator down but almost forgot to get off. He just stood there, replaying the last few minutes while other passengers stepped out and walked away to make room for more people to get on. The closing doors brought him back, signaled him to move, made him lunge through the crowd, hit the safety bar, and jump out. He had no desire to go back up to the floor where Kane lay dead and Melissa stood under arrest.

He felt the stares as he walked through the lobby of the hospital, his jacket still hanging off his shoulder, concealing his Beretta. His shirt had been cut off by the emergency room nurses, so the rest of his chest was bare except for the gauze and dressing wrapped around his middle, and the sling that supported his left arm. He went through the automatic doors and kept going, out into the cold winter air, tugging his jacket onto his

good arm and over his sling, zipping it as best he could.
There was nowhere to go, and no plan for when he got
there. He thought about all that had happened since
Blevins arrived at the hospital and blamed him for the
disastrous turn of events. Everything was fine until he
showed up. Melissa was back with him and safe, and he
was going to live. Kane was dying, but what the hell,
that didn't bother Jamison now. He didn't care about
Kane anymore and regretted saving him from the sidewalk slaughter, hated him just as much as he hated
Blevins.

After a few minutes of walking, he caught a cab and
told the driver to drop him at the front door of
Melissa's building, the one place where he could bring
her back to him. He wandered through her rooms for
several minutes, picking her clothes off the floor. He
stood the shattered bookcase back up, his good arm
and bandaged side straining against its weight. He went
to the bathroom and stared at the spot where she'd
stood wrapped in a towel, realizing now that she was
just toying with him as he stepped out of the shower
and stood naked in front of her, winding him up with
desire and fueling his devotion. He understood what
she was capable of and despised what she'd done to
him. He wanted to exorcise her and walk away from
this whole mess, forget he had ever loved her.

But his heart belonged to Melissa Corley and there
wasn't a damn thing he could do about it, even if she
had never loved him. He felt like a kid in school, in love
with the Homecoming Queen who would never give
him two looks in the same month but loving her anyway, getting sweaty palms and a thumping chest when
she passed in the hall.

He set up a chair, pushed some of the debris away, and sat down to think of what to do next. It wasn't easy. Right now, it was incredibly difficult for him to even imagine a future, much less make plans to get him there. He wanted desperately to live in the past, just a few hours past, when Melissa was beside him and his arm was around her, getting their lives together in a way he'd never thought possible.

And now, suddenly she was completely out of his reach, separated from him by Rich Blevins, the FBI, a murder charge, and ultimately, a set of prison bars. They had come so close, just two hours earlier this morning.

He tried to stop thinking about it, kept trying to focus on his task. He kept brainstorming ideas, trying to think of someone to call, and what he could do to help her. Eventually he came up with a terrible idea that was full of holes and what-ifs, a ridiculously simple scheme but a plan all the same, something he could put into action right now, before Blevins moved Melissa too far away from him. The fact that the plan could be easily implemented made him grasp onto it with a fanatic's determination, and ignore that the probability of failure was overwhelming.

He called Sackett first, said exactly what he needed to say, and didn't care if it offended the man or not. Sackett was on his way out anyway. He was going to testify and then walk. Blevins, in a magnanimous gesture to which Melissa wasn't entitled, would keep Sackett's secret and let him live out his life as a mystery to those who worked for him. He would slip away and disappear.

Then Jamison dialed the squad room and demanded

that the squad secretary go into the interrogation room and pull Blevins out.

"Glad you called, Peter. Sorry about earlier. Where are you?"

"Melissa's apartment."

"That's not smart. We've found some of Kane's assassins, but there are more out there. That would be a pretty logical place for them to look for you."

"I don't care."

"Okay, fair enough, you don't care. She's playing you for a fool, you know, and your pathetic little broken heart is going to get you killed. As your friend, I'm telling you she's not worth it. She's a criminal, plain and simple. You've got to see her for what she is."

Jamison felt his heart break all over again, probably the twentieth time today. Blevins was right; it was foolish even to think about saving her.

"I know she's a criminal. I saw what she did."

"Then get with the program! Get bladed, cover your ass. There are some pretty nasty suckers out there who want you dead."

Jamison looked around Melissa's apartment, amazed to have survived this nightmare, aware that he owed Blevins some gratitude for helping.

"You're right, I've got to pull myself out of this."

"Now you're talking."

"One last thing about Melissa."

"Sure, but make it quick."

"I was wondering if you might cut a deal with her. You could use her testimony to convict a lot of others, let her guide you through your investigation."

"A good thought, Peter. Actually, I already considered it, but murdering Kane was a step too far. I can't plead out a murderer."

"Yeah, well, it was a last-ditch idea."

"Not a bad one, either. Just impossible."

"Last question then. Is the money still available? The money you mentioned in the hospital?"

"Sure, a million bucks, transferred from Justice last night. It's locked up in the armory, and it takes two people to open the door. I didn't use the evidence vault because things tend to get lost there."

"Why's the government being so generous? Why so much money?"

"It's not really that much. They figured you'd have extraordinary expenses for a few years, so they added something to cover those expenses to ten years' worth of your current salary. Rounded that number off at a mill."

"You're right. When you put it that way, it's not much money."

"Better than dying, and all you have to do for it is stay alive to testify about your data."

"Fair enough. So when can I get the money and haul ass out of here? You mentioned Costa Rica and that's fine with me, the sooner the better."

"I can meet you with it later. I just need to finish interviewing Melissa, then stop by the bank to get the money converted into whatever instruments you want besides cash."

"Cash will be fine. Let's just do it. I'm starting to get nervous hanging around here."

"Man, that's a lot of cash. How about some bearer—"

"Cash is fine. I don't want to sit on my thumbs while

you do some half-assed banking. Get me out of here before somebody kills me."

"Just hang on, buddy, I'll come and get you. You're at Melissa's apartment? I'm on my way."

"No, the airport. Make me some new identification, and meet me at Delta ticketing with the money and a ticket to any foreign airport that has flights to Costa Rica. One hour. Okay?"

"One hour. See you then."

Jamison hung up and took one last look around Melissa's apartment, at the life he was leaving behind. He was trading a life of engineering, cherry blossom festivals, and weekends in Georgetown for a low-country life in the lesser latitudes. Losing his name, his past, and his connection to everyone he loved or had ever loved him. Going alone to start over in some foreign country. Blevins said it would only be for a few years, but Jamison knew he couldn't mark time that long. He would have to start building a new life right away or go insane. It would become important to him, so giving it up to come back would mean starting over yet again. As impossible as it was to imagine any of that now, with his heart aching and loneliness settling around him like fallout, he was sure it would happen.

There was nothing in the apartment he wanted. He thought about some pictures of him with Melissa, but passed. He walked out the door and down the stairs to the street, then caught a cab to his bank and made a quick stop to close his account before leaving forever.

As Jamison had hoped, Blevins beat him to the rendezvous and was standing against a small piece of wall at Delta ticketing, watching Jamison walk up to him. Blevins had changed back to working clothes, jacket, and tie with a heavy winter overcoat. A brown briefcase dangled from Blevins's hands, centered in front of him with a plastic shopping bag behind it. His eyes darted to Jamison, then searched the area, came back, then searched again. Eyes that expected trouble. Maybe lots of it.

"Come with me," he said as Jamison got close. "There's not much time."

He led the way to a little niche in the wall. Blevins handed him the briefcase.

"One million dollars cash, buddy. The other bag is some new clothes. Be careful because it's your money now. Tough shit if you lose it. Sign this receipt." He pulled a voucher out of his jacket pocket, grew impatient while Jamison read it before signing.

"Here's a ticket to Mexico City." He handed Jamison a fat envelope. "It's a direct flight, booked under your new alias. I had a new passport and matching identification made up for you. It's all in the ticket envelope. When you land, look for a man holding a sign for Calinda El Torridor Hotel. He'll be one of our agents. He'll make sure you lose anyone who might have followed you. Questions?"

Jamison took the packet. "No questions. When will you contact me?"

Blevins held his hand out. When Jamison shook it, he smiled. It made the scab over his eye wrinkle. Was it only last Friday they'd boxed? Not even a week ago? It didn't seem possible.

"I'll call you after you've had a little time to get settled. Do whatever your contact agent tells you. He's there to help you. That's just about his only job now. I've told him how important you are."

"Will do."

"You'd better go. It isn't smart for us to be standing here. Your plane is loading now so get on it. Want me to come with you?"

Jamison smiled. It was all over. Nothing much left to worry about.

"I'll be all right. Just a short walk and a sit-down. Here, take my pistol before I have to throw it in a trash can."

Blevins took a step back and looked Jamison over, then slid the Beretta out of Jamison's waistband and stuck it under his coat. "You know you look like shit, don't you?"

"Haven't had a shower since you and Sackett came to my hotel room."

"You look even worse than that." He chuckled a little, then preened himself like a gorgeous bird.

"I'll clean up when I get where I'm going. These clean clothes will help a lot."

Blevins had started to leave, made his moves but didn't go. But now he looked ready.

"I'll be seeing you, Peter."

"Take care, my friend."

Blevins waved his hand over his shoulder as he walked away. Jamison watched him leave the terminal and saw a car slow down and stop long enough for Blevins to jump in.

Jamison stood there a moment longer, checked the departure time of the flight, and stared at the destination. He pulled the new identification and passport out, then walked over to the trash can and threw the ticket away.

# CHAPTER TWENTY-THREE

Jamison hurried to the Crown Room, hoping it would be empty as usual. Under normal circumstances it would be a good place to meet. Only Delta members had access and few ever stayed long. It was a nice place to kill time between flights, with free phones and beverages, but not nice enough to hang around longer than you needed. Of course, nothing was normal about Jamison's circumstances, so he walked up to the door expecting anything to happen.

He opened the door with his card, stepped inside, and looked around. He figured all along that this might be another trap, that he might take a few steps inside the door and get killed, but it was something he had to do, something absolutely necessary, like a victim's family needing to meet the person who'd killed a loved one.

Closure, that's what it was. Putting it all behind him, then going forward with whatever portion of his old life survived.

The room was empty except for two people sitting on a sofa at the far end, watching him come through the door. Sackett was one, Melissa the other. Jamison stopped when he saw them and decided not to go any farther until he knew what they were thinking. Would Sackett be holding a gun on Melissa, down low where Jamison couldn't see it? Would Melissa think Jamison helped Blevins set her up and look at him with hate in her eyes? He would wait for these answers before moving closer.

Melissa looked surprised to see him. Sackett allowed her to stand up, which was a good sign. He sat there with one leg crossed over the other, watching Jamison's eyes go soft as if part of his reward for bringing her.

She walked over to Jamison, stopped in front of him, and looked like a sad little girl.

"Hi," she said quietly, as her head went down.

Jamison didn't know what to do or say, but didn't want to start babbling. He had to concentrate on what he had to do. Leave all of the unknowns for later. He lifted her chin gently and smiled a little. Then he stepped around her and walked over to Sackett.

"Did you have any trouble?"

Sackett turned his head and looked out the wall of windows, concentrated on an MD-88 rolling by.

"No. There'll be hell to pay when Blevins gets back, though."

"Nobody questioned why you left with her?"

Sackett smirked and chuckled sadly at some joke in

his head. "I'm the SAC, Jamison, the boss. Why would anyone question me?"

Jamison didn't answer. He was destroying Sackett and hated himself for shredding the last bit of the man's self-respect. Exploiting his sad situation and his love for his family and his needs for the future. He was buying Sackett with blood money and was ashamed of himself for doing it.

"Where did Melissa get the clothes?"

"Just some of my wife's things. I called her from work and had her meet me on our way here. I didn't want Ms. Corley walking around in that bloody dress of hers."

Jamison set the briefcase of cash on the floor in front of the couch. Sackett didn't even glance at it, just kept staring at the jet outside the windows.

"Thank you."

Sackett nodded. "I hope it works out for you."

"Yeah, you too. I hope you buy a good life with this money. I swear I'll never tell anyone where you got it. A million dollars should last a pretty long time if you're careful."

Sackett reached for the briefcase handle, flipped it back and forth a few times before he closed his fingers around it. He stood up, took a deep breath, and gave Jamison a loser's smile.

"It doesn't matter, because I'll know. I'll always know what I've done here."

Jamison bit his lip to cut off the temptation to say something more. He held out his hand and Sackett shook it.

"I've already given Ms. Corley a new passport and

ID. A few thousand dollars, too, so I'd make tracks if I were you. Once Blevins finds out she's gone, he's going to shut this airport down. You know that, don't you?"

Jamison kept biting his lip, feeling even more ashamed of himself than he had a moment ago, wondering if he could possibly sink any lower. Sackett was probably a decent guy, an honorable man who'd made a couple of mistakes. Jamison was the real criminal here. He was capitalizing on Sackett's errors, using them like some pimp might use a woman's drug habit to get her to sell her body. It was a terrible thing he'd done.

Jamison followed Sackett to the door, saying nothing, and closed the door after he'd gone. Then he turned to Melissa. God, she was beautiful. To him, she was the exact definition of the word. He tried to look at her differently now, tried to see her with the world's eyes. Why couldn't he convince himself that he didn't really love her and get the hell out of here? She was free, he had done what he'd set out to do. He should end it here, right now, and he knew it.

But it wasn't going to happen, so he gave up and walked over to her. The room felt as if it were a hundred miles across, giving him time for a thousand thoughts which evoked a million good reasons why he should turn and run away.

She'd dropped her head when he let go of her chin and was still looking down at the floor when he came back to her. He took a deep breath and looked around the room. She still didn't look up.

"Quite a week, huh?"

He waited, but she didn't move. He could almost hear the hands of his watch sweeping the time away from them.

"What do you plan to do now, Melissa?"

No answer. He couldn't take it anymore, standing so close and not hugging her, not putting his arms around her and pulling her close, feeling the press of their bodies against each other, her hair tormenting his face the way it always did.

He walked to the kitchen area, where her gravitational pull wasn't quite so strong, and began to change into the clothes Blevins had given him. She didn't look at him the entire time, not once while he struggled to dress with one hand. He was actually hoping she would look, maybe bring back some of what they'd shared in her bathroom last week.

After he changed, he stuffed his old clothes into the bag, then rinsed his face in the sink. When he raised his head and opened his eyes she was standing right there, just across the counter from him.

"You gave Sackett a million dollars to get me free. I want to know why."

He listened to the question carefully, didn't even reach for a towel, just stood there with water on his face and her question in his ears.

"Just something I wanted to do. Nothing more to it."

She was using her attorney's voice now, not too nice but not quite confrontational, either.

"Rich told me you heard everything I said in Kane's room. Is that right?"

"Yes."

"Then why, Peter? Why would you pay a fortune to save me?"

He picked a towel off the counter, dabbed at his face with his good hand, careful of the scabs. He didn't have an answer she would understand. If she loved him at all, she would have realized already how overwhelming that emotion was, how it forced a person to do things that made absolutely no sense. On the other hand, if she'd never felt it, there was no way to make her understand.

He raked his fingers through his hair, gathered up the few things he had, and got ready to go.

"Do you need money, Melissa? I got a little over thirty thousand dollars when I closed my bank account. If you need some traveling money, it's yours."

She shook her head hard. "Why are you being so nice? I tried to kill you."

"I know, I'm a fool. Do you need the money or not?" He walked around the counter and headed toward the door.

"No," she said, still shaking her head. "My dad left me a lot of money. I've never wanted to use it, but I've got cash stashed all over the place. Would you at least let me repay the money you gave Sackett?"

He shot to her eyes and checked to see if she had offended him on purpose, then decided she hadn't. She looked confused and bewildered, but there wasn't a hint of haughtiness anywhere on her face.

"No, but thanks."

It was time for him to go. Blevins would hear about this soon and hit the ceiling, and Jamison had to be on a flight before then. Melissa should be, too, but he wasn't about to tell her what to do. He put his good hand on her right arm.

"One question, Melissa. Did you ever love me, even a little? Or was it all a lie?"

She didn't know the answer, he could tell by the way her head tilted and her eyes looked at him.

"I . . . I think I may have loved you. Honestly, I've never been sure what love is, but if I've ever been in love, it was with you. I just can't say for sure and don't want to mislead you anymore."

It felt great to hear her confess that maybe, just maybe, she might have shared some part of the feeling he had for her. It made him happy as he turned to leave.

"Well, I love you, Melissa. Don't really want to anymore, but I can't help it."

"Then I should say I love you back. You just paid a million dollars for me. I kind of feel like an indentured servant."

He turned and walked away, leaving her behind, his brain ignoring his heart's demands to beg her to come with him. He wasn't going to turn back now, regardless of what she said.

"Good-bye, Melissa." He stared at the doorknob twenty feet away. "Hope you get to be in love some day. It's a wonderful feeling."

Then he struggled against every power of nature, fought his way to the door as if walking against a beating wind. It took all of his strength to turn the knob but once done, he pulled back on the door and stepped through it. Shuffled away, trying to remember how to find the ticketing area.

"May I help you, sir?"

Jamison looked up. The line in front of him had vanished and the perky woman in the blue uniform was waiting with a smile of forced patience on her face. He slid his paper bag forward with his right foot, then stepped up to the counter.

"There's a flight to Zurich leaving in fifteen minutes.
Are there still seats available?" He'd never been to Zurich before and had never wanted to go there, but it was
the next international departure.

She tapped her keyboard. "Let me see . . . yes, sir, it
goes through JFK. There's a seat in first class." She rose
up on her toes and looked Jamison over, raised her eyebrows as if the words *first class* might cause him to
faint. "One way or round-trip?"

"One-way," Jamison said.

The direction for the rest of his life. Never coming
back. Never seeing Melissa again. One way.

"Your ticket will be 2,642 dollars, sir. Would you like
me to book that?"

"Yes."

"Are you traveling alone?"

Melissa's voice suddenly snapped him out of his
trance. "No," she said. "Make it two."

Jamison jumped a little as she put her elbows on the
counter. The ticket agent looked at Jamison. He closed
his eyes.

He could actually see it happening, could imagine
them rushing for their gate with Jamison carrying
nothing but a plastic bag of dirty clothes and all his
savings. Not exactly the typical first-class-to-Zurich
passenger, but Melissa would be beside him. He
wouldn't even have to look to prove it. He would hear
her feet slapping the tile floor and her voice giggling as
if they were getting away with a silly prank. All the
while his heart would be thumping away with the pleasure of knowing that the next several hours would be
spent sitting beside her.

Of course, tomorrow might be different. Anything could happen. Blevins might be pissed enough to come after them. Melissa might go out for coffee and never come back. She could kill him when they slept together. It was even possible she would discover she loved him.

Tomorrow could wait. Right now was all that mattered, and right now Melissa was willing to come with him, her legs ready to move along with his, their lives, at least for the next several hours, moving in the same direction. The woman he loved would be going to Zurich with him. He would take nothing else for granted. Had never taken her for granted. The essence of love.

"Sir? Will that be two tickets?"

He opened his eyes and looked at Melissa. He loved her so much it hurt, still noticed each and every breath she took, still tried to inhale the air that left her lungs, but she was different now. She wasn't crying on a beach and she wasn't in any danger. She did not need him anymore and didn't care about him. She had given him a chance to love and he would always be grateful, but he had to leave her, had to go somewhere new and start over. There might even be another woman out there for him, someone who would reflect some of the love he gave her. It seemed unlikely, but possible.

"Sir?"

He took Melissa's new passport out of her hand and gave it to the ticket agent. He started counting out the money. "No. Just one."

Melissa put her hand on his arm. "You're not coming? You don't want to be with me now?"

Jamison watched the woman recount the money,

waited as she processed the ticket, and handed it to Melissa. He did not look in Melissa's direction.

"Gate 23. It's boarding now."

"Peter?"

He turned and walked away.